He That Covereth *His* Sins

J. A. ROSS

WESTBOW
PRESS®
A DIVISION OF THOMAS NELSON
& ZONDERVAN

WestBow Press books may be ordered through booksellers or by contacting:

WestBow Press
A Division of Thomas Nelson & Zondervan
1663 Liberty Drive
Bloomington, IN 47403
www.westbowpress.com
1 (866) 928-1240

Scripture taken from the King James Version of the Bible.

ISBN: 978-1-9736-7046-9 (sc)
ISBN: 978-1-9736-7047-6 (hc)
ISBN: 978-1-9736-7045-2 (e)

Library of Congress Control Number: 2019910610

Print information available on the last page.

WestBow Press rev. date: 08/2/2019

Dedication

To Jesus Christ, the One to whom I owe everything.

And to my wife Nancy, whose willingness to be the primary breadwinner for a while made it possible for the dream of being a writer to come true.

And to Dan Elliott and Adam Gittins, my brothers in Christ and my Proverbs 27:17 friends, whose combined personalities inspired the character of Roy Schoening.

Acknowledgements

This book would not have been possible without the help of so many people.

First, I must thank Edna Geise, Robert and Marian Geise, Merlyn and Zeda Ross, and Rue and Ruth Nickle for the endless information they all provided me about what life was really like in Southwestern Iowa during the 1930s. Though almost all of them have passed on, their beloved stories remain alive and well.

Next, I would be remiss if I didn't thank the teachers who have supported my dream of becoming a novelist since its inception way back in eighth grade: Mrs. Cathy McWilliams, Mrs. Shelly Brown, and Mrs. Julie Larsen. A very special thanks goes to Mrs. Julie Handbury, the educator who gave me the keys that unlocked the world of writing. Every woman listed in this paragraph is a credit to the teaching profession, and I remember their individual nurturing well.

The people at Westbow Press have been awesome. I couldn't have done this without them.

A big thank you must go to Trudy Beno, my first cousin twice removed, whose help with the history of the Squirrel Cage Jail in Council Bluffs is greatly appreciated.

And lastly, I want to thank my primary editing team: my aunt Cheri Geise for her astute theological eye; my sister-in-law Susan for being the initial cheerleader and continuity editor; Rhonda Ross, my mom, who offered advice and support; and Leah Shannon, my trusted friend since second grade, who offered much encouragement along the journey and a critical eye at the end. I hope you'll all be willing to perform the same functions for the next novel.

He that covereth his sins shall not prosper: but whoso confesseth and forsaketh them shall have mercy. -Proverbs 28:13

Chapter One

October 24, 1935

"Hello, ma'am. I'm sorry to bother you, but my name is Harlan Jensen, and I just jumped off the train next to your back pasture, and I was wondering if you had any work that a fellow could do for a bite to eat," rehearsed the young man as he trod his way through the last green grass of autumn. This was about the fifth time Harlan Jensen had said these words aloud. Under ordinary circumstances, his stomach might have been tightening with nervousness, but he was far too hungry to notice any adverse physical symptoms caused by anxiety.

"Hello, ma'am. I'm sorry to bother you, but my name is Harlan Jensen, and I just jumped off the train next to your back pasture, and I was wondering if you had any work that a fellow could do for a bite to eat," Harlan repeated.

Harlan shook his head. It was probably folly to have jumped off the train where he had. After he had gotten himself up off the ground, made sure that he had suffered no major injuries, and dusted himself off, he examined several of the fence posts, looking for the telltale marks that hobos who had preceded him might have left. However, he could find nothing—which he considered a bad sign. Surely other men had seen in the distance the well-kept flowerbeds, weedless vegetable garden, and smoke curling out of the kitchen chimney and assumed that it might be a good spot

1

to get a hot meal. At least, he figured, there had been no signs of any hostility at this particular farmstead. Harlan had carefully memorized all of the hobo code that Dirty Darby had taught him at the little hobo jungle he had been in a couple of weeks ago, but he couldn't find anything more than a vacant pair of staple holes along the stretch of fence that ran parallel with the railroad. With that, he had hopped the fence and begun rehearsing his introduction while keeping an eye out for any not-so-amiable bull.

"Hello, ma'am. I'm sorry to bother you, but my name is Harlan Jensen, and I just jumped off the train next to your back pasture, and I was wondering if you had any work that a fellow could do for a bite to eat.

"She'll probably start right in with a bunch of questions, you know," Harlan said to himself. "Are you going to tell her that you've run off from the Civilian Conservation Corps? Are you going to tell her why? That'll get you nowhere and probably take away any chances for anything to eat."

Harlan shook his head and kept walking. Every failure that he had ever experienced was replaying itself in his head and would have successfully prevented him from continuing on toward the small farmhouse except that his empty stomach was in command. Harlan felt that if he could even just get a piece of bread, that would at least get him a little farther down the road to the next farmstead. He wasn't sure when he had eaten last, but he knew that it had been days earlier and that his last meal had been only a part of a can of pork and beans that another bindle stiff had been kind enough to share with him.

The pasture that Harlan had been walking through came to an end at an assortment of feedlots and barn pens. He climbed the sturdy fences agilely but with less energy than he might have had he consumed a square meal in the recent past. All that lay between him and the house then was a short stretch of farmyard, a white wire fence, and a small patch of neatly trimmed house yard.

"Hello, ma'am. I'm sorry to bother you, but my name is Harlan

Jensen, and I just jumped off the train next to your back pasture, and I was wondering if you had any work that a fellow could do for a bite to eat," Harlan repeated in a whisper, fixing his eyes resolutely on the back door of the house.

Chickens, ducks, and geese scattered out of Harlan's path as he walked toward the house. The noise that they created at seeing a stranger pass through aroused a dog that looked like a collie and retriever mix. The dog came trotting toward Harlan with its tail wagging in excitement. It obviously presented no threat, and its welcome gave Harlan a renewed sense of hope.

"That's a good girl," he whispered, patting the dog on the head.

Harlan quietly opened the back gate and strode toward what looked to him like the kitchen door. He knew that at most farmhouses, the front door was merely a formality and that the back door greeted the majority of the traffic. Harlan knocked firmly at the screen door frame. The inner door was open into the kitchen of the house, but he could see no one.

"Now who could that be?" he heard a woman's voice ask somewhere inside.

Harlan thought too lately about taking off his cap, so he didn't have any time to smooth the blond hair that tumbled out from beneath it, but he felt that it was more polite to be hatless when he met the lady of the house.

Harlan heard Elsie Meyer's footsteps coming before she appeared in the kitchen, and he was somewhat reassured when he saw that the lady of the house was a short, matronly woman who was dressed plainly. The dress that she was wearing was covered by a white apron with deep pockets on the sides, and her graying, crimped hair framed a kind face. Harlan could immediately see that above her reading glasses she was scrutinizing him carefully as she approached her side of the screen door. Then, unmistakably, a look of surprise passed over her face which then melted into an expression that seemed to indicate that she recognized him. If he'd had time, Harlan would have been confused by what he had just seen, but suddenly he heard himself speaking.

"Hello, ma'am. I'm sorry to bother you, but my name is Harlan Jensen, and I just jumped off the train next to your back pasture, and..."

He was interrupted before he could finish his well-rehearsed opening lines. "Well, come right in, Harlan Jensen, and go into the washroom here and make yourself presentable while I get you something to eat," said Mrs. Meyer, opening the screen door and directing him to a small room on his right. "You look like you just finished threshing in a windstorm with all of that dust on you, and if I guess right, you haven't had much to eat in the last few days."

Harlan tried to continue the speech he had rehearsed. "I was wondering if you..."

Elsie Meyer had grabbed his arm and was pulling him into the house. "Let me get you a fresh wash rag. You're going to have to get that fuzz off your cheeks, too. I'll not have you at my table looking like a heathen. You'll find everything you need there in the medicine chest." She was bustling about the small wash room as she said all of this and suddenly disappeared back into the kitchen.

Harlan was not sure what to think about what was transpiring, but when he caught a glimpse of himself in the small looking glass above the wash stand, he could understand why Mrs. Meyer had told him to make himself presentable. It had been a long time since Harlan had seen himself in a mirror, and the face that looked back at him from the other side of the glass was certainly a surprise. He remembered enough of the principles of his upbringing to feel shame at his appearance and was suddenly even more shocked that Mrs. Meyer had let him into her house at all. He had only hoped that he would be given a few bites to eat while he sat on the back porch.

Harlan set about the task of cleaning himself up so that he could sit at Mrs. Meyer's table. At least he thought that that was the reason that he was supposed to wash up. Had she said that she was going to feed him? He was a bit dumbfounded with the speed at which he had been invited in. Furthermore, the look of recognition that had crossed her countenance had distracted him, so he was having a difficult time sorting out the events of the last few minutes. Harlan reviewed Mrs. Meyer's words and believed that she had said something about feeding him. As he dampened the washcloth, the sound of the lids of the cookstove being removed and replaced told him that Mrs. Meyer was indeed fixing something for him to eat. Hardly believing his good fortune, he redoubled his efforts to improve his appearance.

When he emerged from the washroom several minutes later, Mrs. Meyer turned from the stove and inspected him once again.

"Better," she said, approvingly. "One could practically call you handsome. You go on into the dining room now, and I'll be there in a minute." She indicated the way with a nod of her head.

Harlan walked into the next room and was startled by the presence of a man in a hospital bed.

"Oh, hello," Harlan stammered.

The man almost imperceptibly nodded his head.

Harlan felt the courtesy he had been taught as a youth urge him to walk toward the man with an outstretched hand. "I'm Harlan Jensen," he said as he approached the older gentleman. "How do you do?"

The man raised his left hand rather clumsily. Harlan did his best to shake it, but since he had been offered the wrong hand, the motion was awkward. The man made no attempt to speak, but he smiled politely.

"I see you've met my husband," Mrs. Meyer said as she entered the dining room with a glass of milk and a dish of sliced apples. "Sit right down here at the table; I'll be right back."

Harlan immediately did as he was told with speed that was not entirely born of his hunger. He didn't want anything that he did to change his hostess's mind about feeding him since she seemed to be happy to provide him with a meal. After all, he had not even asked her for anything to eat. Mostly though, he seated himself so quickly because everything about Mrs. Meyer's manner conveyed the message that she was accustomed to being obeyed, and Harlan was convinced that it would be mighty uncomfortable to cross her.

Once seated, Harlan's eyes did a quick sweep of the dining room. It seemed that this room had not been used much until the addition of the hospital bed and its occupant had made it become as much the center of the household activities as the kitchen. At the end of the table closest to the windows, a pile of mending was spread, and a half-finished garment of some feminine variety lay askew among various pieces of sewing equipment. All of this made it obvious what the day's tasks had been for Mrs. Meyer. An open Bible was sitting in a chair that had been pulled close to the man in the hospital bed, and it appeared that it had perhaps been cast hastily aside when Harlan had knocked on the door. Harlan noticed that the only decorations on the walls of the room were an ornately carved wooden cross and an ugly depiction of some white irises which had the words "As thy days, so shall thy strength be" next to them. Harlan recognized the smaller letters beneath the text as an indication that the words were a Bible verse, but he was unfamiliar with what the smaller letters meant.

"Here we are now," Mrs. Meyer said as she placed a steaming plate of hash in front of Harlan. "If you don't see something you need, just let me know."

"Thank you, ma'am."

Largely due to the presence of the Bible and the picture and cross on the wall, it seemed to Harlan that it might be a good idea to appear to ask grace before he ate. He ducked his head for what he considered an appropriate length of time and then dug hungrily into the succulent hash before him. Mrs. Meyer was looking at him approvingly as she sat down at her pile of mending. It suddenly occurred to Harlan that his hostess would probably start peppering him with questions now that he was seated at her table. His mind began to think of ways to avoid saying much about himself.

"Good gracious!" Mrs. Meyer said, noting the rate at which

Harlan had begun to shovel the food in his mouth. "When was the last time you ate?"

Harlan thought about that for a second. The question seemed safe enough, but he didn't know the answer. "I don't know for sure."

"Go ahead and tell me. You don't have to feel ashamed," Mrs. Meyer coaxed.

"It's not that," said Harlan between gulps. "I don't know what day today is."

"Thursday," Mrs. Meyer supplied.

Harlan figured while he chewed. "Then it was Monday or Tuesday," he said finally.

"You'd better slow down so you don't get sick, then."

"Do you have some work that I can do in exchange for my dinner?" Harlan asked, hoping to keep the conversation in neutral territory.

"You ever spent much time on a farm?"

"Grew up on one until I was twelve," Harlan answered between mouthfuls.

"Well, then you know that there is always work to do around here. It's been especially hard since my husband Al here had his stroke a month ago," Mrs. Meyer indicated the man in the hospital bed with a nod. "His right side is paralyzed and he can't speak anymore, but we're hoping for recovery. He's already much better than he was a few weeks ago, aren't you, Al?" Mrs. Meyer patted Mr. Meyer's hand, and he nodded almost imperceptibly. "He understands everything perfectly, even though he can't respond. I know him so well that I know what he's thinking, though."

Mrs. Meyer paused, and it seemed to Harlan that he was expected to say something. He didn't know what to say, however, so continued eating.

"Marty and I have been doing the best that we can in these last few weeks, but we're awfully slow about getting the corn picked. The neighbors are planning to help us, but we don't want to save it all up until then, so we've been picking together in the mornings.

Then Marty continues in the afternoon while I catch up on the work here in the house. Have you got any experience picking corn?"

"Yes, ma'am," Harlan answered.

"Well, when you get done eating, you go on out and do just that. When it's time to milk, Marty can come on in and help me with that, and if you'll pick until the sun disappears behind the hill, that will leave enough time for you to scoop the corn into the crib before it gets dark, and I'll have a nice hot supper ready for you."

Harlan thought quickly. He hadn't planned to be at this farm all that long. His initial idea was to get a bite to eat, work a couple of hours and be on his way, but the hash had tasted extraordinarily good, and he figured that it couldn't hurt to work long enough to get a second meal from Mrs. Meyer.

The telephone rang at that moment, one long and three shorts.

"Oh, that's our ring," said Mrs. Meyer. "I bet it's my sister. She often calls on Thursday afternoons once her mending is done. You'll have to excuse me."

Mrs. Meyer left the dining room for the kitchen, where the telephone was located, and was soon engaged in sisterly conversation which alternated back and forth between English and German. Harlan was relieved to have the opportunity to eat without being questioned any further about what had been his habits over the last few days. He noticed out of the corner of his eye that Mr. Meyer was intently regarding him as he ate, but he felt nothing hostile in the older man's mute gaze.

Mrs. Meyer returned as Harlan was finishing the last of the sugared apple slices which had served as his dessert.

"Much obliged ma'am. That was very good. Where will I find my work now?" Harlan asked as he rose from the table, picking up his dirty dishes to be polite.

"You can just leave those; I'll get them," Mrs. Meyer said, motioning for Harlan to follow her out of the house. "If you just head straight east of that rear barn there, go along the fence a piece and then turn north when you get to the gate, you'll see

Marty somewhere in that cornfield. We just started that field this morning, so there's a lot of corn to be picked there yet," Mrs. Meyer directed, pointing to the northeast of the house.

"Thank you, ma'am," Harlan said, beginning to depart.

"Now here's a pair of gloves," she said, handing them to him.

"Thank you," Harlan said again, beginning to feel like he knew nothing else to say.

"Go on now. It's getting dark so early these days!"

Chapter Two

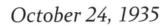

October 24, 1935

A brisk fifteen minute walk lay between Harlan and the location of his work, and as he began the trek, he was suddenly aware of his fatigue. A full belly conspired with the afternoon sun to make Harlan wish that he might lie down somewhere and take a nap, but that authoritative tone of Mrs. Meyer's spurred him on through the long rows of light brown cornstalks with their dried ears pointing toward the earth.

"You'd be a fool not to at least pick a little corn and do a little scooping to pay for not just one but two meals, Jensen," he heard himself saying aloud. He immediately began shaking his head at having heard his own throat giving voice to his thoughts. Harlan was more than a little chagrined by his recently acquired habit of talking to himself. *You've got to quit that,* he thought. *People will begin to think that you're touched in the head, and that will only make it more difficult for you to get back to a normal life.*

Harlan's thoughts were presently interrupted by a train whistle. He lifted his eyes to the railroad track that he had left scarcely an hour earlier and saw another train—a passenger train this time—headed east.

A two o'clock and a three o'clock, he thought. *Good. The track is a busy one—you might have guessed that since it goes all the way to Chicago. That means there will be plenty of chances for a quick escape when the time comes.* Harlan began calculating. He knew that he would be assured of supper tonight at least. After that, if he could beg an apple or two off Mrs. Meyer, he could bunk down in the loft of the rear barn for the night, catch the earliest train that went east in the morning, eat the apples for his breakfast, and be back on his way to . . .

Yup. Good plan, Jensen, he thought sarcastically. *Just where is it that you're in such an all-fired hurry to go?*

Harlan had no answer to that question.

"Doesn't make any difference. Right now you are headed to go pick corn," he heard himself reply aloud once again.

Just then a team and wagon entered Harlan's view. Even from a distance, it was obvious that the pair of Percherons were a well-cared-for example of their breed. Furthermore, they had been well-trained. At intervals, he heard a clipped command issue from someone who was located on the far side of the wagon. The horses obediently stopped and started, thus keeping the wagon apace with the person who was steadily tossing ears of corn into it. Marty Meyer was only a few steps into the two rows nearest the team and wagon, so Harlan hurried forward, beginning to pick the next two rows away from the wagon to quickly catch up with Marty. When Harlan's first few ears of corn flew into the wagon, he saw Marty's head turn back in surprise.

As Harlan approached the young Meyer offspring, he could only see Marty's back, which was partially obscured by the two rows of corn between them. Marty was clad in denim overalls which appeared to be too large, a blue shirt, and a cap. Using height and breadth, Harlan guessed the youth to be about thirteen or fourteen years old. *Probably just finished the eighth grade in the spring,* Harlan thought to himself. *Poor kid. This is a huge job for a boy.*

"You must be Marty," Harlan said once he was abreast of his fellow corn picker.

"That's right," came the reply.

"My name is Harlan Jensen."

"Thanks for helping, Mr. Jensen. You'll excuse me if I'm not much of a talker."

"Sounds fine to me," Harlan returned, relieved that he was evidently in no danger of having to divulge his personal history.

The next two and a half hours passed with only the occasional noise from the team of horses and the regular rhythmic thump of the ears of corn as they were harvested, but the rustling sound of the dry cornstalks and husks kept Harlan's imagination busy. More than once he looked over his shoulder, thinking that someone had come upon him and was whispering loudly in his ear. The sun, which had initially been warm on the corn pickers' backs, cooled rapidly in its westward trek, and the evening promised to be plenty chilly.

"I have to go milk," Marty announced, turning a filthy, dust-streaked face toward Harlan when they reached the end of their rows.

"Your mother said that I was to continue picking until the sun went behind the hill. Then I'm supposed to bring the wagon in and scoop the corn into the crib in the last light," Harlan returned.

"The scoop is hanging on a nail on the south side of the crib," Marty said, starting back to the barn.

After Harlan had done as he was told and scooped the corn into the crib, he walked back to the house, where Mrs. Meyer met him at the kitchen door.

"I've put a wash tub on the floor in the washhouse. You'll find a boiler of hot water on the stove in there, a washrag, a towel and a chunk of soap. Get you a bucket of cold water at the soft water pump there to temper the hot water; then go take a bath. I didn't think you probably had another set of your own clothes, so I hurried over to my sister's while you were picking corn. Her son Charlie is about your size, so I borrowed some of his clothes for you. You'll find them on the chair in there."

Harlan was immediately alarmed at this new development in

his situation. Mrs. Meyer's words made it sound as though he were staying, and he had no intention of that.

"Thank you, but . . ." Harlan began.

"Get goin'! Supper will be ready soon now. Don't dawdle," Mrs. Meyer said.

Harlan opened his mouth to state his case, but that authority in Mrs. Meyer's attitude clapped his mouth shut, and he headed to the rain water cistern.

Harlan had to admit that it felt good to be clean once more as he dried himself by the little laundry stove. He donned the clothes that Mrs. Meyer had left for him and headed to the house.

Upon entering the kitchen, Mrs. Meyer quickly looked him up and down to see that he had indeed washed.

"Good," she assessed. "Go on into the dining room. Marty will be down in a minute."

Again, Harlan did as he was told. Mr. Meyer was seated at the table, his face bathed in the golden light of the oil lamp in its center, and Harlan noticed that even when he was not in his hospital bed, something about his posture indicated that the man was an invalid.

"Hello," Harlan said, feeling foolish as he did so because he knew that Mr. Meyer couldn't speak. "Where should I sit?"

Mr. Meyer nodded acknowledgement, indicated the chair to his right with a clumsy movement of his left hand, and smiled wordlessly at Harlan. It was obvious that even though he was smiling, Mr. Meyer was also intently studying Harlan, making the younger man a little nervous.

"It looked to me like there was only about an acre left to pick and that south slope where we were picking will be finished," Harlan volunteered after an uncomfortable few moments of silence. He remembered that most of the farmers he had ever known always wanted to talk about their crops.

Mr. Meyer nodded.

"If you were the one who built the corncrib on the side of the hill like that, it was smart. It made scooping the corn into it a lot easier than I remembered it being," Harlan continued.

"My Al is a smart fellow," Mrs. Meyer agreed, bringing in a plate of hot biscuits and setting them on the table which was already laid with stewed apples, summer sausage, and butter and jelly.

Quick, light steps were heard descending the stairway just then, and Mrs. Meyer called out, "Marty, can you bring in the milk pitcher?"

"Yes, Mama."

Mrs. Meyer began putting food on Mr. Meyer's plate, carefully cutting everything into bite-sized pieces for him.

"When Al first had his stroke, he was having difficulty swallowing properly, so it has only been within this last week that he is able to have solid food again," Mrs. Meyer explained. "He's really made excellent progress in a short time. Haven't you, Al?"

Mr. Meyer responded with a faint nod. His eyes were still fixed on Harlan, watching to see how he responded to Mrs. Meyer's talk. Harlan began to feel that there was nothing hostile in Mr. Meyer's extended regard of him; he just appeared to be intensely interested in him.

At that moment, a brown-haired young lady entered the dining room carrying a pitcher of milk. She was wearing a faded yellow dress, and her bobbed hair framed a beautifully feminine face. Harlan remembered his manners and stood at sight of her. His response caused the girl to blush slightly and cast her eyes to the floor.

"Thank you, Marty. Now, I think we're ready to sit down and say grace," Mrs. Meyer said, her eyes twinkling a little.

Marty? Harlan almost asked aloud, returning to his seat.

The three of them who had been standing gained their seats so that Harlan was to the left of Mr. Meyer, facing Mrs. Meyer, and Marty was to Harlan's left, facing her father. Harlan found himself staring at Marty, trying to recognize any of the features that he had seen of the youth in the corn field. Mrs. Meyer noticed his confusion.

"You didn't know that our Marty is a girl, did you Mr. Jensen?" she prodded. "'Marty' is short for 'Martha'."

"No, I uh . . . didn't notice, I mean, I had no idea," Harlan stammered.

Mr. Meyer's lips curled into a lop-sided grin.

"I'll ask the blessing now," Mrs. Meyer said. She folded her hands and tucked her head down. The rest of them did the same.

"Heavenly Father, we thank Thee for the beautiful weather that we had today, and for Thy provision of the harvest and this food, but, Lord, we especially thank Thee for sending Harlan to us to help us. In the name of Thy precious Son Jesus, Amen."

Sent? Harlan thought. *Nobody sent me, I just jumped off the train here because I was hungry!*

Harlan might have spent more time contemplating Mrs. Meyer's words except that Marty had started passing food to him. Harlan would not have given Marty a second thought if she had been the thirteen-year-old boy he had originally assumed, but now he found himself wishing that his eyes didn't keep darting over to steal a glance at her. He was trying to find any similarity in her current appearance to what he had seen of her in the cornfield. Apparently, the combination of her overalls and cap coupled with the cornstalks obscured her enough that he didn't notice anything about her. Harlan felt he was looking at someone entirely new to him, rather than someone whom he had worked alongside for a few hours.

All through supper, Mrs. Meyer updated her companions about the goings on at her sister's home. Harlan was relieved by her benign chatter because it kept the conversation off himself. Because he didn't know any of the people that Mrs. Meyer was talking about, his mind was occupied with two thoughts. The first was how surprised he was at Marty's transformation. For the last several hours, Marty had been a boy in his mind, and now he was having trouble making his brain conform to reality. The second thing that was keeping his mind busy was that his plan to quickly depart the Meyer farm had a new glitch: he was no longer wearing his own clothes.

He understood why Mrs. Meyer would not have wanted him to eat supper with the family in the clothes that he was wearing when he arrived. They were filthy after all, and the meal was definitely worth the inconvenience of having to wear the clean clothes that were offered him. For a moment, it crossed Harlan's mind that he could just leave his own clothing here and make his escape in Mrs. Meyer's nephew's clothing; however, he had noted that the clothes that were on loan, while worn, were in far better condition than the tattered CCC-issued outfit he had arrived in. The fact that the borrowed clothing would have also afforded him better anonymity should his troubles catch up with him was a great temptation to Harlan, but alas, it was not an even exchange, and Harlan felt that it would be more than he could handle to add yet another bad deed to his name.

Harlan convinced himself that it was no matter. After supper, he would change back to his clothing in the summer kitchen and leave.

"I took some apples from the tree in the southeast corner of the orchard to Aunt Louise," Mrs. Meyer was saying, indicating the direction of the orchard with a wave of her fork. "She was going to bake a . . ."

Harlan heard no more. He now knew where to find the apple tree so that he could have full pockets when he left.

"I put an extra quilt on the bed in the west bedroom upstairs," Mrs. Meyer said, and suddenly Harlan was aware of the fact that she was addressing him now. "I also laid an old pair of Al's pajamas on the bed for you. I suspect that they will be too big, but I can take them in later."

Harlan was taken aback by Mrs. Meyer's statement. He had no

intention of staying, and even if he had, sleeping in these strangers' house was never his intent.

"Oh, ma'am, thank you, but I need to be moving along," he said. "You've been more than kind to me, but . . ."

"But nothing. The fact of the matter is this, Mr. Jensen. We don't have any money to be able to pay you, but we can certainly provide you room and board, and we just plain need your help right now," Mrs. Meyer said matter-of-factly. "Surely you can stay until the corn picking is done."

"Mrs. Meyer, I've got to be getting along," Harlan reiterated, shaking his head.

"It really won't take that long, and a boy your age needs three good square meals a day," Mrs. Meyer bargained.

"Your cooking has been delicious, ma'am, but I think I really should . . ."

"Why don't you at least stay until it rains? Then we won't be able to pick corn for a little bit. How about that for a compromise?"

Harlan knew that autumn in Iowa could have some rainy times, but he also knew that there could be long stretches of dry weather, and he was not interested in staying with the Meyer family. However, he was also not interested in continuing to argue with Mrs. Meyer. That something in her voice that told him that she was used to being obeyed caused his brain to arrive at a solution to his dilemma. He knew that she was not going to let him go without an argument, but he neither wished to stay nor to argue, so he decided that a little deception would solve everything.

"All right. I'll stay until it rains," Harlan acquiesced, then hastily added, "or for two weeks, whichever is shorter, but I'm sleeping in the barn loft."

"You'll get frightfully cold at night, I fear, but it sounds like a deal to me," Mrs. Meyer said, reaching her hand across the table to shake on it.

Harlan had no intention to make good on the promises which had just crossed his lips. After supper, he planned to head to the barn loft while he knew eyes would still be on him, wait until the house became dark, retrieve his clothes from the summer kitchen, fill his pockets with apples, and be on his way. It was a slick plan, and he knew it would work because even the Meyers' dog wouldn't give him away.

As Harlan shook Mrs. Meyer's hand, he stole yet another glance at Marty. She appeared to be completely embarrassed by her mother's forward personality.

The rest of the meal was filled with Mrs. Meyer's planning of the next day's activities, which included Harlan's labor here and there. This didn't bother Harlan any because his plans certainly didn't coincide with Mrs. Meyer's. When the time came for Harlan to make his exit to the barn loft, Mrs. Meyer equipped him with a kerosene lantern and strict instructions to be careful with it in the loft of the barn and a strict admonishing against smoking up there due to the risk of fire. Harlan assured her that he had no intentions of smoking because he had never been able to afford the luxury.

"Well, good," she had responded. "I'm sorry to hear that money has always been so tight for you, but if poverty has kept you from developing the habit of smoking, it has done you at least one service."

He left her kitchen then and headed to the barn loft to wait until the house became dark. Harlan had no trouble navigating his way up to the loft, and as it was filled with the summer's crop of hay and straw, he had no trouble gaining a view of the house out of one of the high windows. He hung the lantern on a nail in a rafter and carefully blew out the flame. He knew he would not need it later because a bright sliver of moon was beginning its trek across the clear sky, promising him ideal conditions for executing his departure.

Harlan lay down in the sweet-smelling hay with his eyes glued to the windows of the house, and before he knew it, his full belly and tired body had put him into a deep, involuntary sleep.

Chapter Three

October 25, 1935

Harlan woke with a start, first because he didn't know where he was, and secondly because the sun was shining brightly. A swear word escaped him as he struggled to remember what he was about.

Maybe they're not awake yet, Harlan thought in desperation, then realized his foolishness. *No, with the amount of work that they have to do with the old man down, they're probably wide awake. Besides, look how far the sun is up. It has completely cleared the horizon.*

Harlan scrambled through the hay to the windows on the other side of the loft. He scanned the pasture and spotted the dairy cows chomping calmly on the last green grass of the season.

"But the milk cows are still out in the pasture," Harlan said aloud. "Maybe it's not as late as I thought. If I'm careful, I may still have time to get out of here."

In seconds, Harlan was skimming along fence railings and hiding behind various outbuildings on his way to the summer kitchen to find his clothes.

I feel like Tom Mix in that western movie that I saw with Dad just before he . . . don't think about that now, Harlan.

Harlan entered the summer kitchen, expecting to see his clothes hanging on the hooks where he had left them. Instead, he found them soaking in a wash tub of sudsy water. Harlan swore again.

You've got two choices, Harlan. You can either steal the clothes that are on your back and make your escape, or you can pick corn for one more day and leave in your own clothes.

"I guess I'll add theft to my list of faults," he said aloud, looking down at the clothes he was wearing.

You know you're already in trouble. Why add to your miseries by stealing from people who have treated you decent?

"Looks like you're picking corn again today, Harlan," he mumbled. "Better go see what Mrs. Meyer has in store for you."

He left the summer kitchen and headed into the house. The kitchen was vacant, but he happened to glance at the clock on the wall and was shocked to note that it was after nine. He walked through to the dining room, expecting to see Mrs. Meyer there again with Mr. Meyer. Instead, Mr. Meyer was alone in his hospital bed, looking out the bay windows, and Harlan realized at that moment that Mr. Meyer had watched all of his furtive movements on his way from the barn to the summer kitchen. Harlan felt his blush rising into his cheeks at being discovered.

"Good morning, Mr. Meyer," Harlan said, shamefaced.

Mr. Meyer nodded his greeting. Then he motioned toward a piece of paper on the dining room table. Harlan saw that it was a note bearing his name.

Harlan,

Marty and I are out in the field. Your breakfast is in the warming oven. Come on out when you're finished eating.

-E.M.

"That lady thinks of everything!" Harlan said aloud, feeling defeated.

Mr. Meyer began to laugh in silent but quaking chuckles, nodding agreement as he did so.

"Why didn't you wake me up?" Harlan asked as he caught up with the two Meyer women a few rows over from where he had quit picking on the previous evening.

"Marty tried to," Mrs. Meyer responded, "but you were out cold."

Harlan was immediately embarrassed. He didn't know what he looked like when he slept, but he remembered seeing how undignified several of the boys in the CCC camp looked while they were sleeping, and he was surprised to find that he didn't like the idea of Marty having seen him like that.

"We figured if you could sleep through all the racket that we made rattling buckets around and whatnot while we were milking right beneath you, you must have needed your sleep, so we thought it best just to let you get rested up. We won't be so kind about it tomorrow morning," Mrs. Meyer continued.

So the milk cows weren't still in the pasture, they were back *in the pasture,* Harlan thought, chiding himself for his stupidity.

Mrs. Meyer was picking the two rows or corn nearest the wagon, putting Marty between herself and Harlan.

"Did you find your breakfast?" Mrs. Meyer asked.

"Yeah," Harlan answered, beginning to throw ears into the wagon at a respectable speed.

"That's good," she returned. "I don't normally do any washing on a Friday, but I've put your clothes to soak, and I'll get them washed out right after dinner."

"Thanks," Harlan said, mostly because he figured that he was obliged to appear grateful.

He stole a glance at Marty, who was just a few feet away on his right. She was wearing the same clothing as she had worn in the field the day before, and he could see no resemblance to the girl with whom he had eaten supper on the previous evening.

There was a pause, and Harlan feared that the topic of conversation might turn to him, so he began to think of excuses and fibs to keep the Meyer women both at bay and in ignorance.

"Sometimes Marty and I pass the long hours in the field by singing. Do you mind if we sing, Mr. Jensen?" Mrs. Meyer inquired.

Harlan could think of nothing better because the singing was a guarantee that he would not have to answer any questions.

"No, it's fine," he responded.

Mrs. Meyer began to sing in a rather reedy soprano that was a bit shaky around the edges.

Sowing in the morning, sowing seeds of kindness,
Sowing in the noontide, and the dewy eve.
Waiting for the harvest, and the time of reaping,
We shall come rejoicing, bringing in the sheaves.

Marty joined her mother with a rich and well-tempered alto voice which caused Harlan to look over at her. He was surprised that such a sound could come from such a small person, and though he didn't recognize the song that they were singing, he felt that he could easily listen to them for several hours.

The south slope was finished in short order, and not long after they crested the hill, the wagon was full.

"We'll take this load in, and I'll start dinner while you scoop it into the crib," Mrs. Meyer said, signaling that Harlan should drive the team while she and Marty would ride on top of the load. "Then, you two can come back out this afternoon."

Harlan skillfully guided the beautiful pair of Percherons down to the farmstead, driving to the house first to let off his passengers. As he was again scooping the ears of corn into the crib, he heard the familiar sound of an ax being used to split firewood. *Mr. Meyer must really be feeling good today,* he thought. Harlan unhitched the horses, led them to the water trough, and then put them back in their pen to rest. As he headed toward the house to see if Mrs.

Meyer had another job for him while he waited for dinner, he saw that it was not Mr. Meyer who was wielding the ax. Instead, it was Marty. She was chopping pieces of silver maple into stovewood for the kitchen. It was yielding easily since it was soft, but sweat had beaded on Marty's forehead, and her brows were knit with the effort of the task.

Something in Harlan rebelled at the sight of Marty occupied in this manner, and he strode quickly to her side and took the ax from her.

"Let me do this," he almost commanded, the tone of his own voice startling him. She surrendered the ax without argument.

"Thanks," she said, looking at him eye-to-eye for the first time.

Harlan knew now why he had mistaken her for a young boy. With her hair concealed by a cap and the heavy denims that she wore disguising her decidedly feminine figure, it was an easy mistake. However, when her eyes met his at that moment, he knew that he would never think of her as a boy again.

"Why are *you* chopping wood?" Harlan asked before he had time to stop himself.

She looked at him wryly. "Whom else would you suggest?"

Realizing the silliness of his question, he turned to the chopping block and picked up the task where he had interrupted her. When he paused to put a new log on the block, Marty took advantage of the moment of safety to pick up an armload of firewood and carry it into the kitchen. Harlan was surprised to discover that he wished that she had stayed outdoors with him.

Noon dinner proved to be a similar experience to the previous night's supper as far as conversation was concerned. Harlan dreaded the Meyers asking him questions about himself, but they did not. He wondered why they didn't, but he was not about to draw any attention to himself by asking. Marty participated minimally in the dinner conversation, and Harlan was beginning to wonder if his presence caused her to be so quiet or if she was normally this way.

Harlan was relieved to see Mrs. Meyer stay behind while he and

Marty returned to the field after dinner. He was hoping that she would make good on her promise to finish laundering his clothes. With them back in his possession, he could cut and run whenever it was convenient.

Harlan and Marty had been picking corn silently and steadily for about an hour when Marty suddenly spoke.

"I'm glad to see that you are a man of your word, Mr. Jensen," she said, catching him off guard.

"What do you mean?"

"I figured that when we saw you heading to the barn last night after supper, that would be the last we'd see of you, so I'm glad to see that you are a man of your word and that you are staying to help us pick corn," Marty explained.

Harlan was silent for a little while.

"I had every intention of leaving," he admitted slowly. "The only thing that kept me here was that I didn't think it was right to steal these clothes that belong to your cousin since they're nicer than mine."

A new thought suddenly struck Harlan. "Say, your mom didn't put my clothes to soak just to try to make me stay, did she?"

Marty snickered a bit. "You give Mother too much credit. She's sharp, but she's not what one might call wily. Fact is, I don't think I've ever seen her say or do anything with an ulterior motive. If she decided to wash your clothes, you can rest assured that the only thing crossing her mind was that they were dirty and needed it. You were pretty rank when you arrived yesterday."

Harlan's fair skin turned pink. "Sorry. It had been quite a while since I'd had the chance to get a bath."

"How long had you been riding the rails?" Marty asked.

"Don't really know," Harlan said quietly, getting nervous because the topic of conversation had turned to his history.

"Had it been just a few days, or had it been weeks, what?" Marty pressed.

"Time, uh...all kinda begins to run together," Harlan shrugged.

"Where had you been before you got on the trains?" Marty continued to interrogate innocently.

Harlan sensed that the conversation was soon going to be in dangerous waters, and his defenses were rising.

"Here and there," came his evasive answer, his voice sounding a little more curt than he had intended.

His tone caught Marty off guard, and she turned to face him.

"I'm sorry, Mr. Jensen. I didn't mean to—I mean, I…" Marty stammered.

When Harlan looked at her eyes, he could see that his brusk inflection had frightened her, and the look of fear in her eyes nearly broke his heart.

"No, I'm sorry," he cut off her in a much more calm tone. "Call me Harlan, please. I had been a part of the Civilian Conservation Corp, working in—well, let's just say north of here. I don't want to talk about that, though." Harlan's eyes scanned the northern horizon just then because talking about his past renewed his fear that eventually someone would find him.

"Well, I'm sorry I brought it up," Marty apologized again. "At any rate, we are very grateful for the help you've given us."

Marty became silent then, and Harlan realized that his brusqueness had caused her reticence. If she couldn't ask him questions about his past without the possibility of being snapped at, why would she want to engage him in conversation? Harlan also knew that questions about his future would be as futile because even he didn't know anything about that. However, suddenly Marty's silence—for which he had hitherto been thankful—seemed unbearable to Harlan. He began racking his brain for topics of conversation with which he could safely engage her.

"I guess I misjudged your mother on her motives for washing my clothes, but I know I'm correct when I say that she is one good cook," Harlan ventured, figuring that it was always safe to complement a girl's mother.

"That she is," Marty agreed, her voice sounding cheerful again.

"There are a lot of little things that I've noticed around the farm that tell me that your father was a pretty good farmer, too," Harlan continued.

"*Is* a good farmer," Marty corrected, with special emphasis on the present tense.

Harlan immediately felt his blunder. "Now it's my turn to be sorry," he said. "I didn't mean to…I mean, I just meant…."

"I know what you meant," Marty rejoined, her tone conciliatory. "I should have said thank you. You are right that Dad is a good farmer, or was, or…" Marty's voice broke a little, and Harlan felt even worse. His brain worked frantically to figure out what to say.

"Here. Let's start over," he suddenly heard himself saying. "Hi, my name is Harlan Jensen. This sure is lovely weather we're having today."

Marty chuckled a little at what she recognized as Harlan's way of putting everything at ease again. "Nice to meet you, Mr. Jensen," she returned, forcing her tone to be lighthearted again too. "My name is Martha Meyer, but you can call me Marty."

With his confidence boosted by how quickly she picked up on his cue, Harlan continued, "Well, Martha Meyer, I've heard tell that you have a beautiful singing voice. Would you mind singing a little right now? Some people say that singing sort of lightens the work, you know?"

"Do you really want me to sing?" Marty asked, leaving her affected tone aside.

"Talking doesn't seem to be working out very well," Harlan said a bit bashfully.

There was a moment of silence in which Marty appeared to be considering what to sing, then her lush voice broke forth.

Be not dismayed, whate'er betide.
God will take care of you.
Beneath His wings of love abide.
God will take care of you.

26

God will take care of you,
through every day, o'er all the way.
He will take care of you.
God will take care of you.

After the supper dishes had been cleared that evening, it was obvious to the Meyer family that Harlan was not as exhausted as he had been on the previous night, so Mrs. Meyer retrieved a checkerboard and set it on the table between Mr. Meyer and Harlan.

"While Marty and I do up the dishes, would you be so kind as to play a game of checkers with Father? The doctor says that anything we can do to stimulate his brain and his coordination is helpful."

"I guess so," Harlan said, a bit nonplussed about the prospect of playing checkers with a mute stroke victim; it seemed like such a trivial thing to do with his time.

"Whatever you do, don't just let him win. Make him work for it," Mrs. Meyer admonished.

Harlan turned to Mr. Meyer to see his lop-sided smile shining back at him. Harlan placed both sets of checkers on the board, and motioned for Mr. Meyer to start. He made his first move with his shaky left hand, and the game had begun. Mr. Meyer proved to be a worthy adversary, and Harlan found that he had to concentrate in order to make sure that Mr. Meyer had to "work for it."

As the game slowed and the two had to think longer before making each move, Harlan began to study Mr. Meyer. Harlan guessed him to be in his early fifties, and it was easy to tell that before the stroke, he had been the picture of health. Evidence of his former might was still present in his thick arms and shoulders, but a month of paralysis had caused them to begin to atrophy. He was balding with a ring of salt and pepper hair still present around the sides of his head. What struck Harlan the most about Mr. Meyer's appearance, though, was his face. Harlan had had only minimal experience with people who had physical limitations, and what he had always seen in their faces was either vacancy or frustration. Mr.

Meyer's face was different, and Harlan was trying to decide why, a process that was made more difficult by the fact that the right side of his face sagged a little.

Mr. Meyer tapped one of his checkers to be kinged.

"Here you go, sir," Harlan said jovially as he supplied the additional piece. The light tone of his own voice surprised him. He had been drawn into the game more than he expected and was actually enjoying himself, and then it dawned on him. What he had seen in Mr. Meyer's face was joy and peace, but for the life of him, Harlan couldn't figure out why a mute cripple would possess either one.

The game of checkers concluded with a hard-fought victory for Harlan. Mr. Meyer reached for Harlan's hand and patted his congratulations. Mr. Meyer's touch surprised Harlan so much that he almost jumped. How long had it been since another human being had touched him with anything other than hostility?

The two women emerged from the kitchen just then.

"Marty is going to read to us for awhile before prayers, Mr. Jensen. You're welcome to stay and listen," Mrs. Meyer invited.

"No, thank you," Harlan returned. "I think I'd better get to sleep if you're going to make good on your promise to not go easy on me tomorrow morning." With that, he made his exit to the barn loft.

Chapter Four

October 26 & 27, 1935

Harlan easily woke to the sounds of cattle lowing beneath him the next morning. The light from the eastern horizon was beginning to paint the black and white shadows in the barn loft with the colors of the day, and Harlan was aware that he felt cold. This sensation reminded him of Mrs. Meyer's initial invitation to sleep in the house, and for a second he thought maybe he should take her up on it.

Wait! You forgot that you aren't staying here, Harlan chided himself. Then he was struck by the realization that he had not thought about leaving since yesterday morning when his plans had been foiled by Mrs. Meyer laundering his clothes. Harlan lay there recalling the conversation that he had with Marty in the cornfield the day before. She had thanked him for being a man of his word.

What was your word anyway, Jensen? Harlan worked to recall what he had promised Mrs. Meyer. *Two weeks or rain, whichever comes first. That was dumb. Two weeks and your past could easily catch up with you. Then what?*

In that moment, he heard commotion below the hayloft. He climbed down to the lower level of the barn and discovered Marty there by herself, tying cattle in their stalls.

"Good morning!" she said cheerily when she heard him alight

from the ladder. Her back was to him as she was pulling a lead rope through its hole in the manger.

"Morning," Harlan returned groggily.

"You ever milked a cow before?"

"Only from the time I was seven until I was twelve," he returned.

"Good. It'll come right back to you. Mother said to have you help me with the milking so that she could take care of the poultry and get breakfast, and then we'll be able to get out to the field that much faster."

Harlan grunted his assent.

Marty turned to hand him the bucket of water to wash the cows' udders, and at sight of him her face broke into a broad grin.

"What?" Harlan asked suspiciously, a bit startled by how attractive he found her smile.

"You've got a little of your bedding in your hair," she laughed, pointing to a couple of pieces of brownish green hay adorning his blond locks.

Harlan felt the blood rushing to his face again. Two mornings in a row now, this girl had seen him in embarrassing situations: once asleep in the hay and now wearing the hay in his hair.

He brushed the dried brome away quickly.

Seeing him blush, Marty felt bad and sought to change the subject. "You start with Betty over there. Dad always used to be the one who milked her because she likes men better than women. Mother and I have been able to manage her for the last month, but it's been tense."

"Maybe it's change that she doesn't like," Harlan said dubiously. "So boss, so boss," he murmured calmly as he approached the cantankerous cow.

Betty turned her head and cast her deep brown gaze on the tall man at her rear flank, lowed a little, and then turned her head back toward the manger in front of her. With a gurgling belch she began calmly chewing her cud.

"Nope. It's women that she doesn't like," Marty observed firmly. "I can tell already that you two are going to get along fine."

The day passed exactly as the previous one had, but as it was Saturday, field work was stopped a little earlier so that as soon as the evening chores were done, Marty and Mrs. Meyer could take the cream and eggs into Underwood and do whatever trading was necessary for the week. Harlan wondered nervously if there were any chance that they would see his name and face on a wanted poster at the post office.

Harlan was to be left alone with Mr. Meyer, and no sooner were the two ladies on the road than he motioned for Harlan to come to him. Pantomiming, Mr. Meyer made it known that he wanted help to get to his feet. Harlan helped him into a standing position, and then it was obvious that Mr. Meyer wished to walk, but Harlan could tell by the amount of weight that Mr. Meyer was putting on his arm that Mr. Meyer would not be able to walk on his own.

Mr. Meyer indicated that he wanted to go out the door to the front porch. Getting through the front door was a challenge as it was not wide enough for the two of them together, but once on the porch, Harlan learned that Mr. Meyer's plan was to practice walking by supporting himself on one side with the porch railing and with Harlan's assistance on the other. It was extremely slow going, and in the space of a quarter of an hour, the two had traveled the length of the porch only four times, but Harlan was surprised at how patient he could be with Mr. Meyer. He could not help admiring Mr. Meyer's determination, and the time passed more quickly than Harlan would have guessed.

When they eventually returned to the dining room and Harlan had deposited Mr. Meyer in his bed again, Mr. Meyer pointed to the front porch, put his finger in front of his lips and then pointed to the kitchen.

"You don't want me to say anything about your walking practice to Mrs. Meyer, huh?"

Mr. Meyer nodded. As Harlan turned to go sit in a dining room chair, he felt Mr. Meyer catch his hand and squeeze his thanks. Mr. Meyer's kind touch caught Harlan off guard for the second time. It caused Harlan's mind to recall images of his father, but he quickly pushed them back.

Mr. Meyer motioned for Harlan to bring him the Bible which was resting on the table. Harlan obeyed, and Mr. Meyer began awkwardly flipping pages until he found a place that satisfied him; then he handed the Bible back to Harlan, pointing to the place where he wanted Harlan to read.

"I'm not much of a Bible reader, Mr. Meyer. I..." Harlan began to protest.

Mr. Meyer used a series of hand gestures to indicate that he wanted Harlan to read aloud to him.

"Oh, I'm not very good at reading out loud, either, Mr. Meyer," Harlan continued to protest, but the disappointed look on Mr. Meyer's face changed Harlan's mind. "I guess if you don't mind me stumbling through it, I could probably..." Harlan finished his sentence with a resigned shake of his head.

"In the beginning was the Word, and the Word was with God, and the Word was God," Harlan slowly read where Mr. Meyer's finger had pointed. "The same was in the beginning with God."

"Aren't you two quite the pair?" Mrs. Meyer chuckled, coming into the dining room from the kitchen while removing her coat.

Harlan awakened with a start at the sound of her voice, the Bible which had come to rest in his lap nearly spilling to the floor. Mr. Meyer, snoring audibly and with his chin resting on his chest, remained undisturbed by his wife's entrance.

"What time is it?" Harlan yawned.

"Half past nine, sleepy head," answered Mrs. Meyer. "Must have been real exciting around here after we left," she grinned.

"I guess we fell asleep," Harlan observed sheepishly.

"I guess you did," Mrs. Meyer laughed.

"Where's Marty?" Harlan asked, seeing no sign of her but glad that she hadn't been able to observe him in yet another compromising sleep-related state.

"Oh, we ran across Roy Schoening in town, and he asked her to go to the picture show at the Phoenix Theatre up in Neola with him."

Harlan yawned in response.

"Al, wake up, honey. We've got to get your pajamas on." Mrs. Meyer shook Mr. Meyer, but he didn't rouse from his slumber.

"Harlan, can you help me? He sleeps so soundly since his stroke, and I can't handle him by myself when he's dead weight like this."

Harlan nodded his assent and got out of his chair to help Mrs. Meyer. As the two of them maneuvered Mr. Meyer into his pajamas, Harlan noticed how tenderly, yet efficiently, Mrs. Meyer handled Mr. Meyer. He wondered if his mother had treated his father that way when he was still alive. Then, before he could stop it, his mind jumped to whether a woman would ever touch him so tenderly.

You've no right to even think about that after what you've done, Harlan Jensen. You shouldn't even be walking around free!

Harlan snapped his thoughts back to the present as he became aware that they had finished their task and Mrs. Meyer was talking to him again.

"Were you planning on going to church tomorrow?" she asked.

The question struck Harlan as being very strange. Mrs. Meyer had asked it as if she and Harlan had had this conversation every Saturday evening for several years. Others had strongly urged Harlan to go to church before, but nothing in Mrs. Meyer's tone had indicated that she cared one way or another what his decision would be.

"I guess I wasn't planning to," Harlan replied, bracing for an argument with the formidable Mrs. Meyer.

"Well then, would you mind staying with Al again tomorrow morning? I haven't been able to go to church since his stroke because I haven't been able to leave him, and I really want to go."

This request was not at all what Harlan had anticipated.

"I think I could do that," he replied.

"Bless you," Mrs. Meyer said. "You have no idea what a Godsend you are to us."

You only think that because you don't really know me, Harlan thought.

"I guess I'll head out to the barn now," he said quietly and made his exit.

Harlan awoke in the early morning to the sound of rain pelting the barn roof.

Good. This is your opportunity to get out of here.

The sun had not yet risen, and with the thick layer of clouds overhead, darkness still cloaked everything. Harlan felt his shirt collar to make certain he was wearing his own clothing rather than those which belonged to Mrs. Meyer's nephew, and then made his way down from the barn loft and out into the rain. The apple tree that Mrs. Meyer had mentioned was on the opposite side of the house from the barn, so Harlan began to make his way there.

If I can just fill my pockets with apples, I'll be able to make it a couple days before I have to find some other food, Harlan thought to himself.

It was raining hard enough that Harlan's clothing was fairly wet by the time he reached the house yard, and he was sorely wishing he had a jacket or overcoat of some kind as the north breeze began pricking at the exposed skin of his face and hands.

Harlan Jensen, you're an idiot to think that this is a good day to leave. What do you think it will be like sitting up on the railroad tracks waiting for a train? Harlan's mind immediately switched gears, though. *But this is your chance to get out of here and leave these people alone. You don't want to bring any trouble on them when you're finally found out.*

Upon reaching the apple tree, Harlan filled his pants pockets with as many apples as possible, stuffed some in his shirt, and carried two more in his hand for his breakfast. He began his trek to the railroad tracks at the north side of the farm by crossing through the house yard. As he rounded the southeast corner of the house with the dining room bay windows, he thought of Mr. Meyer who was slumbering on the other side of the glass—at least, Harlan *hoped* he was slumbering. Mr. Meyer had already seen him sneaking around the farmyard once, and Harlan was not interested in having him witness any more of his furtive attempts to escape the farm by rail.

What difference does it make? Harlan asked himself. *He knows that I was only going to stay until it rained; plus he won't be able to tell anyone if he saw me leave.*

Harlan took a few more strides away from the house and into the chilly wind.

You said you'd stay with him while Mrs. Meyer went to church. Harlan's conscience was beginning to prick him along with the cold raindrops. *Think of all that woman has done for you: fed you, clothed you, washed your clothes. And all she wants to do is go to church. To church!*

"She doesn't need to go to church," Harlan whispered aloud. "She probably knows the whole Bible inside and out."

Harlan steeled himself against the north wind, bent his head, and plodded up the hill to the railroad tracks. He wracked his brain to remember the train schedule that he had been trying to memorize for the past couple days.

But you haven't been awake this early in the morning, you rube. You have no idea when the next train will go through.

In the blackness of the cloudy night, Harlan found it difficult to discern where fences and other obstacles lay, so his exodus was slow and treacherous. More than once, objects in the farmyard made painful contact with his shins, but he finally managed to get himself into the north pasture and thus on a clear path to the railroad tracks. After crossing the fence, Harlan situated himself on the north side of the tracks so that the wind was to his back. He huddled down as much as possible and began to contemplate which direction he wanted to go.

A train headed west from here will most likely take you into Omaha; one going east will land you in Des Moines perhaps or then on to Chicago. Hopefully not Des Moines—there may be people looking for you there. Omaha and Chicago are both out of state if that matters, but in Chicago your chances of blending in and getting lost are better.

Harlan instinctively looked down the western section of the tracks, hoping to see the headlight of a locomotive coming toward him.

Nothing.

"Just wait. Fall asleep if you can; the train will wake you," he said aloud to himself, summoning as much determination as he could muster.

Time passed, and the frigid rain began to erode Harlan's resolve with a speed that Harlan found disconcerting. He ate both of the apples that he had designated for his breakfast, hoping that food in his stomach would help warm him, but the effect was minimal. He had just decided that it no longer mattered which direction a train was traveling, that he would try to board anything that came by, when he saw that a lamp had been lit in the Meyer farmhouse below him. From his position on the north side of the tracks, if the sun were shining, he would have had the same view of the Meyer farmstead that caught his attention a few days earlier. The longing to be warm and dry was only made stronger at sight of the tiny yellow glow, and the knowledge that the Meyers seemed to want him to be there only exacerbated his predicament.

You told them you'd only stay until it rained. Well, now it's raining, so it's your time to go. They are expecting you to go.

A few moments later Harlan's body started shivering in earnest. He stood and began to rub his arms, stomp his feet, and turn in circles with the hope of getting his blood to circulate warmth to his extremities.

This is stupid, and you're stupid, Jensen. You could be down there where you'd be dry, warm, and assured of a hot breakfast, but you've got to be up here, risking pneumonia to hop a train and go.... Harlan swore. *Just where is it you're going?*

"Chicago," Harlan said aloud.

To do what?

"Chicago, to start over and forget what you did!" Harlan shouted. Startled at the force of his own voice, Harlan whipped his head around to look toward the farm again, thinking that the wind may have carried his voice down the hill and given away his location.

The bay windows of the dining room now glowed with yellow-warm lamplight of a kerosene flame, and Harlan knew that Mrs. Meyer was there taking care of her invalid husband. Just then, the glow of a lantern began its voyage toward the barn, made intermittent by a pair of legs and two milk buckets on the opposite side.

Harlan thought of what Marty would think when she discovered that he had disappeared. First, she'd probably think he was oversleeping again. When he didn't show, she'd head up to the hayloft and see that he was gone; then she'd need to go to the house to get her mother to help her with the milking.

Just then, Harlan heard the far off shriek of a train whistle coming from the west.

"Finally!" Harlan rejoiced a little. "And it's going the right direction."

He stood and gathered himself in order to be ready to hop the train when it came, but then thought better of being so visible to the approaching engineer and fireman, so crouched back down a little way from the track. The locomotive was laboring up the slight incline, and Harlan could tell that the train was loaded and moving fairly slowly. Soon its headlamp pierced the darkness of the track, and within a few seconds the air was heavy with the smell of black coal smoke. Then freight car after freight car lumbered past him, the tracks squeaking and heaving with their weight.

Harlan had only to take a few steps forward and grab the ladder of any car, but he remained motionless on the ground.

Chapter Five

"What just happened?" Harlan cursed as he watched the caboose vanish into the dark morning. He was shocked that he had not moved a muscle while his ride out of captivity on the Meyer farm rolled past.

As if breaking free from ropes that had held him in place, Harlan rose from his crouched position and bounded toward the tracks, intent on catching up with the train. However, his toe caught the edge of a railroad tie, and in order to prevent himself from falling face first onto the iron rails, he threw his weight backward and landed hard on his side in a puddle of rainwater, his pocket full of apples bruising him savagely.

Harlan swore loudly and felt the urge to cry coming on.

"Stop it, you baby!" he shouted.

Harlan quickly weighed his options: he could crouch down and wait for the next train, he could begin walking, or he could return to the Meyer household. Though he couldn't understand why, the last option was the only one that seemed logical, and before he had time to change his mind, he realized that his feet were already carrying him toward the lantern that was glowing in the barn window. Harlan was angry and confused, but it was the fact that he was cold which was foremost on his mind.

Both Mrs. Meyer and Marty peered at Harlan around the rear legs of the cows they were milking when he entered the milking parlor of the barn. He wrung out his cap, wiped the rainwater from his forehead, picked up Mr. Meyer's milking stool from between two studs of the outer wall, retrieved an empty bucket, and walked silently into Betty's stall. He felt grateful for the warmth that emanated from the cow as the streams of milk began pinging against the bucket.

No one spoke while the three of them finished milking, and as soon as Mrs. Meyer was able, she headed to the house to make breakfast, leaving Harlan and Marty to finish by themselves. The two continued in silence until they found themselves on opposite sides of a full milk can, about to share the burden of hauling it to the cream separator in the house.

Marty's eyes quickly surveyed the mud and other debris that was clinging to Harlan's clothing, and Harlan was instantly ashamed of his morning appearance once again.

When she noticed the discomfort in his eyes, Marty shifted her focus to the ground in front of her. They hoisted the can and began the slow, awkward trek to the house.

"What made you decide to come back?" she asked quietly.

"I don't know," Harlan sighed.

Marty waited until they were outside of the shelter of the barn and nearly to the house before she spoke again.

"I'm really glad you did," she said, glancing toward his face.

The rain had made the roads muddy enough that driving the car to the church seemed a somewhat risky proposition, so Mrs. Meyer and her daughter set out on foot soon after breakfast. Before breakfast, Harlan had done his best to make himself presentable once again, but he feared Mrs. Meyer would not welcome him to her dinner table if he didn't make a little more effort.

After his ablutions, he entered the dining room to sit with Mr. Meyer, thinking that perhaps the two of them would enjoy another game of checkers. However, when he entered, Mr. Meyer was sitting up in his bed with his Bible open to the book of John once more. Mr. Meyer motioned for Harlan to take the book.

"Again?" Harlan questioned, a slight edge in his voice.

Mr. Meyer nodded insistently.

Harlan reluctantly took the book and sat down in a chair. He noticed that the Bible was opened to the third chapter of John this time and began reading haltingly.

"There was a man of the Ph-Phar-i-sees, named N-Nicod-Nicodemus."

Harlan looked up at Mr. Meyer. His eyes were closed, but he didn't appear to be sleeping.

"Mr. Meyer, you know I can't read out loud well, and these names are hard! I'm making you miserable. I can tell that by the look on your face. You don't need me to read it to you because you probably already know what it says. Why don't we play checkers?"

Mr. Meyer's eyes opened briefly; he shook his head and pointed again to the Bible in Harlan's lap. Everything in his posture indicated that he wanted to hear Harlan read aloud.

"All right," Harlan acquiesced, "but I don't understand it."

Mr. Meyer shook his finger toward the Bible, indicating that he wanted Harlan to commence.

The morning's rain had tapered off before noon, but the northerly wind continued to usher in cold air under a thick blanket of clouds. By the time Harlan and Marty had finished the evening's milking, snow flurries dotted the air, and the livestock chores were completed with collars raised and caps pulled low around the ears.

"Now, I'm not letting you sleep in the barn loft on a night like this," Mrs. Meyer admonished Harlan over a supper of bacon, fried apples, and toast. "You'll catch pneumonia for certain."

"Well, if it's all right with you, I figured I'd just take one of those old horse blankets hanging with the other tack and keep warm under it. I could also bring the dog up to the barn loft with me, and she'll keep me warm. I'll be fine," Harlan said.

When the temperature had begun to drop in the afternoon, he had begun thinking about ways to stay warm out in the barn loft. Harlan had suspicioned that Mrs. Meyer would extend an invitation for him to sleep in the house, and the thought made him uncomfortable. He still planned to leave as soon as could be managed, and it would be much more difficult to sneak away if he were sleeping right above Mr. and Mrs. Meyer.

"You're a man, not a horse," Mrs. Meyer objected, her voice thick with disapproval, "and haven't you heard that when you lie down with dogs, you'll rise up with fleas?"

"Maybe it's time that I…," Harlan started, intending to take this opportunity to make a clean exit from the Meyer farm.

"I don't want to be lying in here worried about you. I need my sleep, and so do you. No sense in sleeping outside when you've been offered a clean warm bed."

"But I…," Harlan started.

"It's not polite to argue with an old lady, Mr. Jensen," said Mrs. Meyer evenly but directly.

Mrs. Meyer's tone let Harlan know that the discussion was over. He also felt like he was a little boy, and he could feel the color rising in his neck and cheeks. He glanced up at Marty and saw that she also was blushing a little and that she had focused her gaze intently on her supper plate. With horror, he realized that she was probably embarrassed because he would be sleeping upstairs—where her bedroom was—and she would only be across the hall from him, a veritable stranger. He hated the fact that he was responsible for her nervousness and riveted his eyes to his supper plate as well.

The four of them ate in silence for a moment.

"You never told us about the picture show last night, Marty," Mrs. Meyer said, obviously endeavoring to ease the tension. "What did you and Roy see, and did you enjoy it?"

Marty raised her eyes. "We went to see *This Is the Life*. It's that new movie with little Jane Withers and John McGuire in it. She plays an orphan who is a very talented entertainer and..."

Harlan didn't hear a word of what she said because of the turmoil he was in regarding his situation. *I have to get out of here!* kept ringing in his mind.

When the supper dishes had been cleared away, Mr. Meyer made it known that he wanted Harlan to play checkers with him again. This was a welcome diversion to Harlan as he figured he would have time to plot his escape in silence while waiting for Mr. Meyer to make his next move. The elder gentleman was in fine form; however, and Harlan was amazed at how quickly first one and then another round of checkers elapsed. Even more to his surprise, Mr. Meyer handily won the third game.

"You've beaten me!" Harlan exclaimed in shock.

Mr. Meyer's face spread into his lopsided smile.

"Well, Father, I'd say that noggin of yours must be improving if you can outsmart a young buck like Mr. Jensen, here," Mrs. Meyer said proudly from the kitchen doorway. She crossed the room and gave Mr. Meyer a peck on the forehead. Marty entered from the kitchen too and surveyed her parents with a fleeting grin.

"How about you read to us this evening, Marty?" Mrs. Meyer asked. "On a night like this, I always like to hear Longfellow or Whittier."

"Oh, Mama, maybe Mr. Jensen doesn't like poetry as well as we do." The tone of Marty's voice revealed her embarrassment at her mother's suggestion. "We could play Rummy."

"I'm afraid I'm too tired to think that hard," Mrs. Meyer returned. "You read so beautifully that I'm sure Mr. Jensen will enjoy it."

Something about the tone of Mrs. Meyer's voice reminded Harlan of seeing parents urge their toddlers to repeat some performance that adults had found amusing. When he had witnessed those situations, his sympathy had always been with the youngster, and now that he found his presence causing Marty discomfort for the second time that evening, his mind grasped desperately for some way to ease her tension.

Harlan's own voice surprised him when he heard himself saying, "I don't mind if you read out loud. I had to memorize a lot of poetry when I was in grade school. Miss Stanton, the teacher, was a bit of a fanatic about that."

"I did too! Do you remember any of it?" Marty asked, her face lighting up.

Harlan instantly regretted having spoken. He had not only given the Meyer family information about his past, but he feared he had also made it sound as though he were educated.

"Abou Ben Adhem (may his tribe increase!)/awoke one night from a deep dream of peace." Harlan seemed to no longer have control of his own mouth, and words committed to memory a decade ago began pouring forth. "And saw within the moonlight of his room/making it rich like a lily in bloom/an angel writing in a book of gold.

"Exceeding peace had made Ben Adhem bold . . ."

At that moment, Harlan's eyes met Marty's. His performance had caused an unmistakable expression of joy on Marty's face, and the realization that he had put it there caused Harlan's mind to stop.

"I...I don't remember any more," he said after a long pause.

"And to the presence in the room he said/'What writest thou?' The vision raised its head/And, with a look made of all accord/Answered, 'The names of those who love the Lord,'" Marty continued.

"You had to memorize that one too?" Harlan asked.

"Yes," Marty nodded.

"I don't think that was the end of it, though."

"You're right; it's not, but the rest of it is rather incomplete theology, so it doesn't bear repeating."

Harlan had no idea what Marty meant by that.

"Do you remember any others?" she asked.

"The only other lines I remember are 'The outlook wasn't brilliant for the Mudville Nine that day/the score stood four to two with but one inning left to play," quoted Harlan, rather chagrined.

Apparently, Marty's embarrassment was sufficiently mollified since she walked into the living room and retrieved a book from its place in the colonnade. On the spine, Harlan saw the name "Lowell" written in richly embellished letters, and the edges of its cover were rounded with much use. As Marty spread it open under the lamp on the dining room table, she had to be careful that the loose pages didn't slip out of place. She searched for but a few seconds, found something that suited her fancy, drew herself into a very erect posture, and began.

"He spoke of Burns: men rude and rough/Pressed round to hear the praise of one/Whose heart was made of manly, simple stuff/As homespun as their own...."

As Marty sat across the table from Harlan, the yellow light pouring from the Rayo lamp cast fascinating shadows on Marty's lowered eyelids and deepened the rosiness that passion for poetry brought to her cheeks. Her voice registered several notes lower than usual, making the reading of the poem seem almost an act of intimacy. In seconds, any thoughts that Harlan had previously entertained about leaving the Meyer home that night had vanished. Vague hopes that no one would ask him what he thought of the poems neared the surface of his consciousness occasionally, for all he could do was follow the intoxicating hills and valleys of her voice.

Marty read various selections from Lowell for nearly a half hour then gently closed the volume of poetry and rose from the table to return it to the shelf. As she did, she repeated Isaac Watts' prayerful verse:

> *"How precious, Lord, Thy sacred Word,*
> *What light and joy those leaves afford*
> *To souls in deep distress!*

Thy precepts guide our doubtful way,
Thy fear forbids our feet to stray,
Thy promise leads to rest.

Thy threat'nings wake our slum'bring eyes,
And warn us where our danger lies;
But 'tis Thy Gospel, Lord,
That makes the guilty conscience clean,
Converts the soul, and conquers sin,
And gives a free reward."

By the time she finished her recitation, she had returned to the dining room table with the family's Bible and had turned it to the sixty-second chapter of the book of Psalms.

"Truly my soul waiteth on God: from Him cometh my salvation."

Harlan leaned toward Mr. Meyer. "This will be much easier to listen to than when you have me read," he whispered conspiratorially.

Mr. Meyer smiled a bit, but his attention was focused on his daughter's reading of the Word. Harlan listened intently, still enjoying Marty's voice, but what he was hearing had little meaning to him. However, he could not help noticing the shift in the Meyer family's demeanor. An almost palpable feeling of contentment and rest had settled over the three of them, and it was as if they were drinking in the words that Marty was reading. Harlan wondered at this for a moment, but settled back into the warmth of Marty's voice.

As Harlan burrowed into the first bedsheets that he had slept between in weeks, his mind was working rapidly. There had been no physical labor to tire him out on this day, so his brain took the opportunity of wakefulness to torment him.

It had been such a strange day! Just that morning, he had been waiting along the railroad tracks, executing his plan for leaving the Meyer farm, nearly freezing to death it seemed, and now he was sleeping in one of the beds inside their house. The irony of this situation was not lost on Harlan, though he may not have been able to articulate that. To further confound him, his brain was alternating between the sense that he needed to leave the Meyers as soon as possible and new thoughts of wanting to stay indefinitely.

As a result of spending his first real evening in the Meyer family's company, he suddenly felt connected to them in a way that he had not experienced since he had been a little boy at home with his parents. Furthermore, he could not shake the recollection of how they had all acted while Marty was reading from the Psalms. Harlan wanted to know more about why they seemed so glad to hear words that they had undoubtedly heard many times before. His curiosity was piqued.

And then there was Marty.

Harlan had spent large chunks of the last three days working at her side, but something had happened in Harlan's mind as he had watched her read aloud in the golden lamplight.

Stop! he nearly shouted aloud, startled at how close he had come to creating a disturbance in the quiet house. *You are only here because of some colossal accident! You shouldn't even be walking around free right now, and the fact that you are here in this house at all is a danger to these people!*

The jolt back to reality was poignant enough to start tears leaking from Harlan's eyes.

This brought another thought to the forefront of his mind: for what earthly reason would Mrs. Meyer trust him so implicitly that she would let him spend so much time alone with her only daughter? Why did these people trust him so thoroughly?

Just across the hall from him, lying in the safety of her own bed, was one of the sweetest personalities he had ever run across, but he himself was one of the most dangerous people he had ever known.

Harlan recalled the last words of Psalm 62 which Marty had

read: "For thou renderest unto every man according to his work." What could that mean but that God would see Harlan punished for his evil? He knew he certainly deserved it.

How can you even think about the possibility of staying? What you have done is going to haunt you for the rest of your life, and you're going to have to run from it for many, many years. And God will know where you are anyway. Harlan's conscience abused him.

Do you even believe the Bible? Harlan considered this for a moment. He didn't really know what it said, and he had certainly never spent any time trying to find out. He decided that he didn't know the answer to that question, but he knew the Meyers believed the Bible. That fact was written very clearly on their faces just a few moments earlier, and he had never met people who were more sincere about living by it than they seemed to be.

Harlan steeled himself in his resolve: *You have got to get out of here!*

Chapter Six

October 29 - November 1, 1935

"Shh, now. You're fine; just lie still. Shh, now," Marty said in low, hushed tones. "It's just me, Marty Meyer. I'm not going to hurt you."

Harlan became aware that a woman was prying his fingers away from something that was firmly in his grasp.

"There, there," Marty said as if talking to a toddler. "You can let go of my arm; I just want to freshen your wash rag."

Alarmed that he had grabbed hold of a woman, Harlan loosened his grip and felt that his arm was too heavy to hold up any longer, letting it fall to his side. A cold, wet cloth was placed on his forehead, and Harlan managed to open his eyes just enough to take in the fact that the bedroom he was in was dimly lit by a small finger lamp on the dresser.

"What happened to me?" Harlan managed to ask, closing his eyes again. He ached all over, his throat felt very dry, and his voice sounded unfamiliar even to him.

"You've been very sick," Marty said in hushed tones. "Here, drink some water. The doctor said that we needed to get you to drink as much as we could."

"Doctor?"

"Dr. Wyland was here to see you twice yesterday. You gave us a good scare."

"Twice yesterday?" Harlan wondered in a whisper. "What day is this?"

"It's about four o'clock on Tuesday morning," Marty answered.

Harlan opened his eyes halfway and looked at Marty. "What happened to me?" he repeated.

"When I knocked on your bedroom door to wake you on Monday morning, there was no response. I thought maybe you had sneaked out of the house in the night, so I opened the door. You were still here, but you were burning up with fever. I called for Mama right away, and she has hardly left your side since then.

"She just went down to try to get a little sleep a little while ago, so I came to sit with you until I have to go do the milking," explained Marty. "Mama could tell your fever was finally coming down, and she'll be relieved to find out that you woke."

Harlan digested this for a moment. "You shouldn't have gotten the doctor," Harlan mumbled crossly. "I can't pay him."

"We can't either, but lucky for you he has a penchant for Mama's sour cream butter and thinks that we have the best tasting stewing hens in the county," Marty replied.

Harlan opened his eyes narrowly. "What did he say was the matter with me?"

"He figures that you had gotten pretty worn down before you got here, so you were still weak when you got yourself soaked to the bone trying to leave Sunday morning in that cold rain."

Marty paused for a moment. "You ought to be very thankful that he didn't cut your leg off," she said almost mischievously.

"Cut my leg off?" Harlan croaked, his eyes opening wider than they had been in many hours. "What's the matter with my leg?"

"Well, when he was examining you, trying to figure out what could be the matter, he discovered that your upper leg was all black and blue and swollen. He thought maybe that had something to do with why you were ill until Mama discovered the remains of some apples in your trouser pockets and put two and two together."

Harlan closed his eyes in embarrassment at having been caught stealing fruit.

"It was also lucky for you that Mama didn't let you sleep in the barn loft. I don't know how we would have gotten you down out of there and into the house with as sick as you've been."

Harlan was surprised at Marty's volubility; it appeared that her sense of relief was so great that it had loosened her tongue. However, the shame that he felt conspired with his overpowering fatigue to cause him to fall asleep again—but not before he realized that for the fifth morning in a row Marty had seen him at far less than his best.

Harlan remained confined to bed for another three days, resting in a drowsy stupor. Dr. Wyland visited an additional time to pronounce him "out of the woods but still in the brush for awhile yet," and Mrs. Meyer seemed never far away. Harlan couldn't help but notice that she was a very efficient and capable nurse, and whatever feelings of frustration he had harbored toward her for entreating him to stay were dissolving beneath her tender care, but he was also conscious of the fact that his sense of obligation to her was growing almost hourly.

As his health improved, he found himself craving more and more of the delectable food that she continually proffered. Thirst had returned with a vengeance, too, and he felt he might never get his fill of warm apple cider. The thing he found himself craving most, however, was more time with Marty, but she had absented herself from his room since that first morning of regained consciousness.

Harlan summoned the courage to ask about her while Mrs. Meyer was retrieving his dirty breakfast dishes on Friday.

"I haven't seen Marty since Tuesday morning," Harlan hinted broadly.

"Oh, well the weather turned so nice again that she's been putting in really long days outdoors. With both you and Al laid up, she's had to do almost all the chores by herself, and then she's been picking as much corn as she can, shoveling it into the crib by lantern light after supper. By the time she comes inside at night, you've been long asleep," replied Mrs. Meyer.

Harlan was silent for a moment. "I think I could probably help with this evening's milking."

Mrs. Meyer appraised him through narrowed eyes for a moment. "We'll see how you feel this afternoon. There is no sense in overdoing it before you're ready," she said with finality.

As Harlan lay in bed throughout the rest of the day, thoughts of Marty picking corn by herself, then coming back in to milk, and then shoveling the corn into the crib alone plagued Harlan's imagination, and when it seemed to him that the sunlight in his windows indicated about five o'clock, Harlan got out of bed and began to put on his work clothing.

Every languishing muscle let Harlan know that it had been idle for too long, and his bruised thigh hurled unjust accusations at him. But when Marty saw him waiting in the barn as she brought the cows in from the pasture, the look on her face made him forget any discomfort his body was feeling.

Her words gave him no joy whatsoever, though.

"Mr. Jensen!" she exclaimed. "Betty will be so glad to see you."

Harlan hoped that he had not let his face show how deflated he felt.

As the streams of Betty's milk began pinging on the side of his bucket, Harlan felt free to sulk in his disappointment. Obviously, Marty's willingness to talk to him as freely as she had when he first woke up had faded with his restored health. But then, what reason did he have to hope that it would have been any different?

You need to remember who you are, anyway! Harlan thought. *All of this lying around in bed has made you forget your situation. Figure out how long you need to stay in order to make up for the doctor's bill and then get your —- offa this two-bit farm!*

What right do you have to be disappointed in that girl's reaction?

Harlan berated himself. *You're not fit to shine her shoes, and besides, you know that the only thing you can offer her is danger. In fact, if that doctor ever looks at any "Wanted" posters, your time here is limited anyway. And besides, she's not a bit interested in you. You know that she's already got a fella: Roy Whatever-his-name-was.*

Tonight during supper, you just be up front with these people. Tell them that you aim to stay long enough to make up for whatever they have to give Dr. Wyland, and then you're gone. You don't have to wait for any train, either. Just put one foot in front of the other until your stupid carcass is somewhere else! These are nice people; you don't belong here, and they don't want you forever anyway.

Harlan continued to wallow in self-pity, and when he heard Marty begin to hum softly, his attitude became even more foul. No words were exchanged between the two until once again they found themselves on opposite sides of the full milk can on the way to the cream separator back at the house.

"I'm glad you're well enough to milk again," Marty said sincerely. "Betty is obviously glad too."

Harlan's temper flared, and cross words bubbled up in his throat, but he swallowed them and responded with only a disbelieving grunt.

"No, I'm serious. I've been sent sprawling twice this week," Marty confessed.

Harlan was alarmed. "She actually kicked you?"

"Oh yeah. And put her foot in the bucket three times. I told you she doesn't like women. It's not been much fun out here without you."

"Are you all right?" Just moments ago Harlan had felt quite nonchalant, but now even he was surprised at how obvious the concern was in his voice.

"I'm a little sore, but nothing that won't heal in short order now that you're able to be the one that milks her."

Something in Marty's tone was very satisfying to Harlan, and he felt a rush of chivalry.

"That cow really ought to be sold," he remarked decisively.

"Why?" Marty asked, suddenly defensive. "She gives more milk than any of the other cows."

"What if she had hurt you? Your folks couldn't get by if you had been injured bad enough. And if Betty really doesn't like women, what are you going to do after I leave?"

"Well, by that time Dad'll be able to..." Marty stopped suddenly, and Harlan saw tears beginning to puddle in her eyes. Marty turned her face away from him, and all of his resolve to leave the Meyer farm as soon as possible drained away once more.

Supper that evening seemed to restore quite a bit of Harlan's strength, and he went out with Marty to help her shovel the corn into the crib. The shadows created by the yellow lantern light offered a hiding place for emotional faces and gave Harlan courage.

"I'm sorry I upset you earlier tonight," he ventured to apologize.

Marty didn't respond right away, and Harlan wasn't sure that she had understood him.

After she had cast a couple more shovels into the crib, she stopped and leaned on her scoop.

"It's not your fault. You're probably right about Betty; it's just hard to hear," Marty admitted.

Harlan sensed that she was taking him into her confidence and sat down to rest on the pile of ear corn still in the wagon.

"It's hard to know what to do right now," she continued in a lowered voice. "Mama thinks that Dad is getting better, and he is certainly better than he was right after the stroke, but I don't know that he will ever be able to do everything that he did before. If that is the case, then we do need to make some changes around here."

"Yeah," agreed Harlan evenly, staring at the corn at his feet.

"Do you really have to go?" Marty asked, her voice thick with trepidation.

At that moment, everything in Harlan wanted to remain at the

Meyer farm forever, but he remembered the dark clouds that he was sure would soon catch up with him.

Harlan took off his cap and smoothed his blond hair back before returning it to his head. "If you really knew me, you wouldn't want me to stay," he answered quietly, raising his eyes to meet hers.

Marty looked away suddenly in order to compose herself.

"How long *can* you stay?" she finally asked.

"Well, I was meaning to talk to your folks about that at supper tonight. I don't want to leave any debts behind, so I need to know how many days' labor will make up for whatever they have to pay Dr. Wyland. I gathered that you're going to pay him in produce rather than cash, but the cream and the hens could have been turned into cash, so I'm hoping your mom can figure out what would be fair. Once that is taken care of, I'll be on my way."

"Where will you go?" Marty asked, turning her shadowy face back toward Harlan.

There was that nagging question again. A little over a week ago, it would have been Harlan's turn to be defensive, but he felt that Marty was somehow some kind of friend now, and there was no edginess in his voice when he replied.

Instead, his tone was utterly honest as he said, "I don't know—Chicago maybe."

Marty took that in for a moment. "To do what?" she asked.

Run from what I've done is what Harlan wanted to say, but what came out was simply, "Don't really know."

Harlan got up and started shoveling corn into the crib again, and Marty followed suit. When the job was done and the scoops were leaned against the crib, Marty picked up the lantern and the two headed back toward the house in the crisp autumn air.

"What about you?" Harlan asked, seemingly out of the blue.

"What about me?" Marty asked, confused.

"What will you do? I mean, I know you don't know what you're going to do right now because so many things depend on your dad, but take that off the table for a minute. If Mr. Meyer had never had a stroke, what were your plans?"

"That's kind of a bold question," Marty returned.

"Is it?"

"Well, it seems like it to me," she said, but Harlan could hear no annoyance in her voice.

"Sorry. I was just curious," Harlan shrugged.

Marty's steps slowed slightly. "You'll probably laugh at me."

"I doubt it."

Harlan could sense Marty straining to see his face in the darkness.

"All right, I'll tell you what my plans were," she began, evidently deciding that Harlan could be trusted. "Before Dad had his stroke, my plan was to follow God's leading and to obey Him wholeheartedly.

"After I finished the eighth grade, we talked about me going to high school, but I'm an only child; Dad and Mama needed my help. They didn't feel like it would pay to take on a hired man, so it seemed to make sense that I stay home. So for the last five years, I've just been working with them here. I felt like that was where God wanted me during that time, but I also felt like there was something more coming.

"Now maybe I know what that was because I feel that God's plan for me now is definitely that I need to be here to take care of Dad and Mama, so I'm doing that wholeheartedly now. When and if that changes, I trust God will let me know."

Harlan didn't know what to say to this, so he remained silent as they continued on their way to the house.

After a short while, Marty observed, "You're not saying anything."

"I'm not laughing either," Harlan said gravely.

"No, you're not. Thank you for that at least."

"Religion is all new to me," he said at last, "and your family is so religious. I don't understand how you would know what God wants."

"The first thing you do is look to His Word, the Bible," Marty began to explain, "and it tells you that the Lord wants to have a relationship with you."

"I doubt that He'd want to have anything to do with me," Harlan muttered and silently added *especially after what I've done.*

"That's not true at all," Marty argued. "What makes you say that?"

Harlan was beginning to feel trapped and began to think of ways to avoid confessing what was really on his mind. "I didn't go to church much when I was younger, and now I haven't been for such a long time. If God exists, I'm sure that he has forgotten all about me."

"Harlan, do you believe in God?" Marty gently asked.

"I don't know," he answered honestly. "I suppose so."

"Well, for the sake of argument, let's say you do believe in God."

"All right."

"Now," pressed Marty, "by the very definition of God, wouldn't He have control of everything?"

It appeared logical to Harlan. "I guess so," he acquiesced.

"Now think about what happened to you just a few days ago. If you had gotten on that train on Sunday morning and then gotten sick on some boxcar somewhere, you could easily have died because there would have been no one to take care of you. Don't you think that maybe God had something to do with the fact that you're still alive?"

If God were in control of everything, why did He let me get sick? Harlan wanted to ask. However, what kept him silent at that moment was the fact that as the train had gone by in front of him that Sunday morning, he had felt as though he were tied to the ground beneath him. Every part of his will and every cell of his body had been poised to jump aboard, but as railcar after railcar had lumbered on into the darkness, Harlan had remained inexplicably paralyzed beside the track.

Chapter *Seven*

November 1 & 2, 1935

Discussion with Mr. and Mrs. Meyer when Harlan and Marty returned to the house determined that an additional four days of corn picking would be fair compensation for whatever expenses Harlan's visits from Dr. Wyland had incurred. Thus, depending on the weather, Harlan would remain with the Meyer family until Thursday morning of the following week. He would pick all day Saturday; on Sunday there would be no field work; he would pick on Monday, Tuesday, and Wednesday; and then he would be free to leave after chores and breakfast on Thursday.

Part of the conversation also had been about what to do with Betty, and it had been decided that shortly after Sunday dinner Harlan would lead her to the Neumanns, Mrs. Meyer's sister and brother-in-law, where they could board her in exchange for her milk until Mr. Meyer's future prognosis was more obvious. With these arrangements made, Harlan felt that his departure could be executed in good conscience.

Saturday's weather was perfect, and Harlan, Marty, and Mrs. Meyer were able to harvest a great deal of corn that day, even though Mrs. Meyer only picked in the morning and Marty quit early again to go into town with Mrs. Meyer to do their week's trading. The frank conversations that had occurred the evening before and the solidity of Harlan's plan to depart on Thursday had eliminated any tensions that might have existed between Harlan and the Meyer family. Therefore, conversation in the cornfield that day was light and easy, and when it was just Harlan and Marty alone in the afternoon, the two sounded a little like school chums working together. Neither of the Meyer women asked Harlan any questions about his past or his future, which also contributed to his sense of ease.

That evening had been nearly identical to the previous Saturday, complete with Harlan escorting Mr. Meyer on his laps around the front porch as soon as the women had disappeared down the road and Harlan had taken a quick bath. Mr. Meyer was able to move a bit more efficiently and with slightly less assistance from Harlan, but this only served to make him want to walk longer. When he had finally tired of his exercise, the two returned to the dining room, and Mr. Meyer once again took the Bible and fumbled through the pages until he found the passage that he wanted Harlan to read aloud.

This time the text was the book of Romans, and Harlan felt like what he was reading was very deep and difficult to understand, but he also began to feel that it was written about him. In the language of the latter verses of Romans 1, Harlan could see names that he had called himself in the solitary darkness of boxcars rumbling along the tracks.

Forgetting that he was ostensibly reading to Mr. Meyer, Harlan read verse 32 aloud twice: "Who knowing the judgment of God, that they which commit such things are worthy of death, not only do the same, but have pleasure in them that do them."

I don't take any pleasure in other people doing what I've done, he thought to himself, *but I knew that what I was doing was wrong.*

He sensed Mr. Meyer scrutinizing him carefully, and continued reading before any suspicions might have risen.

Later, for reasons unknown to him—and certainly indefinable by him—Harlan felt some kind of relief as he read the words from Romans 5:8, "But God commedeth his love toward us, in that, while we were yet sinners, Christ died for us." What did that mean, and why did it give Harlan a sense of hope? He could not answer these questions and couldn't take time to ponder them because more text stretched ahead of him and his job was to read to Mr. Meyer.

Harlan was thrown into despair again when he read "For the wages of sin is death." His brain stopped there, having a vague understanding that the word "death" in this case was referring to the second death and eternal damnation, but his mouth continued on its task. Since the two parts of him were no longer operating in tandem, Harlan's oral reading skills—already tenuous—began deteriorating quickly so that by the time he reached the word "concupiscence" in the seventh chapter of the book, the word was completely obliterated and Harlan thoroughly frustrated.

"Can I stop, Mr. Meyer?" Harlan fairly begged. "I don't know, I must be getting tired or something, and these words aren't coming out right anymore." This was something of a lie because Harlan knew that his reading difficulty at this moment stemmed not from his lack of skill but rather his distracted state since all he could think about was "the wages of sin."

Mr. Meyer nodded and shot Harlan one of his lopsided grins in an apparent show of support; then the Bible was closed and the checkerboard retrieved.

What Harlan had believed would be a welcome distraction from thinking about sin proved ineffective since his worried thoughts continued to hammer against him while he waited for Mr. Meyer to move his pieces across the board. So many questions were roiling in his brain, and he wished that he could ask them of Mr. Meyer, but Mr. Meyer's muteness was not the only thing preventing such a conversation from happening. Harlan couldn't have figured out how to ask any of his questions without revealing more information about his past than he considered prudent.

As Harlan looked into the warm, albeit half-fallen, face in front of him while he was kinging Mr. Meyer's checker, another verse resurfaced which he had read a few moments back: "For all have sinned, and come short of the glory of God." If this were the case, then wasn't Mr. Meyer, who, in spite of his muteness seemed to be the epitome of goodness and godliness, also guilty of sin, and if so, what in the world could have caused the joy and content that was so evident about him? Mr. Meyer certainly did not have the demeanor of a man who was doomed to eternal suffering.

He can be happy because the sins he has committed aren't as big as yours, Harlan thought to himself. Using his worldly sense of justice and righteousness, Harlan was trying to reconcile what he had read in Romans with what he observed in real life without realizing the futility of such an effort. *You've done the worst thing you or anyone else could do. Now you're going to have to live with the consequences...forever.* This sudden awareness caused Harlan to panic.

"Mr. Meyer, I've got to go to the outhouse," Harlan said, rising quickly and almost running out the back door.

The chilly outdoor air hit Harlan's face as he jumped off the back porch and tore through the yard, and he became aware that tears were streaming down his cheeks.

But you didn't mean to do it! Harlan's mind whirled, but his conscience convicted him. *That's not true. You did mean to do it. When you had your hands on that fellow, you meant to hurt him; you just didn't mean to hurt him that bad.*

Harlan's more usual lines of thinking began to restore themselves as he walked toward the privy. He remembered the question that Marty had asked him the night before.

"Harlan Jensen, get ahold of yourself!" he hissed aloud. "You don't even know if you believe in God. And if there is no God, there is no Hell, so don't be getting all worked up. When you die, you die. That's it. There's no proof of anything more.

"These people are getting under your skin somehow, and you've started to believe things you've never believed before. What kind of sway do they have over you? Sure, they've taken you in and fed you, and they cared for you when you were sick, but you've worked your hind end off for them in exchange. There's no sense in going gaga over their religion.

"The rest of it was all a gigantic accident. No use crying over spilt milk."

Harlan was blissfully unaware of the Biblical accounts of what befalls men whose hearts are hardened against God, so he felt some relief at his own words.

The headlights of the Meyer car swung into the driveway at that moment, and Harlan quickly slipped into the outhouse to make his swift exit of a moment ago appear completely natural. He didn't stay long, though, thinking that he ought to offer to help the Meyer women carry the fruits of their marketing trip into the house as this would afford him more time with Marty, a thing he was unconsciously growing to covet more and more.

When Harlan arrived at the garage in time to help carry the meager supplies into the house, Martha Meyer was no where to be seen.

"Where's Marty?" Harlan asked.

"Oh my goodness, Mr. Jensen! You nearly scared me to death!" gasped a very startled Mrs. Meyer.

"Sorry," Harlan replied diffidently.

"What are you doing frightening a poor old lady in the dark like that?"

"I was just up at the outhouse. I was…um…taken short."

"Why in the world would you go up there with a perfectly good toilet in the house?" Mrs. Meyer asked incredulously.

Harlan suddenly felt rather stupid. In his rush to escape Mr. Meyer he hadn't remembered that the Meyer farmhouse was equipped with an indoor toilet.

"Well, I…um…"

Mrs. Meyer waved away any need for an explanation and hastened to answer his question about Marty. "Roy Schoening was in town again—which I don't believe was any coincidence, mind you—and he asked her if she wouldn't go with him to the dance hall over in Weston. I guess some little orchestra from Red Oak is going to be playing there tonight, and rumor has it that they're pretty good." Mrs. Meyer paused to try to see Harlan's reaction, but couldn't make it out in the darkness. "I kind of had some reservations about letting her go to a dance hall, but Roy's an awfully good young man and I've known him since he was born."

Mrs. Meyer abruptly changed the subject. "Can you believe that this is all I could get with the money from the eggs? Prices for produce are so low right now!" Harlan could see Mrs. Meyer's head shaking. "I don't know what is to become of the farmers."

Harlan was unsure about what to say but felt that a response was required. "Times are tough for everyone right now."

"Yes, but for the farmers they haven't been anything but tough for a good long time now," Mrs. Meyer added. "Can you bring in the ice for the icebox?"

Harlan responded in the affirmative and an awkward silence prevailed while Harlan and Mrs. Meyer walked from the garage to the house.

"Does Marty dance?" Harlan asked, more to break the silence than anything else, but as soon as he had asked the question, he felt that his tone made him sound a little too interested in Marty's activities.

"I don't know that she does, but she enjoys the music. I understand, though, that Roy can "cut a rug" as the young folks say. How about you?"

"Afraid not," Harlan muttered as he held the back door open for Mrs. Meyer.

"Well, I wouldn't consider that a big loss if I were you," she said offhandedly.

Mrs. Meyer opened the upper left compartment of the icebox for Harlan to slide the large block of ice in and then deposited her purchases on the kitchen table before heading straight into the dining room to check on Mr. Meyer. Harlan followed her. As Harlan passed by Mr. Meyer on his way to a vacant dining room chair, Mr. Meyer grabbed his hand and squeezed it meaningfully. Something about Mr. Meyer's touch conveyed to Harlan that the older man knew he had not left to go to the outhouse for any physical reason. Harlan found it unnerving to know that Mr. Meyer was somehow aware of the thoughts that were plaguing him, and he was suddenly glad for Mr. Meyer's muteness.

"Marty and I ran across Roy Schoening in town again tonight," Mrs. Meyer said to her husband as she removed her hat and shawl and set about straightening the pillows behind her husband's back. "I think our little girl has a suitor, Al."

Mr. Meyer did not respond in any way; instead, Harlan could feel the gentleman's eyes studying him.

"Furthermore, Roy, bless his heart, was asking about you, and he wondered if you wouldn't like to go to church tomorrow." Mr. Meyer's eyes flew to his wife's face. "He said that he would round up a couple of the other young men to carry you into the building if we could just get you there. Do you think that Marty, Mr. Jensen, and I could get you out to the car somehow?"

Both Harlan and Mrs. Meyer couldn't help but notice the expression of joy on Mr. Meyer's face. He nodded an emphatic yes, and motioned for Harlan to talk to Mrs. Meyer.

"He can make it to the car. We've been practicing," Harlan said.

Mrs. Meyer's eyebrows rose in surprise. The plan was in place.

Strange things began to happen in Harlan's mind as he lay in bed later that evening. Marty had not come home yet, and it had felt awkward to remain alone with Mr. and Mrs. Meyer downstairs after Mrs. Meyer had read Scripture and prayed. Thus, Harlan had claimed fatigue due to his recent illness and ascended the stairs to the bedroom he had occupied for the last week.

The sheets and quilt that had been such a luxury to him just the night before seemed to be quite constricting on this particular night—so much so that he found himself somewhat wistful for the hay loft. He poked a bare foot out from under the covers, hoping to feel some relief. He wondered why he felt like he was having trouble breathing, thinking that he was perhaps relapsing into sickness again, but nothing felt the same. Harlan assessed his physical state and concluded that he was healthy in that regard.

No, your problem isn't you, Harlan Jensen. Your problem is that fool Roy Schoening. The admission was simultaneously startling and liberating. At least the root of the problem was now out in the open so that he could evaluate it head on.

First, why couldn't this Schoening fellow court Marty straight out rather than making it appear coincidental when they met in town? This seemed cowardly to Harlan. Secondly, what had kept them out so late tonight? Respectable, church-going people like these needed to be in bed early on a Saturday night, didn't they? And lastly, why did Roy Schoening—of all people—have to be the one to orchestrate Mr. Meyer's first trip to church in over a month? What business was it of his?

Though Harlan wouldn't have been able to articulate it very well, the time he had spent alone with Mr. Meyer had caused him to begin feeling a little possessive toward the elder man. Consequently, Roy Schoening had become undesirable competition on two fronts.

I'll bet that fellow doesn't really care whether Mr. Meyer gets to church. He's just doing all this to get Marty's attention. He probably doesn't really think that Mr. and Mrs. Meyer would take him up on the offer, and poor Mr. Meyer will be humiliated when he gets all the way to the church and has to stay in the car because Schoening doesn't know how to get Mr. Meyer inside.

Harlan's mind quickly began to accuse Roy Schoening of all sorts of fantastic villainy when suddenly he heard a car slowing down to enter the driveway. In a few seconds, he heard Marty entering the house followed by the muffled sounds of a short, low conversation between Marty and her parents. Marty then climbed the stairway almost noiselessly, and Harlan realized that she assumed he was asleep and was trying not to wake him.

The door to Marty's bedroom closed softly, and Harlan could

hear her moving about as she prepared for bed. He recognized the squeak of her closet door opening as her "town dress" was hung inside, and he heard tinkling noises as she tossed her few hairpins in a glass dish. These sounds he had memorized over the course of the last couple of nights when he had been well enough to pay attention to the noises that drifted across the upstairs hallway. But then he heard a different sound. It was Marty's voice, barely audible through the two closed doors and the expanse between. Was she talking to him?

Harlan was just about to call out a reply when he realized that what he was hearing was indeed Marty's voice, but that she was absentmindedly humming a tune—no doubt some catchy melody that the orchestra had played that night as she and Roy Schoening had whirled endlessly around the dance floor, lost in each other's eyes and locked in each other's embrace.

And what difference does it make to you anyway? Harlan asked himself. *You're leaving on Thursday morning like you've been wanting to all along. None of this has a single thing to do with you.*

That may have been true, but misplaced male jealousy took over Harlan's thinking in that moment, and he made a rather rash decision.

I'll show that Roy Schoening! Won't he be surprised when I show up to church with the Meyers tomorrow morning! He'll have to make good on his fake promises to get Mr. Meyer into the church building because he's going to be the one helping me!

Harlan's mind pointed out that he didn't have any dress clothes to wear in the morning.

That doesn't make any difference, he thought defiantly.

What if someone recognizes your face from some wanted poster? His brain kept providing excuses.

Nobody would believe that a criminal would show his face in church, so you're safe there too, he reasoned.

Harlan's final thought was his least theologically sound: *Boy! God will be twice as surprised as Roy Schoening when you show up in church tomorrow!*

Chapter Eight

November 3, 1935

"I'd like to go to church with you," Harlan announced at the breakfast table the next morning.

Mr. Meyer's face broke into his lopsided smile, and Marty's fork, which had been halfway to her mouth with a bite of fried egg on it came clattering back down to her plate while her hand remained in mid-air.

"Oh, pardon me," she mumbled quietly, the color rising up her neck.

Mrs. Meyer was completely unruffled and took in his request as if she had been expecting it all along. "I'm glad, Harlan. We'd love to have you. That will make it much easier to get Al into the building, too. Thank you."

The differing ways in which the Meyer family members had reacted to his request were interesting to Harlan. Mr. Meyer wore an expression that unmistakably showed his happiness at the prospect of Harlan coming to church. Harlan honestly found that rewarding, but he naively assumed it was because Mr. Meyer was relieved that someone familiar would be helping him with his mobility.

Marty seemed to be completely shocked at his request and kept casting furtive glances at him from the corners of her eyes. Harlan was pleased that he had managed to take *her* off guard for once.

Mrs. Meyer's reaction interested him the most, however. She didn't seem the least bit surprised that he had asked to go to church with them that morning. But then, Mrs. Meyer never seemed surprised when it came to Harlan, not even that afternoon a few days ago when he had first shown up at her back door.

When everyone was primped and readied for church, Mr. Meyer took great pleasure in showing the womenfolk how much improved his walking was with Harlan at his side. Though the words of praise and encouragement were directed toward Mr. Meyer, Harlan felt satisfaction at having played a significant role in Mr. Meyer's progress.

The foursome was soon loaded into the car and headed down the road to the small, white country church with Harlan at the wheel and Mr. Meyer beside him. The two ladies occupied the back. It had been a long time since he had driven a car, and the feeling of power that it gave him was quite welcome. He had been feeling pretty self-conscious regarding his clothing, but being able to drive again erased that.

The trip was not long, however, and as Harlan brought the car to a halt amidst the others which were parked in the church yard, he actually felt eager to meet Roy Schoening and see what could be done about exposing the interloper's foolishness. Harlan's spirit soared when, after surveying the other cars present, Marty announced that the Schoenings had not yet arrived.

He probably had no real intention of helping Mr. Meyer into the church at all, thought Harlan.

"Should we just wait here while you two go on in?" Harlan asked.

"We'll all just wait for a little bit," Mrs. Meyer said calmly. "It's plenty early yet." She took a tiny mirror from her purse, examined her hair, and tucked a few strays back under her hat.

"What if this Schoening fellow doesn't show up?" Harlan asked, almost antagonistically.

In the rear view mirror, he saw Marty's eyes fly to his face in response to the edginess in his voice.

"Oh, he'll be here. The Schoenings never miss church," Mrs. Meyer answered.

They waited only a couple minutes more while Harlan's satisfaction with himself grew exponentially. Then, a shiny black Buick Series 40 pulled into the churchyard.

"There he is," Marty said. "Oh, he's got Miss Porter with him!"

Harlan's heart leapt at the thought that Roy Schoening had arrived with an unmarried female companion who was different from the one with whom he had spent the previous evening. He felt vindicated in all of his suspicions toward the young man; it seemed clear that Roy was a two-timing cad.

He turned his head in time to see Roy exit the car and walk around to the passenger door to assist his lady friend out of the car. First, she was obscured by the car door and then by Roy's person. When Miss Porter was on her feet and Roy stepped aside to let her pass, Harlan's heart descended to his shoes.

"Who's Miss Porter?" he asked.

"She's a spinster teacher who has had the Maple Grove School for the last twenty-five years," Mrs. Meyer supplied.

"She was my teacher all through school," Marty added. "Everyone loves her. I wonder why she didn't drive herself."

As soon as Miss Porter was out of the way, Roy shut the car door and made a beeline for the Meyer vehicle, drawing up to the driver's side first. Harlan rolled down the window and was chagrined at what he saw coming toward him. He had hoped to encounter a short fat fellow with a cigarette permanently bobbing between sets of yellowed teeth or a wad of tobacco bulging behind his lower lip. Alternately, he had envisioned a towering, chisel-featured athlete clad in a tailored suit who looked as if he had just stepped from a page of the Sears catalog, but who was just as one dimensional.

In reality, Roy Schoening was neither of these. Instead, the young man striding toward him wearing a warm smile was a shade shorter than Harlan with closely cropped brown hair and a trim build. He was obviously wearing his Sunday best, but his clothes wouldn't have been considered fancy by anyone's standards.

"You must be Harlan," he said, thrusting a hand through the open window. "Marty's told me a lot about you—all of it good—and it's nice to put a face with the name."

Harlan hoped that his confusion wasn't showing on his face. The only reason that he had wanted to come to church was to put this young man in his place, and now he felt completely disarmed as he cordially shook Roy Schoening's hand.

Roy leaned down to look past Harlan. "Hello, Mr. Meyer! It's certainly good to have you with us this morning!" And then to the ladies, "I'm sorry I'm late. Miss Porter discovered a flat tire on her car this morning, and the Nelsen's that she boards with are gone visiting their daughter in Atlantic today." Turning his attention back to Harlan, he continued, "Could you drive right up to the church steps there? That will make things easier."

Harlan nodded and did as he was told. Once there, Roy orchestrated everything very smoothly so that he and Harlan held onto each other's arms and made a human chair in which the two strong young men carried Mr. Meyer up the front stoop and into the church effortlessly.

Once past the stairs and into the vestibule, they set Mr. Meyer on his feet and Harlan said, "We can walk from here. We've been practicing."

Harlan was unprepared for what happened next, however. As soon as Roy opened the doors for them to walk into the sanctuary, those who had already assembled there were waiting to extend an enthusiastic welcome to Mr. Meyer, whom they had not seen in church for several weeks. As the flood of people moved toward them, Harlan felt quite self-conscious since he was suddenly at the center of the throng.

Most of the people who greeted Mr. Meyer then turned to welcome Harlan to the church, and he was astonished at the fact that they seemed no less excited to see him than Mr. Meyer. To say the least, it was embarrassing for him to discover that Marty and Mrs. Meyer—or perhaps Dr. Wyland—had evidently talked about him enough when they were away from home that he had achieved a somewhat legendary status. It also did not escape his notice that a knot of three young ladies were assessing him from across the sanctuary and whispered to each other behind gloved hands.

As quickly as could be managed, Mr. Meyer was deposited in the Meyer family's customary pew on the right side of the aisle, and as Mrs. Meyer had slid in next to him, Harlan extricated himself from the throng and began walking around to the side aisle so that he could enter the pew from the opposite end. Roy Schoening intercepted him before he arrived, however.

"Thanks for bringing him to church," Roy said, sidling up to Harlan but keeping his eyes on the commotion surrounding Mr. Meyer. "It's good for both the congregation and Mr. Meyer for him to be here."

"It looks like he's pretty popular," Harlan observed.

"Al Meyer is one of the pillars of this church," explained Roy. "Up until he had his stroke a month and a half ago, he had been our Sunday School Superintendent for over twenty years. He's been instrumental in leading a number of these people to Christ."

Roy's terminology was unfamiliar to Harlan, so he didn't understand what Roy meant by his last statement. To try to keep his ignorance a secret, Harlan felt that he ought to remove himself from Roy's company, so he began to enter the Meyer pew, but Roy stopped him by gently grasping his arm.

"Our Sunday School class is held up in the balcony," Roy explained.

"Oh." replied Harlan flatly. He had had no intention of attending Sunday School as well as church.

"Rev. Martin himself is our teacher. He's great," Roy continued, steering Harlan toward a narrow winding staircase at the back of the church. The two ascended, discovering that Marty was already there and was the center of a knot of young people. Harlan and Roy slid into the pew behind her, and a few of the people who had been in the group that was greeting Mr. Meyer below filtered in after them. The talk was all about Mr. Meyer and had been directed toward Marty.

"It sure is good to see your dad in church again," said one young lady.

"I'll say," another girl added. "I didn't know that your father was walking again."

"I didn't either until this morning," Marty responded. "Apparently he and Mr. Jensen had been practicing when Mama and I weren't looking." Marty turned around so as to include Harlan in her conversation. "You're a great one for secrets, aren't you?" she addressed him.

Harlan took extraordinary pleasure at something he heard in Marty's tone, but he alone understood the full irony of her statement because only he knew the extent of his secrets.

"We only practiced a couple of times," Harlan demurred, his eyes falling to his shoes.

"Well, still, it was quite a surprise," Marty smiled.

Rev. Martin appeared at the top of the stairs just then, clad in his traditional black shirt and white clerical collar. He strode directly to Harlan and extended his hand.

"Mr. Jensen, it's very nice to see you," he said welcomingly. "I'm sorry I haven't had the opportunity to meet you yet. I was over to visit with Al the other day, but you were ill upstairs."

Harlan found this statement rather embarrassing and wasn't sure how to respond. "I guess I was pretty sick," he said lamely. He wondered how these people could know so much about him when he had only been in the area for a week and a half.

A high-pitched bell tingled somewhere below, and everyone stood up, so Harlan followed suit. A young man about Harlan's age stood at the front of the church and blew into a pitch pipe, and then the congregation broke into song. Harlan didn't recognize "I'll be

71

a Sunbeam," which they sang first, but the strains of "Oh, How I Love Jesus" were familiar to him because he had heard Marty and Mrs. Meyer sing it while they were picking corn. After a couple more songs, the young man who had begun the singing prayed aloud and everyone sat down again to commence their Sunday School lessons.

"If you will all turn with me in your Bibles to the book of Galatians..." began Rev. Martin.

Harlan was momentarily embarrassed again because he didn't have a Bible, but Roy noticed this and held his Bible so that it was between the two of them, also locating the book of Galatians for them both. Harlan was grateful for Roy's finesse at putting people at ease.

"...we pick up where we left off in our study in the middle of the fifth chapter," Rev. Martin continued. "The last verse that we read last week was number fourteen. It is such a good one that I think we need to read it one more time. Esther, can you read fourteen for us?"

The girl sitting to the right of Marty read, "For the law is fulfilled in one word, even in this: Thou shalt love thy neighbor as thyself."

Harlan felt the relief of recognizing the verse being discussed. He thought he had heard it—or a similar verse—often repeated when he was in school. He did his best to follow along with Rev. Martin's teaching, but he became distracted upon discovering that it was the class's tradition to read the Scripture in round-robin fashion. As soon as the pattern of readers was obvious, his mind was busy calculating which verses might be his to read so that he could practice them silently ahead of time. This was difficult, though, because Rev. Martin was grouping the verses together in ways that fit how he was going to expound upon them. Thus, Harlan put all of his efforts into reading the verses ahead. When he got to the nineteenth, twentieth, and twenty-first verses, he felt sure that those would end up being his. He had no idea what fornication, lasciviousness, emulations, and seditions were—let alone how to pronounce them—but there was one other sin listed there that he was more worried about than any of those. He knew what it meant and how to say it; he just didn't know whether he could read it aloud without his voice giving away too much information about his past.

Harlan was busy sounding out the challenging words in his head when Roy tapped him and pointed to verse eighteen.

Harlan felt all kinds of relief as he read, "But if ye be led of the Spirit, ye are not under the law."

Rev. Martin stopped there to speak a little more, so Harlan was spared the embarrassment of having to stumble over difficult words among strangers. It was Roy who had to read the next three verses aloud, and Harlan noted that he didn't stumble over any of the words.

The last part of what Roy had read rang in Harlan's brain as loudly as what he had read the night before to Mr. Meyer. "That they which do such things shall not inherit the kingdom of God." Wasn't that further evidence that he, Harlan Jensen, would not be going to Heaven? But the other sins listed there—some of them didn't seem so bad. "Envyings" and "revellings," for example, seemed common enough to Harlan. Surely these relatively small sins wouldn't keep people from going to Heaven, would they? Harlan concluded that there had to be more to all of this than he knew or understood. Certainly not all of these joy-filled people he had seen greeting Mr. Meyer this morning were completely innocent of sin!

But what difference does it make? Harlan's guilt-wracked conscience was asking him. *You are guilty of the worst sin. You're doomed to suffer forever!*

Harlan began sweating rather profusely as these thoughts worked on him, and the urge to take flight began to consume him again, but he couldn't make a smooth exit from this group. Furthermore, he didn't want to raise any suspicions with Marty, who would have certainly found it odd if he left at that moment.

Last night, you read something that made you feel hopeful, though, too. What was that? Harlan began reading ahead, searching for words of comfort, but found nothing in the remainder of Galatians which fit that bill. Had he been listening to Rev. Martin more closely, he would have heard reason to have hope, but he was too distracted by his fear.

At the appointed time, someone rang the large bell in the steeple, and the Sunday School classes dispersed. People who had not been present for the Sunday School hour began to pour into the church so that the main floor of the sanctuary was filling rapidly.

Marty rose from her place in front of Harlan and turned around to face him. "Are you going to sit with Dad and Mama, Harlan? If so, you'd better get down there before the pew is full. I stay up here to sing in the choir," she said.

At that moment, the girl whom Rev. Martin had earlier addressed as Esther not-so-subtly nudged Marty's arm while smiling up at Harlan. Harlan saw the action, but as any man who was so pre-occupied with his eternal state may be expected to do, he did not recognize Esther's intent.

"I guess I better get going then," Harlan said awkwardly and began edging out of the pew.

Esther nudged Marty again with a little more force, but Marty didn't respond.

"Oh, Mr. Jensen," Esther said sweetly, catching his elbow, "would you mind helping me down the stairs? They're so narrow, and I have a loose heel on my left shoe."

Harlan shrugged his assent as Esther latched onto him.

"My name is Esther Stempel," she said. "It's so nice to finally meet you...."

Even in his distracted state, Harlan noted that it had been a long time since he had smelled a woman's perfume.

Within moments of finally taking his seat next to Mrs. Meyer, someone began playing prelude music on a reed organ in the balcony, and the church service had begun. Harlan had not been in church for a very long time, but this service felt different from what he remembered. The congregation sang with fervor, the music was rendered a little faster than he expected, and the congregation seemed extremely attentive to Rev. Martin, but those things alone didn't define the atmosphere of that country church.

Harlan decided that it was Rev. Martin's preaching that was different from anything he had heard before. Harlan gathered that that Sunday's sermon was a continuation of a series entitled "The Attributes of God," and the day's topics were God's beauty and purity. Among others, Rev. Martin had used Psalm 27:4 and Habakkuk 1:13 and described the heavenly Father in such a way that caused Harlan to admit to himself that perhaps he believed in the one true and living God. And if he did, he also was guilty of sinning against Him.

Harlan hoped desperately that no one could see the tear that was slowly traversing his jaw.

Chapter Nine

November 3, 1935

Over Sunday dinner it was determined that Marty would make the mile and a half trek east with Harlan to deliver Betty the cow to her aunt and uncle's farm. If Betty were to get stubborn, Marty would be equipped with a cattle switch to offer encouragement at a safe distance from the rear, and if Betty were to get loose, there would be two people there to bring her back into captivity rather than just one.

Thus, the afternoon sun was warm on their backs as the errant bovine walked with Harlan's authoritative grasp on the halter at her cheek and Marty flanking her rear. Betty showed no signs of even being tempted to revolt, but rather seemed to enjoy the idea of a stroll beyond her normal scope of existence.

After nearly a half mile of silence, Marty jogged up to Harlan's side. "Are you all right?" she inquired.

Harlan cast a sidelong glance at her. "Why?"

She shrugged. "I don't know. You've been awfully quiet since this morning."

"I've just been…thinking," Harlan responded.

They traveled a few more rods, and then Marty broke the silence again. "Did you enjoy church this morning?"

"Is church something that people *enjoy*?" Harlan asked. "I've always thought of it more as something you *do*."

Harlan assumed that Marty didn't know what to make of this statement as she didn't respond to it at all and silence again prevailed.

"Do you have any questions about anything you heard at church?" she prodded a few steps later.

Unbeknownst to Marty, Harlan was fighting an internal desire to completely unburden himself on her. He was quite confused by this since he had hitherto been working so hard to keep everything about himself a secret. While nothing about a full confession seemed prudent at that moment, a rebellious streak overtook his tongue and Harlan did confess one thing.

"Really, the biggest reason I went to church this morning was to meet Roy Schoening," he said.

"Oh?" Marty responded with interest. "Why's that?"

Harlan's tension manifested itself in his speech. "I wanted to see if he was good enough to be your boyfriend," he said daringly.

Harlan could feel Marty's hackles rising even though she didn't say anything right away. Just before the pause in the conversation became awkward, Marty said through tight lips, "If Roy Schoening told you that he is my boyfriend, he might've at least had the decency to let *me* know first."

Her words and tone soothed something in Harlan, and he decided that he'd better back-pedal to safer ground.

"Don't worry; he never said a word about you," he admitted. "And if he had, I'm sure it would have been nice. He seems like a real gentleman."

"He is," Marty agreed.

Harlan decided to press his luck a little further. "To tell the truth, I expected to hate him, but I couldn't find any reason to. Have you known him for a long time?"

"We were in school together," Marty explained, "but he went on to high school in town and graduated last year.

"As long as we're playing this game," she went on with

antagonism, "did you get your new friend Esther down the stairs safely?"

"I guess so," Harlan said absently.

Marty could immediately tell from the expression in his voice that Harlan had not recognized Esther's shameless ploy to attract his attention earlier that morning. She didn't say anything for a few minutes, but then asked again, "Are you sure you're all right, Harlan?"

"Yeah, why?" he asked, but his tone did not match his words.

"It's just that most boys your age would have noticed how badly Esther wanted...I mean, you don't seem to have caught that...." Marty was having great difficulty as to how she should best choose her words.

"There are so many things I just don't understand," Harlan interrupted, his frustration ringing loudly in his voice..

"Well, I wouldn't worry about it. It doesn't really make that much difference if you understood Esther's flirting with you today or not."

"Wait. What? Esther was flirting with me? What are you talking about?" Harlan asked, a note of desperation in his voice as if he had just awoken from a nap and didn't know where he was.

"You just said that there were so many things you didn't understand, and I started to say..."

Harlan waved her off. "No, you asked earlier if I had any questions about anything at church this morning. That's why I said I'm so confused. My first question is why everyone at church seemed so happy. I mean, the Bible verses I read to your dad last night and the verses that we read in church today are not happy with all their talk about sin and how people will rot in Hell for lying and drunkenness and all those other things that were listed there. I'm sure a lot of the people in your church aren't guilty of very many sins, but none of them are perfect."

Harlan's words were coming fast now. "And what about people like me? I'm a..." Harlan caught his tongue before he came to a full confession. "I'm a...terrible person. You asked if I enjoyed church. How could I when all I heard about was the fact that I'm not going to 'inherit the Kingdom of God'?"

Marty caught Harlan's elbow and pulled him and the cow to a halt, turning Harlan so that he was looking her in the face. She was wearing a joyful smile that Harlan immediately misinterpreted.

"You're laughing at me!" he said derisively, wrenching his arm out of her grasp and resuming his trek at a much faster speed. Bitter feelings of betrayal surged through him, and Betty sensed the change in his demeanor. She had been calm before, but her fear instincts engaged, causing her to stop in her tracks and plant her feet.

"Harlan, wait!" Marty called, running to his side. Her speed, coupled with the urgency in her voice caused Betty to sidle away from Harlan, stretch the lead rope, and drag him into the middle of the road.

"Get back over here, you fool animal," Harlan spat at Betty.

"Sorry," said Marty quietly. A car was coming along the road, so the two of them had to work together to get Betty calmed down and back on her eastward journey toward the Neumann farm. A few minutes after the car had gone by and Betty seemed to be more relaxed, Marty approached Harlan's side again.

"Harlan, can we talk again?" she asked timidly.

"Don't have much choice right now, do I?" he responded peevishly.

"I don't suppose you do," admitted Marty, "but you need to listen to what I have to say."

Harlan grunted.

"I wasn't laughing at you at all. Please understand that right up front. The reason I was smiling was because I have good news for you. Actually, I'm smiling because of *the* Good News," Marty began explaining.

"You're talking in riddles," Harlan accused, but Marty could tell that he was listening.

"You hit the nail on the head when you said that none of the people at church are perfect, but you were wrong when you indicated that you are a worse sinner than any of them. The Bible says that *all* have sinned and fallen short of the glory of God—every one of us with no exception.

"The Bible also says that the wages of sin is death. This means that everyone—*every* human being—deserves eternal damnation because of our sin," Marty clarified.

"Yeah, I read those verses to your dad last night. And you call this good news?" Harlan asked sardonically.

"Patience," she commanded. "So, we know from the book of Genesis that God has created us in His own image. That's what makes us different from animals and other living things. It's why we're more important than Betty here. We're so important to God that He wants to have fellowship with us, but our sin keeps us separate from Him. It is also what makes us unfit for Heaven. See, God is holy, so he can't have any impurity with him in heaven.

"So God sent His Son Jesus to take away our sins so that we are no longer separated from God. You might have heard John 3:16, which says 'For God so loved the world that He gave his only begotten Son that whosoever believeth in Him shall not perish but have everlasting life.' That's good news. God sent his son to die for our sins, and he rose again. Believing in him means that we trust him for our salvation and turn from our sins. When we have put our faith in Christ, we are no longer damned for eternity. Damnation is still what we deserve; it just isn't what we're going to get, and that is called grace.

"Do you see now why the people at church are happy? We know we deserve to 'rot in hell' as you put it, but because we have put our faith in Jesus who has taken the punishment we deserved, we have been saved from that fate, and that's a whole lot of reason to be happy."

"But you don't know what kind of a horrible sin I'm guilty of," Harlan argued.

Marty chuckled, but then checked herself lest she offend Harlan again. *"You* don't know what kind of horrible sins *I'm* guilty of," she retorted.

"Like what? Cutting paper with the cloth scissors?" Harlan asked in disbelief.

"I only did that once, I can assure you," Marty laughed. "How did you know?"

"My mother sewed," Harlan answered.

"Well, anyway, it doesn't make a difference what your sin is, Harlan. Jesus' blood is bigger and can wash it away."

After a pause, Harlan asked, "How do you know all of this is true? I mean, how can you be sure? Can you even be sure that the Bible is true?"

Marty paused to choose her words carefully. "That's the nature of faith, isn't it?—believing in things you cannot see, or in this case can't scientifically prove. If you want well-researched answers for those questions, you need to speak with Rev. Martin. He can give you all kinds of reasons that the Bible is reliable, but for me two are sufficient.

"The first is that as I study the Bible, I always check it against itself, and it stands every time. Secondly, did you ever stop to think about the fact that no one has ever been able to prove without a doubt that the Bible is false? Sure, many people have tried over the centuries, but no one has been successful. I think that is amazing.

"You must believe in the Bible already," Marty pointed out. "Otherwise, you wouldn't be upset about what it says about going to Hell."

Harlan was unprepared for Marty's perceptive analysis of his character.

"I'm not sure what I believe," Harlan said aloud, but internally he was remembering the convictions he had felt in the morning.

"As far as the transforming power of Jesus Christ, the biggest reason I have to believe is the knowledge of what he has done in

81

the lives of people I know. I received Jesus into my heart as a very little girl, so I don't really remember what I was like before that. However, Roy Schoening, for example, didn't come to faith until a couple of years ago. You just mentioned what a gentleman he is, but if you had met him about three years ago, you would never have said that about him."

"Roy Schoening didn't grow up in the church?" Harlan asked, surprised. "He walked around there today as if he'd been born in one of the pews."

"Oh, Roy grew up in our church all right; his great-grandparents were charter members, but just because you are standing in the henhouse doesn't mean you're a chicken. A person has to make his own individual decision to follow Jesus Christ, and Roy didn't do that until he was seventeen. Before that, he was a different person."

The phrase "a different person" held an appeal for Harlan that Marty Meyer could not have known. How he had longed to be a different person than what he was! However, Harlan's skepticism was too powerful and wouldn't allow him to believe that the Lord had the power to change him. He also suspicioned that yielding to Christ might cause some changes in his life that he did not desire.

Harlan felt a little less confused, but he also felt a vague notion that Marty might begin pressing him to make some kind of decision or other. To avoid that, he wanted to control the conversation for a while.

"So, do you think Roy could be *the one?*" Harlan asked. He was amazed at his own nerve.

"You're awfully bold this afternoon, Mr. Jensen!" Marty reproved, but she kept her steps even with his. She was silent for several steps, and just when Harlan was going to apologize for having been too pushy, she spoke again quietly.

"If you're asking whether I think I could be married to Roy

Schoening, I suppose the answer is yes. But I don't believe that he is *the one*—as you say."

"Why would you marry him if he isn't *the one*?" Harlan asked, confused.

"Because I don't believe in *the one*," she answered.

Harlan felt it was reckless for Marty and him to be so frank with each other about this topic, but at that moment it was more comfortable for him than having her preach about Jesus.

"What do you mean?" he asked, looking over at her.

Marty focused her eyes on the road ahead, but Harlan could tell that she wasn't seeing it. "I think there are any number of men God has prepared to be good husbands for me—men I could be very happily married to. My responsibility is to pick which one I will continually choose to love and who will continually choose to love me until one or the other of us dies."

Harlan shook his head. "I have no idea what you just said." He was beginning to become a little frustrated by the fact that nothing seemed to be simple with Martha Meyer.

"Maybe a better way to put it is that love is a choice—an action," she paused. "I guess I view it like you view church. Love is something you *do*. I know Roy very well; I could see myself choosing to love him as a husband, and I feel like he's the sort of person who would choose to love me as a wife. However, it doesn't appear to me that either of us have made that choice yet."

A question popped into Harlan's head which he figured would keep Marty occupied for quite a while. He was immensely pleased with himself for thinking of it because he was sure her answer would consume the remaining time until they reached Betty's new home. If he had thought more thoroughly about how it would sound to a woman when a man asked this question, he would likely never have asked it, however.

"So what are you looking for in a husband?" Harlan asked. The smoothness with which he had asked the question was noticeable even to him.

Marty, however, acted as though the question were as natural as dandelions in the spring.

"Oh, the list is long," Marty laughed. "I want a husband who is a man of kindness, someone who is hardworking. I want him to be somebody who will read poetry with me in the evenings, someone who will be a loving father to our children. I want to marry a man whom I can respect and who respects me; I also need him to respect my parents. Since I'm an only child, they will be my responsibility when they're no longer able to care for themselves, so I need him to be prepared for that.

"Above all, though, I want him to be a Christian who earnestly seeks to do God's will in everything. And, truthfully, if that were the only characteristic I find in the man, it would be sufficient. What about you? What are you looking for in a wife?"

Harlan had not thought about the possibility that his own question would be returned to him, and he was taken completely off guard. He suddenly didn't feel as though he were in control of the conversation anymore.

"I don't know," Harlan said.

"Well, that wasn't a very fair question then," she chided him. "Don't you ever think about getting married?"

"No," he admitted.

"Why not?" she pressed. "Do you think you're too young? How old are you, anyway?"

"Twenty," he answered before he had thought well enough to keep his mouth shut.

"There you go. If you don't think about what you want in a wife now, how will you know if you've found someone you could marry?"

"I'm not sure if I'll ever get married," Harlan said, trying his best to affect a nonchalant attitude. After all, he could not tell her that he used to think about getting married until the sin that he was so worried about had made him feel completely unworthy of any wife. He hurried on, "Anyway, we're not done with you yet. You never told me what you wanted your husband to look like."

Marty thought for a second, "I don't really care what he looks like," she said finally. "He could have a face only a mother could love." She paused, then added, "But it wouldn't hurt anything if he had blond hair."

Harlan blushed a deep crimson.

Chapter Ten

November 3-5, 1935

When Harlan and Marty had finished leading Betty, the cow, to Marty's aunt and uncle's home, Marty's cousin Charlie, whose clothing Harlan had been wearing, offered to drive them back to the Meyer farm in their Studebaker, but Marty had turned him down, saying it was far too beautiful a day to drive such a short distance when a walk would be so pleasant.

This had surprised Harlan very much, but he was pleased with her decision because it meant that the two of them would spend another hour alone together. He had fully expected Marty to take advantage of this time to push her faith on him, but she had not said a thing that alluded to Harlan's need for a savior, the sin that haunted him, or anything else about his spiritual state. Instead, the two had leisurely walked home, and there were moments that he thought maybe Marty was just on the edge of flirting with him. He felt he must have been misreading her signals, however.

But then, he couldn't get past her comment about liking blond men. Wasn't that directly aimed at him? Surely not. It was too bold a statement.

On Monday morning, after Mrs. Meyer had left the cornfield to go to the house and prepare the noon dinner, Marty was again alone with him as they picked corn with such speed that an onlooker would have imagined them to be mad, but even that hour and a half had a sweetness to it about which Harlan was keenly aware. During all of their time together, they had either talked about nothing of consequence or Marty sang. Harlan had been treated to rousing renditions of "Wonderful Grace of Jesus," "Since Jesus Came into My Heart," and the like, and he found that he enjoyed listening to Marty sing as much as he enjoyed their conversations.

Thus, as Harlan slid into bed on Monday night, his body was completely exhausted from a full day of corn picking, but his mind was so busy that he knew sleep was still far in the future. Confusing emotions were tormenting him, and he was glad for a time when his body could remain still so that his brain could sort them out.

Be honest. You've fallen in love with her, his conscience accused as he stared at the dark bedroom ceiling. *You can't wait to pick corn again tomorrow because it will mean more time alone with Marty. Falling in love was kind of a foolish thing to do, Harlan Jensen. It doesn't make any difference if you love her. You're leaving on Thursday morning because you're on the lam, anyway.*

His conscience was much easier on him regarding this situation with Marty than it was regarding his sinful past. He had not acted inappropriately and had no intentions of doing so. Instead, their time together had been pleasant, comfortable, and easy.

That's another thing! All this time you've had with Marty alone. Yes, she's an only child, and yes, her father has recently become a cripple, but what parents in their right minds would let their daughter be alone with a young man close to her own age for so much time? Though it had not been his choice and nor had it been at his arrangement, Harlan was shocked at the number of hours he and Marty had been left alone together. Except that he knew that there had been no untoward behavior on anyone's part, he felt that he and Marty should really have been chaperoned much more closely. After all, he had indeed lost his heart to her. He couldn't help but wonder what explanation there could possibly be for how much trust her parents had had in him. After all, he was a complete stranger to everyone, and they didn't know what awful things he was capable of.

Harlan's lines of thought began to shift a little. *You know, you've been here for several days now, and not a single person has recognized you. You're basically in seclusion on this farm, and it doesn't seem like any of the people around here are the sort who would pay much attention to wanted posters. What about just staying? You don't have any real plans for where you're going on Thursday anyway. All you're thinking about doing is going to Chicago and blending in. Why couldn't you just do that here? Maybe your chances of being discovered are smaller if you stayed put.*

Besides, you know that the Meyers would be glad to keep you. They need you.

But did they really? Once the corn was picked, Marty and Mrs. Meyer would be able to manage the farm over the winter, and Mrs. Meyer had just complained on Saturday evening about how few groceries she was able to buy right now. *Maybe they really couldn't afford to keep you on,* Harlan mused.

He thought a while longer, his mind becoming a little more clear. *The problem is that you wouldn't be satisfied just being the hired man, Harlan Jensen. Right now, it's fun to be with Marty, and you're enjoying her company, but could you just be the hired man forever? Could you continue to behave so innocently, just working alongside of her when you really want to reach out and touch her, hold her in your arms? You'd have to keep her at arm's length. You can't marry her—not with the possibility of your past dragging you away at any moment. And it isn't fair to her, no matter how you look at it.*

No, your best bet is to let everything stand as it is with you leaving on Thursday, and spend the next two days pretending that she's your girl. That's harmless. Just enjoy the next two days as much as you can while living in a fantasy.

Thinking that he had resolved the situation satisfactorily, Harlan settled more deeply into the soft mattress, intent on spending the remaining time he was awake imagining how his life would look if Marty Meyer were indeed his girlfriend. These thoughts were so distracting that he was embarrassed to discover that he was humming very softly. Stopping immediately, he hoped that no one else in the house had heard him. Despite the fact that he had ceased humming aloud, the tune was still stuck in his head. What was it, though? Where had it come from?

At first, Harlan thought it might be some popular tune he had heard somewhere, but bits and snatches of lyrics were attaching themselves to the musical notes, and Harlan recognized that what he was hearing was a hymn that Marty had sung in the field that day.

Of all the hymns that Marty had sung as they had worked, she had no way of knowing that the hymn that resonated with Harlan the most was "Whiter Than Snow." Marty always sang that hymn with a plaintive note in her alto voice, and though Harlan didn't understand the full meaning of the symbolic words, he identified with something about the hymn writer's request: "Lord, Jesus, let nothing unholy remain, Apply Thine own blood and extract every stain; To get this blest cleansing, I all things forego—Now wash me, and I shall be whiter than snow."

If the sin in my past had never happened, I wouldn't have to be lying here imagining what it would be like to be courting Marty; I would feel free to just do it! he thought.

The problem was that Harlan's worldly outlook would not allow him to believe that he was forgivable, that his sin could be erased. To combat the sadness that accompanied this distorted thinking, Harlan tried vainly for a moment to convince himself that he did not believe in God. This task was becoming impossible, however, especially since the Meyer family's lives were constant reminders of his existence.

Tuesday's weather dawned crisp and beautiful, perfect for harvest. Harlan and Marty worked side by side through the day, picking corn as efficiently as possible from the time morning livestock chores were completed to when they could no longer see. Neither felt that conversation ever lagged, even though they did not talk the whole time. Sometimes Marty sang as they worked, sometimes she recited poetry, and sometimes they only listened to the breeze rustling through the dried corn shucks. All the while, Harlan's brain was indulging in the fiction that Marty Meyer was his girlfriend and that they were destined to have all the time in the world together.

Just after the supper dishes had been cleared and Harlan and Mr. Meyer had settled down on either side of the checkerboard, a pair of headlights swung into the driveway.

"I wonder who that could be," Harlan heard Mrs. Meyer say as she hung her dishtowel on its hook and began opening the back door. "I hope everything is all right."

The foreboding note in Mrs. Meyer's voice activated Harlan's imagination. Thinking that he had finally been found out, Harlan's stomach dropped. He suddenly felt as though he were trapped in the house and jumped up from his place at the table, fairly running into the kitchen.

Marty looked up from the dishpan, alarmed at his speed. The frightened expression on her face caused Harlan to stop in his tracks. He realized that running out of the house under the pretense of having to use the outhouse the way he had escaped her father's eyes a few days back was an impossibility, for it would cause Marty great distress. He was indeed trapped and would have to face whatever was going to happen.

"What's the matter?" she asked.

"...N...Nothing..." Harlan stuttered. "I...I just wondered who's here," he finished lamely.

"Hello, Elsie," an older gentleman's voice called through the darkness. "It's just Roy and I coming to pay a quick visit."

"Why, Karl Schoening, what brings you out so late? Is Dora with you?" Mrs. Meyer asked from the back porch.

Harlan's emotions were completely confused. On the one hand, he was relieved beyond measure that it was not the state police who had arrived to cart him away, but on the other hand, could Roy Schoening have come with his father to officially ask if he could court Marty? The idea seemed to tarnish the bliss that he had been feeling all day as he imagined his life stretching on forever with Marty as his wife.

"No, no. She's trying to finish canning applesauce today, so she's home poking cobs into the stove," Mr. Schoening replied as he stepped up onto the back porch. As Mr. Schoening came into the yellow square of lamplight pouring out of the back door, Harlan recognized him as being one of the men he had seen at church on Sunday. Both he and Roy were dressed in their overalls, which still bore the dust of the day's work.

"I should be doing the same thing," Mrs. Meyer admitted, "but other things have taken priority."

Harlan saw Roy and Marty exchange furtive smiles as Roy entered the kitchen behind his father.

"Well, that's why me and Roy are here," said Mr. Schoening. "Seems kind of rude to be talking here in the kitchen without Al. Is he near?"

"Surely. Come on into the dining room," Mrs. Meyer said, leading the way.

Mr. Schoening followed Mrs. Meyer in to see Mr. Meyer, leaving the three younger people to follow.

This situation seemed uncomfortable to Harlan because he wanted to be the one who stood nearest to Marty; in fact, he was fighting the instinct to put a possessive arm around her. However, Marty smoothly dispelled any awkwardness that may have arisen between the two of them by motioning for both to walk into the dining room ahead of her while she played the role of hostess and entered after them and then stood behind her father.

"I say again, it was good to see you in church on Sunday, Al," Mr. Schoening said as he shook Mr. Meyer's hand. "Looks to me like you're making excellent progress, but I guess that's only natural when you've got the support of a good wife and daughter and the help of this fine young man here," he said, pointing at Harlan.

"Anyway, if this weather holds, a bunch of us neighbors are planning to get together and have a corn picking bee for you on

Thursday. Hansens, Neumanns, and Schultzes and us are all going to bring our teams and wagons, and there should be a good many more who will be here to help pick. Most of the men of the church will be here. Does that sound good? We're sorry we didn't get around to it sooner, but you know how it is this time of year, so we're getting around to it now. We figure we can have everything you've got left picked inside of one day unless something unforeseen happens. Does that sound all right?"

It appeared that Mr. Meyer was struggling to keep his emotions in check as he reached for Mr. Schoening's hand to communicate his assent and gratitude.

"It's just your turn, Al," Mr. Schoening said consolingly. "Think how much corn you've picked for other folks, and unfortunately, this wasn't a great year since it's been dry, so we won't have nearly as much corn to pick as we should have.

"And now, Elsie, Dora has lined up several of the ladies to help you on Thursday morning. She said to tell you that they're each bringing a pie, so you don't have to worry about dessert," he continued.

"I'll be ready to feed a crowd," said Mrs. Meyer, her voice thick.

"We're all glad to do it," Roy chimed in. "Everyone we talked to is excited. Basically, it's going to be a big party."

"It *will* be fun; a corn picking bee always is," Karl Schoening agreed. "But for now, we should get out of your way. We'll be back as early as possible on Thursday," he continued, beginning to shuffle back toward the kitchen.

The two Schoening men quickly left, and Harlan and the three Meyers reconvened in the dining room.

"We've certainly got some wonderful neighbors," Mrs. Meyer said, dabbing the corners of her eyes with her apron hem. "They've talked all along about doing this, but when you finally hear them put a date on when it's going to happen, it becomes a real thing, you know?"

Marty's hands were gently stroking the tops of her father's

shoulders as his head nodded his agreement with his wife. Harlan noted the faraway expression on her face and couldn't decide whether she was also struggling with her emotions or was mentally calculating something.

"Instead of picking corn tomorrow, Marty, I'll need you to help me get ready to feed all those people. We'll dress a few chickens and make a big batch of chicken and dumplings. We can easily stretch that to feed however many people show up on Thursday," Mrs. Meyer began to make plans. Her words seemed to snap Marty out of her reverie. "We'll cook up a bunch of carrots to go in it for a vegetable. We've got a lot of squash too, but no, cooking that much squash would be..."

Marty interrupted her mother. "Please don't leave on Thursday morning," she fairly begged Harlan, taking him completely off guard.

"Why not? We already agreed..." Harlan automatically began to protest.

The urgency in Marty's voice as she explained herself tugged mightily on Harlan's heart. "If you are here, you can be the one that all those guys will answer to on Thursday. You can be our representative outside. If you're gone, that job falls to me, and I just don't feel comfortable doing it. It's a man's job, and it will feel awkward to be the one who's kind of in charge of all those fellows."

"You'll do fine," Harlan attempted to reassure her kindly. "Roy would do a good job of it, and I'm sure he would be happy to do it." He was surprised that there was not a trace of malice in his intent nor his tone.

"Please!" Marty pled, coming from behind her father and placing a hand on Harlan's forearm. "You know the way we've been doing everything. It's just one more day."

The warmth of her grip on his arm had an almost electrical effect on Harlan, and when he looked down into the two soft brown eyes that were imploring him, he knew his plans were changing.

"I can stay," he acquiesced.

The relief and appreciation in Marty's eyes was enough reward that Harlan would have agreed to stay for another five days just to feel responsible for giving her those emotions again. Mr. Meyer also reached out and squeezed Harlan's free hand to show his gratitude, but it was Mrs. Meyer's reaction that truly puzzled Harlan. While Mrs. Meyer was smiling and appeared genuinely glad that Harlan was staying another day, there was something about her which made Harlan feel as though she had expected him to remain through Thursday all along. Once again, Harlan wondered what Mrs. Meyer knew that he did not.

Chapter *Eleven*

November 6, 1935

It had been quite a while since Harlan had helped dress chickens, but on Wednesday morning as soon as he dipped one of the headless carcasses into the steaming water to scald it before plucking, the odor that assaulted his nostrils brought memories rushing back. Plucking chickens was a job that he had helped his mother do, and he was suddenly extremely homesick for her. He had not thought about her for a long time, and he wondered whether she were even still alive.

Then, of course, the smell reminded him too of a fellow hobo he had met in a hobo jungle just a few days after he had run off from the Civilian Conservation Corp. The man had been given the moniker "Dirty Darby," and Harlan had not kept company with him long enough to figure out whether he was called that because of the filth that concealed his face and hands or because of his lack of scruples. Dirty Darby was a wiry fellow who slunk about with intimidating liquidity, and it was well known that he occasionally borrowed things he had no intention of returning. One night shortly after Harlan had arrived in camp, Dirty Darby had "borrowed" a chicken whom he said wasn't roosting comfortably. Harlan had watched hungrily as he converted the bird into the main attraction in a large pot of very thin soup.

"You there, with the yella hair," Harlan remembered Dirty

Darby saying. "You'd better have a good sample o' this. It don't look like you'll make it through the night without a little somp'n in your stomach." With that, Dirty Darby had handed him a large portion of the unseasoned consommé in what remained of a broken crockery bowl. A whole wing, which was not completely devoid of its pin feathers, was floating in the middle of the bowl.

With shame, Harlan remembered devouring it both greedily and gratefully. It was some of the worst food he had ever tasted, but he wondered if that were partly because he had been feeling so guilty at the time—guilty about the thing that haunted him as well as the fact that he was eating stolen food. Even so, he felt like Dirty Darby's horrible concoction had probably saved his life that night and winced at the memory.

"You all right?" Marty inquired at his elbow, her hands working vigorously to denude a chicken of its feathers.

"Yeah, why?" Harlan asked quietly.

"Well, this is kind of a disgusting job, and the look on your face made me think you were about to be sick."

"The work's not that bad; it just reminded me of something else," Harlan said dismissively.

"Must have been something pretty unpleasant. We're going to be at this for a while so you might as well share it and make this job more interesting," she prodded playfully.

Familiar feelings of being trapped were rising in Harlan, but he knew that he couldn't find it in himself to be curt with Marty and cut her off. In a panic, he decided that it would be safer to talk about his mother than about his jungle experiences as a new tramp.

"The last time I helped dress a chicken was with my mother," Harlan explained.

"You don't have very pleasant memories of your mother then, judging from the look on your face," Marty pressed further.

"No, I do," Harlan contradicted.

"Is she still alive?" Marty asked sympathetically. Had it not been for the kind tone in her voice, Harlan would have curtailed these inquiries into his past.

"I don't know," he admitted calmly.

"What was she like?"

"She was tall and thin. Very light hair and skin—almost a towhead. She spoke in a thick Danish accent so that all of her "v's" and "w's" were mixed up." Harlan was speaking slowly as different recollections came to him. "She made the best meatloaf in the world, and when she got mad she turned the prettiest shade of red."

"Did you give her lots of occasion to turn such an attractive color?" probed Marty.

"No more than any other boy would have," Harlan retorted, thrilled to detect that faint note of flirtation in Marty's voice once again.

"What's your favorite memory of her?"

Harlan thought for a moment. "When we still lived on the farm and she would pack our lunches for school, she would take a wax crayon and write notes to us on the paper that she wrapped our sandwiches in."

"Who's 'we'?"

"My little sister and I," Harlan answered.

"You have a sister?"

"*Had* a sister," Harlan replied. "She died of pneumonia when I was 11."

"I'm sorry."

"Me too," Harlan said. "Mom and I both believed that losing her is what killed my dad."

"How old were you when he died?"

"Twelve. He had a heart attack one cold morning while he was feeding the hogs. By the time Mom found him, the hogs had already eaten his ears off and badly mangled his face."

Marty shuddered.

"We had to move off the farm then," he continued. "We rented it on a sharecropping agreement, and without Dad, our landlord didn't want to let us stay because he didn't think that Mom and I could turn a profit alone," Harlan related. "He was probably right." This last was said with a note of resignation in his voice.

"So that's why you know how to do everything around here!" exclaimed Marty.

"You didn't know I was raised on a farm?" Harlan was surprised. "I guess I told your folks when I first got here, but you weren't in the house then."

"You must have liked farming in order to have learned so much by such a young age," she observed.

"Yeah, I did. Times were tough for us—I guess the Twenties were tough for most farmers, and the Thirties haven't been any better so far—but we always had plenty to eat and Dad and I were always together. I think he would have made a great schoolteacher because he was always teaching me things.

"Overall, the farm was good for us. When Mom and I had to leave it, we moved into an apartment over a millinery store, and she worked there until times got real bad a few years ago and it closed." Harlan was surprised at how much information he was letting out. It probably wasn't safe, but it felt good to talk about this part of his past with Marty.

"So what happened then?"

"Well, after Dad died, I had quit school in order to do the farm work until we moved. After that, I found work at odd jobs or as a farmhand where I could, and that was what kept us fed. Mom tried to find other work so that we could continue to rent the apartment, but jobs were hard to come by. It got pretty bad, and then the people who owned the store building sold it to a family who were going to move their appliance business there and live in the apartment. So, we were relieved when the CCC expanded further into the Midwest in July of last year and I was able to get signed on. I went off to camp, and Mom moved in with an old lady to be her caretaker and have a place to stay."

"I'm sure the money that the CCC requires its boys to send home each month came in quite handy to her," Marty said.

Harlan grunted his affirmation. Pangs of guilt were poking his heart because his mother hadn't received any money for the last month.

"How come you don't know whether she's still alive then?" Marty bravely inquired.

"Well, the older lady she was living with has a daughter who is pretty well off and lives in Cedar Falls. The daughter wanted her mother to come live with her, so Mom was going to make the trip to Cedar Falls with the lady, and then she was supposed to come back and prepare the lady's house to be sold. Then Mom was hoping to find someone else who needed help, but I don't know...." Harlan couldn't say anymore.

"Would you like to find out if she's still alive?"

Harlan was silent for a while, hoping the emotions roiling inside him would calm down. He felt the strong and familiar instinct to run away rising from his toes, but after a glance at Marty he pushed it down again. He could not run away from her.

Marty mistook Harlan's silence for indecision, and recklessly pushed her point forward. "I'm just thinking about this from your mother's point of view. If she's still alive, she's got to be worried sick about you. It's really not fair..."

"You don't understand," Harlan interrupted through gritted teeth, the urge to run becoming even stronger. He was angry with himself because he had been careless and told Marty too much; now, his misjudgment had resulted in him being trapped in a dangerous conversation.

"What do you mean?" asked Marty.

"I can't..." Harlan started and stopped. "If Mom...." Harlan took a deep breath and began again. "I can't try to find Mom for the same reason that I can't stay here."

"You're referring to your big sin again, aren't you?" Marty said perceptively. "I don't mean to press you, but won't you let me help

you make it right? I *know* that whatever you did can be made right."
Her words were coming quickly now. "At least make it right with
God, Harlan. The Bible says in Proverbs 'He that covereth his sins
shall not prosper: but whoso confesseth and forsaketh them shall
have mercy.'"

"Don't you think I..." Harlan began in a raised voice, but Marty
raised her hand to stop him.

"What sin does is make us lose our fellowship. We lose our
fellowship with God, of course, but we lose it with each other
too, and your unconfessed sin has made you lose fellowship with
your own mother who loves you and whom you love!" she said
emphatically.

Harlan wished desperately that he could undo what he had
done. "Some things can never be made right," he groaned, thinking
that other facets of dressing chickens besides the smell brought up
bad memories.

Marty did not go to the cornfield with Harlan that afternoon
since she had been pressed into service in the house, helping Mrs.
Meyer clean and prepare for all of the women who would be
arriving to help serve the meals the next day.

Harlan noticed that he didn't pick corn as quickly by himself
as he did when Marty was with him. His conversation with Marty
that morning, the homesickness for his mother, and the unpleasant
memories that had surfaced tormented him all afternoon since he
did not have Marty there beside him to divert his thoughts. He
was deeply regretting the fact that he had divulged so much to
Marty, but as he went over and over their exchange in his mind,
Harlan was relieved that he had never mentioned the name of the
town where he and his mother had lived, and surely Cedar Falls
was large enough to have several well-to-do women whose elderly
mothers lived with them. Marty wouldn't be able to find his mother
herself. After all, he felt he had done his mother a great service by
not running home to her right away.

Harlan figured that the authorities had already tracked down his mother through the information that the CCC would have had on where his monthly pay was to be mailed, but she could answer truthfully that she had no idea where he was. Yes, it seemed quite obvious that his mother's home would have been the first place that they would have tried to find him, and he was sure that his mother wouldn't want to have anything to do with him once she had been told what he had done.

However, Harlan had no concept of his own naiveté in that regard. Having no children of his own and having spent no time thinking about it, he had an incomplete grasp of just how powerful a parent's love is, and this deficiency in his understanding of love prevented him from having any concept whatsoever of the deep love that God the Father has for His people. Harlan was walking in darkness in so many ways.

Harlan stopped harvesting corn earlier than usual that evening because he wanted to have enough daylight left to try to neaten up the farmstead before all of Mr. Meyer's neighbors converged there the next morning. In the short time that he had known Mr. Meyer, Harlan had become quite attached to the man, and he felt like he owed it to Mr. Meyer to help him preserve as much of his dignity as possible since he was sure that it was going to be quite humbling to have so many people helping the Meyer family out. After the sun sank low and the Meyer women had lit a lamp in the house, Harlan could see Mr. Meyer watching him through the bay windows in the dining room.

Though Mr. Meyer's face was not visible, Mr. Meyer's posture as he stared out the window was sufficient to let Harlan know that the elder man was troubled. When it was time for Harlan to go to the house, wash his hands, and fetch the milking equipment, he discovered the Meyer ladies completely engrossed in chasing the last bits of dirt from the back porch with scrub brushes. He tiptoed past them so as to be sure that he wasn't tracking any dirt into the house and went straight to the dining room. Mr. Meyer was still facing the windows, peering blankly out at the gathering darkness.

"You all right, Mr. Meyer?" Harlan asked.

Mr. Meyer shifted his weight uncoordinatedly and turned to face Harlan. Tears were welling in his eyes.

"Mr. Meyer?"

Mr. Meyer pointed to his chest with his left hand and then pointed out the windows.

"You want to go outside?" Harlan asked.

Mr. Meyer's face brightened a bit as he nodded his head.

There was something heart-wrenching about Mr. Meyer's countenance, and Harlan could completely understand the crippled man's frustration. Until only a matter of weeks ago, he had been a successful farmer, respected among his peers and operating independently. Now, he was the beneficiary of his neighbors' charity, even though they were happy to help him. More than that, he had been a strong and capable man, leading and teaching others; now he could neither walk nor communicate without help. Harlan possessed an admiration for Mr. Meyer that rivaled the feelings he still harbored for his own father, and upon seeing tears in Mr. Meyer's eyes, Harlan would have moved Heaven and Earth for the man.

Harlan spoke with conviction. "Let me see what we can do about that."

What followed was a flurry of activity while Harlan and Mrs. Meyer worked together to get Mr. Meyer into clothing that was suitable for a trip outdoors, and then, because only Harlan was strong enough to maneuver Mr. Meyer, the two men made the arduous walk to the corn crib while the two women did the milking. A good twenty minutes elapsed between the time that they stepped gingerly off the back porch steps and arrived at the corn crib a few yards away, and both of the men had exerted a great deal of energy to remain upright along the way.

Mr. Meyer inspected the fullness of the corn crib, and then

through a series of pantomimed gestures made his wishes known to Harlan regarding how he wanted the events of the next day to be organized. The dialog between the two was slow and convoluted at times, but both remained extremely patient with the other, and Harlan's astute intuition eventually afforded Mr. Meyer and him a shared vision. The two men arrived back inside the house in time for a late supper of waffles and canned fruit.

"Well, Father, you must be worn out after all the work you did today," Mrs. Meyer said as she cut Mr. Meyer's waffle into bite-sized pieces for him. She had made the comment in all seriousness, and even someone who didn't know her well would have been able to detect the pleasure in her voice.

Mr. Meyer responded with his lopsided grin.

"Did you two get everything prepared for tomorrow?" Marty asked.

"We sure did," Harlan said happily. Working with Mr. Meyer and seeing the satisfaction that he had afforded the older man in doing so had given Harlan's mood a humongous boost. "Mr. Meyer had some good ideas about how to keep the wagon traffic running smoothly as well as keeping things safe."

"Well, I'm sure glad you've been here, Harlan, and I'm so thankful that you are staying around tomorrow," Mrs. Meyer said appreciatively. "You just have no idea what a blessing God sent when He brought you to us. The farm work that you have done has been great, but the thing I thank you for the most is your help with Al here. You have done so much to speed his recuperation from the stroke—things Marty and I couldn't have done ourselves. You've got a real decent streak in you, and I don't know as I've ever met another man your age who has half so much patience with a couple of old people like ourselves."

Mr. Meyer reached over and squeezed Harlan's arm to indicate his agreement, and the smile on Marty's face was unmistakable.

Harlan did not agree with Mrs. Meyer about his having a "decent streak," but he did find it thrilling to be the Meyer family's hero that evening, and he hoped that the work he was going to do the next day would further ingratiate him with these people before his time with them came to a close. He didn't know if he had ever felt as important as he did just then.

"Thank you," Harlan said demurely.

Chapter *Twelve*

November 7, 1935

Just after the sun crept over the horizon on Thursday morning, teams, wagons, and men began to arrive at the Meyer farm. Women lagged behind a little, waiting for pies to bake while they washed their cream separators in preparation for the evening milking. The feeling of camaraderie and shared sense of purpose lent a festivity to the crisp morning that made it seem much more of a holiday than a day of intense labor. Harlan, the Meyer family, and even the Schoenings were shocked at how many people had come to help. While nearly every able-bodied person from the Meyers' church family were present—including Rev. Martin—the workforce present that day was also drawn from the Meyers' neighbors and friends who either went to church elsewhere or not at all. The presence of so many people was a testament to how well Mr. and Mrs. Meyer were regarded in their community.

Harlan's instinct would have let him be most content as a peasant farmhand on this sort of day. Instead, as Marty had predicted, he was elevated to Lord of the Manor as all questions about how and where things should be done were deferred to him. He was extremely thankful that Mr. Meyer had felt well enough to engineer the whole event the night before. After all, it was much easier to begin answering each question with the phrase "Mr. Meyer wants us to..." because no one would argue the merits of whatever he said after that. His word had already become law. Harlan noticed the effect that evoking Mr. Meyer's name had on people, and, without jealousy, he wished that he possessed that kind of power.

Older men for whom the actual picking of the corn had become challenging were employed in driving the teams and wagons in a continual rotation between field and crib. Harlan noticed with possessive pride that none of the visiting teams of horses under the direction of these men were quite as beautiful and well maintained as the Meyer Percherons. With the exception of Harlan and Roy Schoening, every other able-bodied man was sent out to the fields. Roy and Harlan were to remain at the farmstead to scoop out the wagons as they brought their yellow cargo in for storage, and between wagonloads, they were engaged at the corn sheller with the goal of filling the small wooden granary that stood nearby with as much grain as they could and carting the pink cobs to the fuel bin at the back of the summer kitchen.

As the two were hauling their first bushel baskets of shelled corn to the granary, Roy began a friendly conversation with Harlan.

"I was kind of hoping that the Andersens would bring over their McCormick-Deering picker. That thing would really make quick work of this job, but my Dad discouraged them. He said that half the fun of a picking bee was the competitions that the guys get into about who can pick the fastest and who can tell the tallest tales while they're out there. Said that a corn picking machine would take all the fun out of it," Roy chuckled.

"Oh?" Harlan said, not really sure what the expected response was.

"Dad's kind of a stick in the mud that way. He says that our hills are too steep for corn pickers, that they leave or drop too many ears, that they are too expensive, and he levels all kinds of other complaints against them, but I think they are the way of the future, don't you? One man can only pick around an acre of corn in a day, but Andersens can pick almost fifteen acres in the same amount of time with that picker. I think in only a few years when you and I are farming our own places, everybody will be picking corn by machine.

"There are some folks who think we won't even be using horses anymore—say tractors will provide all the power. That'll change everything—no stopping to rest or switch teams. We'll be able to winter over more cattle because we won't have to hay horses. Think how things will be different for us!"

Harlan was taken off guard and sort of amused by the fact that Roy Schoening assumed that he was planning to be a farmer, but Roy's conversation was both amicable and safe, and Harlan couldn't help but feel at ease with him.

"Maybe, but I'll miss the horses," Harlan said.

The two worked efficiently together until Marty dropped off a pair of old lard cans with a piece of coffee cake and a pint mason jar of hot coffee in each on her way out to the field to take more of the same to the men who were picking.

"They're taking good care of us today!" Roy remarked jovially.

"It's the least we can do," Marty replied, her appreciation evident in her voice. "When Dad saw all these people arrive this morning, you should have seen the tears run down his face! I can't believe how many people you got to show up!" she said as she continued on her journey.

"We didn't ask all of them," admitted Roy. "We were just as surprised as you."

He addressed Harlan after Marty was no longer in earshot. "Dad and I talked to the folks at church, of course, and a few of the other near neighbors, but apparently the word spread like fire."

"Well, it looks to me like Mr. Meyer is pretty well respected around here," observed Harlan as he put half of his piece of coffee cake in his mouth at once.

"Understatement of the year!" replied Roy, opening his jar of coffee.

"Everybody is doing exactly what I told them to do right now—it was kind of a weird feeling to have that kind of power this morning—and it is only because they know the orders came from Mr. Meyer. That's a lot of honor, in my book," Harlan said. "I know they wouldn't all have obeyed my orders if they hadn't come from him."

"Probably so," Roy assented.

When it came time for noon dinner, everyone came in from the fields to the house for an hour's break. So many men were present that they had to eat in shifts. Mrs. Meyer and her crew of neighbor women had somehow managed to move Mr. Meyer's hospital bed into the living room. Then, they had stretched the dining room table out to its fullest length and added folding tables on either end. This made for a very cramped dining space, but it was the only way to accommodate such a crowd. Had the weather been warmer outdoors, trestle tables would have been set up in the yard, but it was too late in the season for that.

While the older women staffed the kitchen by plating the food and washing the dishes, Marty and a few other girls her age were stationed in the dining room to serve and clear. Esther Stempel, whom Harlan had escorted down the stairway at church the previous Sunday, was among the young ladies in the dining room. Her face brightened when she saw Harlan take his seat at the table when it was his shift's turn to eat.

"Why, Mr. Jensen," Esther said as if she were surprised at his presence, "what can I get you to drink: coffee, tea, water, or milk?"

"Milk, please," Harlan replied. He tried frantically to suppress the blush that began rising in his neck at her overly attentive tone. Now that Marty had made him aware of Esther's interest in him, he felt very awkward around her, and it didn't help that he was surrounded by so many local men whom he didn't know.

"From what I've heard the men say, everything is going just as smoothly as possible, and you deserve all the credit," Esther attempted to flatter him.

"Oh, no. I would have botched it all if Mr. Meyer hadn't spent a lot of time yesterday showing me how to organize all this," Harlan demurred. "Isn't that right, Mr. Meyer?" he asked, tossing his head toward the elder man who was seated in a chair between the colonnades that separated the dining room from the living room.

Mr. Meyer acknowledged this with a broad, lopsided smile.

"Still, you've had to be in charge out there today, and that's a big job," praised Esther.

"Well, it is easy to be in charge of such a great crew," Harlan responded, pleased with himself for quickly thinking of what to say to avoid taking any credit.

"We should be done well before evening milking at the rate everything is going, Al," a middle-aged man at the end of the table said to Mr. Meyer. "The best corn we've seen has been down in the valleys, of course. With the dry year we've had, that's no surprise. You might be getting twenty bushel to the acre on the low ground. Isn't that what you gents would estimate?"

"Too bad it's not worth anything!" another farmer put in.

Harlan was glad for the distraction of the masculine talk that followed, but as Esther put Harlan's glass of milk in front of him, she rested her free hand on his shoulder in what amounted to a very obvious and lengthy caress.

Clearing his throat very loudly first, a man across the table said, "I'll have coffee please, Esther." His tone made it obvious that he felt she had spent a little too much time and attention on Harlan. At this, Harlan lost his battle with his blush.

Just then, Marty came through from the kitchen, leading a parade of young women her age who were burdened with plates of steaming chicken and dumplings, bowls of peas and carrots, and platters of hot biscuits. Sauce dishes of apple salad had already been placed at each spot on the table, and the crew of harvesters dug in. The meal was rich in starch, but the men needed it for the physically demanding work of the day.

For dessert, everyone was given his choice of pie. The vast majority of the hearty pastries were made of the seasonal apples and pumpkins, but a few of the wives had given thought to how much a little variety can be appreciated and brought mincemeat and raisin. One particularly generous woman had opened a quart of her home-canned cherries to make the filling for her pie, and the dark red filling stood out like a beacon on the plate. Groans of satisfaction emitted from the men as they got up to make way for the next shift of workers and Marty and Mrs. Meyer came in to the dining room to express their gratitude.

The afternoon work sped along smoothly under pleasant sunshine. The rattle of wagons laden with ears of corn came more frequently to Harlan and Roy's hearing as the men who were picking came nearer and nearer the farmstead. The corn crib was approaching capacity, as was the granary, and the fuel bin on the summer kitchen was looking better too.

During one of their trips back to the corncrib from the fuel bin after emptying their baskets of cobs, Roy said, "You know, I've been thinking about what you said earlier about how everyone only took orders from you today because they knew they came from Mr. Meyer."

"Yeah?" Harlan responded.

"You might be selling yourself a little short there, but I was reminded about how my dad says that sometimes it's not what you know but who you know," mused Roy.

Harlan felt that Roy expected some kind of response from him there, but nothing in his words had demanded it, so he remained silent.

"I was thinking that the Christian faith is like that, you know? A person can know all of the basic tenets of the Christian faith—which is the 'what'—but if one doesn't know Jesus Christ as Lord and Savior—the 'Who'—it's all for nothing."

Harlan grumbled inwardly. *Does everyone around here have to bring religion into everything?* He was immediately uncomfortable.

"Do you know Jesus, Harlan?" Roy asked.

Not wanting to directly answer "no," Harlan evaded the question and said, "Marty's been talking to me about that too, and

Mr. Meyer's been making me read the Bible to him when we've been alone in the evenings."

Roy chuckled. "Wow! Even as a mute that man has figured out a way to witness! 'Faith cometh by hearing, and hearing by the word of God.'" Roy shook his head in amazement. "God has used that man mightily.

"All I can say is that receiving Jesus Christ as my Lord and Savior was the best thing I ever did. I rebelled against the calling of the Holy Spirit for awhile, but yielding has given me more joy than I ever thought it would."

"And you still go to dance halls?" Harlan asked, not accusatorially but surprisedly.

Roy laughed again. "That's good exercise!" he said. "In all seriousness, I don't go in for any dancing that's at all suggestive. I'll admit that a couple of years ago, it was a lot different for me. But now, mostly I like the fast stuff. The Bible says that even David danced before the Lord. But, just so you know, when Marty and I went to the dance hall in Weston last Saturday, we didn't dance at all, just listened to the orchestra."

Another wagon to be unloaded arrived just then, much to Harlan's relief.

At a quarter after three in the afternoon, Marty and a couple of other young ladies, including Esther Stempel, came by the corncrib again and dropped off the same lard cans containing lunches on their way out to the picking crew with larger baskets of food. This time, though, Marty was more careful about their placement, saying "This one on the south is yours, Roy. I'll put Harlan's on the north side of the crib. Mama and those ladies are really spoiling you all today—egg salad sandwiches and fresh donuts for your lunch."

This little speech struck Harlan as odd since she had not made any distinction between the two pails when the morning coffee had been delivered and the contents of the buckets had been identical.

Esther lingered while the other girls walked on right away.

"Don't you think that we ought to do all of our corn picking this way like we do with threshing, Roy? We could just all move from farm to farm until everyone's harvesting was finished. It's been so much more fun to have everyone together." While the comment was apparently addressed to Roy, Harlan could feel that Esther's eyes were resting on him the whole time she was speaking.

"Come on, Esther! We don't have enough donuts without the basket you're carrying," one of the other girls called back to her. Esther listlessly began walking again, picking up speed only after she was past Harlan.

Roy shook his head in amusement at Esther's lack of subtlety.

After the wagon they had been unloading and its successor had been emptied, the two young men were finally able to eat their lunches.

Harlan seated himself on the ground with his back propped against the wall of the crib. He opened the lard can and his face broke into a gigantic grin. His sandwich was wrapped in waxed paper, and he could see a note written on it in crayon.

Thanks for staying! - M.M.

Roy approached Harlan with his lard tin at that moment, so Harlan crumpled the waxed paper into a wad and shoved it in his pants pocket. Roy sat down in identical posture a couple of feet away from Harlan and opened his lunch. Harlan noted with satisfaction that Roy's sandwich paper had no writing on it. The two were hungry again and ate in silence for awhile, enjoying the tangy egg salad and the sugared donuts, washing them down with the cool water from their respective mason jars. Harlan expected Roy to begin talking about Jesus with him again at any moment, and the thought made him resentful because he preferred concentrating on the thoughtfulness that Marty had shown with the note to him.

"She's fallen in love with you, you know," Roy said around a mouthful of egg salad.

Harlan assumed Roy was talking about Esther. "She doesn't even know me," Harlan disagreed. "I just met her in Sunday School a few days ago."

Roy's head snapped toward Harlan. "I'm not talking about Esther, you idiot. She's not in love with you. Infatuated, yes, but not in love. I'm talking about Martha Meyer. *She's* in love with you."

Harlan was shocked by both Roy's statement and his boldness. "What?"

"Isn't that who wrote that note on your sandwich paper?" Roy said.

"You saw it?" Harlan asked.

"I only saw you reading it and the big ol' grin it put on your face," Roy revealed. "But it was from Marty wasn't it?"

"How did you know?" Harlan was a bit sore that Roy had discovered Marty's sweet gesture.

"I see the way she looks at you. And let me tell you something else. When a boy takes a girl out on two separate occasions and all she can talk about is another boy, you don't have to work too hard to figure out what's going on," Roy said.

Harlan's mind was reeling, and he had no idea what to say.

"Whatever you do, please don't hurt her. She's a wonderful girl," Roy said almost inaudibly.

The intensity in Roy's voice scared Harlan a little, and he was silent for a moment. He wanted to say that he had done nothing to encourage her, but he felt that that might be an untruth. Certainly, he had fantasized about Marty falling in love with him, but he had not really pursued her, had he?

"I've no intention of hurting her." Harlan's voice was thick. "I'm scheduled to leave tomorrow morning after chores. I would have been gone this morning, but she asked me to stay and help with everything today."

Roy didn't comment further, and another wagon full of corn rumbled to a stop.

Chapter Thirteen

November 7, 1935

Along about four thirty in the afternoon, Roy and Harlan looked up to see a veritable herd of men, horses, and wagons coming their way. The corn had all been picked.

The wagons that didn't belong to the Meyer farm were unloaded by as many people as there were shovels, everyone else standing around watching the process and congratulating themselves on a job well done. The women who had not had to leave to be present when the schoolchildren came home filed out of the house to join the men at the corncrib.

"I'll unload Mr. Meyer's wagon after milking," Harlan said, signaling the end of the picking bee.

"We thank you all so much," Marty shouted to the crowd. "Dad, Mama, and I appreciate this more than we can say."

Choruses of "You're welcome" and "Our pleasure" were returned from the crowd.

"Reverend Martin, where are you?" a male voice shouted. "How 'bout a prayer?"

Reverend Martin was produced and hoisted into an empty wagon so that he could be heard.

"Let us speak with our Creator and Lord," he intoned. Heads bowed and hands were folded; a few men knelt on the ground. "Heavenly Father, we thank and praise Thee for the work Thee gave us to do today. This has been a wonderful day! What a blessing these many hands have been, and what joy we have experienced! May what we have done for our Christian brethren here today bring Thee glory.

"Lord, we have relished the fellowship that we have shared today, and we thank Thee for keeping everyone safe. We humbly ask Thee to bless Al Meyer as he continues to recover from his stroke, and we request traveling mercies as we head home. Most of all, Father, we thank Thee for Thy Son and the precious gift of salvation that is offered us through Him alone. It's in His holy name that we pray all of this. Amen."

Another "Amen" rumbled from the throats of the crowd, and then they began to disperse. Harlan, Marty, and Mrs. Meyer waited until the last guests were gone; then Mrs. Meyer went to the house to get the egg basket, Marty went to fetch the milking equipment, and Harlan went to bring in the cows.

Harlan and Marty were alone as they milked, but neither said anything, much to Harlan's surprise. He knew the reason he wasn't talking was because his mind was so busy that he didn't have any spare brain capacity to handle a conversation with anyone other than himself. Marty's reticence was much more of a mystery to him, but he put it down to fatigue or perhaps having used up all of her words for the day with her friends as they went about their many tasks. Either way, her silence didn't bother him because he had too many other things to consider. The idea that Marty was in love with him as much as he was in love with her opened all kinds of possibilities in his mind.

Why couldn't you stay? Harlan was asking himself. *None of the people around here seem a bit concerned about your past, they don't seem the sort who are going to spend any time looking at wanted posters, and no one in authority would ever think of looking for you here. Mrs. Meyer and Marty can be the ones who go into town to take care of any necessary business. After all, this might be a safer place for you than Chicago, and you have no idea what you are going to do there anyway.*

But then there was the problem about what to do with Marty. Harlan figured that if he stayed, their relationship would only advance—which was what he wanted—and he wanted to have her as his wife. The problem was that getting a marriage license would make his whereabouts a matter of public record.

What if you changed your name? Harlan asked himself. No amount of deviousness seemed too extreme if it would allow him to spend the rest of his life with the woman he loved. *You could tell the people that "Harlan" was just a nickname that you have used for so long that you consider it your name but that your real name is something else. "Jensen" is such a common last name in Iowa that surely you could just blend in. Keep your nose straight and there would be no reason to fear.*

No! Think about what you are doing! If you start a new identity now when you've already been living for so long under your correct name, you're just building a house of cards. And remember, if for some reason you're found out, you'll be carted away to the state penitentiary. Do you care so little for Marty that you're willing to put her at risk of that? You told Roy that you had no intention of hurting her, and that would kill her for sure!

On the other hand, if Roy is right and Marty really does love you, it's going to hurt her badly if you leave for good tomorrow anyway. Which is worse? If you stay, even though there is risk, you have the chance to make both of you happy for a long time. If you go, it is certain that neither of you benefits, and can you really live without her anymore?

It was along these lines that Harlan's mind was waffling back and forth. His conversation with Roy had removed any of the joy he had found in pretending that Marty was his girl because now he knew that her feelings were mutual, so merely imagining the possibilities of a relationship with her no longer satisfied him. Now, he felt that he must figure out a way to make his dreams come true since it seemed that there was a chance.

Chores were finished mechanically, supper was eaten in a stupor of distraction and fatigue, and then Harlan went back out to scoop the last of the corn into the crib by lantern light. He was thrilled to hear Marty's footsteps coming toward the wagon in the chilly fall air.

"It's been a long day, hasn't it?" she asked as she came into the yellow circle of lantern light.

"Yup."

"A long day but a good day," she sighed. She walked over to the side of a the corncrib where another grain scoop was resting, retrieved it and began walking toward the wagon.

An idea struck Harlan at that moment. "Hey, can you go get a feed bucket out of the barn?"

"Yeah, why?"

"Well, I was just thinking about your dad. He went to all the work to plant, cultivate, and care for this crop, and now he doesn't get to have anything to do with harvesting it. He's kind of been robbed of the best part. I thought maybe I'd fill a bucket with ears of corn, and then tomorrow morning I'll help him walk out here and he can throw them into the crib. That way he can say that he at least put part of the crop in the crib," explained Harlan.

"I think that's a great idea—sort of a symbolic harvest," Marty agreed, turning to go fetch a bucket.

Upon her return, the bucket was filled, and then Marty climbed into the wagon to help finish scooping the ears of corn into the corncrib. All the while, Harlan's mind was working feverishly to figure out what to say to Marty. Nothing as eloquent as he wanted was coming to mind, and the pregnant silence between them was making him nervous.

When the wagon was emptied, their grain scoops were hung on nails by the crib doors. A bright harvest moon had risen in the east while they were scooping, so Marty blew the lantern out, and the two began the trek back to the house. Their unison steps were slow with both exhaustion from the day of hard labor and sorrow at the knowledge that their time together was coming to a close.

"I'll hitch the team tomorrow morning and put the wagon in the shed," Harlan planned aloud. "Roy and I got the granary almost full of shelled corn today, so all you've got to do is grind it, and there should be enough for the poultry for quite a while."

"Thank you," responded Marty in an unmistakably melancholy tone. "Thank you for everything you've done for us. You've been such a godsend."

The dolefulness of her voice brought Harlan to a stop. He turned and gathered her into his arms, and she did not resist. Instead, she laid her head against his chest and squeezed him back. This action on her part steeled Harlan's resolve and loosened his tongue.

"Marty, I've been thinking things over." The resoluteness of his words surprised even him. "There's nothing that says I have to go. Over these last several days, I've fallen in love with you, and I want to be by your side until I die."

She took a step back so that she could search his moonlit face. "I...I don't understand. What are you saying?"

Harlan's mind was working fast, but not necessarily very clearly at that moment, and all he could think to do was plunge ahead on the path he had apparently chosen. He took both her hands in his and knelt down in front of her.

"Martha Meyer, will you do me the honor of becoming my wife?" he asked, his sincerity evident in his voice. "I'm sorry I don't have a ring or anything, and I know it seems crazy because we've only known each other for two weeks, but..."

Marty dropped to her knees in front of him, simultaneously bursting into sobs. This reaction was not entirely surprising to Harlan as he had heard stories of women crying in response to a marriage proposal, but like any man, women's tears made him feel helpless, and all he could think to do was to try to stop them. Knowing no other course of action, Harlan leaned forward to embrace her. His heart sank when she wriggled away to keep him at arm's length. It crossed his mind that maybe Roy Schoening had been incorrect in his assessment of Marty's feelings toward him.

"What's wrong?" he asked.

It was a moment before Marty had sufficiently collected herself to speak. "I'm so sorry," she sobbed. "I've made a horrible mess of things."

"What?"

"I'm so sorry," she repeated. "This is all my fault."

"Your fault?" Harlan asked incredulously.

"I shouldn't have led you on."

"Led me on? You mean you don't really love me?" The pain in Harlan's voice was obvious.

"No, I *do* love you. I love you more than you know." Confession was calming Marty down, but her hands were still trembling and her voice tripped as she spoke. "You don't know how I've longed for you to take me in your arms as you did just now, and I've dreamed over and over of the day when you would ask me to marry you, but…" she paused as if trying to steel her nerves, "but even though I want to so badly, I just can't marry you."

Harlan shifted from kneeling to sitting on the ground. He felt thoroughly confused, but oddly not without hope. He couldn't figure out what to say, however, and Marty took his silence as a demand for further explanation.

"I'm so sorry," she said again. She scooted over so that she was sitting beside him on the ground and took one of his hands in both of hers. "I shouldn't have behaved the way I have been, mooning about and flirting with you. It's just that I…." She stopped, seeming to suddenly think that further confession along the vein she was on was unwise. "You've been so good to all of us, especially Dad, and here I've given you the impression that I could…." She stopped again, releasing his hand and putting it on his leg. "I'm just so sorry, Harlan, that's all."

Harlan's mind had gotten stuck on the fact that she had said that she wanted to marry him, and the rest of what she said seemed to be confusing nonsense that was really irrelevant in the face of their mutual desires for marriage.

"If you love me and I love you, and if you want to marry me and I want to marry you, why can't we get married?" he asked simply.

"Marriage is not as simple as just two people who love each other," Marty began.

This statement seemed the veriest of nonsense to Harlan, and his mind began to jump to conclusions. "You're worried about my 'big sin' as you called it yesterday, aren't you? I should have known!" Harlan's voice was deep with bitterness.

"No!" Marty said vehemently. She took his hand back in hers to emphasize her sincerity. "As far as I'm concerned, your life didn't begin until you came to us, and since then, you have been nothing but a decent, respectable human being."

"Then I just don't understand," Harlan admitted, his frustration obviously mounting.

A certain serenity had overtaken Marty, and her nerves had calmed enough that her fingers no longer shook as she began affectionately tracing the veins on the back of Harlan's hand.

"Harlan, the Bible says in 1 Corinthians that a Christian is not be be unequally yoked with an unbeliever," she said patiently.

Harlan's first instinct was to groan and complain about her overzealousness, but something in him prevented the outburst.

"If I were to marry you, as much as I would like to, I would be committing a sin that I would feel so very guilty about that I don't think it would be long before I'm no longer the person that you've fallen in love with. You of all people know how powerful guilt can be. Besides, it may not be long before our different beliefs are in conflict, and we may become quite unhappy together because we seek different things."

Harlan watched her slender fingers gently travel his veins in the moonlight.

"I shouldn't have been throwing myself at you like I did. I'm sorry about that," she continued.

"You haven't thrown yourself at me; that was Esther Stempel," Harlan contradicted her.

"But you didn't even notice her until I pointed it out," Marty said. "I flirted with you too much, acted too familiar, and that wasn't right."

"Why did you do it then?"

"I don't know," Marty almost wailed. "You've just treated me so nicely from the beginning, and my folks loved you immediately. I thought...."

"Looks to me like Roy Schoening has treated you very nicely too," interrupted Harlan.

"He has," Marty acquiesced, her mood evening out again. "But I don't find him nearly as attractive...." she stopped abruptly, catching herself flirting again. "I guess I was hoping...."

"Hoping what?" prodded Harlan.

"I was hoping that you'd become a Christian and that we could live happily ever after, all right? From the moment you arrived beside me in the cornfield I've been hoping that."

"You've been in love with me that long? I didn't even know you were a girl until supper that night!" Harlan confessed.

"I know," Marty said dryly.

"What a surprise that was!"

Marty giggled softly.

"Speaking of surprises," Harlan continued, "why is your mother never surprised by anything that I do?"

"You'd have to take that up with her," Marty answered as though she was familiar with her mother's situation but unwilling to discuss it.

There was a pause in the conversation while Harlan reversed the position of their hands such that he was now holding hers.

"So all I have to do is become a Christian, and then we can get married? I can do that, can't I?" Harlan asked, prepared to do whatever it took in order to win the girl he desired.

Marty sighed. "I wish it were that simple, and I appreciate the fact that you would do it for me, but it probably wouldn't be genuine if that were your thinking. Harlan Jensen, you need to receive Jesus Christ as your Savior, but you need to do it for you and for him.

You need to trust him because he loves you so much, not because you love me. You need to want to love him and let him be the Lord of your life; you need to recognize that he is the only one who can take away your sins—big ones and little ones.

"To be fair to you, I want to warn you, too, that receiving Christ as your Lord and Savior doesn't mean that all your problems are suddenly gone."

"What do you mean?" Harlan asked.

Marty seemed to be searching for the right words to explain her statement. "I mean three things. The first is that you've got to repent of your sins. To repent literally means to turn away from them and then trust in Christ alone for your salvation.

"As a believer in Jesus Christ, he demands unconditional surrender. You might remember that from some of what you read to Dad in Romans. He asks people to follow him and to do things that are counter to their human nature. If you become a believer, you need to follow Christ even when it's difficult because that is his perfect will. You *will* have the Holy Spirit's help, however. Eventually—and it may not be until you get to heaven—being obedient in these difficult things will bring you a joy that will be far greater than whatever satisfaction you may have gotten out of being disobedient.

"The third thing that happens is that Satan pursues you with new vigor. When you are outside of Christ, the devil's already got you, so he can afford to leave you alone. Your life can be pretty easy—that is, until you die. But when you receive Christ, you become a target for Satan. Therefore, you have to 'put on the whole armor of God, that ye may be able to stand against the wiles of the devil.'

Now, the Lord will help you with all of these things when you ask for his help and protection. But do you see? It's too big a decision to make just for me."

Harlan let go of Marty's hand and looked away, his attitude shifting to one of despair.

"I just can't do it," he mumbled.

"Why, Harlan?"

He looked at the bright moon and thought for a minute.

"I guess for one thing, I don't know whether I believe any of it. It all just seems so far-fetched. Secondly, if I did believe in God, I can't see that he would be willing to forgive me. My 'big sin,' as you call it, is just too big."

"Have you ever stopped to think, Harlan, that whether or not you believe in God has absolutely no bearing on whether or not he exists? The true and living God does not magically come into existence just because you decide that he is a possibility. Quite frankly, you don't have that kind of power. No. God's reality is not dependent on your belief. Our faith in God doesn't change God; it changes us.

"And I say again, whatever you have done, whatever colossal wrong you have committed, the blood of Jesus Christ is all sufficient."

Harlan wrested his eyes from the moon and looked at Marty for a second.

He shook his head resignedly. "So where does this put you and me?"

She thought for a moment. "I think the only thing that has changed tonight is that we have been honest with ourselves and each other about our love for one another. And I'm thankful for that."

Harlan rose from the ground and turned to help Marty to her feet.

"After milking and chores tomorrow morning, I'll bring your dad out to look at the corn crib and to throw that bucket of ears in," Harlan spoke evenly. "Then, I'll be on my way."

Chapter Fourteen

November 8, 1935

Friday morning dawned mild, bright, and beautiful; but the mood of the people on the Meyer farm was in direct contradiction to the weather. Everyone was very quiet, and when Harlan and Marty did the milking alone together, the awkwardness of the situation was palpable. Breakfast was consumed in near silence, the tinkling of silverware against china seeming almost deafening.

Upon draining his coffee cup, Harlan said, "It didn't seem right yesterday that you didn't get to harvest any of the crop that you had planted, Mr. Meyer. So, I've saved a bucket of ears for you to throw in the crib. After I finish feeding the stock, I'm going to hitch a team and put the wagon in the shed; then I'll come in and walk with you to the corncrib so that you can throw the bucket of ears in and see what kind of a crop you had. Does that sound all right?"

Mr. Meyer smiled a little and nodded his appreciation.

"That was very thoughtful of you, Harlan," Mrs. Meyer put in. "Throwing with his left hand won't come easy to Al, but it will be good therapy for him."

As Harlan completed the tasks that he had listed, he noted how slowly he was working.

"You're tired," he said aloud to himself, shaking his head as if trying to wake up. He had spoken the truth. Harlan had not slept much during the night for thinking about the conversation he and

Marty had had during the evening. Judging from the darkness he had observed around Marty's eyes, she hadn't slept much either. However, he thought maybe his sluggishness was also due to the fact that he wanted to delay his inevitable departure.

When Harlan arrived back at the house, it was nearing nine-thirty in the morning, and Mrs. Meyer was washing the cream separator. Its disks were piled up on the drainboard, and its sundry other parts were strewn about the kitchen. She was later than usual at this task because she had been engaged in helping Mr. Meyer get ready to go outdoors. She followed Harlan into the dining room to help get Mr. Meyer into a standing position.

"Well, Father, that was the easiest you've gotten up in weeks!" Mrs. Meyer observed, patting her husband on the shoulder.

Harlan also noted how much less effort he himself had had to exert in order to help Mr. Meyer up. "I'd say you'll soon be up and walking on your own, sir," added Harlan.

The two men walked slowly out to the corncrib, the autumn sun beaming down on them with extraordinary warmth.

"This Indian summer was sure handy to finish the harvest," Harlan commented.

Mr. Meyer nodded his agreement. Not knowing what else to say, Harlan then lapsed into silence for the remainder of the trek. They stopped first at the granary so that Mr. Meyer could see how much corn had been shelled already, then walked on to the crib, where Harlan pointed out the part of it that was still empty because of the poor crop.

Mr. Meyer communicated his disappointment by shaking his head. After that, Harlan retrieved the bucket of ear corn for Mr. Meyer to throw into the opening at the top of the crib. Harlan noted how carefully Mr. Meyer first examined the ears of corn, counting the rows of kernels and how many kernels were in each row. Mr. Meyer was what he considered a very good farmer, and for the thousandth time in the last two weeks, Harlan wished that Mr. Meyer could speak so that he could have learned more from him.

Then, throwing the ears into the crib proved to be a challenge since Mr. Meyer was not naturally left handed. Harlan had to retrieve more than one ear which had not reached its intended destination so that Mr. Meyer could try again. Mr. Meyer became a bit frustrated, and Harlan could see his jaw clenched stiffly in concentration while perspiration began beading on his forehead. It was obvious through the process, though, that Mr. Meyer appreciated the opportunity to complete his symbolic harvest. When the bucket was empty, Mr. Meyer was worn out from the exertion. He latched onto Harlan's arm, and the two began the arduous voyage back to the house.

"Mr. Meyer, I want to thank you for all that you've done for me while I've been here," Harlan began. It seemed like Mr. Meyer was walking much slower than he had on the way out to the corncrib, and Harlan became aware that he was supporting Mr. Meyer more than he had earlier. "You've been a great example of...Mr. Meyer?"

Mr. Meyer's entire weight was suddenly leaning against Harlan, stopping his progress and threatening to knock him over.

"Mr. Meyer?" Harlan said loudly.

Harlan did his best to gently lay Mr. Meyer on the ground.

"Mr. Meyer!" Harlan shouted, shaking the older man's arm and lightly slapping his face.

The elder man did not respond.

"Mrs. Meyer! Marty! Come quick!" Harlan bellowed. "Wake up, Mr. Meyer! Can you hear me?"

Mrs. Meyer, who had been watching them from the kitchen window when Mr. Meyer collapsed, ran to her husband's side immediately, hollering for Marty the whole way.

"Al, honey, wake up!" she urged, shaking him, but no response came from the man. Moving quickly, she put her ear on his chest to listen for a second. "Help me turn him over," she commanded Harlan.

By the time Mr. Meyer was on his stomach, Marty had arrived from the poultry houses where she had been working.

"Go call Dr. Wyland!" Mrs. Meyer barked. Marty flew to the house in obedience.

Mrs. Meyer deftly folded Mr. Meyer's arms under his head and began trying to resuscitate Mr. Meyer with the Holger-Nielsen method. After a few repetitions, she put a finger on his neck and felt for a pulse. She motioned for Harlan to help her roll him onto his back again; then she listened to his chest once more.

"He's gone," Mrs. Meyer announced. She scooted forward and cradled Mr. Meyer's head in her lap, tears beginning to softly fall from her eyes.

Marty returned with a sprint, immediately understood the situation, uttered an indescribable whimper, and crumpled to the ground between Harlan and her father.

Harlan felt his legs begin to twitch with the instinct to run. The scene before him was harrowingly familiar, and every impulse urged him to disappear fast. He rose to his feet and took long, quick strides toward the railroad tracks, his legs carrying him several feet in a mere fraction of a second.

"Harlan!" Marty wailed. He turned to look back at her and stopped. Her flushed face was contorted in grief and tears poured from her eyes. She stretched her arms toward him, and in that instant he knew that he was forever done running from Martha Meyer.

Upon his arrival, Dr. Wyland only confirmed Mrs. Meyer's assessment. He helped carry Mr. Meyer's body into the kitchen, where the separator parts were quickly removed from the kitchen table so that it could be temporarily converted to an embalming bed. The quick-thinking telephone operator had started Rev. Martin on his way to the Meyer farm in response to Marty's initial call to the doctor, and a second call to the operator resulted in the undertaker being summoned to perform his ancient art and the neighbors being notified of their loss.

"You have my sympathies, Elsie," Dr. Wyland said as he

prepared to leave. "A massive stroke like this was the best that we could have hoped for in the state he was in. I also feel it incumbent upon me to say that you have been an outstanding wife to him for many years, but during these last six weeks you have shown a mettle that I've seen in precious few people. It was an honor for Al to have you for his wife, and he knew it."

"Thank you, Doctor," Mrs. Meyer returned shaking her head in disagreement, "but the honor was in being the wife to such a godly man."

Dr. Wyland and Rev. Martin met each other on the sidewalk, exchanged a few quick words, and the doctor was on his way to his next call by the time Rev. Martin entered the kitchen. Rev. Martin had been called to the side of many a deceased parishioner in his years at the local church, but when he beheld Al Meyer's dead body, the man who had been his mentor in many ways, it affected him deeply. He held Mr. Meyer's hand for a moment, and when he was finally able to control himself, he croaked, "Well done, good and faithful servant."

Fresh sobs came from Mrs. Meyer and Marty at that, and Harlan's eyes dropped to the floor.

Within moments, several neighbors, all of whom had been present the previous day, began to arrive. Harlan recognized every face but only a few of the names, and since he felt like an outsider, he retreated to the fringe of the group. Few people knew how close to Mr. Meyer he had come to feel, fewer still could have imagined the depth of his grief, and absolutely none could have fathomed the poignancy of the guilt he suffered. After all, it had been his idea to have Mr. Meyer throw the ears of corn into the crib. He had orchestrated the whole excursion. He had been the only one to see the sweat beading on Mr. Meyer's forehead as each ear had been awkwardly launched into the air. In his mind, he alone was responsible for the corpse lying on the kitchen table, and it was his fault that Martha Meyer had tears in her eyes that refused to be quelled.

When the mortician arrived, everyone present was ushered out of the kitchen and into the dining and living rooms. Mrs. Meyer, ever the administrator, recognized the need to rid the dining room of Mr. Meyer's hospital bed so that there would be room for his casket and enlisted the help of the neighbors in getting that job done. It was in the middle of that chaos that Roy Schoening approached Harlan, took him by the elbow and ushered him out the seldom-used front door, past the porch, and into the west side yard where they were away from everyone else and no one would think to find them.

"What happened?" Roy asked in a sympathetic tone.

Harlan's eyes fell. He explained the series of events which led up to Mr. Meyer's passing and then, meeting Roy's eyes, said, "I was planning to leave right after I got him back to the house, but when this happened..."

"Now you can't leave—at least not for a while," Roy said. "It'll kill Marty if you do."

Harlan thought for just a second about telling Roy of his and Marty's conversation from the previous evening because in some strange way it seemed like it would justify his continued presence. However, disclosing the details of their exchange would have felt like kissing and telling to Harlan, and he decided that what had been shared between Marty and him was no business of Roy's.

The two young men stood in awkward taciturnity for a few moments until Roy finally spoke again. "I'm sorry for your loss," he said, tapping Harlan's arm. "I could tell you thought very highly of Mr. Meyer, and I think this is probably harder on you than most people imagine."

Harlan was touched by Roy's kindness once again, and tears began stinging his eyes.

"I just can't help thinking about this from Mr. Meyer's point of view, though. Just think, he got to meet Jesus this morning!" Roy said in awe. "Al Meyer's race ended today, and he was victorious!"

Harlan had never heard this kind of talk after someone had

died, and he raised his eyes to make sure that Roy wasn't being irreverent.

"And after being mute for all these weeks, I bet that man is shouting praises to the Lord at the top of his lungs! Not being able to talk had to be really tough on him, even though you made things better after you arrived."

Harlan considered Roy extremely naive with his last sentiment. *If I'd never arrived, Mr. Meyer would still be alive!* he thought.

"Listen," Roy went on. "There's nothing we can do inside, and Earl May said on the radio this morning that he believes the weather is going to turn colder tomorrow. When we were here yesterday, it didn't look like there was much to the woodpile here. Let's do what we can to help by chopping some wood."

The two moved to the north side of the house and worked diligently at splitting the many logs that Mr. Meyer had stacked there. Upon hearing the rhythmic ring of the sledge and splitting maul, Mrs. Meyer's nephew Charlie Neumann joined them at the task.

While the undertaker did his job in the kitchen, the neighbor women who lived the closest made quick trips home to bring enough back to feed the gathered crowd. When the body had been prepared for viewing and was lying in state in the dining room, the neighbors who had gathered pronounced the mortician's work satisfactory and left for home in time for evening chores. Mrs. Meyer finalized the arrangements for the funeral to be on Monday at the church, but Mr. Meyer's body would remain at the Meyer home until then so that Sunday's worship would be unbothered.

Roy Schoening left in the afternoon with his folks, as did Charlie, but Harlan persisted at the woodpile, pausing only to milk and complete the evening chores. The clang of the sledge hammer against the wedge continued into the darkness because in Harlan's mind each heavy blow was part of the penance he was paying for the lifeless body in the house and the feminine tears which were being shed over it. According to his logic, the events of the day were the result of his poor decision making, and he was resolved to do whatever he could to make amends.

"You need to come in and eat some supper," Marty said, startling him with her presence. He had not heard her approach.

"Not hungry."

"You might not feel hunger, but you can't put in the kind of labor that you've done today on only a meal of pancakes, eggs, and oatmeal over twelve hours ago," she reasoned. When he laid the sledge hammer down to put a new log in place, Marty picked it up along with the wedges and held them resolutely. She could see a look of frustration cross Harlan's face in the moonlight, but she held her ground, and he wearily surrendered to her will. They both picked up armloads of wood and carried them into the house.

Once he had washed up, Mrs. Meyer set a bowl of soup and a piece of bread in front of him at the kitchen table. In all the time that he had been with the Meyers, he had never seen a meal eaten in the kitchen, and the reason for the change of venue made the food less appetizing. Marty had apparently gone into the dining room to be near her father's remains, so Mrs. Meyer and Harlan were alone when she brought a pitcher of milk to the table and filled Harlan's glass. As she did so, she rested her left hand on Harlan's shoulder in a maternal gesture. In Harlan's mind, the irony of being treated affectionately by the person whose grief he had caused was beyond understanding, and his guilt was compounded.

When his glass was full, Mrs. Meyer sank into a chair opposite Harlan. Though Harlan couldn't bring himself to make eye contact with her, in his peripheral vision he saw her dabbing her eyes with her handkerchief. The sight was so pathetic that Harlan's heart was moved to ask her forgiveness.

"Mrs. Meyer, I'm so sorry. I..." he started.

"Oh, Harlan," Mrs. Meyer sighed, mistaking Harlan's apology for an expression of sympathy. "I've got to stop all this blubbering because it is so selfish."

Harlan could see that Mrs. Meyer had misunderstood his intent, and started again. "But, Mrs. Meyer, you don't..."

"These are selfish tears, and I know it," she interrupted. "I'm only crying because I'm going to miss him so. I'm not crying for Al's sake, for his sake I'm happy. You know, the Bible says in Romans 'if you confess with your mouth the Lord Jesus and believe in your heart that God has raised Him from the dead, you will be saved,' and I don't know anyone who had believed in the Lord Jesus Christ and his resurrection as strongly as Al. And I have to stop thinking about myself and start remembering that my husband is with his Lord in paradise.

"He always had as good an attitude as possible after his stroke. I mean, he would get frustrated at times because communication was so difficult and he couldn't do all of the things he wanted to anymore, but I never saw any evidence that he felt sorry for himself. Even at that though, the life he was living at the end was no kind of way to live for any length of time. Now, he's experiencing real joy, and I need to concentrate on that."

Harlan didn't know what to say in response to Mrs. Meyer, but the urge to confess had passed because it somehow felt inappropriate at that moment. Mrs. Meyer's words had done nothing to assuage his guilt, however.

Chapter *Fifteen*

November 9, 1935

Very little sleeping occurred in the Meyer house that night. Two people didn't sleep because of their grief, and the third couldn't sleep because of his remorse. Harlan could hear Marty sobbing quietly across the hall, and the feeling that he was responsible for her sadness caused Harlan to be on the verge of crying himself. He was afraid that Marty or Mrs. Meyer would hear him, however, so he swallowed the urge which turned it into a whanging headache.

Earl May had been correct in his prediction of chillier weather, and Saturday dawned cold and grey with a biting north wind. Neighbors and friends of the Meyer family began dropping by shortly after morning chores, bringing with them a wide array of foods. They were coming to pay their last respects and to view the body, but Harlan had not been able to bring himself to enter the dining room since Mr. Meyer's remains had been in repose there.

As quickly as could be managed, Harlan escaped the house and sought work outdoors to continue trying to make amends for having precipitated Mr. Meyer's death. He purposely looked for the most unpleasant jobs to do and decided that mucking out the barn was the most appropriate task for him that day. This chore had obviously been slighted during the last several weeks due to the pressure of harvest and Mr. Meyer's convalescence, so Harlan had enough work to keep him busy.

Harlan had had every intention of remaining outside during the noon meal, but Marty had come to the barn to retrieve him, and he could think of no way to refuse to follow her back to dinner. Thus, he unhitched the horses from the manure spreader and put them back in the barn before heading to the house.

A petite woman whom Harlan had never met was present when he entered the kitchen. She was very smartly dressed, and Harlan could easily see that she had exercised no financial restraint when she had chosen her clothing.

"Aunt Amanda, this is Harlan Jensen. Harlan, this is Dad's sister Amanda Engel, from Council Bluffs," Marty completed the introductions.

"Very nice to meet you, Harlan," Mrs. Engel said, extending him a dainty hand which was clearly not accustomed to doing difficult work. "I've heard nothing but wonderful things about you, and I want to thank you for all that you've done for my brother and his family since you've been here."

Harlan's emotions were completely muddled. Simultaneously, he felt pleased that the Meyers had spoken so highly of him, embarrassed because he was sure he was undeserving of their praise, nervous since Mrs. Engel was obviously of a social strata far greater than he, and guilty because he assumed responsibility for her brother's death. The result was that he became tongue-tied and could only offer a mumbled "Thank you" and drop his eyes to the floor.

Other neighbors were again present, and the various foods that people had brought to the Meyer family were arranged on the kitchen counter in an informal sort of buffet so that people could fill their plates at will. This created a rather uncomfortable situation for Harlan since assembling his dinner plate meant that he had to walk about the kitchen and interact with other people rather than sink into oblivion at the corner of the kitchen table. Furthermore, as he moved around the kitchen to choose his dinner, he felt Mrs. Engel's eyes following him quite intensely. Harlan was afraid that her scrutiny was perhaps due to the fact that she recognized him from a poster or a newspaper story.

When Harlan finally sat down to eat, Mrs. Engel and Mrs. Meyer disappeared into the dining room. He heard the two of them engage in a conversation in German, and then they both entered the kitchen again so that Mrs. Engel could bid farewell to those she knew before she departed for home, saying that she would return early on Monday morning.

Harlan ate as quickly as he could and was relieved that he could retreat to the barn for the rest of the afternoon. Just as he was exiting the back door, however, Mrs. Meyer caught his attention.

"Harlan, Roy Schoening and my nephew Charlie are going to be dropped off by their folks this evening to go with you into town. I need you to do our trading this week for us, and they are going along to introduce you to the grocer and be sure that you get a fair price for the eggs and cream. You'll drive our car like you did on Sunday, so plan accordingly, please."

The prospect of going into town concerned Harlan because he had convinced himself that it was far safer for him to remain anonymous and be sequestered on the farm, but that same old note in Mrs. Meyer's voice that indicated her expectation of obedience was present again. Since Harlan felt that he had already caused her so much undue grief, he decided not to protest. However, he felt a nervousness in his stomach as he walked out to the barn that had not been there before dinner.

The afternoon's hard physical labor distracted Harlan from this uneasiness, but each successive car that pulled into the lane reminded him of his culpability in regard to the body which lay silently in the house. He was glad to finally see Marty approach the barn with the milking buckets, but she did not speak beyond what was absolutely necessary while they completed the chores, and Harlan mistook her reticence as anger toward him.

Thus, he was feeling quite miserable when, after he had bathed and donned his only other set of clothes, he, Roy, and Charlie loaded the Meyer car with the week's eggs and cream and pulled onto the dirt road in the direction of the town.

"We'll go to the store first and take care of Mrs. Meyer's list there," Roy said from the passenger seat as he perused the paper that Mrs. Meyer had written her list on for them. "Then we'll go fill this baby up with gasoline," he said, patting the car door affectionately.

"Did you get your car's problem figured out?" Charlie asked Roy from the back seat.

"I cleaned the poles on the battery and replaced a spark plug, and things seem to be working well again," replied Roy. "I tell you, earlier in the week I had to fix the flat tire on Miss Porter's car, too, and once we get our corn picking finished, Henry Carlson wants me to work on his tractor. I'm thinking about starting a garage, man!"

"Seriously?" Charlie asked.

"Nah, my dad would be disappointed. He's been planning on me farming with him forever, and I don't think there's really enough business for another garage around here, but it's kind of fun to think about," Roy admitted.

The masculine conversation between Charlie and Roy continued and was refreshing for Harlan. He did not partake in it, but he was listening very actively. He noticed that Roy and Charlie's exchange was much different than what he was used to hearing from other men his age. The topics were pretty much the same, but for one thing, it was completely devoid of cursing, and then neither of them made any disrespectful comments about members of the fairer sex. This struck Harlan as odd, and he would have wondered about it more except that each mile which brought them closer to town made him more nervous and distracted.

"Meyers trade at Martin's," Roy said as he pointed to a large brick building at the center of the three-block main street.

Harlan gently guided the car to a stop on the street in front of the store, and the three young men carried in the eggs and cream that Mrs. Meyer had sent with them. Another farm family was selling their produce ahead of them, so they had to wait for a bit.

"Hey, Roy and Charlie, come take a look at this poster," an older female voice called behind them.

All three turned around to see who had addressed the two natives, and the blood left Harlan's face when he realized that the voice had come from behind the post office cage in the corner of the store. The owner of the voice was shoving a white piece of paper with photographs on it under the barred window. Harlan could make out the word "WANTED" across the top.

Harlan's mind began working quickly, assessing how he might exit the building as quickly as possible. It had been dark when they pulled up, so he hadn't been able to see any other door on the building except the front one they had come in. His head whipped back to that door, but through its glass he could see a family approaching it on the outside, and two women were visiting on the inside of it. There was no way he could exit back through that door without creating quite a ruckus. He began searching the rest of the building for signs of another exit. *There has to be another way out!* he thought.

He spotted what appeared to be another exterior door on the other side of the counter. The distance between him and the door was relatively clear, and he knew he could cover it in an instant. Harlan bent to put the egg crate he was carrying on the floor and make a run for it when laughter erupted from Roy.

"That man is something else!" he heard Charlie say in an amused voice. "He doesn't let up for anything, does he? Tell him I'm planning on joining, at least. I'll try to get my cousin Martha convinced; after all, she's the best alto in the area, but she's got to get through the next few days before I can say anything to her."

Harlan was confused as to what Charlie was talking about, but his sense of impending danger passed. He heard the post mistress offer her condolences to Charlie after his allusion to Mr. Meyer's death, and watched as all three people's moods sobered at this mention.

"What was that all about?" Harlan asked when his companions returned to their places in line, Roy carrying the poster that the lady had handed to them.

"That's Thelma Verpoorten, the post mistress. Her husband is trying to get some kind of community choir scraped together to put on a Christmas program next month, and she showed us the "wanted" poster that he went and had printed." Roy showed it to Harlan before folding it to put it in his shirt pocket.

"Oh," Harlan said, trying hard to sound indifferent when in reality he had never been so relieved in his life.

Roy and Charlie oversaw the process of selling the eggs and cream to Martins, purchasing the few items that Mrs. Meyer had put on the list, depositing the remaining cash in Harlan's pants pocket, and filling the Meyer car with gasoline at the small gas station. A block of ice was bought and attached to the side of the car where there was no danger of it melting in the frosty evening air, and then the three men stood beside the car while Roy consulted Mrs. Meyer's instructions under the street lamp.

"Now to Mr. George's tonsorial parlor," Roy announced.

"What?" Harlan asked.

"The barbershop, Harlan. We're going to the barbershop. All three of us. Your treat," Charlie chuckled.

Harlan was bewildered. "You two go on ahead, I'll wait here," he said, embarrassed to admit that he could not pay.

"Oh no you don't!" Roy said, holding up Mrs. Meyer's list. "Mrs. Meyer has it written right here that we are all three to get a shave and a haircut, and I don't know about you, but I don't want to cross her."

Harlan could see no way to avoid divulging his situation to the others. "But I have no way of paying for it," he confessed.

"Yes, you do," Roy grinned mischievously.

"No, I don't."

"What's this in your pocket?" Charlie asked, thumping Harlan's thigh where Mrs. Meyer's egg money jingled in response.

"That's Mrs. Meyer's money, not mine," Harlan protested, thinking that his two companions were urging him to steal from his benefactress.

"Look here," Roy said, showing him the list from Mrs. Meyer and still grinning.

In Mrs. Meyer's antiquated script, Harlan read, "Shaves and haircuts for all three of you. Harlan is to pay for them out of the egg money."

"Why?" Harlan asked.

"Because we are serving as half of the pallbearers on Monday," Roy revealed.

Harlan's face blanched, and he was glad that the other two men could not see him very well in the darkness. They turned and began walking toward the barbershop.

"I'm supposed to be a pallbearer, too?" he asked in disbelief.

"Yup," confirmed Charlie.

"I can see you two doing that; I mean, you've known Mr. Meyer for a long time," Harlan said to Roy and then turned to Charlie. "And you're his nephew, but I only knew the man for two weeks."

"I think the Meyers really appreciate how much you've done for them since you arrived," Roy said.

"And Aunt Elsie is a woman who knows her own mind," Charlie added. "If she didn't really want to have you be a pallbearer, she wouldn't have asked you."

"But I don't have clothes that would be good enough to do that," Harlan pointed out.

"Did Amanda Engel look you up one side and down the other when she was at Aunt Elsie and Uncle Al's earlier today?" Charlie asked.

Harlan nodded in the affirmative.

"Then you'll have clothes that are nice enough by Monday morning," Charlie prophesied.

"How do you know?"

"Aunt Elsie has been hatching a plan since yesterday. After we got done with chores last night, Mama measured me all over because my clothes fit you so well. She wrote everything down on a piece of paper which I had to deliver to Aunt Elsie this morning while you were out in the barn. Amanda Engel was coming out to see Uncle Al's body anyway, but Aunt Elsie had already enlisted her help in this plan. Amanda Engel is married to some bigwig with the railroad. They have no children of their own and plenty of money to burn, and you could probably tell by looking at her that clothing is one of her hobbies. So Amanda has your measurements—well, mine really—and she has seen you face-to-face to get a feel for your style. Mark my words, you'll have a new suit on Monday morning in time to wear it to the funeral."

Harlan shook his head in amazement.

After the gentlemen had been suitably groomed and Roy had treated them all to nickel ice cream cones, Harlan guided the car back toward their part of the countryside, dropping Charlie off first. Harlan felt more comfortable with Roy since the two of them had spent so much time alone together and had already had some very honest conversations, and he felt the need to unburden himself a little.

"I still can't figure all of this out," Harlan began.

"What do you mean?" asked Roy.

"I mean, I feel bad about Mrs. Meyer paying for my haircut and Mrs. Engel buying me a new suit," Harlan answered.

"I wouldn't feel bad about it if I were you," Roy reasoned. "If they want you to be a pallbearer and they want you to look a certain way, I don't see any reason to feel guilty if they decide to pay for it when they know that you don't have any means to do it yourself. You've done an awful lot of work for the Meyers, anyway. Why the manure you spread just today was more than enough labor to earn a haircut!

"And let me tell you something: Amanda Engel is well-known for her generosity. The Engels have more money than they know what to do with, and with no children of their own, they have no heirs, so they enjoy their money now by giving it away. I wouldn't feel a bit bad about getting a new suit from her since you're going to be a pallbearer at her brother's funeral.

"Take a left here," Roy motioned, giving Harlan directions to his home.

"But that's just it," Harlan said. "I even feel bad about being a pallbearer at Mr. Meyer's funeral. I mean, I'm the one who's..."

Harlan was on the verge of confessing his perceived guilt in Mr. Meyer's death, but Roy misinterpreted his words and interrupted him.

"You're the one who's worked his tail off for the Meyers for the last several days and continues to do so, and you're the one Mr. Meyer was last witnessing to. You have a special place in the Meyer family's heart."

"Right, I understand that, but I don't deserve it at all. They've got no good reason to love me as much as they do. Why, I'm the one who..." Harlan tried again to confess, but Roy cut him off once more.

"That's the nature of grace, though, isn't it?" Roy said. "Grace is when we get something good that we don't deserve."

"But," Harlan inserted, trying to take back control of the conversation.

"No 'buts' about it," Roy pressed on. "You know, I think that is one of the hardest things for some people to believe about Jesus Christ."

Here we go again! thought Harlan as he rolled his eyes in the darkness.

"People are so accustomed to our earthly ways of thinking— to our earthly sense of justice, if you will—that we stumble over the concept of grace. We think that we have to work our way into heaven because that is the only way that makes any sense to us humans." Roy was talking fast now. "We think of our admission into heaven as a tabulation of what we've done wrong subtracted from what we've done right, and if the end result is a positive number, then we're in. But, the Bible makes it clear that it's nothing like that at all. Did Mr. Meyer ever make you read Ephesians? You should sometime if he didn't, but don't you see? It's the same thing with you and the Meyer family. You think you have to earn everything they give you, and they're trying to extend grace. Just don't fool with it, man. Like my mother always says, 'Be a gracious receiver.'"

Chapter *Sixteen*

November 9 & 10, 1935

When Harlan entered the Meyer house later that evening, Mrs. Meyer met him at the kitchen door with one finger over her lips and the other pointing to the second floor.

"Marty's asleep upstairs," she whispered. "She hasn't slept much the last couple of nights, but I heard her breathing heavily a little bit ago, so I'm sure she's out, and I don't want to wake her. I told her that I'd do the milking with you in the morning so that she can stay in bed a little longer."

When Harlan had removed his cap and was finally close enough to the lamp that she could see him clearly, Mrs. Meyer surveyed his haircut. "You look very nice," she said.

"Thanks, and thank you for the haircut," Harlan said very quietly. "Mrs. Meyer, why didn't you tell me that you wanted me to be a pallbearer?" he asked.

"Roy and Charlie filled you in on the plans, I see," Mrs. Meyer observed. "I would have told you, but we haven't had a moment's peace around here, and you've been keeping your distance since Al died."

Harlan knew that this last was true but said nothing.

"I have another favor to ask you about tomorrow," Mrs. Meyer continued. "Please understand that I would love to have you in church with us in the morning, but even though I know it sounds silly, in fact it *is* silly, I just don't feel right about having no one at home tomorrow morning while Al's body is still lying in the dining room. And the problem is that I feel like Marty and I need to be in church tomorrow. Would you be willing to stay here during church?"

"Sure," Harlan replied. He wasn't really convinced that guarding a corpse was any better than having to go to church, but he considered it his responsibility to do what he could for Mrs. Meyer since his poor judgment had resulted in her premature widowhood.

"Sometime tomorrow afternoon he will be moved to the church," she went on, "and while I know it's not really Al that's in the dining room anymore, I want to sit up with him for a while longer since this is the last...." Mrs. Meyer's voice broke, and she covered her mouth with her handkerchief and hurried out of the kitchen.

There was nothing left for Harlan to do but creep softly upstairs to bed.

Harlan was still outdoors tending livestock when Marty and Mrs. Meyer left for church the next morning. When he was being honest with himself, he had to admit that he was avoiding the house. He had successfully stayed out of the dining room since Mr. Meyer's body had been lying there. It wasn't that he was scared of dead bodies. He had figured out that what he was afraid of was his emotional reaction to seeing Mr. Meyer's lifeless state once more. However, as Harlan plugged away at little odd jobs that he saw outside, he kept thinking and began to realize that being alone when he first viewed Mr. Meyer's body would allow him to avoid any embarrassment he might feel if others saw him distraught.

Thus, Harlan steeled himself and entered the back door of the house. He removed his jacket and worn, dirty boots and washed his hands more thoroughly than he usually would have. Then, he walked to the swinging door that divided the kitchen from the dining room and paused.

"Come on! Get it over with," he prodded himself aloud.

He pushed the door open but kept his eyes on the floor. In his peripheral vision, he could see that the casket was set up in front of the window seat in the same location that Mr. Meyer's hospital bed had occupied. Slowly, Harlan padded to the casket and lifted his eyes to look inside.

Mr. Meyer's body looked as unlike himself as every other corpse has since Abel. Gravity had misshaped the mouth, the pose that the body had been put in seemed unnatural, and the cosmetics applied to the skin lent it an artificial color.

Harlan reached for the cold hand that had so frequently squeezed his in the past few weeks. He clasped it for just a few seconds and then affectionately squeezed it, returning the gesture for the first and last time.

"I'm so sorry, Mr. Meyer," Harlan said, trembling. "It really wasn't a good idea to have you go out and throw ear corn into the crib. I know that now."

Harlan surrendered the battle to keep his emotions in check and gave way to reckless sobbing. Hot tears began flowing down his cheeks. "I wish you had told me that you didn't feel well. We could have stopped any time." Harlan's fist came down hard on the edge of the casket. "I didn't know! If you had just said something, we could have stopped any time!"

Harlan suddenly grasped the foolishness of his words and actions. How could Mr. Meyer, a mute, have alerted anyone of his own illness? What business did Harlan have being so disrespectful as to strike a dead man's coffin? And how could he be so base as to blame Mr. Meyer for what only Harlan himself was responsible? These realizations caused a fresh wave of guilt to rack Harlan's frame.

"I'm such a terrible person, Mr. Meyer," he groaned. "You're the second man whose death I've caused in the last month and a half, but you didn't deserve to die, and I didn't mean to hurt you at all. I'm a murderer, plain and simple. That's right, a murderer whose been sleeping under your roof for the past two and a half weeks. What's worse is that this murderer has fallen in love with your daughter, and she has fallen in love with me. I'm also sorry about that; I didn't mean for that to happen either.

"What am I going to do, Mr. Meyer? I don't know if I can live with this guilt much longer."

There. He had said it aloud for the first time. Actually, he had confessed two things: what he was and how he felt. His mind had been accusing him of murder for the last several weeks, but this was the first time that either his mind or his conscience had given voice to how much of a burden his self-condemnation had become. Hearing himself say that he wasn't sure how much longer he could live with his guilt birthed a new idea in Harlan's already warped thinking. In his earth-bound view, dying was the only way that he could see to get out from under the oppressive remorse which was his constant companion, and he was sure he didn't have the patience to wait for his life to end naturally.

Contemplating his own death afforded Harlan a sense of relief that he had not experienced for quite a while, and his crying subsided. His eyes darted back to Mr. Meyer's face. As dissimilar as it was to what it looked like in life, it bore no evidence of any kind of strife, and Harlan envied that. However, standing next to the body of a person who had been so holy convicted Harlan of how wrong his new vein of thinking was, so he moved away from the casket and slumped into a dining room chair.

"You're already going to Hell—if there is such a place," Harlan addressed himself. "What difference does it make if you get there sooner than you thought? You've got nothing to keep you here. Your mother probably already thinks you're dead; you might as well make her correct. The only girl you've ever been really interested in has said that she won't marry you, so there's no reason to stay here. Once you leave, you have no plan except to keep one step ahead of the law—which you already know is no kind of life since you were living it for the weeks between leaving the CCC and showing up here. So what are you waiting for?"

Harlan's grief and guilt were quickly turning into anger. His eyes traveled up to the lifeless visage in the casket, and his conscience pricked him. He couldn't give voice to these kinds of thoughts in the presence of Mr. Meyer's body.

"Sorry, old man," Harlan said, not irreverently, and exited the dining room for the kitchen. Absentmindedly, he poked a couple of pieces of split wood in the cookstove and began pacing back and forth.

"So how will you go about it?" he asked himself aloud. *I've seen no gun here anywhere, though there is likely to be one somewhere in order to shoot pests. No. Too messy. What about the barn loft? Plenty of good thick rope attached to the hay grapple in the loft, and it would be very easy to do. Lots of guys have done that over these last few years.*

All of this could be over in just a few minutes. You're not doing anyone any good anyway. Before this hour is over, you won't feel any guilt anymore! You won't feel anything anymore! What a relief that will be! No more guilt!

Harlan looked down and saw his hands tying his bootlaces, and he realized in a hazy way that they seemed like foreign objects as they mechanically completed their task. He could see no reason to don a jacket since in just a few minutes he wouldn't feel the chill air anymore either. In seconds, Harlan was marching toward the barn, and the Meyers' dog raised its head to watch him as he strode by. Usually, the dog could count on the occasional scratch to her ears from Harlan's hand, but at that moment, even the canine detected Harlan's acute sense of purpose.

No more guilt!

He reached the barn loft in short order, scrambled up the giant mound of hay to where the ropes for the grapple fork descended from the hay trolley on its track. Harlan viewed the ropes as his keys to relief and took them in his hands. Though he had seen pictures of nooses before, he had no knowledge of how they were tied. After a few fumbling attempts to recreate what he knew to be a proper hangman's halter, he gave up his pursuit of perfection.

"What does it matter anyway so long as it gets the job done?" he asked aloud. All he could think about was the relief that he perceived would soon be his.

No more guilt! continually drummed through his brain. *No more guilt!*

Harlan slid to a shallow spot in the hay, haphazardly tied the free end of one of the ropes low on a rafter brace there, and then worked his way back to the top of the mound.

No more guilt!

In the middle of the slack rope, he carelessly fashioned a loop which was big enough to go over his head. He figured that if he jumped from the top of the haystack with the loop around his neck, his weight would be sufficient to tighten the rope and accomplish his goal.

No more guilt! was all he heard as he slipped the coil over his head. It seemed as if the earth's rotation had been accelerating rapidly, and Harlan had a feeling similar to what one experiences just before an automobile accident when one knows a crash is imminent.

No more guilt! he thought again, and hurdled his body from the top of the hay.

Harlan's eyes fluttered open, and for a moment all he could see was the wood rafters and shakes of the barn roof. Then, in the fuzzy edge of his sight, he detected movement; it was the rope still swinging spectrally from the hay trolley.

Shooting bolt upright, Harlan looked at the lower end of the rope. Somehow, it was no longer tied to the rafter brace. His knees buckled at the sight, and he crumpled into a heap on the hay.

Harlan swore violently, spewing every morsel of profanity he had ever heard. When he had exhausted his supply of obscenities, he screamed, "You can accidentally kill two other men, but you can't even manage to successfully end your own life when you set out to do it! What kind of moron are you?" His anger became greater than what he could channel into words, and he dissolved into convulsive sobs once again.

Harlan ran his hands around his neck. Why couldn't he feel any rope-burned skin? Why wasn't his neck sore at all? Nothing made any sense. With the foolishness of one who can't think of anything to do but repeat what had already been proven ineffective, Harlan slid down the hay once more and tried to retie the rope to the rafter brace, but his prolific tears blinded him and rendered his efforts useless.

"Forget this; I'm going to look for a gun!" he seethed.

His new resolution dried his tears and restored in him a certain poise. He recklessly jumped out of the hayloft, ignoring the ladder entirely, and rocketed headlong toward the house again. On the other side of the back door, he turned to look above its frame for some sort of firearm. Nothing. He felt behind the various coats and other outdoor clothing that hung on hooks near the door. Nothing.

"If I were the Meyers, where would I keep a pistol?" he asked aloud.

"Dad always kept his in the drawer of the dining room buffet," Harlan replied to his own question.

A few strides carried him to the dining room again, and Harlan was instantly rifling amongst table linens and silverware, but to no avail.

"What about the top dresser drawer?"

Harlan easily gained entrance to Mrs. Meyer's bedroom as it was tucked in the northwest corner of the main floor behind the kitchen and he had never seen the door of it closed, let alone locked. He walked straight to the dresser and pulled out the top drawer.

Right on top of all the other contents was a framed photograph of Marty. Harlan came to a sudden halt, snapped out of his self-absorption by the calm and trusting expression on the grey and white depiction of the face he loved.

Harlan Jensen, you are some special kind of idiot! his conscience derided him. *How can you have said three nights ago that you love this girl and then you plot to leave your dead carcass for her to find while her father's lifeless body is lying in a casket in her dining room? Are you trying to kill her, too? Yes, she turned you down, but she also said that she loves you. And just because she rejected you didn't stop you from loving her. What are you thinking?*

"Suicide is the ultimate act of selfishness," he remembered hearing Miss Stanton, his teacher, say while teaching about the atrocities of the Roman Empire. He had never given that statement much thought at the time, but those words came flooding back to him.

But what about your guilt? his conscience asked. *You know you can't live with it much longer. You said that just a few minutes ago. What are you going to do with the truth of that statement?*

"Well, add selfishness to your list of sins then," he shouted to himself.

Harlan had to think. He shut the drawer, turned to leave the bedroom, and caught the reflection of his face in the mirror. Walking closer to examine it, he couldn't believe that there were no marks on his neck whatsoever. Nothing seemed to make sense, and tears of frustration and shame began to flow again, burning his exhausted eyes as they leaked out.

There are lots of ways to end your life, Harlan reflected, slowly calming. He sought a kitchen chair and sat down to contemplate. *You're not in so much of a hurry that you can't wait until you leave after Mr. Meyer's funeral. There is no point in causing Mrs. Meyer and Marty any more pain than you already have. Once you've met your obligations tomorrow, you'll surely be able to leave soon after. Two or three more days here, hitch a ride on a train and ride for a day so that when you make your final exit from this life, the two Meyer ladies will never get wind of it, and it will be all over. That's the best way to handle it all. You can handle two or three more days of this guilt.*

Harlan rubbed his eyes to rid them of their tears. When he

stopped, they happened to be focused on the floor, and he realized at that moment that he had tracked dirt through the kitchen and into the bedroom. Since he didn't want to raise Mrs. Meyer's suspicions in any way, he brought the broom and dustpan out of the washroom, took them to the bedroom, and began sweeping away the only external evidence that his suicidal thoughts existed. He had swept the bedroom and was halfway finished with the dining room floor when Marty and Mrs. Meyer arrived home from church. Mrs. Meyer caught him with the broom in his hands.

"Why, Harlan, how kind of you!" she said with appreciation. "That was very thoughtful."

Raising his eyes to meet hers, he deprecatingly began, "Well, it really wasn't; I had tracked…"

At sight of his puffy red eyes while he was standing next to Mr. Meyer's casket, Mrs. Meyer jumped to the conclusion that Harlan's tears had all been shed for her husband.

"Come here," she said, advancing toward him with a strong maternal note in her voice and her arms stretched wide to receive him in an embrace. "I should have thought! It wasn't right of me to leave you here to be alone in your grief. I'm sorry. I should have called someone else to sit with him."

Once again, Mrs. Meyer interpreted his actions to be more pure than they were. She was constantly giving him the benefit of the doubt. While he let her hug him, Harlan realized that he was extremely grateful that there had been no witnesses to his emotional outbursts, for this way there would be no one who would thwart the plans that he had put in place to deal with his all-consuming remorse.

He decided more firmly that, one way or another, there would be no more guilt for Harlan Jensen.

Chapter Seventeen

November 11, 1935

No one spilled any unnecessary words in the Meyer household on Monday morning. The routines of milking and livestock chores were carried out with hushed automaticity. As he and Marty milked in silence, Harlan realized that she had exchanged only whatever words were absolutely necessary with him since their heart-to-heart conversation on Thursday evening in which she had turned down his marriage proposal. This caused a twinge of bitterness to take root in Harlan's heart, and after his outlook had taken such a dark turn the day before, he was in a mood to nurse a grudge. However, in his foolishness, he did not take into account that he had barely spoken to Marty either.

Amanda Engel arrived shortly after chores were finished with her husband Otto. She unceremoniously presented the predicted set of new dress clothes to Harlan, explaining that they were his to keep as her gift for how nicely he had treated her brother at the end of his life. Harlan found the irony of this sentiment to be a little much, but decided to keep his mouth shut about it. Instead, he set out to honor Mr. Meyer's memory the best he could by taking extra effort on his personal grooming so that he would be worthy of the new clothes. He had never done such a meticulous job of shaving, combing his blond hair, and making sure that his fingernails and calloused hands were as free from as much of the rich Iowa soil as he could.

The suit from Marty's aunt fit perfectly, and Harlan, though he was not well-versed in the finer points of men's apparel, mentally noted that he had never seen—let alone possessed—such a finely tailored set of clothing. He was most impressed with the shiny black shoes and the black necktie. His CCC-issued boots had become quite dilapidated, and while he had worn clothing of varying degrees of worth and condition in his life, he had never owned a pair of black dress shoes. He found that these new wing tips constantly drew his attention to his feet. The silk tie presented its own set of problems in that Harlan had never learned to tie a windsor knot. After a bumbling attempt in his bedroom mirror that only confirmed his ignorance, Harlan decided that he would have to ask Mrs. Meyer to take care of it for him.

"Mrs. Meyer?" he called as he descended the stairway to the kitchen, his new shoes clicking expensively with each tread. "Mrs. Meyer? I need help."

The kitchen was empty, so he pushed open the swinging door to the dining room.

"Mrs. Meyer, I need help with my..." Harlan stopped suddenly. Dressed in black crepe with her back to him as she was pinning on a charcoal grey cloche hat in the mirror of the hall tree, Marty was the picture of femininity.

"Mother wanted to get to the church before anyone else, so she left with Aunt Amanda and Uncle Otto in their car," Marty said, concentrating on her reflection. "I waited here to go with you in our car."

"I see. Well, I need help with my tie," Harlan explained. "I'll ask someone at the church."

Apparently satisfied with her appearance, Marty removed her gaze from the mirror and turned to face Harlan. A soft "Oh!" escaped her lips and accompanied her wide-eyed expression the moment she beheld him in his new suit.

"Don't I look all right?" Harlan asked, thinking that she had seen a flaw. He did not realize that Marty's reaction had been occasioned by how shockingly attractive she found him in that moment.

"No, no. You look just fine," she said, shaking her head to snap herself out of her reverie. "Here, let me help you with that." She took his tie from his hand, put it around his neck and began tying it for him.

Harlan had had so little experience with ties that he did not realize what an extraordinary display of talent this was. As Marty worked at her task, the scent of her light perfume rose to him and thwarted his earlier hostility toward her. Harlan felt that there ought to be some conversation occurring between the two of them while they were so near each other, but for the life of him, he couldn't figure out what to say.

Marty apparently experienced the same feeling, and she finally broke the silence. "Aunt Amanda certainly has good taste in clothing."

"And expensive taste," Harlan agreed.

"She can afford it," Marty said dismissively.

She began unbuttoning the top of Harlan's vest in order to place the tie beneath it, an act that he considered extremely familiar even though two more layers of clothing still separated his flesh from her fingertips. This gesture reminded Harlan of the evening several days prior when he had helped Mrs. Meyer prepare Mr. Meyer for bed and he had observed the tenderness with which she had handled her husband. At that time, Harlan had wondered if he would ever be on the receiving end of such warmth, and here it was happening to him in the very same room. Some instinct in Harlan caused him to want to gather her into his arms at that moment, but memories of their previous conversation and consciousness of the day's occasion prevented him.

"There. All finished." Marty had re-buttoned the vest as well as the suit jacket and absentmindedly smoothed them across his chest with her hands. She stood back then and took in his appearance. "You look..." Marty stopped, obviously catching herself from paying Harlan a compliment. "Thank you so much for staying and helping us with the funeral. Dad would have wanted you here, and I appreciate your choosing to honor him by agreeing to be a pallbearer."

Many things came to Harlan's mind that he would have liked to have said at that moment, but all that reached his lips was a simple "You're welcome."

★★★★★★★★★★★★★

"Albert Edwin Meyer was born on July 13, 1883, to the late Edwin and Olga (Schiltz) Meyer on the home farm here in rural Pottawattamie County, Iowa. Al attended Maple Grove School through the eighth grade, graduating in May of 1896. After growing up in this church, Al received Jesus Christ as his savior on July 20, 1897, and was baptized shortly after," eulogized Rev. Martin after the organ prelude and opening prayer.

Harlan listened to these words from his place among the other men who were serving as his fellow pallbearers. They were seated together in the front pew on the left side of the church with Harlan next to the aisle. All of them were dressed in their best black suits with an embroidered red rose pinned to their lapels which signified their function at the funeral ceremony. Harlan noticed with a certain amount of embarrassment that his suit was the sharpest looking of them all, and he felt keenly the fact that he didn't deserve that distinction.

"Mr. Meyer was united in holy matrimony with Elsie Heinrichs on June 6, 1910. To this union was born two children, the first a stillborn son in 1912, and a daughter Martha Louise in 1917. Albert Edwin Meyer entered into Paradise on Friday, November 8, 1935, having attained the age of fifty-two years, three months, and twenty-six days."

Mrs. Meyer and Marty were seated in the front pew across the aisle, flanked by the rest of the Meyer and Schiltz relatives. Occasionally, Harlan's eyes darted over to them to see how they were doing.

"Mr. Meyer was preceded in death by his parents, brother Adolf, and infant son. He is survived by his wife of twenty-five years, Elsie, daughter Martha, sister Amanda Engel of Council Bluffs, two nieces and two nephews on his wife's side, and a host of friends and neighbors."

The small country church was overflowing with people; in fact, several middle-aged and younger men were standing along the outside walls and on the balcony stairs in order to accommodate the crowd. When Harlan and his fellow pallbearers had been escorted to their pew by the funeral director, his guilt multiplied at the sight of so many lives which had been disrupted by Mr. Meyer's death.

A woman whose face Harlan recognized but whose name he did not know rose and sang "Sweet Hour of Prayer" in a powerful soprano voice. The first two verses were familiar to Harlan because Marty and Mrs. Meyer had frequently sung them in the cornfield, but the third verse that the lady sang caught his attention.

> *Sweet hour of prayer! Sweet hour of prayer!*
> *May I thy consolation share,*
> *Till, from Mount Pisgah's lofty height,*
> *I view my home and take my flight*
> *This robe of flesh I'll drop, and rise*
> *To seize the everlasting prize,*
> *And shout, while passing through the air,*
> *"Farewell, farewell, sweet hour of prayer!"*

When she was finished, Rev. Martin entered the pulpit again. "Hear these words spoken by Jesus the Christ as recorded in the Gospel of John, chapter eleven, verses twenty-five and twenty-six: 'Jesus said unto her, I am the resurrection, and the life: he that believeth in me, though he were dead, yet shall he live: And whosoever liveth and believeth in me shall never die. Believest thou this?'"

Rev. Martin cleared his throat loudly before continuing.

"Brethren, I have been the pastor of this church for fifteen years, and during that time I have presided over the funerals of many people whom I considered dear friends, but I think you'll understand what I mean when I say that today I am presiding over the funeral of a man whom I considered one of the heroes of the faith, a man whom I looked to for advice and guidance, for encouragement, and for Christian fellowship. I say all this to make clear that the earthly death of Albert Meyer has been an occasion for great mourning on my part. The large number of people in this church building today is, I believe, a testimony to the fact that I am not alone in my feelings toward this brother in Christ."

The pastor's words were making Harlan feel worse about the role he had played in Mr. Meyer's passing.

"But *I* believe, dear friends," Rev. Martin continued, "that today—nay, that this very *moment*—needs to mark the turning point in our emotions regarding the death of this man. We have spent the last three days largely mourning Mr. Meyer's death. We could not help doing so. A man we all loved and took comfort and inspiration from has been removed from our presence here on Earth. It was right that we mourned.

"But it is only right that we mourn for a short while. Now, I'm not saying there won't be difficult times ahead: those moments when we think, 'Oh, I'll just ask Al what I should do,' or 'I want to be sure and tell Al whatever it is that is on our minds,' for example. I can assure you there will be times in the days, weeks, months, and years ahead when we will miss him quite sorely. However, I challenge you that when you find yourself in those moments, miss him for a second or two and then remind yourself of the fact that he is in the presence of Jesus, his beloved savior. Let me just say that again. Al Meyer is *in the presence of Jesus!*" The inflection in Rev. Martin's voice did full justice to what a wonderful place that is.

"And when we think of that in connection with Al Meyer, it should bring us *joy!* Today, I challenge us to start walking in the joy that is Al Meyer's as he is with our savior and to reflect on the joy we had in knowing the Al Meyer that we did.

"I have met very few people in the course of my life who have had stronger faith in Jesus Christ than Albert Meyer. Let me remind you of our scripture: 'Jesus said, "I am the resurrection, and the life: he that believeth in me, though he were dead, yet shall he live: And whosoever liveth and believeth in me shall never die."' Albert Edwin Meyer *believed*, my friends!"

At Harlan's left elbow, Roy Schoening and another young man his age further down the pew voiced a quiet but firm "Amen!"

"Albert Edwin Meyer *believed* in Jesus Christ," Rev. Martin echoed, gaining a certain rhythm to his speech. "He *believed* that Jesus Christ is the resurrection and the life. And now, though his earthly death has occurred, yet shall he live! And, my friends, the beauty of God's love for us is that *whosoever*—that's you and me now—*whosoever* liveth and believeth in Jesus Christ shall never die. Believest thou this?

"Al Meyer did. Al Meyer loved Jesus, and Al Meyer loved people. And when you love Jesus and you love people, you tell people about Jesus.

"When I first came to this congregation as a young whippersnapper right out of seminary, I had a conversation with Al that I will never forget. I had grown up in downtown Chicago and had a great deal to learn about agriculture in general, and I had only been here a couple months when Harold Kloeckner lost his life in a farming accident. Most of you remember that awful day.

"'You know, Rev.' Al said to me a couple days later. He always called me 'Rev.' He said, 'You know, Rev., farming is a very dangerous occupation. You may be called upon to bury me at any time, and I want you to know a few things about my funeral wishes beforehand. The first thing is, I want you to remind the people who come that they aren't there to bury the real me.' Of course, I had to ask him what he meant by that.

"He said, 'The real me was a little weasel who was going nowhere, and he was getting there on his own steam. The real me trusted Jesus Christ way back when he was fourteen years old. The real Al Meyer was crucified with Christ that day, and he was put to death. Since then, the Holy Spirit has been living in me, and I have tried with his help to live as a reflection of Jesus Christ. Now, the Lord knows I haven't always been as successful at that as I might, and my wife could probably tell you about a few times when I haven't looked anything at all like Jesus, but there is one thing I've noticed about people who attend funerals: no matter what kind of a skunk is lying in the casket, all the people gathered 'round will carry on about how kind and good and wonderful the fella was. As that seems to me to be human nature, I imagine people will come to my funeral and do the same. But, Rev., it's your job to make sure that if anyone does that, they are reminded that I want all the glory to go to God. He is the one who is kind and good and wonderful, and whatever good there was about me was just a small reflection of him.' Then he chuckled a little and added, 'And anything about me that people might bring up that wasn't any good was no reflection of him, but a little glimpse of the old me that the good Lord hadn't got finished sanctifying yet.'

"He went on to say, 'And the second thing, Rev., is that you be sure and share the gospel with the whole kit and bilin' of 'em who show up.' Wasn't that just like Al? I'm told that even after his stroke rendered him mute, he was witnessing to Harlan Jensen, who has been such a help to the Meyer family these last few weeks, by having him read passages of Scripture aloud when they were home alone together," Rev. Martin continued, indicating Harlan's location in the front pew.

Harlan blushed violently at being pointed out amongst the crowd and wished that he could disappear. His embarrassment was so acute that he could no longer focus on what Rev. Martin was saying as the pastor followed Mr. Meyer's wishes that the Gospel of Jesus Christ be shared at his funeral. Later, the only thing Harlan was able to recall from Rev. Martin's presentation was that it was punctuated with the frequent repetition of the question "Believest thou this?"

After Rev. Martin finished his sermon, he prayed, and then the whole congregation sang "When We All Get to Heaven" with such throaty enthusiasm that Harlan could feel the floor shaking beneath his feet.

Mrs. Meyer insisted on helping the other church ladies wash the dishes and coffee cups after the funeral luncheon in the church basement had largely disbanded. They protested loudly, but she responded by saying that the work would be therapeutic for her. Mr. and Mrs. Engel had departed for Council Bluffs, so Harlan was obligated to stay to drive Mrs. Meyer home when the work was done. He was troubled by the fact that he had not seen Marty for a while and couldn't locate her among those who remained in the church basement. He searched the small main floor and balcony to no avail, and then went outside to see if she were already in the car. As he was walking to the vehicle, he spotted her solitary figure standing at her father's grave in the cemetery.

The pathetic sight of her there alone aroused his guilt once more, but he found himself irresistibly drawn to her, and his legs were spanning the distance to her before he could stop them.

Marty was not noticeably crying, but she was sniffling, and her handkerchief looked as though it had outlived its usefulness. Harlan dug in his pocket and produced the brilliant white hanky that Amanda Engel had been so thoughtful as to provide with the suit.

"It's damp, but only with tears," he said apologetically as he offered it to Marty.

She accepted it, blew her nose discreetly, and tucked it into her sleeve while he stood there helplessly.

"I'm sor..." he started.

"Shhh," she whispered. Without warning, she squeezed him hard around his middle and laid her cheek on his breast.

Harlan felt that it was impolite not to return the embrace, so he wrapped his warm, strong arms around her quivering frame.

Chapter Eighteen

November 12-15, 1935

The three occupants of the Meyer farm felt as though the cloudy days following the funeral were lived in a trance. Perhaps it was due to the lengthening nights, or maybe it was because nobody in the Meyer home was sleeping very well and their shared fatigue cast its own unmistakeable pall over the household.

Mrs. Meyer stayed occupied at the house with the time that she would have spent caring for Mr. Meyer now devoted to writing the necessary correspondence that his death occasioned.

All outdoor work fell to Harlan and Marty, but Marty's time was divided between that and a few responsibilities in the house as well.

For his part, beyond what was daily necessary for the livestock, Harlan tried to look for jobs that needed to be done around the farm before winter. By Wednesday, all of the fences had been inspected, and the cattle were turned out onto the cornstalks for the winter. It was obvious to Harlan that weaning the most recent litters of pigs had been put off due to Mr. Meyer's stroke and the subsequent corn harvest, so that job was completed after the cattle had been moved. Truthfully, Harlan could see no end to the work that needed to be done, but he tried to figure out which jobs would be most difficult for Mrs. Meyer and Marty to complete once he was no longer there.

Since the funeral on Monday, he had been looking for opportunities to take his leave, but none had presented themselves yet.

The evenings saw the three of them in the living room, the two women seated near the lamp at the center table either continuing through the endless mail that Mr. Meyer's passing brought to their box or sifting through insurance policies, legal papers, and farm records to learn about their financial status. As he figured that none of this was his business, he asked no questions about it, which caused the two women to assume he was uninterested. What Harlan did consider his business were the expressions of concentration that they wore as they trudged through this work. He perceived their knitted brows as signs of anguish, and whenever he saw them, his sense of culpability was renewed. He longed to see Mrs. Meyer and Marty spend an evening in the old familiar pursuits of needlework and poetry reading, and his feelings of guilt were exacerbated by his own idleness while the two women toiled.

The only thing that seemed right about the evenings was when Marty and Mrs. Meyer decided that enough was enough and put the business aside so that Marty could read aloud from the Bible for a while before they went to bed. However, even this was soured for Harlan by the fact that Marty was purposely seeking passages regarding Heaven, and while they obviously offered comfort to Mrs. Meyer and herself, they only served to remind Harlan of his damnable state. He was especially upset on Thursday evening when she read Revelation 21. He recognized the fact that the fourth and fifth verses soothed her hurting heart: "And God shall wipe away all tears from their eyes; and there shall be no more death, neither sorrow, nor crying, neither shall there be any more pain: for the former things are passed away." But it was the eighth verse that he heard most loudly: "But the fearful, and unbelieving, and the abominable, and murderers, and whoremongers, and sorcerers, and idolaters, and all liars, shall have their part in the lake which burneth with fire and brimstone: which is the second death."

Harlan knew that this "second death" was his destiny, but in his ignorance of what all it implied for him and in his belief that it would relieve him of the guilt that he carried, he freshened his resolve to hasten its coming.

On Friday morning, unfamiliar commotion filled the kitchen at breakfast time. The usual aromas of sausage, hot cereal, and pancakes mingled with the anachronistic odors of onions, beef, and tomatoes, and Mrs. Meyer exhibited an air of nervous energy as she rushed through tasks on which she usually spent great care.

"Marty and I are going to Council Bluffs as soon as she's done with the poultry and I can get the separator washed," Mrs. Meyer said, determination evident in her voice. "I've put a pot of chili together for your dinner, which I'll leave on the back of the range so it will be hot and ready for you at noon. There's a new loaf of yesterday's bread in the breadbox, and I've opened a jar of peaches for you and put them in the cooler. I'll load the firebox on the stove before we leave, and if you'll occasionally feed the fire while we're away, I'd appreciate that. It'll make getting supper that much faster whenever we do get back. Oh, and when you fuel the fire this afternoon, take a peek in the chili pot each time to make sure that it isn't getting too dry. If so, add some hot water from the teakettle. Understand?"

Harlan nodded his assent as he shoveled another forkful of pancakes into his mouth, and for the first time he was thankful for the few weeks that he had been assigned to the mess hall in his CCC camp.

"I don't know when we'll be back," Mrs. Meyer continued, "but my guess is that it won't be until close to suppertime, but we could be quite late. We'll try to be home by milking, but I just can't promise anything."

Harlan thought this might be his opportunity to depart from the Meyer farm and put into motion his plan to end his life. He knew that his relationship with Marty—strained and undefined though it was—prevented him from running away without warning, so his mind was working quickly while he ate his breakfast.

"Maybe today ought to be the day that I move on," Harlan ventured.

Marty's face paled, and she stopped eating, but nothing in Mrs. Meyer's demeanor indicated that she had actually heard him speak.

"My plans got put on hold when Mr. Meyer died, you know, and I don't want to be a drag on the two of you," Harlan pressed. "So maybe today I should go on my way."

Mrs. Meyer did not look at Harlan at all. Instead, she acted as if this topic of conversation was a part of their regular breakfast routine.

Harlan was beginning to feel a little deflated when he continued lamely. "I won't leave until the morning chores are finished, of course, but then I..." he trailed off, waiting for Mrs. Meyer to acknowledge him.

"Marty and I are going into Council Bluffs to take care of business at Pottawattamie County Farmer's Mutual regarding Al's passing. We're also going to pick up a new pair of boots for you. That's the least we can do for all that you've done for us. The ones you have aren't going to make it another day," said Mrs. Meyer.

The decaying state of Harlan's boots had actually been on his mind lately. Though his hobo days had been relatively short, they had quickly taught him how important sturdy footwear is to a transient. And while Amanda Engel had made it clear that his new outfit of dress clothes was his to keep, he knew the new wingtips would not withstand the stress of even the few days of travel he intended to use to distance himself from the Meyers.

What's one more day if it will get you a new pair of shoes? he asked himself. But then, as if on cue, his guilt kicked in again, and he thought about what a waste it would be for the Meyers to spend money on a pair of shoes that he would only use for a few days. *No point in arguing, though,* he thought. *She doesn't hear me anyway.*

Nothing else was said during breakfast, but Harlan noticed

that Marty only picked at her pancakes. What remained of them and most of her hot cereal landed in the dog's pan on the back step.

While he was pouring the morning's skimmed milk into the trough for the feeder pigs, Marty nearly made him jump out of his decrepit boots when she tapped him lightly on the elbow.

"You *will* be here when we get back, right?" she asked timidly.

"Yeah," Harlan grunted. "How come she doesn't even hear me talking?" He implored, turning to face her.

Marty shrugged helplessly. She stared at Harlan for a couple of seconds, then turned on her heel and hurried away.

Elsie Meyer's chili was superb when Harlan came in from the blustery outdoors at noon. As he sat in the warmth radiating from the kitchen stove and downed two bowls of chili, a thick slice of buttered bread, and a bowl of peaches, it occurred to him that Mrs. Meyer would have no way of knowing just how much food he consumed for his noon meal. She had commented on his healthy appetite a couple of times before, so it would not surprise her if there was less chili left in the pot when she arrived home than she might have expected.

Thus, Harlan lit a barn lantern and ventured down into the cellar. He was able to quickly find what he sought: a wide mouth pint canning jar with lid and rubber seal. He washed them quickly, filled the jar with boiling chili, and sealed it with the lid and rubber ring. The weather was cool enough now that the chili would keep for a couple of days outdoors, so Harlan squirreled it away in the barn where he could grab it on his way to catch a train. If he could manage to board a train without breaking the jar, he would be able to survive on that one meal long enough to get a sufficient distance away to execute his final plans.

Harlan might have felt a pang of guilt about stealing the food and the jar, but, truth be told, he was a little angry at Mrs. Meyer. It had appeared to Harlan that she was manipulating him that morning at the breakfast table, and it made him feel rebellious. Even if he was wrong about that—as he had been when he had believed that she was laundering his clothes just to keep him around to pick another day's worth of corn—he resented the fact that she didn't appear to be listening to what he was saying at all.

Furthermore, he was getting very tired of the fact that nothing he did or said seemed to surprise Mrs. Meyer. He was befuddled by this trait of hers, and his confusion gave a foothold to distrust.

Harlan quit oiling harness at a little before five o'clock. There was still no sign of the Meyer women, so he set about the routine of evening chores by himself. Of course, everything took double the amount of time than it usually did, and hauling the full milk cans to the separator in the house was extremely difficult since he was alone. It was long past seven and had been dark for a good hour and a half when he was finally in the house to stay for the evening. The extra effort required of him fed his current bitterness toward Mrs. Meyer because he felt more than ever that she was taking advantage of him.

He rummaged in the icebox and found a variety of leftovers that sufficed for his supper when supplemented with a couple of fried eggs. He didn't feel guilty about eating what he found because there was enough chili remaining in the pot for Marty and Mrs. Meyer if they had not yet eaten once they got home.

After he had eaten, Harlan put his supper dishes in the sink on top of his dinner dishes and then retired to the living room. Harlan wished for a radio to listen to, but the Meyers didn't own one. He saw the family's Bible on the lamp table and felt drawn to read it for a moment, but then decided that he'd had enough of the Bible recently, especially since it seemed to him that it only spoke of his coming doom. Instead, he pulled the volume of James Russell Lowell's poetry off the shelf. That was the book that Marty had read from on the evening before he got sick, an evening that was a very pleasant memory to Harlan.

He thumbed through the pages and randomly landed on

"Sumthin' in the Pastoral Line," but when he got to the word "precerdents" in the second line, he gave up on it. He flipped pages again and landed on "Without and Within." He started reading that one, but was turned off when he reached the second stanza which says "Flattening his nose against the pane,/He envies me my brilliant lot,/Breathes on his aching fist in vain,/And dooms me to a place more hot." Harlan was beginning to feel like he was seeing an inordinate number of reminders regarding his place of residence in the afterlife.

He flipped the pages of the book one more time and landed at a poem entitled simply "A Parable." Harlan read the first stanza: "Said Christ our Lord, "I will go and see/How the men, my brethren, believe in me." However, Harlan knew that he didn't believe in Jesus, and the verse had the strange effect of making him feel angry and guilty once again. He returned the book to the shelf in frustration and consulted the clock.

"Nine o'clock," he sighed aloud. "I wonder where they could be." He reminded himself that Mrs. Meyer had predicted they would be late, but Harlan had not figured they would be this late.

His imagination began to feed on his fears, and Harlan began to wonder if someone in Council Bluffs had alerted Marty and Mrs. Meyer to his identity and true nature. Perhaps they were frightened to come home again until they could bring the authorities with them to arrest and haul him away. If the two women *hadn't* been apprised of his villainous past, then what had happened to them? Harlan figured they must have had some trouble, but he had no way of finding out or coming to their aid.

Harlan's mind ran wild for a few minutes; then, he decided that borrowing trouble from tomorrow was pure foolishness, so he decided to go upstairs to bed. After all, Mrs. Meyer had been very vague about what time they would return; he had no real cause for concern yet. It did seem somehow wrong to go to sleep when the women were not back yet, though, so he promised himself that he would stay awake until they returned.

It was not long, however, before exhaustion from the day's labor sabotaged his resolve.

"Harlan?" a timid voice inquired from the other side of his bedroom door. "Harlan, are you in there?"

No response was uttered from inside the room.

"Harlan?" Marty called again, this time also knocking softly on the door.

Again there was no response, so Marty gingerly turned the knob of the bedroom door and gained entrance. She had done the same a few days prior when she had discovered that Harlan had become ill. Once the door was open, she could see the lumpy outline of what appeared to be a body in the bed. However, the room was far too dark to detect movement, and she could neither hear breathing nor make out a face. She had heard stories of people strategically placing pillows or other paraphernalia in a bed to make it look occupied.

Very anxious and also quite scared, Marty reached down and grasped what she hoped was a foot.

Harlan woke with a start and inhaled so loudly and deeply that he sounded like a drowning man who had just come to the surface. He started thrashing around defensively, striking at his feet, but Marty had immediately let go and stepped back. The reason that she couldn't make out his face upon entering his room was because his head had been under the pillow, and this caused him to be disoriented upon waking.

"Shhh!" Marty whispered. "It's just me. I'm sorry I scared you. I just wanted to be sure that you were still here."

Harlan took a moment to regain his senses and blinked repeatedly, trying to get Marty into focus.

"I told you I would be here when you got back," he said finally, his peevishness evident even in his whisper.

"I know, and Mama said you'd be here and that I was not to wake you, but I wouldn't have been able to fall asleep until I knew for sure. I hope she didn't hear all of this commotion downstairs. Sorry."

"What time is it?" Harlan asked.

"After eleven thirty," Marty replied.

"Eleven thirty!"

"I'm sure we frightened all of the neighbors by driving by at this time of night, but we left the Bluffs much later than we had planned, and then Mother swerved to miss a cow that had gotten out onto the road and put us in the ditch. We had to walk to the nearest farmhouse to get help." Marty whispered all of this information as if she were somehow accountable to Harlan.

"Are you both all right?" Harlan inquired neutrally.

"Yes, and the car is fine too. Just a little extra dust and grass that will have to be removed," she related.

Harlan couldn't think of anything more that needed to be said, but it appeared that Marty expected a response. Finally, he replied, "Well, that's good."

"Yeah, it was a scary ride." She lingered a few seconds, seeming as though she wished to converse longer, but finally she turned to go. "Good night. I'm sorry I woke you."

"G'night," Harlan mumbled, snuggling back down into his covers. The adrenaline rush of being awakened in such an alarming way did not allow Harlan to fall asleep again immediately. While he lay there waiting to become drowsy again, he reflected on the conversation he had just had. He had noticed Marty's apparent need to confess her whereabouts to him, but he was distressed and annoyed at the fact that she obviously did not trust him to have kept his word about staying.

Well, it doesn't matter anyway, he thought. *You are leaving as soon as you can, so don't get all bent out of shape about it.*

Chapter Nineteen

November 16 & 17, 1935

In the morning, Harlan discovered that his old boots had disappeared, and in their place stood a new pair. They were stiff but fit well, and Harlan was suitably grateful.

"We had quite the evening last night," Mrs. Meyer began over breakfast after Harlan and Marty had returned to the house from milking. She related the same story that Harlan had already heard from Marty, but with much greater detail. Harlan looked at Marty briefly, and her eyes begged him to not reveal that he was already aware of the previous evening's excitement.

The chronicle of putting the car in the ditch was finished by the time Harlan was onto his second stack of French toast, but it was evident that Mrs. Meyer was just warming up. "Of course, the reason we were so late was because we had so much to do. Then, we spent a lot of time visiting with Marty's uncle Otto. He's got a good business head on him, you know. After you and Marty finish with the rest of the stock chores, I want you to come back in the house so we can all talk about what we learned yesterday. Do your boots fit?" These last two sentences were said without a pause between them, and were somewhat surprising to Harlan, but Mrs. Meyer was using that old familiar tone again, so there was no room for debating the future events of the morning.

"Now, the reason that Marty and I had to go into the Bluffs yesterday is because we had to take Al's death certificate into the insurance office," Mrs. Meyer said later over the empty kitchen table. "Al was never one to tell me a whole lot about the details of the business side of things. I don't know why, really. I think he thought I wasn't interested. Anyway, while we were there, we learned quite a bit, and then we went to the Engels' to talk it all over with Amanda and Otto. The long and the short of it, though, is that through some smart decisions with insurance, Al left us in pretty good shape money wise. We're not rich—in fact, I wouldn't even call us comfortable—but unlike so many people these days, we are going to be all right if we don't lose our heads."

She paused and looked at Harlan long enough to determine that he had no idea why she was telling him any of this.

"The reason we wanted to talk to you is because we now know that once Al's life insurance money comes in a few days, we'll have enough that we can start paying you for all of the work that you've been doing around here," Mrs. Meyer said.

"Oh, you don't need to worry about that. You've fed me and taken care of me when I was sick," Harlan demurred. "I think we can just call it even. I should move on as soon as possible anyway."

"No, you don't understand," Mrs. Meyer said. "We want to take you on as our hired man. Two ladies can't run this farm all by themselves. We don't want to sell it—at this time anyway, with land prices so low—and with the markets and weather like they are right now, I'm not sure that we could get anyone to rent it. You've been just excellent help, Harlan. We trust you, and, truth be told, we're attached to you, so we are hoping you'll stay."

Harlan was completely taken aback. His eyes darted back and forth between Mrs. Meyer and her daughter. Marty wore an expectant expression, but Mrs. Meyer acted like it was already concluded that Harlan would stay. For his part, Harlan was confused. This was not at all a part of his plans.

"Please say you will," Marty implored.

"Well, I...I just don't know," sputtered Harlan. "This is a surp...I need to think about it."

"Suit yourself," Mrs. Meyer said. "We sure have appreciated all that you have done for us since you arrived. I say again, you've been such a godsend. He really answered my prayers when he sent you."

As Harlan continued the task of oiling harness after dinner, the sun disappeared behind a dark grey layer of clouds, and the air took on an uncomfortable dampness. The weather fit Harlan's mood perfectly.

Before Mrs. Meyer and Marty had presented their offer that morning, Harlan thought he had planned the last few days of his life. What's more, he thought he had begun to feel some real peace with these plans, too. Now, everything was mixed up in his mind.

"But why is it mixed up?" he muttered aloud to himself. "Nothing has changed really. You're still who you are; you're still a guilty little cuss, and you're still stuck working your hind end off for these women."

However, if Harlan were being truthful, he knew that something had indeed changed. This time when the Meyers had asked him to stay, they were offering him genuine employment. Harlan realized now, too, that they had not been trying to manipulate him when they ignored his hints about leaving the day before. The two of them had been hatching this plan for some time. He now knew that they truly wanted him to stay. With money on the table, they could have their pick of farmhands, but they had asked him, and the idea that he was really and truly wanted muddled his plans to end his life. It had struck him as ironic that they trusted him, but that thought was strangely comforting too.

"Just remember, Harlan, they don't know what you are, and they haven't even figured out that you killed Mr. Meyer," his toxic conscience caused him to hiss aloud. "If they ever put it all together, you'll be sent out of here faster than you can..."

"Harlan, are you out here?" Marty called from the yard.

"In the barn," he returned.

She arrived at his side shortly with a wheelbarrow and pitchfork in tow.

At sight of her equipment, Harlan inquired, "What are you doing?"

"Most of the chickens should be done laying for the day, so I'm going to take some fresh straw up to put in their nests."

Harlan nodded his understanding.

Marty picked up a part of the harness that he had already oiled and appeared to inspect his work closely. She acted like she wanted to say something, but Harlan was not in the mood to make it easier for her by prompting her. She continued fingering the harness a while longer.

In the pregnant silence, Harlan stole a couple of glances at her. She had changed somehow in the last week; now there was a vulnerability about her that tugged at his heart. He reflected that prior to her father's death, whenever someone mentioned his handicapped state, she responded sensitively. Now it was different. Harlan credited it to the fact that before Mr. Meyer had died, there was still a faint hope that he would recover, and by all accounts there had appeared to be progress in that direction. Now that Mr. Meyer was deceased, Harlan perceived that this hope had transformed into a nagging fear about what her future held.

Again, Harlan's sense of responsibility for Mr. Meyer's death made him feel as though he were also the one who had sewn the seeds of Marty's insecurity. With the advent of these ideas, Harlan wished desperately that he could do something more than oil harness for the young woman at his side. This desire was at conflict with his quest to get permanent relief from his guilt, though, and Harlan became aware that with Marty Meyer standing beside him, he was all kinds of confused.

"Harlan," she murmured, breaking the silence, "I know things haven't been as easy between us for the past week as they had been."

He wanted to ask her what she meant by that, wanted to open

up that vein of conversation in order to see where it would lead, but he intuitively knew what she was saying and decided it would be better to let it go.

Marty continued, "But, I want you to know that I really do hope you'll decide to stay. I promise that I'll behave myself better so that things won't be uncomfortable for either of us. I think you'll agree with me that we work well together, and I think that together we can make this farm support the three of us.

"Mama and I talked about all the other possible fellows that we could have asked to be our hired man, and none of them could hold a candle to you. Also, we know how close you and Dad had become, and that means a lot to us because he was a very good judge of character. We feel like he would have wanted you to stay.

"I'll respect whatever decision you make, but I just wanted to say all of this to you, and I couldn't do it in front of Mama."

She turned away to climb into the loft so that she could retrieve the straw for the chicken coop, and Harlan was left alone at his task of oiling harness once more.

Times are tough, Harlan reflected, *and if Marty and Mrs. Meyer hire the wrong man, that could be disastrous for them. Maybe by sticking around, you can partially make up for the fact that you killed Mr. Meyer. Besides, they'd be paying you. You haven't had any money since...*

What about your "big sin"? his conscience asked yet again.

None of the people around here seem to be very interested in your past, though, and they don't seem to be excited about looking at "Wanted" posters, either. You've already wondered if this might be the safest place for you to keep away from the law anyway. You're pretty isolated here, you know.

What about your guilt? Can you go on living with it?

I've been living with it this long. Why not try?

Then his biggest question surfaced in his mind: *Can you continue to live with Marty when you're in love with her, you know she's in love with you, and she's told you that there is no future to your relationship?*

That I don't know, Harlan answered himself honestly.

"Do I look all right?" Harlan asked, entering the kitchen from the stairway door on Sunday morning.

"You look very fine!" Mrs. Meyer said enthusiastically as she fixed his tie. "It was wise of you to not wear the jacket and vest. They would have been a little much, but the pants and shirt are enough to make you look smart for church."

"Thank you," Harlan returned. "Are you ready to go? Where's Marty?"

"She left a half hour ago. Anna Kloeser picked her up early because they are singing a couple of duets today and they wanted to practice before anyone else got there to listen to them."

Harlan drove Mrs. Meyer to the church where he took an ornery sort of delight in seeing the surprised look on Marty's face when he appeared at the top of the balcony stairs just before Sunday School started. This time, he was also more aware of Esther Stempel's obvious pleasure in seeing him again. Places were available next to both Marty and Esther, but Harlan slid into the pew with Roy Schoening since he knew that Roy would share his Bible with him.

This week's Sunday School lesson started with Galatians 6:10: "As we have therefore opportunity, let us do good unto all men, especially unto them who are of the household of faith." This verse spoke loudly to Harlan since he was still trying to decide what to do about the Meyer women's proposal. Clearly, the Meyers were "of the household of faith," and Harlan clearly had the opportunity to "do good unto" them. The situation seemed much more complicated than just that, however, and he wished that he could discuss it with someone other than the two Meyers.

Harlan's preoccupation prevented him from listening intently to what Rev. Martin had to say regarding the remainder of that book, and he was surprised at how quickly the Sunday School hour passed.

It felt strange to sit in Mr. Meyer's place in the family's customary pew, but at the same time Harlan felt an odd sense of guardianship toward Mrs. Meyer, which in turn gave him a feeling of importance.

Harlan wished that Marty was in the pew with them, but as she was singing the duet with Miss Kloeser that morning, the two of them were in the balcony near the organ.

Rev. Martin continued his sermon series "The Attributes of God" by preaching about God's love for people, drawing his largest amount of text from 1 John 4. Marty and Anna Kloeser sang Stainer's "God So Loved the World" for their first musical offering that morning, and later in the service they rendered a haunting version of "What Wondrous Love Is This." Anna's clear, high soprano voice blended beautifully with Marty's alto line in intricate close harmony. The congregation sang a rousing "And Can It Be That I Should Gain?" at the end of the service, and Harlan stood for the benediction with the sentiment that if all church services were like this one, church would be a very enjoyable experience every weekend.

After the service, while the congregation fellowshipped, Harlan sought Roy Schoening's company. Harlan felt that he needed to explain his continued presence on the Meyer farm to Roy since he was the one person whom Harlan had told of his original plan to leave. It had also dawned on Harlan that Roy was someone whom he felt would give him honest advice about whether he should take the Meyer women up on their offer of more permanent employment, in spite of the fact that Roy—at least at one time—had had designs to court Marty.

"Let's go visit outside," Harlan said once he had located young Mr. Schoening.

"Sure."

Roy followed Harlan out of the warm building and into the damp outdoor air. Clouds had darkened the sky during the church service, and the occasional snow flurry made a jagged trek to the ground.

"What's on your mind?" Roy asked, once the two of them had walked to the Meyers' car.

"I don't know why, but I just wanted to be up front with you about the fact that I'm still here. I know I had told you that I was planning on leaving the Friday before last, and then Mr. Meyer passed away. After that, even you said I couldn't leave for a little while. Well, I was planning to leave again last Friday, but Mrs. Meyer and Marty both detained me. It was kind of weird the way they did it, but the reason they asked me to stay was because they wanted to figure out their money situation, which they did. Then, yesterday morning, they asked me if I wanted to stay on to be their hired man," explained Harlan.

"Oh," Roy responded. It was obvious that he was listening to Harlan with his full attention, a fact which Harlan attributed to his own interest in Marty's future plans. "What did you say?"

"I said I'd have to think about it," replied Harlan.

"Have you?"

"It's about the only thing I *can* think about," Harlan admitted. "What do *you* think?"

"It doesn't make any difference what I think," Roy said indifferently.

"Fine, but that doesn't mean I don't want to know."

Roy considered for a moment before replying.

"First, I think there are probably a half dozen other fellows around here who would give their eyeteeth for that job. But I'm sure that the Meyers know that, and you could have guessed it. Secondly, you do good work; I've seen that for myself. If you wanted to, you could easy get a job working at some other farm around here based solely on what we all saw from you a couple of Thursdays ago, in spite of the fact that times are hard. It's obvious that the Meyers want you to stay.

"From here, it looks like it's a foregone conclusion that you should remain there—unless you had other pressing plans, that is. The only problem I see with it is what we talked about at the picking bee," Roy said, his voice now lower to make sure no one else could hear him. "Have you thought about how you're going to handle that part of the arrangement? All I ask is that you don't do anything to hurt Marty."

Harlan whispered, "She turned me down."

"What?" Roy's shock was written all over his face and his tone.

"After you told me that Marty was in love with me, I asked her…" Harlan was suddenly embarrassed to admit that he had proposed marriage to Marty, so he soft-pedaled the account of his conversation with Marty a week and a half ago. "I asked Marty if she and I had any chance together, and she told me no."

"You're kidding!" Roy whistled incredulously. "What reason did she give?"

"Something about being unequally yoked. Said I'm not a Christian."

Roy nodded his understanding. "That would be the best reason not to marry someone." He saw the dejected look on Harlan's face and added, "You could change that, you know."

Harlan grunted. Then, because he was enjoying the confidence of another male and felt a certain kinship with Roy, Harlan recklessly added, "She did tell me that she could see herself choosing to love you for the rest of her life."

Harlan immediately regretted these words! As soon as they were out of his mouth, he felt as though he had betrayed a confidence that Marty had shared with him, even though she had not explicitly said her thoughts were a secret. Furthermore, what was he thinking, opening the door for another suitor of the woman he loved himself?

Roy's eyes darted to Harlan's as if he were gauging how serious the comment was. Roy inhaled to begin speaking, but at that moment he saw Marty and Mrs. Meyer approaching the car.

Chapter Twenty

November 17 & 18, 1935

"I have decided to take you up on your offer to take me on as your hired man," Harlan said at supper that evening.

Marty's face immediately broke into a broad grin, but Mrs. Meyer acted as though Harlan had merely said something as inane as "Tomorrow is Monday."

"Can we bring Betty home tomorrow?" Marty asked enthusiastically.

Harlan couldn't help but chuckle. "You're the one that cow kicked several times, and you can't wait to bring her back home? That doesn't make any sense."

"Well, she never kicked *you*, and like I said when we agreed to take her over to Aunt Louise and Uncle Vernon's, she's the cow that gave the most milk. It's just good business to get her back as soon as possible."

"Probably a good idea to get it done before it gets any colder, too," Harlan added. "I suppose that makes sense." Harlan tried to keep his voice even, but he was excited about bringing Betty back since it meant a three mile round trip walk alone with Marty.

"Good plan," Mrs. Meyer agreed. "The other thing that needs to be done is that we need to finish culling the chickens before the weather gets too cold. After that, we need to work on firewood;

I'll order coal as soon as we can sell either some fat cattle or a load of hogs."

After the supper dishes were finished, Marty read aloud that evening, and it was easy to tell that a slight smile danced around the corners of her mouth. Her mood was lighter than it had been in several days, and Harlan felt that things in the Meyer household were settling back to what he considered closer to normal. He also felt that his decision to stay had something to do with that.

On Monday morning, a skiff of snow lay on the landscape like a white summer bedsheet. The air was brisk but was not moving, and the sun was shining from a clear sky.

Harlan and Marty left Mrs. Meyer alone in the steamy washhouse poking cobs in the laundry stove with two wash boilers on top of it. Her morning's work lay in piles around her, and her mouth was set in determination. Harlan had started the Maytag multi-motor on the washing machine for her before he and Marty took off on their eastward trek to the Neumann farm to retrieve Betty, and everything appeared to be right with the world.

The first several rods of their journey were traveled without speaking. Harlan felt that this reticence was a waste of their precious time together, so he finally broke the silence.

"It sure is chillier today than when we made this trip two weeks ago," he observed.

"That *was* a beautiful afternoon, wasn't it?" said Marty. "This is the time of year when everything begins to change so rapidly, though."

"Do you like snow?" asked Harlan, kicking a bit of it with the toe of his new work boot.

"Yes," she reflected. "I know that too much of it makes for problems, but I love how clean it makes everything look."

"I never thought of it that way, I guess. I always liked it because I like to sled," Harlan responded.

"We've got a toboggan hanging on the wall in the toolshed,"

Marty said. "When I was little, Dad would take me sledding in the back pasture. We had lots of fun, but we never stayed out long because there was always so much work for him to do."

Harlan was afraid that Marty was going to become melancholy with reminiscing about her father, and he didn't want that sort of thing to spoil their time together, so he quickly tried to divert her with what he considered a happy thought. "Maybe when we get enough snow to sled on, you and I could take the toboggan into the back pasture."

"Maybe," Marty shrugged. Her indifferent tone deflated Harlan as much as sadness regarding her father would have, and he was effectively silenced for a while.

They crested the tallest hill between the two farms, and Harlan, frustrated by the perception that they were squandering their time together, broached another topic.

"When we work on cutting firewood, where will we get it?" Harlan inquired.

"We own about twenty-five acres of timber farther to the east and a mile and a half south. Dad bought the ground a few years ago so that we would have a woodlot," answered Marty. "Like Mama said, she'll order some coal, but we burn mostly wood, and there isn't any timber to speak of on our farm except for the little that you see in the creek bottoms."

"That was a smart move on your father's part," Harlan said.

"Yeah, he got a really good deal on the ground because it is too steep to till and is completely covered in trees. There isn't a whole lot of timber around here, so it's rare to find some ground like that. He always wished it was closer, but it's not so bad. The only thing is, we usually would have gotten a lot more wood gathered in before this late in the fall."

"Hopefully we won't get too much snow before we can get more harvested then," Harlan said. "Do you go mushroom hunting on that ground in the spring?"

"Yes."

Harlan had hoped that Marty would expound on the mushroom hunting subject, but she did not offer any further comment.

"Do you like mushrooms?" he asked, trying to keep her talking.

"Yes."

Again, Marty lapsed into quietude.

"How do you folks usually prepare them?" Harlan prompted, beginning to be a little peevish about Marty's reserve.

"Mama washes them, soaks them in salt water to draw off the bugs, dips them in beaten egg, rolls them in soda cracker crumbs, and then fries them in butter."

"That sounds good," Harlan returned. "My mother used flour instead of cracker crumbs, but I bet Mrs. Meyer's way tastes a little better." Harlan hoped that by giving Mrs. Meyer a compliment, Marty's tongue would be loosened to talk a little more. Instead, the two continued in silence for several more steps.

As the sun rose higher on its course across the sky, the snow became slushy at their feet, and each step made the collection of it on their toes become a longer and longer point until it became too heavy to remain attached and fell away. Thus, Harlan's eyes were glued to his feet as he walked beside Marty, watching the continual collection and sloughing of snow on his boots. All the while, he was trying to think of some topic that would keep her talking, something that would keep that voice, which was music to his ears, pouring forth.

"Harlan?"

His heart jumped in his chest at the realization that she had spoken his name and initiated conversation. "Yeah?"

"I've been thinking a lot lately about your mother," Marty started.

Harlan's excitement vanished. This was not the sort of topic that he wished to talk about.

"You know, Thanksgiving is next week already," she continued, "and that is a time when one always thinks about family. I know I'm going to miss having Dad around on Thanksgiving very badly, but I know where he is. Your poor mother has no idea what has become of you, and since you're an only child now, that has to be awful for her."

Marty's thoughts were tumbling out of her mouth at a rapid pace, but they weren't the sort of thoughts that Harlan wanted to hear.

"At first, I was thinking that maybe we could scrape together enough money to get her train fare to come here for Thanksgiving, but then I thought it may take too long to get her located and get the travel arrangements made. So what do you think about bringing her here for Christmas? That could be Mama's and my gift to you. I know Mama would be happy to have her, especially if she knew that it was relieving your mother's fears—or at least the fears that I'm sure she must have—and it would make Christmas really special for all of us. I mean, the first Christmas without Dad is going to be so hard, and having you be reunited with your mother would kind of counteract that, you know?

"When I think about how much I miss Dad, I just feel so sorry for your mother. She's got to be just beside herself with worry. When you described her to me the other day, she seemed like such a nice lady, and I know that both Mama and I would enjoy meeting her. What do you say?"

Waves of refreshed guilt were pouring over Harlan, and by themselves they would have successfully rendered him mute, but the situation was much more complex than just his infinite remorse. He could not let his mother know where he was for fear that the authorities were seeking to find him through her. Further, he could not let Marty know why he could not contact his mother for fear of her finding out that he was responsible for the death of another man besides Mr. Meyer. He had no idea what to say and was desperately trying to figure it out when Marty spoke again.

"If you think of it from your mother's point of view, you can see how important it would be to her, can't you?"

"I...I don't think that's a...a good idea," Harlan finally choked out, surprised at the size of the lump in his throat at the thought of his mother.

"Why not?" she asked innocently.

Harlan paused for just a moment, trying to think of an acceptable answer to her question, but he only said, "It just isn't; that's all."

They walked without talking for a short while, but words were boiling up in Marty, and they were so charged that Harlan could feel them coming.

"I don't understand you, Harlan," Marty finally said, giving vent to her frustration. "What you said about your mother led me to believe that you love her and that she loves you. You indicated that she was a good mother who did everything that she could to provide for you. You haven't had any kind of falling out with her. The whole time I've known you, you have been so good, so kind, so thoughtful to me, to Mama, and to Dad. I don't understand how you can be so cruel to her as to not let her know that you are all right."

Harlan's familiar urge to run was making his legs tingle, but he now felt trapped because he knew he couldn't run from Marty. The feeling of being cornered, his overpowering sense of his own wickedness, his fear of being apprehended, his longing for his mother, and his disillusionment regarding his love for the girl at his side connived to give birth to intense anger in Harlan's breast.

Ignorant of this, Marty fervently pressed her point. "You are the flesh of her flesh, Harlan! She has a right to know that you are alive.

"I'm not asking you to confess what we've called your 'big sin' to her. I don't think you have to do that, and I don't believe that whatever sin you committed was against her. I'm convinced of that, but even if it were, you surely can understand how a mother— especially a good mother like she is—would be able to forgive you anyway. The poor woman probably goes to sleep every night thinking that she is absolutely alone in the world. You're not being fair to her at all."

Harlan became conscious of tears scalding his cheeks on their path to his prominent jawline. The embarrassment of crying in front of Marty only served to further agitate him.

Marty turned to Harlan, stopped him, and grasped his left forearm with both of her hands in order to emphasize her plea.

"Please!" she entreated. "Let's find her, let her know that you're all right, and invite her for Thanksgiving or Christmas. I know that deep down you know it's the right thing to do."

Something snapped inside of Harlan as he looked into Marty's imploring eyes. In the space of just a little over a minute, Marty had managed to hit every sensitive button in Harlan's machinery. He would not run from her, but he was not going to permit this kind of interference from her either. His instincts were those of a trapped animal who can see no other option but to fight.

"Shut up, woman!" he hissed, wrenching his arm violently from her grip. "You have no idea what you're talking about. My past is none of your business; my mother isn't any of your business, and how I handle either of them is also none of your business! You said that you weren't interested in being my wife, so you've got no right to meddle in any of this. I'm tired of your constant reminders of how good you are and how bad I am. We're not talking about any of this ever again! Do you understand me? I can take care of myself. I don't need you to tell me what to do!"

Marty's face had lost all of its color, and the beseeching expression she had been wearing transformed into one of abject terror.

Harlan turned his back on her and took a couple determined steps toward their destination. Sensing that she had not followed him, he turned around and shouted, "And wipe that pitiful look off your face!"

Marty burst into turbulent sobs at Harlan's brutality, but her feet moved obediently forward. She remained a few steps behind Harlan as he tromped recklessly on.

Suddenly, Harlan stopped, did an about-face, and began walking back toward the Meyer farm; he would have trampled Marty except that she moved agilely aside.

"Harlan, what are you doing?" she asked in alarm.

He did not answer, but continued to walk westward in headlong fashion. Marty turned to follow him.

"Harlan, wait!" she yelled. "Where are you going? Aren't we going to bring Betty home? I'm sorry I upset you. I didn't mean to make you so mad; I just thought…I was just trying to…"

Harlan was picking up speed, preventing her from catching up with him, so Marty broke into a run.

"Harlan, please talk to me! What's going on?" Marty shouted.

Harlan froze in his tracks for a moment, then turned around and faced Marty. Tears were still running down his face, and his body was quivering with silent, convulsive sobs.

"We're not bringing Betty home today," he said in a frighteningly intense whisper. "I don't think it is going to work out for me to stay on with you."

Marty bent at the stomach as if Harlan had just delivered her a physical blow, but Harlan turned and began to jog toward the Meyer farm.

"No! Harlan, I said I was sorry! I didn't mean to make you so angry. Please, can't we talk about this?" she begged. "Why are you so angry? What did I say that upset you so?" In desperation, she ended with "I'm sorry I said anything!"

The tone in Marty's voice yanked at Harlan's heart, but again it only managed to harden it. The culmination of his emotions in this supreme moment of anger was crushing any tenderness he had felt for her.

"Leave me alone!" he screamed. "Just leave me alone!" Harlan's hurt took control of his tongue just then and let fly with shocking unkindness. "Isn't that what you wanted? Isn't that what you said we would do: just leave each other alone? So do it then. If I'm not good enough to be your husband, just leave me alone!"

At this, Marty emitted a shriek of pain that Harlan had never before heard any human being make; it was somewhere between the cry of a mountain lion and the howl of a coyote. The strangely unnatural ruckus switched off his rage. Instinctively, he stopped running to see whether she were being devoured by wild animals. He turned around in time to see her sink to her knees at his words as if she had been shot by enemy artillery.

Marty looked small and helpless and utterly beaten. She was crying too, but hers were quiet sobs of resignation, hurt, and loss.

"What have I done?" Harlan gasped. "What have I done?" One hand removed his cap, and the other began tugging on a fistful of blond hair. "What have I done?"

Harlan's anger resurged, but this time it was focused on himself. Marty had been reduced to weeping by his venomous tongue, his thoughtlessness had killed her father, he had grossly neglected his own mother, and another man lay dead because of his uncontrolled rage.

I don't deserve to live! Harlan realized. He walked back to where Marty still rested on the ground. At his approach, she attempted to quiet her sobs, and she raised tear-filled eyes to look at him. For unknown reasons, Harlan could not bring himself to come within arm's reach of her; instead, he addressed her while still several feet away.

"I'm sorry," he said with alacrity. "I'm sorry for everything. Just please know that I'm sorry."

With that, Harlan turned on his heel and started toward the Meyer farm at a dead run. His intention was to accomplish what he had attempted in the barn loft two Sunday mornings ago. Marty sensed the foreboding in his changed attitude and immediately rose to pursue him.

Once they were on the western slope of the hill they had climbed only moments ago, they could run much faster as gravity pulled them toward the valley where the Meyer home rested. "Harlan, wait! What are you doing?" she yelled.

No answer other than another "I'm sorry" which was

punctuated with heavy, rapid footfalls came from Harlan. The space between Harlan and Marty narrowed a little, but she could see that she would not be able to intercept him before they reached the farmstead because the distance to it was diminishing fast.

"Help, Lord!" Marty prayed simply.

"Harlan, stop!" she called again. "What are you going to do?"

She could see him throw his head back to shout a response, but the words were lost in the air as a Buick Series 40 met them traveling east.

Harlan turned into the Meyer lane and ran straight toward the barn. Adrenaline had enabled Marty to keep within twenty strides behind him, but that span was sufficient for him to have disappeared up into the barn loft before Marty could see where he went.

When Marty entered the building only a couple seconds behind him, it was as if he had disappeared entirely.

"Harlan!" she called between gasps for breath. "Harlan, where are you?" Confused panic was beginning to overtake her when she saw the extension ladder leading to the hayloft suddenly ascend through its opening as if propelled by rockets.

Chapter Twenty-One

November 18, 1935

"Harlan!" Marty frantically yelled up the hayloft opening. "Come down! What are you doing? Harlan?"

The barn door opened again, and Roy Schoening bolted in, followed by Mrs. Meyer.

They were at her side in an instant. "What's happened? Are you all right?"

"I'm fine, but Harlan…"

"Did he hurt you?" Roy asked urgently.

"No, nothing like that," Marty shook her head, "but I'm afraid he's going to hurt himself!" She pointed to the opening into the barn loft that was bereft of its ladder.

Roy sprang from the ground in an impressive leap and managed to latch his fingers onto the edge of the loft floor. In a feat of athleticism, he pulled the rest of his body up and disappeared from view.

The two women heard Harlan roar, "Leave me alone!" above their heads, at which Marty dissolved into fresh sobs.

"Let's go to the house," Mrs. Meyer said soothingly to her daughter, and, putting her arms around Marty's quaking body, she led her outside. Mrs. Meyer started to pray aloud before the two had traveled even a foot away from the barn.

"Leave me alone!" roared Harlan from the peak of the haystack when he saw Roy's head emerge from below. Harlan had the rope from the hay trolley in his hand, and a stout knot had been tied in it. It was not the traditional hangman's noose, but Roy could tell at first glance what Harlan was up to, and he knew that the knot would suffice.

"Harlan, have you lost your mind?" Roy asked incredulously and began scrambling up the hay.

"I haven't lost my mind. I've lost everything else, but I haven't lost my mind," Harlan mumbled. His hands were working at a feverish pace, testing the strength of the knot and the flexibility of its loop. "This is the smartest, sanest thing I can do."

"Stop right now!" Roy commanded, but Harlan acted as if he had not heard.

Roy approached the top of the hay, and Harlan shouted menacingly, "Leave me alone, I said!"

"Harlan, just talk to me a minute," pled Roy, trying to strike a soothing note as he struggled closer.

"No. It's over for me. I've ruined everything; it's time for me to be done." With his foot on Roy's shoulder, Harlan shoved Roy back down the stack of hay and shouted, "Stay down!" Undaunted, Roy immediately began the slippery climb again as Harlan widened the loop enough to accommodate his head.

"Don't you dare!" Roy ordered.

Summoning all of his strength, Roy bolted far enough up the hay to yank the rope out of Harlan's hand and send it swinging to the other side of the loft.

Incensed at this audacious move, Harlan swore loudly and backhanded Roy in an attempt to knock him off the mountain of hay once more. While Roy tried vainly to regain his balance, Harlan quickly reached out, ready to catch the rope when it returned to him on its pendulum-like arc.

Roy's feet slipped out from under him just then, and as he began to slide down the hay a second time, he grabbed one of Harlan's ankles and dragged him down with him. At the bottom of the valley where the hay and straw met, both engaged in a bloodthirsty skirmish.

"Let me go!" clamored Harlan as Roy clung perniciously to the ankle he had originally grasped even as Harlan kicked him in the eye.

"Not on your life, you idiot!" came Roy's reply through his clenched teeth.

Harlan had the advantage of a couple inches of height, but Roy had the experience that is incumbent with having a brother, and he was soon the dominant competitor. From above, Roy delivered a punch to Harlan's abdomen that took his breath away and effectively immobilized him.

"Listen," Roy gasped, winded with exertion, "I'll let you hang yourself—at this point, I may even help you do it—but you're going to talk to me first."

Roy rolled Harlan onto his stomach and pulled both of his arms behind his back.

"Just let me go," Harlan hissed. "I deserve to die."

"Well, you've got that right," Roy agreed, placing his knee squarely in Harlan's back to keep him from going anywhere. "But it doesn't seem like you ought to do it in a barn loft that belongs to a woman who is freshly widowed and whose daughter loves you."

"Not anymore," Harlan croaked from beneath Roy's weight.

"All right. So you've got a story to tell. Start talking."

"It's none of your business. Let me go!" protested Harlan angrily.

Roy responded by shoving his knee more deeply into Harlan's back. "When I drive by a friend of mine chasing another friend of mine down the road while bawling her eyes out, and then I find one of those friends trying to hang himself in the other friend's barn loft, I'm sorry, but I consider it all my business, so you might as well tell me your side of the story."

"I'm not your friend," argued Harlan.

"Fine," Roy said evenly, "but I'm being a friend to you, and anyway, you're not going anywhere until I move. And I'm not planning on moving until I know what's going on with you."

Harlan was quiet for a moment, deciding just how much he should tell Roy. "I've messed everything up with Marty," he finally confessed. "Yesterday, I agreed to stay on as the hired man, so we were walking to her aunt and uncle's to bring Betty the cow back. She said something about my mother that upset me, even though she didn't mean it that way, and I blew up at her. The look on her face told me that she's all yours now."

"You're such an idiot!" Roy said exasperatedly. "She doesn't want me; she wants you."

"No, she's too good for me; I don't deserve her."

"Right again! Second time this morning," Roy interjected sarcastically. "But I'll wager she doesn't see it that way." Roy tugged on Harlan's arm's again. "You still haven't given me sufficient evidence that you ought to hang yourself. Keep talking."

Harlan grunted in pain. The physical hurt he was suffering was making it difficult to think clearly. How much could he safely tell? But then again, what did he have to lose?

"I killed Mr. Meyer!" Harlan blurted, breaking down again.

"You what?" Roy bellowed. In one deft wrestling move, he turned Harlan onto his back, leaving his arms restrained behind him and keeping him pinned under his knee. With one hand, he grabbed Harlan's shirt collar and twisted.

"I killed him, Roy," Harlan divulged, locking eyes with his captor. "I thought he would want to feel like he had at least harvested a little of his own corn crop, so I kept a bucket of ears back and brought him out to the corn crib so that he could throw them in. It was too hard for him. I saw the sweat on his face; I saw how hard he was working. I should have stopped him. I should have seen that a heart attack was coming. The whole thing was my idea, and I..."

Roy was studying Harlan's face during the confession and could see how his remorse was torturing him. He let go of his fistful of Harlan's shirt. "What about your mother?" Roy probed.

Harlan's eyes fell. "Marty accused me of mistreating her because I haven't let her know where I am, that I'm still alive. It's all very complicated, and I didn't think…"

"What made you decide to hang yourself?" Roy asked; he was in no mood to listen to trivialities.

"I wanted to get away from all the guilt," Harlan replied, tears running down his cheeks once more. "I can't stand it any longer."

"I can understand that," Roy said, pausing a second. "Answer me one question: if I hadn't climbed up in here and stopped you a few minutes ago, where would your soul be right now?"

"Oh, don't get all religious on me," Harlan snapped. "You know I'm going to hell."

"I'm not 'getting religious' on you. I'm asking you a serious question. And where is your soul going to be in a few minutes when I let you go and you climb that hay pile and follow through with your plan? Answer me that."

"It's going to be in hell, all right?" Harlan said furiously. "What difference does it make *when* I get there? If I had gotten there five minutes ago, or if I get there three minutes from now, the way I look at it is that I'm going to hell anyway, so I might as well get there and get this suffering over with."

"But Harlan, you don't have to go to hell," argued Roy.

"Yeah I do," Harlan countered. "My sins are *huge*. I killed someone! It's not like telling a few lies or stealing something. I took someone's life!" He had not confessed everything to Roy because he could see no point in that, but he felt that his intention behind these words conveyed sufficient meaning for Roy to understand his condemned state.

Roy shook his head incredulously. "You're awfully full of yourself, aren't you?" he accused.

"Huh?"

Roy could tell that his accusation had shocked Harlan enough that he had Harlan's full attention. "Sit up," he commanded contemptuously, releasing Harlan and drawing a tiny book from his pocket. "I don't think I've met anyone who thought more highly of himself than you."

"What do you mean?" Harlan asked defensively. "I just told you that I'm such a worm that I might as well just die. That's what I was trying to do until you ruined everything. I'm not full of myself!"

"Yes, you are," Roy returned authoritatively. He was thumbing quickly through the little book he held. "Here. This is 1 John 5:17. Read the first half of that out loud, just to the colon." Roy handed the little book to Harlan, pointing to the verse that he wanted him to read.

"I'm not good at reading aloud," Harlan said, trying to evade the request.

"Full of yourself *and* stubborn!" Roy muttered, shaking his head disgustedly. "You're good enough. I've heard you do it in Sunday School. Read it before you make me so mad that my fist lands in your gut again," Roy threatened.

The pain that remained in Harlan's stomach caused him to capitulate. "All unrighteousness is sin," he read slowly.

"Tell me what that means," Roy demanded.

"I don't know."

"Read it again then."

"All unrighteousness is sin," Harlan repeated.

"Now, what do you think that means?" Roy pushed.

"I don't know! I guess that everything people do wrong is sin," Harlan muttered. "So what?"

Roy was flipping pages again. "Here, now we're in Romans 3. Start with verse 10."

"As it is written, there is none righteous, no, not one," Harlan read.

"Now skip over to verse 23 and read that."

"For all have sinned, and come short of the glory of God," he continued reading.

"All right, tell me what those verses mean," Roy ordered.

"I suppose you're trying to show me that everyone has sinned," Harlan grumbled, "but I'm telling you: my sins are worse!"

"Which is why I'm telling *you* that you are one of the most arrogant people I've ever met!" Roy exploded. "You have the unmitigated gall to believe that you are so special that you could be worse than anyone else. That's arrogance if I ever heard it!"

Harlan was offended by Roy's accusation, but he was listening with intense interest because what Roy was saying was beginning to make sense in a twisted sort of way.

"Here, now read Romans 6:23 and stop before the word 'but.'"

Harlan obeyed. "For the wages of sin is death," he read. "I remember reading that verse to Mr. Meyer one night."

"And what does it mean?" pressed Roy.

"It means that sin damns people to hell. See, I was right about me going to hell!"

Harlan threw Roy's pocket New Testament across the barn loft, used his elbow to shove Roy aside, and began to get to his feet, but Roy pounced on him. The two wrestled in the hay for the space of only a few seconds before Roy once again gained the upper hand and had Harlan's blond head locked in the crook of his arm. Harlan's bottom lip had been cut, and a red streak was running down his chin and neck, making its way to Roy's shirt sleeve.

"You are the beatenest…fella I think I've ever run across," Roy complained breathlessly, almost reverting to the language he would have used before his conversion. "I'm sure you've blacked *both* of my eyes now. Much more of this and I *promise* I'll help you hang yourself if that's still your plan after we're done talking."

Roy stopped a moment to catch his breath and then went on. "At this moment, you're right. If you die today, you're going to hell. And you're also right that you deserve it, but I've got news for you: I deserve to go to hell, Marty deserves to go to hell, Mrs. Meyer deserves to go to hell, and even our beloved Mr. Meyer deserved to go to hell. The verses you have read tell us that we have all sinned;

those of us who are living continue to sin even though we try not to, and we learned from the earlier verses that no sins are bigger or smaller than others. Do you believe Mr. Meyer went to hell?"

"No," Harlan croaked.

"All right then," grunted Roy. He dragged Harlan across the hay mow by his neck until he retrieved the little testament. He found the page they had been on again and held it in front of Harlan. "Now read Romans 6:23 again, only now read the whole thing."

Harlan reached for the book.

"Nope, I'll hold it this time if you don't mind," Roy said, yanking it away from Harlan's reach for a moment. When Harlan's arms were relaxed again, Roy held the book in Harlan's line of vision.

"For the wages of sin is death," Harlan read in a choked voice since Roy's arm was still around his neck, "but the gift of God is eternal life through Jesus Christ our Lord."

"Harlan, Mr. Meyer deserved to go to hell. In God's eyes his sins weren't any better than yours, but he is in Paradise right now because he had faith in Jesus Christ." Roy thumbed through some more pages. "Here, read John 3:3 to me."

"Jesus answered and said unto him, 'Verily, verily, I say unto thee, Except a man be born again, he cannot see the kingdom of God.'"

"How did Mr. Meyer get to enter the kingdom of God then?" Roy asked.

"He was born again," Harlan answered.

"Right. Now tell me, Harlan, why did Jesus come to die?"

Harlan thought for a moment, reaching back to the teachings of his childhood and what he had learned in his more recent reading from the Bible. "Jesus came to die for our sins," he finally said.

Roy turned some more pages in his Bible, a feat which was difficult considering the fact that one of his arms was still tightly encircling Harlan's neck.

"Now read John 14:6 to me," Roy said.

"Jesus saith unto him, 'I am the way, the truth, and the life: no man cometh unto the Father, but by me.'"

"What does that verse mean?" Roy asked.

"Jesus is the only way to be with God?" Harlan guessed.

"Amen, brother!" interjected Roy, turning to Romans 10:9-11. "Read these three verses now."

"That if thou shalt confess with thy mouth the Lord Jesus, and shalt believe in thine heart that God hath raised him from the dead, thou shalt be saved. For with the heart man believeth unto righteousness; and with the mouth confession is made unto salvation. For the Scripture saith, Whosoever believeth on him shall not be ashamed," Harlan read.

"What does that mean to you?" Roy asked.

"I don't know!" Harlan tried to shout, but he was squirming so much against Roy's arm that his words did not come loudly.

"Read it again, this time maybe a little slower," Roy said imperatively. Harlan did as he was told, and then Roy once more asked, "What does that mean to you?"

"I don't know! If a person says he has faith in Jesus and really believes that God raised him from the dead, then he won't have any shame?" Harlan guessed.

"Fine. I've got only two more passages that I want to share with you, and then I promise that I won't make you read anymore. Here is 2 Corinthians 5:15. Read it aloud."

"He died for all, that they which live should not henceforth live unto themselves, but unto him which died for them, and rose again."

"What do you think that means?" Roy questioned.

Harlan quit struggling against Roy's arm. "Jesus died for everyone, and we shouldn't live for ourselves anymore but for Him."

"Good. Here are the last verses I want you to read: Mark 1:15."

"The time is fulfilled, and the kingdom of God is at hand: repent ye, and believe the gospel."

"You know what I think, Harlan? I think that this incredible guilt that you have been feeling has been because the Lord has been convicting you, which shows you that He loves you. He's been working *on* your heart and *in* your heart, making you feel so bad that you now know something has to change. In your human way of thinking," Roy tapped Harlan's head with the spine of the tiny New Testament, "you couldn't figure out any way to be freed from this horrible guilt except to kill yourself. Really, you weren't far wrong. You *do* need to die, but in a different way than you thought. It's your old self that needs to die, not your body. You need to repent and become a new creation in Christ Jesus."

Roy noticed that Harlan's body had completely relaxed, so he removed his arm from around Harlan's neck and gently laid him on the hay.

"I just don't think I'm good enough. You don't know the half of what I've done," Harlan mumbled in an aggrieved voice.

"Well, you and I are in the same boat then," Roy chuckled. "You don't know the half of what *I've* done, and, like I said, I'm not good enough either. Fortunately for both of us, that is what grace is all about. Ephesians 2:8 and 9 say 'For by grace are ye saved through faith; and that not of yourselves: it is the gift of God: Not of works, lest any man should boast.' There is nothing that you can *do* to ever be good enough, Harlan."

Harlan stared into the rafters of the barn.

"I know I told you that I was done making you read Bible verses, but will you read one more? Here is Romans 10:13." Roy handed Harlan his miniature book.

"For whosoever shall call upon the name of the Lord shall be saved," Harlan read.

"Does it sound like that could include you, Harlan? Today, you can go ahead and end your old life and be born again." Roy let that sink in for a little while as he watched an array of emotions pass over Harlan's face; then he asked, "Harlan, are you ready to pray?"

Chapter Twenty-Two

November 18, 1935

"Dear Lord," Harlan repeated after Roy through tears, "I am a horrible sinner, and my sins are not only against people, but they are against you. I believe in my heart that Jesus Christ came to die for my sins and rose again from the dead. I want him to live in my heart. I give my life to him now, and I want to serve him from now on. I pray these things in Jesus' name, Amen."

Both Harlan and Roy were on their knees in the hay, and when they finished praying, Roy clapped Harlan on the back.

"If you truly meant what you just prayed," Roy said, "we are brothers in Christ, and I believe we've got a friendship that will last into eternity."

Harlan was struggling to see through eyes that were dripping profusely, but there was a lightness and a peace about him that was new.

"I have to say, though," Roy laughed, brushing hay and straw from his clothes, "being your friend today has been a pretty rough time!"

"You look terrible!" said Harlan, wiping his eyes. "Sorry about that."

"You're not looking so good yourself," Roy said, pointing to Harlan's bloody chin and neck.

"What happens now?" Harlan asked sheepishly.

"What happens is that everything changes," answered Roy. "Whom are you living for now?"

"Jesus," Harlan answered.

"I'm not going to sugarcoat anything, Harlan, you're not done battling yourself. You are going to be fighting your sin nature for the rest of your life; the difference is that you're not fighting alone anymore. The Holy Spirit is on your side now. But we've got all kinds of time to talk about that later. Right now, we need to go to the house and get cleaned up; there are also a couple of ladies who are probably pretty worried about you at the moment."

"Do you think I ought to tell them about killing Mr. Meyer?" asked Harlan.

Roy studied Harlan with a knowing look in his rapidly swelling eyes. "Yes, I do."

"And I owe Marty a big apology," Harlan reflected.

"You got that right!" Roy agreed.

Harlan got painfully to his feet. "You've got a powerful right hook!" he said rubbing his stomach.

"Aren't you glad!" Roy scoffed, lifting the ladder from where it lay in the hay and putting it down the opening in the floor again. "Ready?" Roy motioned for Harlan to go down first.

"Just a second," Harlan said. He climbed the haystack and once again caught the rope from the hay trolley; this time, he untied the knot, straightened the rope out, and gave it a playful swing.

As the two men approached the house, Mrs. Meyer and Marty tumbled out of the kitchen door upon seeing their beaten and bloody state. Marty bore the evidence of having been crying just seconds before leaving the house, but Mrs. Meyer exhibited the same serenity that she always did.

"Are you two all right?" Mrs. Meyer asked.

"Never better!" came Roy's reply as he grinned from ear to ear. "There's a new name written down in glory, ladies. Let me introduce you to our newest brother in Christ, Mr. Harlan Jensen."

"Praise God!" Mrs. Meyer shouted while Marty's tears started afresh. Mrs. Meyer jumped forward and hugged Harlan so tightly that he discovered the locations of a few more bruises that Roy had given him. "God is so good! My! When I think of all the prayers that have been answered..." she trailed off, standing back to once more look at Harlan's face. "You're a wreck. Let's get this hay and straw off you both so we can get you inside and washed up. What in the world happened up there in the loft? Why, Roy, you're going to look like a raccoon tomorrow morning with two black eyes."

Mrs. Meyer's volubility continued as she mothered the two young men, consuming all of their attention. Marty remained slightly distanced from the three of them, studying Harlan's face through tears that seemed endless and feeling as though she were in shock.

Once they were sufficiently brushed and dusted, Mrs. Meyer—acting and sounding like a mother hen—herded the two men into the washroom off the kitchen, brought warm water from the reservoir, and generally clucked about Harlan as she cleaned away trails of tears, dirt, and blood. During this process, Roy waited his turn and related the series of events that had transpired in the barn loft with Mrs. Meyer laughing and interjecting words of praise to the Lord for the work that he had done in Harlan's life.

As there was not room for three people, let alone four, in the washroom, Marty listened to everything that was said from the kitchen where she stood in a stupor of amazement over the events of the last hour. More than once, she wondered if she were in the middle of a bizarre nightmare that had eased into a dream. She knew that everything was real, however, when Harlan emerged from the washroom after Mrs. Meyer had finished with him and moved on to tending Roy's wounds. He approached her bashfully, his eyes on the floor, but when he was near enough, he raised his arms and enclosed her in a warm embrace.

"I'm so sorry," he said huskily, his voice shaky once again. "I treated you very badly. Will you forgive me?"

Marty's emotions prevented her from speaking at that moment, but she returned the hug and did not seek release from his hold until it sounded like Roy and her mother were about to enter the kitchen.

"I don't know about all of you, but I need a cup of coffee and a chair!" Mrs. Meyer sighed on entering the kitchen. Soon cups and plates had been distributed and some sugar cookies were passed around the table.

"Harlan has something he wants to tell you about Mr. Meyer," Roy prompted.

Nervously, Harlan took the cue and began unburdening his heart regarding Mr. Meyer's death, repeating what he had told Roy in the barn loft. "So it's all my fault," he concluded. "If I had stopped him when I saw how much work he was going through to throw the corn into the crib, he would still be here with us today, and everything would be different. Again, I'm sorry."

Mrs. Meyer reached for Harlan's hand across the table. "It looks to me like God used your guilt about Al to bring you to faith in Jesus, so I'm glad we never had the opportunity to speak about this before, but, Harlan, I need to tell you something. When you came in that morning and told him that you had saved a bucket of ears for him, he didn't react much while we were at the breakfast table, but after you and Marty went back outside, he was so excited to go out and toss those few ears in the crib. Remember too that Al could have stopped throwing ears of corn anytime he wanted to. If he had, you know you would have understood and let him rest.

"A stroke like that could have come at any moment after any activity or some less pleasant kind of stress, but because of your compassion and patience with him, Al Meyer passed away feeling like he was still an active farmer—a role that he loved. For that, I'm so thankful."

Mrs. Meyer's words were balm to Harlan's heart, and he brushed tears from his eyes once more, but these were the tears of relief.

"Listen, folks," Roy said after draining his coffee cup, "my dad probably thinks I ran away and joined the circus. I was just on my way home from town with new spark plugs for the Fairbanks Morse that runs our water pump when there's no wind. Of course, when I tell him what I've been up to here, I'll be forgiven, but I gotta get going nonetheless. I'll be back to talk to you soon, Harlan, but I'd like to pray with you all before I leave."

"Absolutely!" Mrs. Meyer agreed.

The four of them bowed their heads together and held hands around the table.

"Father, what a glorious morning this is! Our brother Harlan has accepted the free gift of salvation that you offer us through your Son Jesus Christ, and, Lord, we are so thankful, so excited, so full of joy over this decision. What's also exciting about this is that we know from Jesus words 'that likewise joy shall be in Heaven over one sinner that repenteth,' so there is rejoicing over Harlan both on Earth and in Heaven today. That is truly awesome to think about!"

"Amen!" murmured Mrs. Meyer.

"And now, Lord, you know that there couldn't be a better household for a new Christian to be living in than the Meyer home. I praise you for putting Harlan here at this time. Allow Marty and Mrs. Meyer and me to nurture Harlan in his newfound faith. Put people in his life who will educate him in your ways as well as people who will edify and encourage him. Lord, we ask your protection over him as he learns to live life with you directing his path. This we ask in the name of Jesus our precious savior, amen."

After Roy's departure, it was determined that it was too late in the morning to finish the job of retrieving Betty the cow, so that was put off until after dinner. Mrs. Meyer returned to the summer kitchen to continue with the washing, and Marty went with her to help make up for the time that Mrs. Meyer had lost in prayer and celebration.

For his part, Harlan hardly knew what to do with himself. He felt like he was returning to normal life after some sort of holiday. Though he was in very familiar surroundings, everything seemed somewhat surreal. His mood was light, his mind was distracted by other thoughts, and his dominant desire was to hurry through the day's work so that the three occupants of the Meyer household could be sitting together in the living room listening to Marty read from the Bible. He felt that the answer to any question of consequence must be hidden somewhere in those pages since the alleviation of his guilt felt so complete just now.

He didn't want to go to the barn again until he would not have to enter it alone, so he decided to pass his time at the woodpile. As splitting maul rhythmically met with log or buck saw traveled back and forth in the wood cradle, his bruised flesh complained loudly, but he paid no attention to it because the contentment he felt was so delicious that he wanted to think of nothing else.

When he entered the kitchen after washing for dinner, Mrs. Meyer couldn't resist giving him another hug. "I promise I'll stop soon," she gushed. "You just don't know how many of my prayers were answered this morning! God is *so* good!" Harlan was a little embarrassed by her giddiness—he had never seen Mrs. Meyer behave this way and, in fact, wouldn't have believed it was even in her until now—but he felt so good himself that he understood her excitement.

"Sit right down," she continued to bubble hospitably. "I wish it weren't wash day so that I would have had time to make at least *something* special to mark this occasion since, in a way, it's like your birthday, but a little cottage pudding with canned peaches will have to do."

Pork sausage and sauerkraut were also on the table along with tiny potatoes that were boiled with their jackets on, a meal that Harlan had come to see as standard Monday fare on the Meyer farm, even though it didn't particularly appeal to his Scandinavian palate. Mrs. Meyer asked the blessing, and the three of them began to eat.

"Mrs. Meyer, can I ask you something?" Harlan felt more at ease with her than he ever had due to her present mood.

"Certainly," she invited.

"You've said twice this morning that so many prayers have been answered by me trusting Jesus. Just how long have you been praying for me?"

"Oh, I don't know. I think I started praying for you sometime during the first week of October." Mrs. Meyer's eyes showed that she was viewing a mental calendar as she figured out the answer to his question.

"You mean the first week of November when I was sick probably," countered Harlan.

"No, it was definitely the first week of October."

"But I didn't arrive until October twenty-fourth," Harlan said, confused.

"Well, I began praying for you long before you arrived," explained Mrs. Meyer. "Of course, when I started praying, I didn't know specifically that it was you I was praying for, but they were definitely prayers for you."

"Huh?" Harlan was looking all kinds of confused as he shoveled a forkful of sausage and kraut into his mouth.

"Al had his stroke on the twenty-sixth of September, and once we got him to the point where he was stable, I knew right away that Marty and I were going to need help to run this farm because we couldn't do it without him. I knew we couldn't afford a hired man at that point, so I started to pray then. I told Al about it, and after that he and I prayed every afternoon for someone to come and help us. We had prayed that together for at least two weeks, and you can't imagine how surprised we were when we weren't a half hour after 'Amen' one afternoon and you showed up on our back porch! But when I saw you there with your cap in your hand asking for food, I knew that our prayers had been answered."

Harlan stopped chewing even though his mouth was full of food. His surprise was written all over his face—a fact which caused a hint of a smile to play about the corners of Marty's mouth as she ate in silence. Harlan had almost forgotten Marty's presence altogether, though, because his surprise at Mrs. Meyer's disclosure was so great. Since he was going to speak, he opened his mouth and inhaled at that moment, but a piece of sauerkraut took that opportunity to go down the wrong pipe, and he dissolved into a fit of coughing in order to dislodge it.

"Are you all right?" Mrs. Meyer said, leaning forward and pounding him heartily on the back. "I guess you got saved none too soon if you're going to choke to death on your dinner!"

"Ugh! Excuse me!" Harlan apologized. "What I was going to say was that now I know why you looked at me as if you recognized me that day when I first came. I thought the look on your face was strange, but now I understand it!" Harlan reflected a moment. "Wait. I've seen that same sort of look on your face several times after that, though. In fact, I asked Marty not too long ago why nothing I ever do around here surprises you, didn't I, Marty?"

He pointed an accusatory finger at the girl, who had turned a delightful shade of pink.

"You're—what's that word?—clear- clare-..." Harlan struggled.

"Clairvoyant," Mrs. Meyer supplied. "But, no, I'm not. I don't believe in such things, but I do believe in answered prayer and resting in the providence of God. Believe me, there are lots of things that I've prayed for where God's answer was a resounding 'no'; but I'm sure all of those 'no's' have been in my best interest in the end. 'God works all things together for the good of those who love Him' Paul says in Romans. I trust that you'll find that to be very true throughout your new walk with Him, Harlan." Mrs. Meyer smiled as she thought about Harlan's future.

"So, what all have you prayed about me?" Harlan asked nosily.

"Well, first I prayed that you'd come here, that you'd have the ability to do the work that we needed from you, and I prayed that you'd be a Christian. That was before I knew whom God was sending, of course. When I could see that you weren't a Christian when you arrived, I changed that part of my prayers to asking the Lord to work in your life to get you starting to seek him. Also, when I could see that you could easily do the work we needed and that you were good and kind, respectful, pleasant to live with, you know—well then, I naturally prayed that you would stay."

At these words, Harlan remembered sitting beside the railroad tracks on that rainy Sunday morning watching the train pass by. He recalled how badly he had wanted to jump on it but felt as though he were somehow fastened to the ground and couldn't move. That experience had been an answer to Mrs. Meyer's prayer? The thought was astounding.

"What else have you prayed?" prodded Harlan, almost alarmed.

"Well, now, Harlan," Mrs. Meyer said demurely, a conspiratorial grin playing at her mouth, "a person's prayers are between her and God, aren't they? The rest of my prayers about you haven't been answered yet, so they may be ones that are 'no's.' For right now, there isn't any point in sharing them."

"But..." he began to protest.

"You just eat your dinner and rest assured that I'll still be praying for you," she soothed, "...and I imagine I always will be."

Harlan looked at Marty in an appeal for her assistance in plying her mother, but her eyes were concentrating on her fork as she chased a wayward strand of kraut around her plate.

Chapter *Twenty-Three*

November 18 & 19, 1935

All of the morning's snow had melted and left a thin layer of moist dirt on the surface of the road as Harlan and Marty started off a second time on their trip east to retrieve Betty the cow. Again, they started out in silence, but this time Harlan's mind was so busy that he didn't notice the lack of conversation right away. He felt three things simultaneously: that a burden had been removed from his shoulders, a sense of fear that it would somehow return, and confusion about what had happened to him. He wished that Roy hadn't had to leave so quickly. So many questions were popping into his brain!

Harlan and Marty had crested the largest hill once more before he became painfully aware that he hadn't heard Marty say a single word since she had been yelling at him while he was in the barn loft.

He stole a sidelong glance at her. She seemed smaller and more meek than she had this morning, and Harlan was sure this was because she had drawn into herself after he had beaten her so badly with his words that morning. He was resigned to the fact that it would probably be a while before he had earned back her trust.

"Harlan, I…I have something to say, and I want you to hear me out before you get upset," Marty said softly.

Harlan's heart sank on two counts: he was afraid of what Marty could say that needed an introduction such as that, and the timidity in her voice made him feel as though he had whipped her earlier.

"Okay..." he prompted.

"I...I don't know whether you told Roy anything about your 'big sin,' and I don't need to...and I don't need to know anything about your 'big sin' either," she hastily added. "But I just wanted to make sure that he made it clear that it could be forgiven, that Jesus' blood covers everything," she said earnestly.

"He did," Harlan revealed.

They walked a few more paces in silence with Harlan waiting for the proverbial "other shoe" to drop.

"Is that what you thought would make me angry?" he finally asked.

"Yes."

Again, he felt a pang at how deeply he had hurt her that morning, and in his mind he tried to think of things he could say or do which would restore her faith in him.

"I'm very sorry about this morning," Harlan apologized again.

"It's all right; I shouldn't have been pushing you as hard as I was," Marty said warily.

"You had a point, though, and maybe I..."

"Let's not talk about that right now," she returned quietly. "I just...my heart is full. That's all."

Harlan did not know what to make of this statement, but it appeared that she didn't want to talk at all anymore. She seemed to have taken on a sort of fragility, and Harlan felt like she was going to break at any moment. He knew that this change in her demeanor was his doing, so he resolved to simply enjoy Marty's company in silence as the first step in getting her to feel comfortable with him again. As they walked on and he tried to figure out what else he could do to repair his relationship with her, he thought of the jar of chili he had stolen a few days earlier. He felt that he needed to tell Mrs. Meyer of his actions and motives, and perhaps that would be a step toward reestablishing trust between the Meyer women and himself.

When Harlan and Marty entered the Meyer barn later that afternoon with Betty the cow in tow, both of them felt very awkward since it had been the scene of such ugly drama between them earlier that day. They led Betty to the box stall where she would spend what remained of the afternoon before being reintroduced to the rest of the herd after the evening milking.

"Would you...uh...do me a favor?" Harlan asked as he latched the stall door. "I don't mean to scare you or anything, but would you mind going up to the loft with me? I need to get something from up there, and I...uh...I just don't want to go up there by myself the first time since..."

Marty did not speak but communicated her willingness to help by walking toward the ladder. Since she was wearing a dress, he climbed the ladder and waited at the top to offer her his assistance as she stepped into the hay. Once she was safely planted, he walked past her toward one of the far corners of the loft and retrieved the pint jar of chili he had stashed there on Friday. When he turned around to walk back toward Marty, he saw that she was staring wide-eyed at the rope hanging from the hay trolley, and her eyes were filling with tears.

As is the case for any man, feminine tears sparked immediate distress in him, and he was at her side instantly.

"Shh, shh," he said as comfortingly as he knew how. "Don't. It's all right now."

At the sound of his voice, she threw out her arms and clasped him to her, completely succumbing to the sobs that she had withheld for the last several hours. Harlan dropped the pint of chili onto the soft hay and wound his arms around her and just let her cry. The sight of the rope had shattered the composure she had struggled to maintain since the morning, and her pent up emotions crashed over her in waves.

"I could have lost you—for all eternity," she sobbed.

"There now, don't," he crooned just above a whisper, his hands lightly caressing her back. "I'm sorry. I thought there was no reason for me to live. I figured I had no chance of going anywhere but Hell after I died, so it made no difference when I got there," he tried to explain.

She continued, "Do you know how worried I was? And I was thinking it was all my fault! How was I going to live with myself with *that* over my head for the rest of my life?"

This question was a dagger to Harlan's heart. He had not considered the fact that his method for escaping his overpowering contrition would merely have created similar guilt in those who were closest to him. He was suddenly even more thankful for Christ's divine work on the cross.

"I'm sorry," he reiterated, feeling worse and worse as she went on.

Marty's emotions were rapidly changing from fear and sadness to anger. "You scared me half to death! How could you do that to me?" Marty wriggled to loosen Harlan's hold on her and began taking her emotions out on him by beating his chest with the sides of her fists.

It was the second time that day that Harlan was on the receiving side of fists in that hayloft, but these didn't hurt except when they landed on the locations of Roy's former blows. Harlan was quite conscious of the emotional pain that he and Marty were both in, however.

"Shh, now," he murmured again, pulling her against him and holding her tightly to stop the blows. Her passions were soon spent, and she leaned heavily into him in a state of resigned exhaustion. Her sobs slowly dissolved into very deep and shaky breathing. "I'm so sorry," he mumbled, his mouth pressed against her hair. "All I can say is I'm a new man as of this morning, and Jesus Christ is in my heart. I'll do whatever it takes to prove it to you."

"Therefore if any man be in Christ, he is a new creature: old things are passed away; behold, all things are become new," quoted Marty a few moments later. "Second Corinthians 5:17."

He released her and bent to pick the pint of chili up off the hay. "I need to go give this back to your mother," Harlan said, staring at the word "Ball" in raised cursive on the side of the jar. "I stole this and the chili in it on Friday because I was mad at her for not listening to me when I said that I should leave that day. I hid it up here so that I could take it with me and at least have one good meal while I traveled. I want to ask for her forgiveness.

"What I've taken away from you is your trust in me," he continued in hushed tones, "and it's not something I can just hand back to you, but I do ask for your forgiveness also."

Marty produced a flowery handkerchief from somewhere on her person and began putting her face to rights.

"This isn't going to make any sense, especially in light of my lack of self-control just now, but I actually forgave you when you and Roy came to the house this morning and Roy told us that you had received Jesus. I knew at that moment that He had forgiven you, and I felt that I must too," Marty explained.

"So we—you and I—can start over again?" Harlan asked, cautious hope evident in his voice.

"All things are become new," Marty repeated.

Supper in the Meyer home that evening was entirely different than any meal Harlan had ever eaten there. Mrs. Meyer had moved the kitchen table so that the fourth side was against the tall east kitchen windows, and doing so had made Mr. Meyer's absence a little less noticeable. Mrs. Meyer's jovial mood had carried into the evening, and Harlan's confession regarding the pint of chili had only further convinced her of the sincerity of his conversion. Marty's storm of emotion was only a memory, and any walls that had existed amongst the three of them had been tumbled by the fact that the Son of Man had sought and saved the lost.

When the dishes were finished, Harlan took what had become

his customary seat on the sofa; Mrs. Meyer had a pile of mending at her rocking chair; and Marty was at the lamp table in the center of the room, poring through a volume of Christian poetry which she had extracted from one of the bookshelves in the colonnades. Among the pieces that she read aloud were two poems by anonymous authors.

My Grace Is Sufficient for Thee

When, sin-stricken, burdened, and weary,
From bondage I longed to be free,
There came to my heart the sweet message:
"My grace is sufficient for thee."

Though tempted and sadly discouraged,
My soul to this refuge will flee,
And rest in the blessed assurance:
"My grace is sufficient for thee."

Bought with a Price

Bought with a price, O what a price!
'Twas Jesus' precious Blood,
That bought our pardon, cleansed our sin
And brought us nigh to God.

No other Name, no other way,
For sin could e'er atone;
So Jesus shed His precious Blood
Which saves, and His alone.

When she exchanged the poetry anthology for the family Bible, she turned to the book of John.

"I know you've read a large chunk of this aloud to Dad," Marty said, "but it's the best place for you to start listening to the Word after you are a new Christian.

"In the beginning was the Word, and the Word was with God..." she began reading.

"Wait," Harlan interrupted, rising from the sofa. "I can't just listen. I need to be able to see the words too so that I can understand better." He brought a dining room chair into the living room, placing it next to Marty at the center lamp table so that they could both see the sacred text. Harlan's motives in making this move were exactly what he had described them to be; thus, he was unaware of how powerfully they had spoken to Marty and Mrs. Meyer about the truth of his salvation.

"In the beginning was the Word, and the Word was with God, and the Word was God," Marty repeated with Harlan following her finger across the page.

"Now, why is 'word' capitalized there?" Harlan interrupted.

Marty's heart somersaulted, and a smile played at her lips. "Well, that is a very good question," she answered. "Let's skip down to verse fourteen. Will you read that aloud?"

"And the Word was made flesh, and dwelt among us, (and we beheld his glory, the glory as of the only begotten of the Father,) full of grace and truth," Harlan read cautiously, taking extra care to make sure he had read correctly. "Huh. That 'only begotten of the Father' part sounds like the verse that talks about Jesus being God's 'only begotten Son.'"

"Exactly!" Marty said, nearly trembling with excitement. "'Word' is capitalized because it is referring to Jesus and we know from this verse that He was with God from the beginning."

★★★★★★★★★★★★★★★★★

On Tuesday, much to her chagrin, Mrs. Meyer had to put the ironing aside in favor of culling chickens since the weather was nice. Consequently, Harlan was about the business of beheading and scalding all those birds which Mrs. Meyer had determined were no longer laying and were thereby creating an unnecessary drain on the feed supply when Roy Schoening arrived unexpectedly in his Buick.

"I see you've picked a fun job to do on the nineteenth of November," Roy said brightly as he pulled up his sleeves and began helping Marty with the plucking.

Marty rolled her eyes at Roy's verbal irony. "We should have done this earlier when it wasn't so cold," she said as if apologizing.

"Well, you've had a few distractions," Roy returned.

Harlan couldn't concentrate on the banter between his two younger companions. Having to be the one who did the killing that morning was causing his conscience to work on him regarding his "big sin." He wasn't sure what it was all about, but it had his full attention.

When Mrs. Meyer emerged from the henhouse with the last six short-lived hens held upside down by their feet, she immediately knew the reason and import of Roy's visit.

"Harlan, can you and Roy haul some extra baskets of cobs to the house now? Marty and I can finish this part of the work, but I'm going to need plenty of fuel to get these girls canned," she said, thereby facilitating privacy for the two men so that Roy could minister to the new convert.

After they had exchanged common pleasantries and as they retrieved a couple of galvanized bushel baskets from the barn, Roy brought up the events of the previous day.

"Do you have any questions about what happened to you yesterday morning?" he inquired.

"Yes, but I don't even know how to put them all into words yet," Harlan admitted. "I think the biggest question, though, is how do I know that *all* my sins are forgivable?"

"I know that if you have truly confessed and repented, your sins can all be forgiven," Roy answered.

"But you don't know about my past," contended Harlan, "so you don't know what all I've done."

"Remember, I don't have to know your past," Roy countered, "because I know Jesus' past." Roy dug in his pocket for his pocket New Testament. "Here, this is what 1 John 1:7 says 'the blood of Jesus Christ his Son cleanseth us from all sin,' not just some sins."

"I've just...I've got so much to learn!" Harlan worried aloud.

"We all do," Roy consoled, "regardless of how long we've been in the faith. That's one of the reasons it's so important to have fellowship with other Christians."

Roy waxed reflective. "When I think about God sometimes, I am...I don't know...*overwhelmed* maybe. God is just so complex, so powerful...so *big* that we will never be able to completely understand Him. Our human minds just aren't capable. The prophet Isaiah records God saying, 'For my thoughts are not your thoughts, neither are your ways my ways. For as the heavens are higher than the earth, so are my ways higher than your ways, and my thoughts than your thoughts.'

"It's when I think about God's infinite wisdom and power and might, His infinite creativity, that I most appreciate His love for people. I mean, He is in charge of the whole universe, but He loves people so much that He was willing to give His own Son as the propitiation for our sins so that we could spend eternity with Him. Isn't that amazing?"

"It would be if I knew what 'prepitia...protipia...'—whatever it was—meant," Harlan said, his frustration with himself evident in his voice.

"Propitiation," Roy repeated. "Sorry, that is a hard word, isn't it? It means...hmm...how do I explain? It means the thing which takes away the punishment we deserve for our sins. Does that help?"

"Yeah," Harlan nodded.

"Anyway, to think that when He has created so many wonderful things and beings that He wants to have a relationship with *us* is both humbling and awesome, isn't it?

"Of course, just because we will never be able to entirely understand God doesn't mean that we shouldn't continually learn as much about Him as possible. He gave us His Word, the Bible, so that we can understand at least part of His nature," Roy added, "so we need to study it as much as we can, but even that is often difficult. I think that's why older Christians that I've talked to, people who are long in the faith, will say that they are still learning about God."

Harlan was looking forward to being "long in the faith."

Chapter Twenty-Four

November 19-28, 1935

Despite Mr. Meyer's recent passing, the next several days in the Meyer home were filled with joy. Roy Schoening visited Harlan every other day, answering questions if he could, encouraging him, making sure that he was not bereft of male companionship, and generally supporting Harlan's Christian walk in whatever way was in his power. Also, not long after Harlan's conversion, Rev. Martin visited with the dual purpose of making sure that all was well after Mr. Meyer's death, as well as interviewing the most recent new believer in his parish. His jubilance regarding Harlan's salvation was obvious in his face, mannerisms, and speech the whole time he was in the Meyer home.

Otherwise, the days were consumed with the regular late autumn farm work, but it was the evenings that everyone savored the most. While Mrs. Meyer's needle flew, Harlan and Marty bent over the Meyer family Bible, searching the Scriptures for the spiritual food that Harlan's infant faith needed in order to grow, for the continued learning that Marty needed in order to sustain her older faith, and for the comfort that Mrs. Meyer took in hearing the familiar words and promises over and over again as even she kept growing in faith. A secondary, but very noticeable, benefit to this ritual was that Harlan's reading ability improved as well.

Both Harlan and Marty could easily see the approval in Mrs.

Meyer's eyes as together they grew in their relationships with Christ. What Mrs. Meyer was most pleased about, though, was that she felt that they were laying a solid foundation on which they could build their own relationship with each other. However, in all appearances, the developing romance between the two had stalled. Every conversation between them had been either about necessary farm-related topics or about Biblical matters, and other than the occasional, accidental brush or the sharing of bucket or milk can handles, there had been no physical contact between the two since the emotionally fraught embrace in the barn loft on that fateful Monday a few days prior.

This shift in their relationship had been entirely Harlan's doing, but it was an unconscious act as he was so thoroughly immersed in learning the practical application of his new faith that he had no room in his brain to contemplate anything else. He did occasionally remind himself that he needed to re-earn Marty's trust, and he hoped that his new pursuit of Godly living would serve the dual purpose of serving and glorifying God as well as convincing Marty and Mrs. Meyer that he was indeed a changed man.

As a result of his coming to faith, Harlan was finding that he had a sensitivity to sin that had not existed in him before. For example, while those who knew him best would never have said that he had a filthy mouth, he had occasionally let fly with some colorful language if sufficiently provoked. That habit had all but disappeared in the space of a few short days. All desire to be deceitful about his actions or attitudes was gone, too.

Harlan had been absolved of his culpability in relation to Mr. Meyer's death after talking to Mrs. Meyer about it, but now his conscience was beginning to work on him in earnest regarding his mother. He knew Marty's accusation of being unfair to her was well founded; further, the thought of her facing increased hardship because she lacked the aid of his pay coming to her from the Civilian Conservation Corps ate at him constantly. However, Harlan was truly convinced that if any branch of the law were seeking him, they would most likely have contacted her, and he figured it would be easiest for him to remain hidden if his own mother had no idea where he was.

Then again, the very reason that he was afraid to contact his mother was also wearing on him. Harlan had committed murder, and he was beginning to wonder more and more frequently if he should confess what he had done to *someone*. He knew without a doubt that God had forgiven him, and Harlan clearly did not condone what he himself had done, but he was beginning to wonder if he shouldn't still have to suffer the earthly consequences for his actions.

The problem was that Harlan knew these consequences would be extreme. He remembered vividly the stories he had heard about criminals who had been sent to Anamosa or Fort Madison, and his whole being rebelled at the idea of becoming one of them. After all, he had no intention of killing again, he did not present any danger to anyone else, and his sins had been forgiven in the sight of God. Wasn't that enough?

"Did we remember the cranberry sauce?" Mrs. Meyer asked Marty as Harlan brought the car to a gentle halt at the end of the Meyer driveway.

"Yes, it's right here by my feet," Marty said, juggling a warm pie in each hand.

Mrs. Meyer also had a pie in each hand as well as a casserole dish of hot sweet potatoes in her lap. "All right, then I think we have everything."

Harlan eased the car onto the dirt roadway and turned east toward Marty's Aunt Louise and Uncle Vernon Neumann's farm. Mrs. Meyer and her sister had taken turns hosting Thanksgiving for many years, and this year the noon meal was supposed to have been at the Meyer's, but with Mr. Meyer's recent passing, it had been deemed easier on everyone if Mrs. Meyer didn't have the added stress of a house full of holiday company.

Everyone in the family was excited because two of Louise and Vernon's older three children would be present with their families, one of which included a very recent baby. Harlan approached the whole situation with a certain amount of trepidation, however. A shy person anyway, he would have found meeting new people at a family celebration awkward under any circumstances, but as merely a hired man, it felt to him like he was intruding. Both Mrs. Meyer and Marty had insisted on his presence, though, and, of course, Charlie would also be there, and he felt very comfortable with him.

After the foods from the Meyer house were carried inside, Charlie ushered Harlan into the living room where the men were trying to keep two little children and a baby away from the commotion of the kitchen while waiting patiently for the women to finish getting the meal on the table.

"Don and Karl, this is Harlan Jensen, the fellow who's been working for Aunt Elsie. Harlan, this is my older brother Donald; his wife is Luella. She was the black-haired lady in the blue dress who took the cranberry sauce from you. These are their two children, Little Donny and Luanna," Charlie explained, pointing out two children with pale skin and jet-black, naturally curly hair.

Harlan made a mental note that Donald and Luella were not very creative when it came to naming their children and wondered what kind of a quandary they would be flung into if Providence should see fit to bless them with a third child.

"And this is my brother-in-law Karl Bachmann; he's married to my second sister Verna. She's the one that looks like Marty. This is their daughter Shirley, who was born ten days ago."

Karl was holding a bundle of white cloths which had the tiny face of a baby tucked down into it. Obviously, Harlan had heard talk of this late addition to the family, though this was the first time any of the family except Aunt Louise had seen her. She had been born just before midnight on November 18th, the day of Harlan's conversion, and he had early on recognized the connection between the date of her birth and the date of his re-birth. Seeing little Shirley in the flesh illustrated to Harlan just how young a Christian he was.

"Don and Luella live up by Onawa where Don works at the Lewis and Clark State Park that opened there last year, and Karl and Verna live north of Macedonia on a farm owned by his folks," Charlie explained.

Harlan's focus immediately fell to the floor so that Don wouldn't be able to make eye contact with him. He hoped no one noticed how nervous he suddenly was at the knowledge that Charlie's brother Don worked at Lewis and Clark State Park. His mind was working quickly, trying to figure out what he ought to do about that when Karl strode up to him and extended a hand. *Just blend in*, he thought to himself.

"Very nice to meet you, Harlan," Karl smiled conspiratorially. "My mother-in-law had lots to say about you when she came down after Shirley was born last week." There seemed to be a double meaning in what Karl was saying, and Harlan thought he heard a slight teasing note in Karl's voice.

"Well, I hope she said good things," Harlan returned, not sure what to make of his new acquaintance's veiled statement.

"Oh, it was all good," Karl continued, "all very good." Karl shot a grin to both Don and Charlie that Harlan did not understand, and then he retreated to a rocking chair, motioning for Harlan to take a seat on the sofa.

"Did you get done picking corn yet, Karl?" Charlie asked.

"If everything works right and the weather holds, we should be done day after tomorrow," Karl answered. "We would have been done earlier, but we had a bit of a distraction here." He looked down at little Shirley's tiny face with paternal pride.

"So how's the new corn picker working out for you?" Vernon asked.

"Slick as a whistle," Karl replied.

"What kind did you get?"

"Dad got an IHC #20 on a neighbor's farm sale last spring. The bank foreclosed on 'em," explained Karl. "It's a couple years old, but it's in really good shape, and I think it's working out great."

Deciding that it was a safe topic of conversation, Harlan put his oar in. "That's a two-row, isn't it?"

"Sure is. Dad and I and my uncle raised about three hundred acres of corn this year, so we didn't want to mess around with anything smaller."

"Three hundred acres of corn? Wow!" Harlan whistled in amazement.

"The Bachmann's are big operators down there," Charlie said.

"Mr. Jensen, have we met before?" Don asked. "You look awfully familiar to me."

Harlan's stomach dropped, and his face blanched.

"I don't think so," Harlan responded as evenly as he could manage.

Don responded with a shake of his head and a "Hmm."

Harlan's brain was jumping, trying to figure out what, if anything, could be done. He had been honest when he said that he didn't think he and Marty's cousin Don had met before, but was it possible that Don had seen him from a distance and now recognized him?

"Mother says for all of you to come to the table," Verna instructed, entering the living room and taking the baby from her husband. "By the time we get everyone settled, they'll be ready with the food."

General confusion ensued as the men and children made their way to the dining room and tried to figure out where they should sit. Harlan ended up sitting between Charlie and Marty, which made him feel more at ease until he discovered that he was also sitting directly across the table from Don. This arrangement would make it easier for Don to study his face throughout the meal, and that idea made Harlan very uncomfortable.

In short order, the women brought forth platters and bowls heaped with steaming food. Once everything was on the table,

Marty's aunt took her handkerchief out, dabbed the perspiration from her brow and sighed.

"All right, now before your father asks grace, give me that baby. I've been waiting all morning to hold her again, but I was too busy with the dinner," Louise ordered in a matronly tone.

Laughing, Verna surrendered Shirley to her mother. "It's not like she's your first grand baby, Mother!"

"No, but she's the newest," Louise countered.

It was impossible for anyone present to miss the happiness that exuded from the whole family regarding their most recent addition.

Vernon asked the blessing, and then everyone began consuming the most delicious meal that Harlan had ever had. Nothing on the table was extremely fancy, but all of it was prepared with special care. Except for Donald's unabashed study of his face from across the table, Harlan would have felt completely at ease.

The conversation was easy among the family. They discussed the fact that Vernon and Louise's oldest daughter Margaret was not present because she was hosting Thanksgiving for her husband's family, but as Margaret only lived a few miles to the west of the Meyers, she was hoping to be able to sneak away from her own home in the afternoon to come and meet her newest niece. Someone had pointed Margaret and her husband out to Harlan on the day of the corn picking bee since she was one of the women helping in the kitchen that day and her husband was one of the pickers. However, as she was significantly older than Marty, she did not play a prominent role in Marty's life.

They also discussed their excitement regarding the fact that electricity was to come down their road within the next year.

"I am most looking forward to two things," declared Louise. "An electric motor on the washing machine and a refrigerator."

"You'd love a toaster, too, Mother," Verna put in.

"I think an electric iron is a great work saver," added Luella. "They have such nice ones now, and their soleplates are so much larger than our regular sadirons or even gas irons that the ironing goes much more quickly."

"Well, I think you'll be pleased to get a motor on the cream separator, too," Vernon said, "but you women won't be the only ones who'll benefit. Think what a help it will be to have an electric motor on the pump. We won't have to hook up a gas engine every time we have a couple of windless days in the summer and the windmill doesn't pump enough water to the cistern. That'll be such a relief!"

"Mama, don't you think we could get a radio?" Marty asked.

"Oh, now," Mrs. Meyer said in a tone that was obviously meant to quiet Marty.

"You know, I've been on Dad and Mama to buy a radio for several years, but the excuse they always gave me was that they didn't want to have to deal with the batteries," Marty said, addressing the rest of the family. "Well, now the batteries won't be a problem. I think it would be fun to listen to in the evenings, Mama. You'd enjoy it."

"Oh, Aunt Elsie, there are so many good programs for homemakers, too," continued Verna. "I just love to listen to Mrs. Driftmier on KFNF out of Shenandoah; she always has different hints for wives and lots of good recipes."

"I always listen to KMA to hear the weather report from Earl May," Vernon put in. "It's nice to have a little idea of what the weather is going to do a day or so ahead."

"Well, he doesn't always get it right," Louise harrumphed authoritatively, "and I, for one, miss the evenings that we used to have *before* we got a radio. Margaret would play the piano and we would all sing, or Father here would read aloud to us all. Now that we've got a radio, it's just not the same."

"Part of that is that it is only me left at home, Mom. I'm just not enough to keep you entertained all by myself," Charlie said, affecting a pathetic tone.

The whole family snickered a little at his humor, but Harlan, never one to be that excited about progress, could see Aunt Louise's point. He had grown quite fond of the relaxing evening routine at the Meyer home and didn't want to think about what it would be like if they all had their ears glued to the radio.

Conversations continued on like this through the meal and into the dessert course, when Mrs. Meyer's beautiful pies were brought into the dining room and served with mounds of sweetened whipped cream and a fresh round of coffee.

"Are you sure that we haven't met somewhere?" Donald asked Harlan again while everyone was finishing the last of their pie. "You ever been in Onawa?"

Harlan wanted desperately to be able to lie with a clear conscience, and eleven days ago, he would have, but the new convictions that came along with his conversion prevented him from doing that.

"Well, I just passed through," Harlan answered nervously. His apprehension must have been noticeable in his voice because Marty took up his defense.

"I imagine you passed through a number of places while you were riding the rails," Marty said, trying to change the topic of conversation. "You know, I was talking to Auntie Ella in the post office the other day when she was in there substituting for Mrs. Verpoorten." Marty turned to Harlan. "She's not *our* aunt," Marty explained, "but everybody calls her that. Her house is right beside the railroad tracks there, and she says that she's had as many as seven hobos in a day stop at her house asking for food. It's just a tough time for so many people right now."

"That it is!" agreed Donald. "Roosevelt's been doing his level best to help people with jobs..."

"But that man is going to bankrupt this country with the way he's spending money!" interjected Vernon. "Why, if I ran my farm the way he's trying to run the U. S. of A., I'd be bankrupt before I could say..."

"Vernon! You'll wake little Shirley here," Aunt Louise scolded.

An animated discussion about the state of things in the world followed. There were members of the family who took up both sides of the debate, but the discussion was amicable, and no one's temper got out of hand. Harlan was impressed with the fact that a conversation about politics among people with such wildly divergent opinions could be so friendly. He was trying to figure out how it was possible when Donald suddenly pointed a finger toward his nose.

"I know where I've seen your face before!"

Twenty-Five

November 28, 1935

Harlan's face lost all its color, and the muscles in his legs twitched as the instinct to run was awakened by Donald's pointing finger. He was sure that in a moment his life was going to change drastically as his past would be revealed to the family who surrounded him. Many emotions assailed him at once, but he had no time to concentrate on any of them, for Donald continued speaking.

"Only it wasn't actually your face," Donald went on.

So there were indeed "Wanted" posters out with his image on them! Harlan's suspicions were confirmed. He would have given anything for Marty and Mrs. Meyer to not have learned about his past this way. *I should have been honest with them much earlier. This is going to break their hearts,* he thought to himself. *I still should be the one to tell them rather than let them learn about me this way!*

Harlan turned to face Marty. "I should have told you earlier…"

"Luella, doesn't Harlan remind you of that new cashier at the bank back home?"

"My goodness yes!" agreed Luella emphatically. "They could be twins. I believe that fellow's hair is a shade or two darker than yours, but he's still just as blond as they come."

"What was his last name?" Donald asked, his eyes appearing to search the ceiling for answers.

"Heavens, I don't know, Don. Andersen, Andresen—something like that."

"Jeder hat einen Doppelgänger," Louise said, casting a meaningful glance to Mrs. Meyer.

"And they're off!" Verna called, mimicking the announcer at a horse race. She began laughing along with all the rest who were members of her generation. "I wondered how long it would be before Mother and Aunt Elsie would start speaking to each other in German. My, my, though! It's nearly one in the afternoon. This is the latest they've ever started!"

Harlan's head was swimming; he had no idea what had just happened and was particularly confused since some of the people in the room had begun speaking in another language. Had Donald seen his face on a "Wanted" poster or not?

"All she said was that everyone has a lookalike," Mrs. Meyer defended her sister, trying to sound authoritative and calm the laughter. She was ineffective, though, because a smile was leaking out around the corners of her mouth.

The laughter calmed down enough for Luella to say, "You know, I think it is true that we all have someone that looks just like us. I was in the grocery the other day, and out of the corner of my eye I saw a fellow that looked so like you, Vernon, that I almost approached him, but then he spoke and had a different voice."

"Either way, the new bank cashier in Onawa certainly bears a striking resemblance to you, Mr. Jensen. Do you have a brother?"

"No," Harlan answered quietly.

"Hmm. Well, he's got to be some kind of cousin then," Luella dismissed the topic. "What about Shirley? Whom do we think she looks like?"

With that segue, the family was onto the age-old pastime of searching out family resemblances in babies, with Karl and Verna loving every minute of the attention their daughter received.

Meanwhile, Harlan was so relieved that he was nearly shaking. *What a close call you just had!* he thought to himself. However, with

Donald's curiosity surrounding his identity completely abated and everyone believing the matter to be settled, Harlan felt himself quickly relaxing and truly beginning to enjoy the time with Marty's family.

After everyone had eaten pie, Luella disappeared behind the pocket doors to the parlor in order to rock Little Donnie and Luanna to sleep for their afternoon nap, and Verna moved to the kitchen rocking chair to feed Shirley. Mrs. Meyer, her sister, and Marty set about the business of washing the dishes, and the four men moved to one end of the dining room table and started a game of five-handed Ten-Point Pitch. Harlan loved this game and had played a great deal of it in his lifetime, so it didn't occupy all of his concentration. It didn't appear that any of the men were all that concerned about whether they won since they seemed to be much more interested in the banter being exchanged among them.

Harlan's place at the table was at the end closest to the kitchen, and the door between the two rooms was cocked at an angle which ushered every sound from the kitchen directly into his right ear. Thus, he couldn't help but follow the discussion that the women were having as they cleaned up from the meal. Their conversation started out benignly enough, mostly regarding the quality of the turkey they had just consumed. Then they moved on to other topics, most of which didn't interest Harlan because they had to do with housekeeping and other concerns that were of the feminine realm in Harlan's world. When they moved on to discussing Christmas lists, the conversation soon excluded Marty and Verna and was conducted entirely in German.

At that point, Harlan heard a kitchen chair being moved across the floor, and Marty and Verna took up a quiet conversation not far from the doorway between the kitchen and dining room.

"May I hold her for a while when you get done?" Marty asked.

"Certainly!" Verna replied affably. "I'm sure your mother will want to hold her too."

"Oh, yes," Marty agreed. "She can hardly wait for grandchildren, and before Dad had his stroke, she dropped hints all the time that she thought I ought to be getting married soon."

"It's a little difficult to do that until some man asks you," Verna giggled.

"Yes, but then with Dad the way he was for those last six weeks, she couldn't think about that anymore."

Harlan's interest was piqued. He was sure that neither of the girls believed their conversation was audible to anyone else, but the acoustics of the house brought their voices to his ear easily.

"How about now, though? He's frightfully handsome, and Mother..." Verna pressed.

"Shhh!" Marty admonished.

Verna continued in a whisper, thinking that her words wouldn't carry into the dining room. "Mother tells me Aunt Elsie says that he treats you wonderfully, and now that he's become a Christian, what's the holdup?"

"Verna! He'll hear you!" Marty hissed.

Attempting to justify her lack of tact, Verna said, "Sometimes a man needs a hint."

"And sometimes a man can be scared away!" countered Marty.

"Seriously, though, what's the holdup?" goaded Verna.

Marty made excuse, saying, "Well, it's complicated."

"What do you mean complicated? Don't you want to marry him?"

"Harlan! Dad just called for the king of hearts, do you have it?" Charlie asked, putting a fist lightly into Harlan's upper arm and pulling his attention back into the dining room.

"Oh, yeah, sorry!" Harlan apologized, throwing the requested card onto the table, thoroughly disappointed that he missed Marty's reply.

"You falling asleep on us there, son?" Vernon asked jovially.

"Sorry, I was...thinking about something else."

Karl, his eyes dancing mischievously, said, "Funny, looked to me more like you were thinking about some*one* else."

"Careful, Karl," Vernon warned, his voice full of gentleness and goodwill.

Harlan could feel himself blushing to the roots of his hair. It was at moments like these that he hated being so fair-skinned because he knew that his discomfort was obvious to the other men surrounding him.

"Aw, don't take it so hard, man," Karl half-heartedly apologized. "We've all been there except for young Charlie here. Nothing to be ashamed of."

"And take it from me," Donald said, purposely throwing his voice toward the closed parlor doors, "married life is great if you get the right woman like I did." He turned back toward his male companions and winked. "That oughta get me some special treatment."

"Did *you* get the right woman, Karl?" Verna purred as she entered the dining room and laid her hands on her husband's shoulders.

"You know I did, and now she's given me a perfect daughter," Karl said sweetly, pulling Verna's face toward him and landing a peck on her cheek.

"Good answer, Karl, because there's no way Mother and Dad and I are taking her back!" Charlie jabbed.

Verna boxed her little brother on the ears good-naturedly and told him to be quiet.

After the Pitch hand resumed, Marty entered the dining room with Shirley slung over her shoulder, bouncing and patting her on the back to get her to burp. Harlan couldn't help but notice how feminine Marty looked with the baby and all of her linens draped over her. Marty was followed by her mother and her aunt, and soon Luella emerged from the living room, closing the pocket doors softly behind her.

"Are we ready for prayers?" Louise asked.

"I think so. We can finish our game afterward," Vernon responded.

The family explained to Harlan that their tradition on Thanksgiving afternoon was to have a long family prayer after the dishes were finished in which each of them offered thanks to God for some blessing that they had received over the last year. They always sat in a circle around the dining room table to do this. The prayer was started by the male head of the hosting household, then moved to the left around the group until all the adults had prayed aloud.

Harlan was a bit nervous about this tradition. The first time he had ever prayed aloud had been when he repeated after Roy Schoening in the hayloft ten days earlier, and he had only recently begun making short additions to the prayers that he, Mrs. Meyer, and Marty had prayed together. He could think of something that he was thankful for right away, however, and that was that his seat was not directly to the left of Uncle Vernon!

Everyone bowed their heads, closed their eyes, and folded their hands, some choosing to kneel on the floor.

"Great God, our Creator," began Vernon, "we've set aside this day to give our thanks to You for Your provision, protection, guidance, and goodness to us over the past year. We are humbled by Your love for us, and we just want to take this opportunity to individually express our gratitude to You, O Lord."

Mrs. Meyer was seated at Vernon's left, so she was the first to offer her thanks: "Lord, I am thankful for so many things, but today I thank You especially for Al. You made him into a wonderful man who was a loving husband and a great father. You blessed us with many years together, and I am thankful for that. I am also thankful that through Jesus' work on the cross, Al now rests safely in Paradise. Thank You for the peace of mind that gives us who are left here on Earth."

Luella and Donald were next, but Harlan wasn't interested in what they had to say, so he concentrated on trying to silently compose what he would thank God for when his turn came and asked for divine guidance in the matter.

After Donald, it was Charlie's turn. "Gracious Father, I thank You for my family today. This house can get pretty lonesome for Mother and Dad and me sometimes, especially when we've been so used to so much activity for so many years. Getting together means a great deal to us, and I thank You not only for our fellowship but also for the fact that we all get along so well."

At Charlie's words, Louise had trouble containing her emotions and began quietly digging for a handkerchief and blew her nose in it once it was located. Harlan would have heard Vernon sniffle loudly too if his mind hadn't been so busy figuring out what he was going to say since it was now his turn.

"Dear Lord," Harlan began and then paused. His heart was full. He truly had so many things to be thankful for that he hardly knew where to begin. Suddenly, though, he could clearly see what he was most thankful for, and he felt that his thoughts were being put into words for him. "When I think of all the places that You could have made me hungry enough to jump off a moving train, I thank you that it was at Al and Elsie Meyer's back pasture. And when I think of all of the people I might have first met, again I thank you for Al and Elsie and Martha Meyer, for the fact that they were and are such kind and compassionate people. But Lord, I especially thank you for the dedicated Christians that are with me in this room and for Roy Schoening who played such a big part in leading me to faith in Jesus. Lastly, I thank Jesus for calling me to Himself and for the work He did on the cross for me."

More sniffles were heard around the room, and then Marty commenced her portion of the prayer. "Heavenly Father, I am also thankful for my dad today. It is such a blessing to have a godly father, and Al Meyer was certainly that to me. And Lord, since you saw fit to take him home when you did, I thank you for sending Harlan to us. He has worked extremely hard for us since the first afternoon he arrived, and Mama and I would never have been able to remain on the farm if he had not come. I also thank You for the work You have done in his heart. Continue to put people in his life to shepherd him in Your will and way, and build him into a man who will eventually shepherd others."

A few low "Amens" were heard around the room and then Karl continued the round-robin thanksgiving. When everyone had finished, Vernon closed the emotional prayer time.

"Why don't you and Marty sing the Doxology?" Karl prompted Verna after the final amen. The motion was seconded by several others. The two young women stood, and Marty deposited little Shirley in Mrs. Meyer's arms. Verna then hummed a starting note, Marty found the interval below it for her alto line, and the two sang the ancient song of praise with exquisite precision. Verna's voice blent even better with Marty's than Anna Kloeser's did because of their common heredity, and everyone in the room was blessed by the song they rendered.

> *Praise God, from Whom all blessings flow;*
> *Praise Him, all creatures here below;*
> *Praise Him above, ye heavenly hosts;*
> *Praise Father, Son and Holy Ghost. Amen.*

When they had finished, Karl rose and caught hold of Verna in an unabashed display of appreciation, which left Marty standing awkwardly nearby even though she deserved as much recognition as her cousin. Harlan wished that he could stand and relieve her embarrassment, but his sense of propriety held him back.

"I hate to say this, Mom, since you just got the dishes finished a few minutes ago, but I'd like another piece of Aunt Elsie's pie before the kids wake up," Donald said.

"Today and Christmas are the only days that saying that won't make me angry," Louise laughed, rising from her chair and going into the kitchen.

All of Mrs. Meyer's pies were served once more, and the men resumed their game of Pitch since they were only a hand or two from determining the winner. Little Donnie and Luanna awoke from their nap, but were bleary eyed and timid, so they crawled into Louise's lap where they were welcomed with open arms. While Luella, Verna, and Marty visited and enjoyed each other's company in the parlor, Mrs. Meyer continued to hold Shirley, who was now wide awake. Harlan noted that she lost all her usual reserve and became someone he had never met. Her voice had taken on a more nurturing tone than he had ever heard from her, and her mood was extremely light as she tickled and cooed with the baby.

The Pitch game came to an end in just a few moments, just as Louise and Vernon's older daughter Margaret knocked on the door with her four school-aged children in tow. They had come to meet little Shirley who immediately decided to be less than pleased by the extra noise and commotion their presence brought to the gathering.

With a wailing baby and the excited chatter of Louise and Vernon's six other grandchildren, the dining room suddenly felt extremely small. Harlan picked up as many dirty dessert plates as he could handle, and made his escape to the kitchen under the pretense of helping Louise. He had just finished setting the dishes by the sink when Marty entered the kitchen with all of the remaining plates that Harlan didn't have hands enough to carry.

"Lively group, aren't they?" she said.

"You can say that again!" Harlan shook his head in wonder. "But they are a great family. Vernon and Louise have been very blessed."

"I think so. I've always been glad that they were so close by; otherwise, I would have been extremely lonely growing up."

Marty placed the dishes she carried by the pile Harlan had made, carried a dishpan to the water reservoir on the stove, and began dipping out hot water to wash the dessert plates.

"Are you having fun?" she asked.

"Yes, actually. I thought it would be strange to be the only person here who wasn't a member of the family, but I am having a good time. What about you?"

"Of course I'm having fun!" Marty returned. "It's *my* family."

"Which one would you say you are the closest to?" Harlan asked.

Without taking a second to think, Marty answered, "Verna, definitely. I'm the same age as Charlie, of course, but since Verna is a girl, she's always taken the most interest in me, and we always looked alike. In fact, sometimes when we were together and met people who didn't know us, they thought we were sisters."

Harlan brought the other dishpan over to the reservoir and exchanged it for the one Marty had filled. He carried the full dishpan to the white enameled table where he had seen the ladies wash dishes earlier. He returned to Marty's side, ready to carry the second dishpan for her.

"Well, you two certainly sounded like sisters when you were talking by the dining room door earlier," Harlan teased in a whisper so no one else would hear.

"Har—! You heard us?" Marty uttered in a voice that was barely audible. She turned a horrified face to Harlan's, nearly dropping the dipper of hot water she had just ladled out of the reservoir.

Harlan's mouth broke into an ornery smile. "I just have one quick question. I know that Verna thinks I'm 'frightfully handsome,' but do *you?*"

"I...I...of...cour..."Marty stammered, her face turning an attractive shade of purple.

"Oh, and I wanted to tell you not to worry. I'm not easily scared away."

Chapter Twenty-Six

November 28 & 29, 1935

Harlan had difficulty falling asleep that night because he was thinking about what he had seen at Vernon and Louise's house. The couple had raised a beautifully close-knit family who loved the Lord and each other. Harlan wanted that for himself, and he wanted it for Marty too. As he lay in the pitch blackness of the moonless night, his brain was busy planning. The next day, he would ask Mrs. Meyer if he could begin officially courting Marty.

Harlan realized that the feelings he harbored for Martha Meyer had changed drastically since the evening he had so impulsively proposed to her. On that evening, he had felt very close to her and was sure that he loved her. However, since he had become a Christian and the two of them had spent so much time together in the Word, he had come to realize that his feelings for her on that night weeks earlier were comparatively shallow.

Now, the two of them had a love for Jesus in common, and that fact changed everything! He understood why she had rejected him, why being unequally yoked was a recipe for a disastrous marriage, and he was now thankful for the steadfastness in her that he had found so frustrating before. Their mutual sense of purpose and unity in Christ made Harlan view Marty as a mate in so many different, additional ways. He had come to feel a sureness about their love for each other which was much stronger, even though they had not discussed their relationship since his conversion.

Yes. Tomorrow he would secure Mrs. Meyer's permission to pursue her daughter for his wife. The two of them would soon serve and glorify God together as married people, enjoying each other's company for the rest of their lives, and if God saw fit, they would do what they could to raise children who were as wonderful as Marty's cousins. Harlan finally fell asleep with the pleasant notions of a man who feels that all he could want in life has been put within his grasp.

As the first streams of milk pinged against the sides of their buckets the next morning, Harlan cleared his throat to speak. "So, I have a question for you," he began.

"All right," Marty prompted warily.

"Would it be all okay with you if at breakfast here in a little while I asked your mother if I could begin courting you officially?"

Several seconds went by without a response coming from the stanchion next to him, and Harlan became nervous. After a few more seconds, he asked rather timidly, "Marty, did you hear me?"

"Oh, yes, I heard you," she said kindly. "I'm just thinking."

Harlan was nonplussed at the idea that Marty had to think at all regarding this topic. After more time passed, he finally asked, "Do you mind me telling me what's going through your mind right now?"

"No, I don't mind," she answered. "First, I'd like to know what you mean when you say 'courting.'"

"Well, I mean *courting*, you know what that is. We...are a couple together." Harlan was finding it difficult to explain to Marty just exactly what courting was. "You're my girl, and I'm your man."

"I know what courting means in the usual sense of the word," Marty reasoned, "but I'm confused as to what you think will be different for us if we decide that we are courting. Neither of us have the money to go out to movies or whatever, and already we're together more than a lot of couples just because we're the two main farm workers on this place. I mean, for heaven's sake, you sleep just across the hall from me! I'd just like to be clear about the expectations right up front."

Harlan had to admit that Marty had a point, and he took a moment to think before he spoke again.

Finally, he explained, "Three weeks ago, when I proposed to you the night before your dad passed away, I meant it. Now, that said, I shouldn't have proposed to you then, and I know it now. To tell the truth, I'm glad you turned me down. There's been a lot of water under the bridge since then, though, and with me being a Christian now, everything has changed. I *thought* I loved you then." He paused to think. "No, I *know* I loved you then, but now that we have Jesus Christ in common, there's just...we...I don't know. There's just so much *more* to our relationship now.

"I still want to marry you, but rather than rushing into marriage like I was thinking we should a few weeks ago, I think we need to have time to...to...get to know each other in a romantic way.

"I know we can't afford to go on dates, exactly, but I would like to be able to at least hold your hand sometimes—when we're studying the Bible together, for example. And I'd like there to be an understanding between us because, eventually, I want to propose again, but for real. I want for us what I saw over with the Neumanns yesterday: a family who loves the Lord and loves each other too, and it seems like the first step toward that is to court you."

"I see," Marty responded simply.

"So would it be all right if I asked your mother for permission to court you, then? If she says no, I don't think it's right that we pursue it further."

"I'm not done asking questions yet," Marty said. "The second thing I want to know is how long you are thinking our courtship should be."

Harlan was taken aback. "I don't know," he answered honestly. "I guess I hadn't thought that far ahead yet."

"I have another question," continued Marty. "Do you think that people can learn to love each other after they're married rather than having to do it beforehand?"

"What do you mean?"

"Well, think about arranged marriages. Do you think that people who haven't really spent any time courting—or maybe have no courtship before their marriage at all—can fall in love with each other after they're married?"

Harlan had no idea why on God's green Earth Marty would have asked this question.

"In the book of Ephesians, Paul writes a command about marriage. It is 'Husbands, love your wives, even as Christ also loved the church, and gave himself for it.' And then a few verses later, he says, 'let every one of you in particular so love his wife even as himself; and the wife see that she reverence her husband.' Don't you think if a man and a woman who are both Christians, *and* who were complete strangers, got married but then chose to follow those commands, they could find themselves happy in their marital relationship?"

"I suppose so," Harlan conceded. "I've just never thought of marriage that way before."

"I don't think most people have," Marty went on. "I told you earlier that I think love is a choice—that it's something you *do*. Do you remember that conversation?"

"Yeah."

"Well, now I have another question for you. What kinds of things do people do to show love?"

"Boy! I didn't know that asking if I could ask your mother for permission to court you was going to result in my own personal Inquisition!" Harlan complained.

"Sorry, but I have a point here, and I'm getting to it. I promise. Just answer the question: What kinds of things do people do to show love?"

Harlan had to think a bit before he spoke. "Well, before my

dad died, my parents hugged and kissed. I remember my mom sometimes sitting on my dad's lap. I mentioned holding hands earlier. My dad had blond hair like me only his was really curly, and I can remember my mother standing behind his chair at the kitchen table, just running her fingers through it and tracing the curls. It seemed like she did that because she loved him. And of course, between a married couple there's always..."

"That's a good list," she interrupted him, "but those are all physical things. Can you think of things that aren't physical that people do to show love?"

Harlan felt as if he were back on the recitation bench at school taking some kind of oral exam. It was making him fairly nervous, but he was surprised to note that he was not experiencing any of the resentment that usually would have accompanied such stress a few weeks ago.

He thought for a moment, and then said, "Well, sometimes people buy certain things for people they love, like jewelry and other gifts. Other times they buy things that aren't very romantic but are still a way to show love. For example, when we were on the farm, my dad bought my mom a new Maytag washing machine. He could have bought her a One Minute Washer much cheaper, but he said that it looked like the Maytag would be easier for her to operate, so he spent the extra money. I think he did that because he loved her."

Harlan paused to reflect further and then continued, "But there are other, more simple things that people do, too. Every morning, my dad started the fire in the cookstove for my mother. She could have done it herself, of course, and did later in the day during the summer to make dinner and supper, but I think that was one of the ways that he showed his love for her.

"And then, something I noticed about your folks was the way your mother took care of your dad. I helped her get him into his pajamas one Saturday night when you were out with Roy, and I was impressed by how tenderly she handled him. That looked like love to me."

He paused for a second and then went on, "I think that sometimes when you love someone, you can also just spend time together, and you don't even have to talk. Sometimes love is just letting the other person know that you are always on her side."

"I guess I've just given you examples between married people, but that's what we're talking about here, right?—because I think the ways that parents show their love for their children are sometimes much different than the way spouses show love."

Harlan's speech satisfied Marty. "I like your answer," she said. "Sometimes I think that people put too much emphasis on courting; others put way too much emphasis on the wedding—though we haven't seen as much of that here recently since times have gotten so tough. Really, they need to put the emphasis on the marriage. I mean, I'm sure that courting can be fun and exciting, as can weddings, but they're not reality. A real marriage is full of work, family, money, catastrophes, and often a great deal of sorrow."

"And love, and laughter, and little joys, and the Lord," Harlan contradicted. "You left out the good things."

"Those things, too, of course, but those are easy to get through," reasoned Marty.

"I don't know," Harlan shook his head. "When I was under the conviction of the Holy Spirit, I wouldn't say that the Lord was any too much fun then."

"You'll be under conviction of the Holy Spirit again sometimes, but I don't think it will be as uncomfortable as it was the first time because you have your relationship to Christ as your foundation now. But you're getting me sidetracked. I told you that I had a point with all my questions."

"Have we gotten to it yet?" Harlan asked with mock weariness in his voice.

Marty replied, "We are now. My point is this: you have my permission to ask Mama if it's all right to court me. And I will court you, Mr. Harlan Jensen, but I don't want it to be a long courtship." This last was said with an authoritative air that made Marty sound very much like her mother, especially when she tacked on a very direct, "Do you get my drift?"

Harlan was both shocked and pleased with Marty's boldness. He figured that he would never have to wonder what she was thinking.

"I'm catching you quite plainly," he returned, and the smile on his face could be heard in his voice.

Harlan's mood was extraordinarily light as he carried the milk cans back to the house with Marty a few minutes later. He was humming a particularly joyful hymn that he had heard Marty sing many times over the last few days, and upon hearing his baritone voice repeating the familiar phrases, she decided to sing along with the fourth verse which was her favorite:

> Give the winds a mighty voice,
> Jesus saves, Jesus saves;
> Let the nations now rejoice.
> Jesus saves, Jesus saves;
> Shout salvation full and free,
> Highest hills and deepest caves,
> This our song of victory,
> Jesus saves, Jesus saves!

"That's a good one, isn't it?" Harlan asked after he had continued with his throaty accompaniment to her singing.

"Indeed it is!" she agreed enthusiastically. "I've never heard you sing before."

"You still haven't; that was only humming," Harlan pointed out playfully.

"Well, you hum very well then. Now you need to memorize some of the words so that you can sing along."

"I'm not opposed to that," he returned, his tone sounding flirtatious, "but I'll need you to teach me."

She beamed at him in a way that warmed his heart.

At the breakfast table over a stack of buckwheat pancakes, bacon, and a bowl of cream of wheat, Harlan cleared his throat and spoke.

"Mrs. Meyer, I have an important question for you," he said with a broad smile.

"What's that?" she asked.

"I would like permission to start officially courting your daughter."

Marty's mouth curved into a shy grin.

For some reason, Harlan felt moved to give Mrs. Meyer a little background information about his relationship with Marty. "I don't know whether she told you or not, but I asked her to marry me the night before Mr. Meyer passed away. She wisely turned me down that night, and I'm glad she did. There's been a lot of water under the bridge since then, and my feelings for her have only grown stronger, but this time instead of plunging headlong into marriage, I would like to start with a true courtship. I hope you know that my intentions are honorable, and I will only pursue her if you give me permission to do so."

Mrs. Meyer's joy was written all over her face when she replied. "You absolutely have my blessing! You have no idea how long I've been waiting for you to ask that question. Why, to tell the truth, this conversation is another answered prayer."

"Really? How long have you been praying for *this*?" Harlan asked, surprised.

"That doesn't make a difference. All you need to know is that I've been praying for my daughter's future husband for a long time."

"Now, I hope you'll be praying for the two of us together," Harlan stated.

"Oh, you can be sure I will be," Mrs. Meyer said.

That evening, Harlan and Marty spent their customary time at the lamp table in the living room studying the Bible; only, as good as his word, Harlan's hand coyly sought Marty's. Her capable feminine fingers were dwarfed by his larger, more muscular ones, but the warmth that they shared as they intertwined was unmistakable.

After the three of them had prayed together, Mrs. Meyer yawned, said goodnight, and disappeared into the bedroom, letting her two younger companions have some modicum of privacy. At her departure, Marty rose from her chair at the lamp table and turned the lamp a little lower.

"Come sit on the sofa with me," she said, taking Harlan's hands and pulling him to his feet.

He willingly obeyed, and once they were seated again, Marty took his hand in both of hers and began tracing the veins in the back of it as she had done on that evening so many days ago. Then, she snuggled close so that she could speak in his ear.

"Just so you know," Marty whispered softly, "while you were out mending the apron on the manure spreader this afternoon, Mama and I moved enough of my clothes and things down here that I can sleep with her. It didn't seem right to be following you up to bed at night now that we are officially courting."

Her lips were dangerously close to his ear, and Harlan found it hard to concentrate fully on what she was saying.

"That's good," he mumbled. "I'm glad you thought of that."

Suddenly, her hand was on his cheek, gently turning his face toward hers. She traced his prominent jawline with the back of her fingers, feeling his beard stubble scratch along her knuckles, and then her fingertips ascended to his hair and gingerly smoothed his blond locks.

Sure that he was reading all of her signals correctly, Harlan leaned forward a couple of inches, removing the gap between their lips, and kissed her gently. She kissed him back twice, and then snuggled deeper under his arm.

"Is courting living up to your expectations?" she asked coquettishly.

"Better than I ever imagined," he returned.

A few minutes later when Harlan lay in his cold bed alone upstairs, his mind was again busy planning. Marty had said that she didn't want a long courtship.

I wonder what she considers long, he thought silently. Was a Christmas wedding too soon? June was only seven months away. Maybe that was what she had in mind. Harlan decided to ask her sometime soon. She was direct enough that she would surely tell him. Either way, he was sure that by this time next year, he would be a married man, maybe even with a little one on its way.

For the second night in a row, Harlan fell asleep feeling that his life was laid out before him, and he saw that it was good. It was very good.

Chapter Twenty-Seven

November 30 & December 1, 1935

After chores and breakfast on Saturday morning, Harlan sharpened the ax and then loaded it into the largest wagon in the Meyer fleet along with a two-man saw and a buck saw. He hitched a team of horses to the wagon and drove it down to the house where Marty climbed in and Mrs. Meyer deposited a cast iron dutch oven and a basket of provisions in the back with the other wood gathering equipment.

"Your aunt Louise said on the telephone that Charlie would be waiting at the end of their lane and would follow you once you got there," Mrs. Meyer said. "Please be very careful, Harlan," she continued with concern in her voice. "I'm finally getting close to getting a son, and I don't want a tree to fall on him."

"We'll be careful. Don't worry," Harlan assured her.

The conversation that Harlan and Marty had on their way to meet Charlie was light and inconsequential and peppered with a great deal of youthful flirting, but it served to make their bond grow stronger.

When they reached the lane to the Neumann farm, Charlie was waiting at his designated spot with his team and wagon, and the threesome traveled to the Meyer woodlot southeast of Charlie's home. While Marty set about the task of gathering sticks and starting a small campfire to cook their noon dinner, Charlie and

Harlan blocked their wagons in place and unhitched their teams so the horses could rest for a while before being put back to work in the logging process.

Charlie, who had been to the woodlot on numerous occasions, led Harlan along the narrow wildlife trails which snaked up and down the hills and through the trees as the two searched for dead bur oak and black walnut trees. Those were the best varieties that the timber had to offer for long-burning, hot fires, but both men took secondary mental notes about the locations of silver maples or cottonwoods which could be harvested in order to fill their wagons. The young men applied the two-man saw to a couple of dead trees, bringing them down safely and efficiently; then the smaller branches were trimmed off with axes and buck saws. By the time that was done, they heard Marty calling that dinner was ready, so they began the trek back to where she had built the fire.

"We've gotten a lot done already this morning," Charlie said as they walked.

"Yup. After we eat, we can use the horses to drag everything we've felled down the hill; then we'll cut the trunk into pieces that we can load into the wagons," planned Harlan.

"Sounds good," Charlie agreed. "Any idea what we're having for dinner?"

"No. I'm sure it will be good, though. Is your buzz saw all set up?"

"Dad was working on that when I left," Charlie said. "It'll all be ready when we get there. We'll have these loads cut up in no time."

The men arrived back at the campfire to find Marty stirring a pot of baked beans with a ring of pork sausage sliced into it. She had opened a pint jar of home-canned pears, and Mrs. Meyer had also sent a pan of cornbread that had been baked that morning. To drink, mason jars of the morning's rich milk had cooled in the chill air to a thirst quenching temperature. In all, it was a meal that would replace the energy Harlan and Charlie had burned during the morning as well as keep them fueled through the hard labor of the afternoon.

"Mmm! Looks and smells great," Harlan said as he sidled up to Marty.

"Thanks, but I can't really take much credit for it. I just warmed up what Mama sent along," Marty demurred.

"Who said anything about the food? I was talking about you," Harlan teased.

Marty giggled and gave Harlan a kiss on the side of his chin.

"Whoa!" Charlie interrupted their moment. "What's all this?"

"Oh, didn't you know?" replied Marty in mock surprise. "Harlan and I are officially courting."

"No, I did *not* know. How long has this been going on?" quizzed Charlie.

"Since yesterday," Harlan grinned.

"Well, it's about time! I can't say that I'm surprised; we've all seen this coming for quite a while." He then clapped Harlan on the back and said jovially, "Congratulations, my friend. You've chosen very well for yourself."

"So is this public knowledge? Can I tell the folks?" Charlie asked. "I gotta tell you, after all of you left Thanksgiving to go home for chores, the two of you were all that we could talk about. They'll all be so excited when they find out that you're going together."

"I'd be surprised if Aunt Louise doesn't already know. I'm just about sure that once we left to come out here this morning, Mama got on the telephone and brought her up to date," said Marty.

"She may not have, though, because she doesn't like it when other people listen in on the party line," Charlie countered.

"They might have done it in German, though," Marty said. "That way, only Mrs. Kloeser would have understood, and she's never been one to nose in on other people's phone conversations."

"Well, either way, you're all right with the news getting out?" Marty shot an inquiring glance at Harlan.

"I don't think we're trying to keep any secrets," Harlan shrugged.

"Good!" Charlie returned. "Everyone will be excited. As Dad says, 'That Harlan must have had fine parents because he is a good, honorable young man.'"

Those words rang in Harlan's mind all afternoon as he and Charlie went about their wood gathering work. The two spent a long time on either side of the cross-cut saw, chunking the larger logs into pieces that the three of them could load into the wagons. Then, once their wagons were full, the threesome traveled back to Charlie's home, where Vernon's buzz saw was connected to a gasoline engine so that all of the firewood could be quickly cut into stove length pieces.

Harlan was aware that he should be pleased with the reputation he had earned among the members of Marty's family, but something about hearing their sentiments put into words made Harlan feel that he was being deceitful by letting them believe these misinformed opinions regarding his goodness. With every rhythmic stroke of the cross-cut, and with every scream of the buzz saw, Charlie's quote from his father echoed in Harlan's head. He had been completely caught up in his new life in Christ, and there had been no room in his thoughts for his mother. That made him feel guilty again, and then his conscience bothered him because he knew full well that he was neither good nor honorable.

But then again, hadn't he read in the Bible that all people had sinned and fallen short of the glory of God? Weren't *all* of his sins covered by Jesus' blood? Wasn't the grace of Jesus all-sufficient? Some aspects of Harlan's new faith were very confusing to him. Contemplating these things rendered Harlan exceptionally quiet for the afternoon, but no one noticed it because the work that he was doing was not conducive to conversation.

The three young people worked until there was only enough sunlight left for Harlan and Marty to get their team and wagon safely home in time for chores. On the way, Marty nestled closely against Harlan's side on the wagon seat, so he transferred the reins to one hand and circled his other arm around her.

"It's been a good day, hasn't it?" Marty reflected quietly.

"Uh-huh."

"We still don't have enough wood for the winter," Marty said, "but every wagonload helps, and there will be more days we can cut again."

"Yeah," Harlan replied.

Marty sighed contentedly. "You know, ever since yesterday, I've had this new feeling that all of time stretches before us and we have no reason to hurry through life—like we've got all of our forever, you know." She paused for a moment and then added, "Now, don't take that to mean I've changed my mind about wanting a short courtship, though." She gave Harlan a squeeze, which he returned absently.

They rode a few more yards until Marty poked Harlan and broke the silence. "You've been awfully quiet the whole afternoon."

"Have I?" he asked.

"You have," she affirmed. "A penny for your thoughts?"

"You know me so well already," Harlan returned, focusing his attention more fully on her. "You can keep the penny. I'm just thinking about Charlie saying that Vernon thinks I'm a 'good and honorable man.' and that I must have had good parents."

"And?" Marty prompted after several seconds of silence had again ensued.

"To begin with, I'm neither good nor honorable," Harlan admitted.

"'As it is written, There is none righteous, no not one.' Romans 3:10," Marty quoted.

"I know, I know. It's just..."

"You're thinking about *it* again, aren't you?"

"If by 'it' you mean my 'big sin,' yes," admitted Harlan.

"Harlan, I don't know what it was, and I still don't feel that I need to know, but I want to be sure that *you* know a few things. First, I don't know how the Holy Spirit may be working to convict you regarding all of it, and I don't want you to believe that anything I say overpowers His leading. Remember, though, that Jesus Christ's blood provides us with all-sufficient grace. I know you know that.

"That said, I also want you to know that for me, your life didn't begin until you arrived here, and then it began again when you were born again. I've told you that before, but what I'm trying to say is that I'm willing to marry you for the person that you've been since I've known you and the person that you are becoming in Jesus Christ. That's how much I trust you.

"Lastly, no matter what you decide you need to do about your 'big sin'—if anything—I will stand behind your decision no matter what the consequences are. That's also how much I trust you."

"What about my mother?" Harlan asked.

"You know what I think, but how you handle her is up to you. Clearly I don't know all of the details, so again, I bow to your wishes."

Harlan pulled Marty more snugly into his side and kissed her on the temple. "What was God thinking when he blessed me with a woman like you?" he asked huskily. "I certainly am not good enough to deserve you." Harlan breathed deeply and then continued, "I haven't decided what to do about Mom yet, but when I do, I'll let you know because I may need your help."

They rode in silence for a while longer, the setting sun nearly blinding them as they traveled west toward home.

"Perhaps I just need to let the past be in the past," Harlan reflected at length. "If you are willing to build our future on an entirely new foundation, then I am too."

Marty squeezed Harlan's knee affectionately, solidifying his resolve to focus on building their life together. The two commenced planning for that future during the remainder to the trip home.

As so often happens to humankind, the plans that seemed to

gleam gloriously in the starlight were revealed to be pock marked in the harsh morning sun. A nightmare had awakened Harlan in the morning hours. In it, Marty's cousin Donald's pointer finger was wagging in his face again; only this time he was not being compared to the bank teller in some far away place. His true identity was being revealed, and he was being forcibly dragged away from the Meyer farm.

The dream caused him to be in a foul mood when he got out of bed on Sunday morning. The world that he and Marty had built for themselves in their imaginations the night before was eroding away as memories and fresh revelations were colliding in his mind. He left the house earlier than usual and trudged silently to the barn before Marty was ready to accompany him and mechanically brought the dairy cows to their stanchions.

You're such an idiot! Harlan's conscience tormented him as he sat down on his stool beside Betty. *Building a life with Marty at this point would be like the foolish man building his house upon the sand: one little slip and everything will come crashing down. That isn't fair to her, it isn't fair to Mrs. Meyer, and it wouldn't be fair to any children that you might have. Just think how panicked you were at Thanksgiving dinner when you thought Donald was going to reveal what you truly are! Do you want to live life with that kind of uncertainty—in that kind of fear?*

Then, the other side of his mind engaged in his inner conversation. *All right, but what are you going to do about it? You know very well that if you confess to what you've done, the chances of you ever being happy—for that matter the chances of you ever being free—are all shot to pieces. What about just living here as the hired man for the rest of your life? You can avoid detection, still enjoy Marty's presence and friendship, but not put yourself or her at risk by marrying her.*

It'll never work, his saner side argued. *Both you and she want more from this relationship than to just live out your days as friends, and you know it. As you are right now, you are only offering Marty half a man for a husband because you will be so distracted by your past. Nothing you are doing right now is fair to her!*

What was that verse that Marty quoted to you the other day? Harlan asked himself. *"If we confess our sins, he is faithful and just to forgive us our sins, and to cleanse us from all unrighteousness." That's really what you're going to have to do.*

But if I do that, everything is gone. Everything!

Harlan, Jesus wants obedience in all things, not just some things. Not just the things that we find it convenient to give Him.

Thus was the dialog in Harlan's mind when Marty entered the milking parlor of the barn.

"You're awfully speedy this morning," she commented lightly.

Harlan grunted his acknowledgement of the comment.

"Sure is cloudy outside. Too bad we don't know what Earl May has to say about the weather *this* morning," Marty complained lightly, referring to Thursday's conversation about the lack of a radio in the Meyer household. "What do *you* think about us getting a radio when the electric lines are strung?"

"I haven't really thought about it, I guess," he answered distractedly.

There's another thing you'll be giving up if you turn yourself in: evenings with Marty reading aloud, Harlan thought.

Marty continued trying to engage Harlan in happy conversation for a little while, but as she sensed that he was not in the mood to visit, she stopped. As he gave no sign of being hostile, Marty attributed Harlan's mood to fatigue from the previous day's hard labor and resorted to quiet humming.

The news of Harlan and Marty's courtship had traveled quickly through the congregation of the tiny country church, a good many of the people having been made aware of it through the overactive grapevine the day before. As it was not an official engagement or the like, the news was not accompanied by congratulatory remarks from anyone; rather, the couple merely noticed a large number of covert glances and sly smiles directed their way. During Sunday School, Harlan and Marty could now sit together with the approval of the other young unmarrieds, and Marty took Harlan's hand in hers and fell to her habit of affectionately tracing the veins in the back of it. Harlan would have completely enjoyed the familiar gesture had his mind not been otherwise occupied.

The text for the Sunday School lesson was from the second chapter of 1 John, and Harlan felt particularly convicted when Charlie read the ninth verse aloud: "He that saith he is in the light, and hateth his brother, is in darkness even until now."

Harlan did not feel that he hated anyone *now*, but his "big sin" had been an act of hate, hadn't it? And while it had not been directed at a brother in Christ or a true blood brother, in a sense the sin had definitely been committed against someone who would be considered a sort of brother to Harlan. Further, he was tired of the darkness his sin was causing him. For months now, it had been his own personal storm cloud which followed him everywhere.

Harlan stole a glance at the loving woman beside him. What was it she had said to him almost two weeks ago? It was something about sin causing people to lose fellowship. Harlan realized that even though he had repented and been forgiven, he had a sin in his life which was causing him to lose fellowship. It had cost him his good relationship with his mother, and it was already building walls of nervousness and fear between him and happiness with the woman he loved. Further, if his sin was discovered, it had the potential to rob him of his relationship with Marty altogether.

It was true that the last fourteen days had been filled with the joy of his coming to faith in Christ, but he was never going to be able to completely live in that joy until something changed. Rev. Martin's words became a blur as Harlan realized that even though his sin was forgiven in the sight of God, there were earthly consequences which he alone had to bear.

As drastic as the consequences would be, Harlan knew in that moment that a full confession to both Marty and the authorities was in order. What he had to tell her would break her heart, but at least she would have a chance to take hold of her life again before she was legally tethered to Harlan as strongly as she was emotionally tied to him. Everything in his human nature rebelled at the idea of a full disclosure of the events of his past, and Harlan began to feel very sick to his stomach as he could see his future dissolving in front of him.

Chapter *Twenty-Eight*

December 1, 1935

"Listen, I'm...I'm not feeling very well," Harlan whispered to Marty in the back corner of the balcony after the Sunday School hour had concluded.

His face was indeed flushed and drawn, and even his posture was less erect than usual, so Marty instantly believed him to be ill.

"I...I'm going to walk home. That way you and your mom will have the car after church is over."

"You should let Mama or Roy or someone drive you. I'd go with you, but I have to sing in the choir," Marty protested.

"No, I don't think a ride in a car would be good with my stomach feeling the way it is. I'll be fine walking," he said.

The expression on Marty's face told Harlan that she was afraid he was going to run away or that there would be a repeat of the scene that played out in the barn loft two weeks earlier.

He took both of her hands in his. "Look," he said with urgency, "I promise I'll be home when you get there. I'll be fine; I just...I need some fresh air."

She put a hand on his brow to check for fever. Finding none, she acquiesced, "All right, but please be careful."

"I will," he said. Then, feeling that it might be his last chance to do so, Harlan planted a quick kiss on her forehead and then slipped down the stairs and outside the church building just as the first chords of the prelude thundered forth from the reed organ.

The cold damp November air hit Harlan hard once he was on the other side of the heavy double doors. He had hoped that it would steady his nerves, but it had the opposite effect since it drove home the feelings of loneliness whose tentacles were closing in on his heart.

He started to walk back to the Meyer farm and began praying as he did so, the urge to bargain with God gaining ground in his mind the more he considered what the repercussions of a full disclosure would really entail.

"Heavenly Father, I don't want to confess!" Harlan began aloud once he was out of earshot of the church. "What earthly good will it do? If I let bygones be bygones, no one will be the wiser. You know that I'm not going to commit murder again. I didn't even do it on purpose in the first place!

"If I confess, I'm going to end up spending the rest of my life in prison somewhere completely miserable. If I just let it go, Marty and I can be happy, build a life together that brings glory to you, raise children who love you! Where is the sense in the colossal waste that my life would be if I were jailed?"

Suddenly, a Bible verse that Marty had quoted to him weeks ago popped into his head: "He that covereth his sins shall not prosper: but whoso confesseth and forsaketh them shall have mercy."

"But I've confessed my sin to you!" Harlan cried. "And I've just told you that I've forsaken it!"

"Confess your faults one to another, and pray one for another, that ye may be healed. The effectual fervent prayer of a righteous man availeth much." James 5:19 popped into Harlan's head. He and Marty had read that verse together a few days ago. Harlan did feel the need for healing, but he knew that the cost of this healing would be great.

Besides that, there was something in Harlan which continued to tell him that he *needed* to suffer the earthly consequences for his sin. It made no sense, and he couldn't have defined it if someone had asked him to, but the need was there nonetheless. Full confession was his only choice—as repulsive to his nature as it was.

As he continued to make his way toward the Meyer farm, he imagined what the scene was going to look like when he divulged the truth to Marty and Mrs. Meyer. He figured that Mrs. Meyer's disapproval would be evident right away, and he would be able to withstand that. But imagining the hurt which he would see in Marty's eyes caused him to lose control of his nausea. He left the roadway enough to vomit in a small wild plum thicket along the fence row.

He resumed his journey with stomach acid burning his mouth, and the front of his new white shirt stained.

"All right, Lord. I know what I have to do, but I'm weak and foolish, and I'm going to need you to be with me and give me strength and resolve along every step of the way," Harlan prayed aloud again. "I want to be obedient to you in all things, but, Lord, help me. Help me!"

When Marty and Mrs. Meyer entered the house an hour and a half later, Harlan was sitting in his undershirt and good black pants near the kitchen stove, and his white shirt was soaking in the dishpan. On his knee was a pad of writing paper, and he was penciling notes and details as quickly as he could.

"What happened?" Marty asked, pointing to his soaking shirt.

"I upchucked on the way back and got a little on my shirt. Sorry."

"Do you feel better now?" Mrs Meyer asked, ever the pragmatist.

"Not really."

Marty came to his side and gently massaged his shoulders.

"I hope it didn't embarrass you too much that I left church," Harlan said, patting one of her hands. He realized that for him to leave during church on the first Sunday after their courtship was announced was very bad for appearances, but he figured it would be nothing compared to the shame she was about to endure.

"You can't help that you are sick," Marty responded sympathetically. "What do you think caused your upset stomach?"

"Nerves," he answered flatly. "I need to talk to both of you."

Marty, whose thought processes were completely occupied with their new courtship and the reaction it created in the congregation, immediately assumed that Harlan had been nervous because the people at church were whispering about them. That, coupled with the tone of Harlan's voice, caused her to believe that he was now nervous about their relationship and was about to put an end to it. She saw red and immediately moved into emergency mode.

"Harlan, please don't be nervous about the people at church. They mean well, and with the exception of Esther Stempel, they are all happy for us. They're no reason to call off…"

"Huh? What are you talking about?" Harlan asked, utterly confused by the urgency in Marty's voice.

"Your nerves. The people at church didn't mean to upset you or embarrass you. They just have to get used to us, is all. Why, six months after we're married, not a single one of them will give two hoots and a holler about you and me. *Please* don't make any decisions based on them." The tone in her voice brought his attention to her concern, and it finally dawned on him that she had misunderstood his intentions.

"No, no, that's not why I'm nervous. Nothing about you—or you and me together—makes me nervous. That's not why we need to talk. What's got me nervous is my 'big sin.' I need to tell you about it."

That statement caught Mrs. Meyer's attention, and both women were soon seated at the kitchen table with Harlan.

"At Thanksgiving dinner the other day when your cousin Donald said he was trying to figure out why I looked so familiar to him, he had me really worried because I was at Lewis and Clark State Park about three months ago. I don't remember meeting him at all, but I thought maybe he had seen me from a distance because I was there with a group of guys from the CCC. The Civilian Conservation Corps is scheduled to build a lodge there next year, and I was sent along with two other guys to help gather information for the planning process.

"The other guys in the group were two fellow enrollees who had been in my section for a while. One was named Ben Jensen. He and I were no relation to each other, but because we had the same last name, we joked about being long-lost cousins. Ben was a great guy and extremely smart. You wouldn't know it to look at him or hear him speak. He talked real slow, and he had one eye that didn't focus on whatever he was looking at. But the guy could add huge sums in his head, could remember all of the geometry and other math that he had learned in high school, and just had a real mind for logistics, which is why he was with us on the scouting trip to Lewis and Clark. For example, one time he was serving as mess steward, and he got into this big argument with the cook because he could see that the cook had not ordered enough potatoes to feed all of us. The cook lost the argument when one of the assistant cooks took up Benny's side, but as you can imagine, the whole deal didn't ingratiate him with the head cook much.

"Anyway, Ben was pretty out of place in a lot of the work we did. I mean, he was able to pass his physicals and everything, but he just wasn't built like most of the guys like me who had to operate a shovel most of the time. The higher-ups were just beginning to get wise to Ben's abilities before I left, and there were rumblings that he was going to be promoted to other types of administrative-type jobs.

"But there was this one guy who would give Ben a bad time. His last name was Conti. I don't really know what his first name was because we all called him by his nickname 'Digger.' I always thought everybody called him that because he was always getting his digs into everyone. Others told me that he was called that because he had worked as a gravedigger before getting into the

CCC. I don't know if that was true or not; he certainly was good with his shovel. He could dig circles around any two other guys. At any rate, he was a short, dark-haired fellow with a filthy mouth, who was constantly stirring up trouble.

"The worst of it was, he was one of those guys who would do something nasty when no one was looking, and if anyone said anything to him, he always played innocent. I mean, the guys in charge of the CCC were always trying hard to make sure that we all behaved ourselves, and most everyone was great. But Digger was something else. One time in the middle of the night, I saw him get up and walk over to another guy's bunk and…sorry—that's not a story I should tell to ladies." Harlan's face turned pink.

"Anyway, Digger targeted Ben all the time. For example, if we were spading on a line, Digger would wait until all the supervisors were out of earshot and then he would make fun of Ben, or if they were near each other, Digger would throw every second shovel of dirt he had dug right into Ben's area to make Ben's progress even slower—and he was already awfully slow. "Sometimes Digger would mimic the way Ben talked, and other times he'd make fun of his bad eye. Most of the time Ben just put up with everything, never saying anything, never complaining. I don't know how he did it. I know I couldn't have.

"Sometimes, Digger would get other guys to gang up with him against Ben, but it wasn't often—partly because they weren't as good about keeping everything secretive and partly because they would never go as far as Digger wanted them to. The weird thing about when Digger would get other guys to make fun of Ben with him was that a lot of times, one of the other guys would later apologize to Ben, and I think that was the only thing that kept him from going completely crazy.

"To be completely honest, that's how Ben and I became friends. When our section was first formed and none of us knew each other yet, I was one of the guys that Digger convinced to gang up on Ben. We were sitting around just before lights out, and Digger told us all to parrot whatever Ben said in an exaggerated mockery of the way he spoke. We did it all right, but when I saw the look on Ben's face after he realized that we were making fun of him, I was so ashamed that I vowed then and there that I was never going to do anything to hurt him again. Ben didn't do anything to fight back; he didn't argue—nothing. I found out later that he was raised a Quaker somewhere in eastern Iowa; that's why he didn't do anything to retaliate.

"What he did do that first night was stop talking, and for some reason that ate at me more than it would have if he had started screaming and punching. I lay awake that night because I felt so bad about being a part of such an nasty thing, and I could tell that Ben wasn't asleep either. So, after it seemed like everyone else was asleep, I whispered an apology to Ben and promised that I'd never again do anything to make fun of him. All Ben did was whisper 'Thanks,' but I had heard him speak once more, so I knew he was going to be all right. It was only a few seconds after I had said I was sorry that I heard his breathing indicate that he was asleep too, and then I was able to fall asleep that night.

"That was how we became friends. From then on, I'd try to stick up for him when I could. If I was next to him on the shoveling line and Digger or one of his cronies would throw extra dirt on Ben's section, I'd try to work double quick to help him out. Of course, that made Digger mad at me, so he started trying to treat me the same way he treated Ben. Not being a Quaker and not being a Christian yet, though, I didn't have any qualms about putting Digger in his place in a big hurry, so he kind of laid off me, but it was almost like he dished it out to Ben even worse then.

"The senior leaders and other enrollees began to see that Ben was better suited to other jobs than just the manual labor that we were mostly given, and they started finding jobs here and there that put Ben's brain to work more than his arms. I think that made Digger jealous, but he began to lay off of Ben because the higher-ups were taking more notice of him now that they could see his usefulness.

"Well, come September, the CCC decided to send the three of us over to Onawa to the Lewis and Clark State Park to make plans for next year's project there. I know why they sent Ben. They had given him a list of questions like how many barracks could be set up on such and such a stretch of land, how many men would it take to do this and that, and so on. Ben just ate that stuff up. Well, it was soon obvious to Digger and me that we were only there to be Ben's assistants. I was fine with that, but it rubbed Digger the wrong way, as you can imagine.

"For sleeping accommodations we three had to share a tent together. Well, along about the fourth night a strange noise woke me up, and I discovered that it was Ben crying in his sleeping bag, and Digger was gone. It took some coaxing to get Ben to tell me why he was so upset, and I won't tell you what he finally told me, but there was no way I was going to let what Digger did to Ben go unpunished.

"I got dressed and snuck outside the tent and waited for Digger to come back. When he did, we got into a scuffle, of course, and since I had a good six inches of height on Digger, I got the better of him in short order. I'll also admit that I wasn't exactly fighting fair."

At this point in his tale, Harlan's voice began to change, and he could no longer make eye contact with his two listeners.

"All I wanted to do to Digger was make sure that he was never going to do anything like that to Ben again. I started to tell him that if I even suspected him of repeating his actions, he'd sorely regret that he'd ever been born.

"Then, I remember Digger saying to me, 'What's the matter? It's not like I did anything to *you*.' And, something just snapped inside of me at that moment.

"To make a long story short, I was in such a rage that all I could think about was hurting Digger *bad*. The last things I remember about the fight were my hands around Digger's neck and his body suddenly going limp."

Harlan was having trouble keeping his emotions in check, and his voice was shaking deeply as he recollected the horrible events of that night.

"I didn't mean to kill him, but I had, and I panicked at that moment. I hauled his body off into a grove of trees nearby and ran. I was running from then until I jumped off the train in your back pasture."

Harlan could not bring his eyes up to the faces of the two ladies, but he heard Mrs. Meyer clear her throat, and he saw Marty pull a handkerchief from her sleeve and then blow her nose. Her shoulders were shaking in silent sobs, and Harlan was sure that their courtship was over.

Chapter Twenty-Nine

December 1 & 2, 1935

Silence hung heavily in the kitchen for a few moments, and Harlan had never heard the clock tick so loudly before.

"I know this changes everything," Harlan finally said apologetically. "I understand if you want me to leave right away."

"Leave?" Marty asked frantically. "What do you mean?"

Harlan explained, "I've been living here under false pretenses. I'm a murderer, so if you want to kick me out..."

"Shhh, don't say that!" Marty scolded, scrambling into Harlan's lap so that she could stop his mouth with her fingers.

"But it's the truth," Harlan said. "My plan is to go into Council Bluffs tomorrow and turn myself in."

"No, no, please!" Marty begged, clutching a handful of his undershirt. "Can't we just...Well, I mean if no one has..."

"Marty." Mrs. Meyer said her daughter's name in that grave tone a mother uses to tell one of her children to hush up without saying so directly.

"Oh, Harlan!" Marty wailed and buried her face in his chest, crying quietly.

Harlan's arms wound around around her instinctively. "I'm sorry. I shouldn't have let you fall in love with me, and I shouldn't have let *myself* fall in love with *you* when I've done something so heinous."

"I don't know if I'd call it 'heinous,'" Mrs. Meyer said evenly. "But it certainly is the kind of thing I'm most afraid of."

"Mrs. Meyer, please believe me when I say that I'm in no danger of killing anyone else. You don't have anything to be afraid of."

"No, it's not you that I'm afraid of," Mrs. Meyer explained. "It's the kind of situation you find yourself in. The bad things I'm most afraid of doing are the ones that I don't intend to do, the ones where I've accidentally lost control, like killing someone in a car accident. I wouldn't mean to do it, but I'm still at fault. For some reason, it seems like the guilt associated with those kinds of things is worse than if you'd purposely set out to do someone harm."

"But that's just it, Mama. It *was* an accident. You heard Harlan say that he didn't really intend to kill Digger Conti. And either way, Jesus' grace is all-sufficient, right? If Harlan turns himself in, you know he'll land in prison, and I just can't..."

"Marty." Mrs. Meyer was speaking in her authoritative maternal tone again. "Here is your Bible. Open it to 2 Samuel chapter 11 and start at the second verse." Mrs. Meyer slid Marty's Bible across the kitchen table to the place in front of the chair Marty had vacated when she crawled into Harlan's lap—a gesture that Marty knew meant that her mother expected her to return to her own chair.

Marty did as was instructed and began reading 2 Samuel 11 aloud: "'And it came to pass in an eveningtide, that David arose from off his bed, and walked upon the roof of the king's house: and from the roof he saw a woman washing herself; and the woman was very beautiful to look upon.'

"Mama, this is the story of David committing adultery with Bathsheba. Harlan hasn't committed adultery," Marty protested.

"I know that; just keep reading."

Marty did as she was told, recounting the familiar story of King David's indiscretion with Bathsheba, the baby that was the result, and David's failed attempts to conceal his sin. Mrs. Meyer didn't stop her until she had read the words of the prophet Nathan in the twelfth chapter: "'The Lord also hath put away thy sin; thou shalt not die. Howbeit, because by this deed thou hast given great occasion to the enemies of the Lord to blaspheme, the child also that is born unto thee shall surely die.'

"Mama, I still don't see what this has to do with Harlan's situation," Marty said in frustration.

"After King David confessed that he had sinned against God in committing adultery, having Uriah killed, and trying to cover everything up, Nathan told him 'The Lord hath put away thy sin.' In other words, God had forgiven David for all the terrible things he had done. However, there were still earthly consequences that David had to bear for his sins, and that is why his first son with Bathsheba died.

"I have no doubt that Harlan is forgiven for the sin of killing this Digger fellow, but I think that it's obvious that the Holy Spirit is convicting him regarding the fact that he must suffer the earthly consequences too," Mrs. Meyer explained.

"But Bathsheba's first husband Uriah was an honorable man, and Digger Conti was not. It sounds to me like the world is a better place without him in it," Marty reasoned.

"I agree with everything you said," Harlan put in, leaning forward in his chair so that he could caress Marty's elbow. "The problem is that it was not my place to decide that Digger's life should end when it did, and I only made things worse by running and trying to hide what I had done. Basically, my sin stems from my lack of self-control."

Marty's face melted into grief again, and she sought Harlan's embrace once more. "But everything we've planned...it's all gone just like that," she sobbed.

"I'm so sorry," Harlan repeated, "but don't you see that the way things are is no good either? It's like I'm only half a man because so much of my brain is taken up with remorse. I can't put up with the kind of guilt I've been living with for the next forty or so years, and I don't want to live the rest of my life wondering when I'll be found out and forcibly taken away from you. That isn't fair to you at all. This way, you can still build a wonderful life with someone else."

"I don't want anyone else!" Marty declared, climbing into his lap once more and clinging to his neck as if by weighing him down with her body she could prevent him from being taken away from her.

"I don't either," he breathed.

Marty vowed, "I'll wait for you."

"Absolutely not!" Harlan exclaimed, removing her arms from his neck so that he could look her in the eyes. "You mustn't promise things like that in the heat of this moment. I'll be in jail for the rest of my life; you can't put your own life aside like that. You told me yourself that you believe God has created several men whom you could be happily married to. You have to make up your mind to love someone else. It will be easier in time."

"All right, you two melodramatics," Mrs. Meyer said a bit condescendingly, "we need to look at the facts here before you both get all hot and bothered. First, if everything is as Harlan has described it, we're not even sure that what's-his-name is really dead."

"That's right! We've never heard from Donald that a body was found at the park," reasoned Marty. "Couldn't we get a hold of Donald on the phone? You could give him directions to where Digger's body was when you left, and then he could go look. If it's not there, you're off the hook."

"It's not like the park is small, though, and we had camped in kind of an out-of-the-way place. It was dark when we fought and I left; I'm not sure that I could give him directions to the body. And even if the body isn't there now, that doesn't prove my innocence. Wild animals could have done all kinds of things to the remains by now."

"I still say that he may have just been unconscious," Mrs. Meyer reiterated.

"He was dead," Harlan confirmed.

"All right, let's suppose he is. Now, I'm no legal expert mind you, but it would seem to me that if Ben Jensen can be located, he would be able to testify on your behalf about the horrors that were committed, and that would go a long way to reducing your punishment. What do you think happened to him?"

"I guess I'm not as good a friend to him as I thought because I haven't really considered what might have happened to him once I ran off." Harlan ruminated for a moment. "I suppose that after neither Digger nor I returned to the tent, he might have looked around for us a little bit. I doubt that he would have found Digger's body, so I suppose he would have traveled back to the CCC camp and told his superiors that we had both deserted."

"Well, all right," Mrs. Meyer said with decision. "Harlan Jensen, you've made a humongous mess, so you've got a lot of cleaning up to do. I think you're right to go into the Bluffs tomorrow and turn yourself in at the sheriff's office, but before then you've got some letter writing to do. I'd say you owe Ben Jensen a letter apologizing for what you've put that poor young man through."

Marty asked timidly, "And, Harlan, could you also write a letter to..."

"...my mother? Yes, I will," Harlan finished for her.

That Sunday afternoon at the Meyer household was perhaps even more somber than the afternoon after Mr. Meyer had passed away. Harlan wrote the letters which had been discussed and then finished jotting down as many notes as he could regarding what he could remember of Conti's demise since he figured all the details that he could provide would be important to the authorities.

The rest of the afternoon and evening was spent with Marty clinging to him despairingly. As plans had been solidified for the next day, Marty had insisted on traveling with him into the city since she wanted to be with him until it was no longer possible. They decided that it would be best to take the train into Council Bluffs so that Marty didn't have to drive home alone.

The family's time in God's Word that evening was spent reading whatever passages of comfort Marty could think of. While Harlan was definitely at peace with the decision he had made to turn himself in, and while his chosen course of action assuaged his sense of justice, he was not at peace regarding what the rest of his life was going to look like. He also would have admitted to having a hard time finding any kind of solace in the passages that Marty read from God's Word. Psalm 90 afforded him a modicum of relief when he thought about how brief man's life is on Earth compared to eternity, but the thought of living another fifty to sixty years seemed repugnant when he knew that they would be years of incarceration.

The three prayed long and hard together that evening, too, entreating God to protect Harlan as he followed God's leading for his life and asking for his mercy as well.

After Mrs. Meyer had retired to her bedroom to give them a few moments of privacy on what would be their last evening together, Marty climbed back into his lap on the sofa. Harlan was glad that she did so because he wanted to savor the feeling of her petite body resting in his arms and take the memory of the love they shared with him. He hoped to be able to draw on it for comfort during the lonely nights that he was sure his future would hold. He was, however, unsure of the wisdom of spending so much time together at the end. Surely it would be better for both of them emotionally if they began detaching themselves from each other as soon as could be managed. Wouldn't that make the separation easier? He was powerless to protest, though, because all he wanted was yet another and another minute with the woman he loved.

"It doesn't seem possible that only yesterday I felt like we had all of time together, and now we're looking at a matter of hours," lamented Marty in a whisper from lips which were remarkably close to his ear.

Harlan agreed. "This is certainly not the way I thought our tomorrows would look a couple of days ago."

They rested in comfortable silence for a few minutes.

"You know, we both have talked about what a waste it all seems for me to have come here and stayed so long and fallen in love with you, only to have it all be taken away because I now am led to turn myself over to the authorities. I have to say, though, that I think it was God's plan. He knew that I needed to come here and have your family and Roy minister to me because he planned to use this experience to call me to faith in him.

"I'm sorry that this part of it has to hurt both of us so badly— especially you—but I'm so thankful that I've been here over these last few weeks. If I had turned myself in right away like I should have done according to the law, I don't think it would have changed anything regarding my future here on Earth. I imagine I would still be looking at a lifetime spent behind bars, but at least I can now look forward to an eternity with Jesus, and I might not have had that if I hadn't landed here."

"No," Marty disagreed, "if the Lord had chosen you, he would have put people in your way whom he would use to bring you to faith even in prison. I do agree that God had a purpose in bringing you here and causing us to fall in love with each other, though. But for the life of me, I can't see what it is at this moment for all the heartache."

One of Harlan's hands lightly fondled a dark curl of Marty's hair, memorizing the feel of it. "You know, something has puzzled me from the very first day I showed up here."

Marty shifted to a more upright position so that she could see his face. "What's that?"

"How come your parents have never worried about the two of us being alone? I mean, I was a complete stranger when I jumped off the train here, and your mother hadn't even known me for an hour when she sent me out to the field to help you pick corn. What if I'd have been some kind of monster who was going to hurt you in some way?"

"Were you ever tempted to do anything bad to me?"

"No, but that's beside the point."

Marty's strong but delicate fingers fidgeted with Harlan's shirt buttons. "Remember how Mama had been praying for you to come? I think she trusted that God had sent a man who wouldn't be a threat to my safety; plus, she's a very good judge of character. She knew right away that you wouldn't hurt me."

"Did you know it?"

"No." There was a pregnant moment of silence after that admission. "I was a little afraid of you at first, and I scolded Mama a bit when I came in to milk with her that first evening, but I'd already loved you for over an hour by that point, so I was easy on her."

They both giggled a little at that, and Harlan rested his forehead against hers.

"It may sound strange, but I want to thank you for loving me the way you have," Harlan said huskily. "I'm going to look back on our time together as an example of what a woman should be to a man: someone who challenges him to grow in his faith, someone who pushes him to be what God designed him to be." He kissed her tenderly on the nose. "I wish I would have had the time to return the favor."

"You already have more than you know," she said, her lips seeking his.

Livestock chores were completed in a hurry the next morning with a few of them being left for Mrs. Meyer to finish after Harlan and Marty departed for the train station to catch the 7:36 for Council Bluffs. When Harlan finished milking Betty, he felt deep regret at the fact that she had been brought back to the farm where she would pose a threat to Marty and Mrs. Meyer until she could be sold, but he was powerless to do anything about it now.

Harlan put on the set of work clothes that he had been wearing when he arrived at the Meyer farm, feeling that if they were going to be discarded in favor of a striped uniform, he didn't want the clothes from Charlie or Mr. Meyer's sister to be the casualties of his trip to prison.

It was still dark when Harlan and Marty departed the Meyer farm for the train station, and the car's headlights caught the reflection of tiny flecks of snow dotting the air. Later, as the train rumbled toward Council Bluffs, Harlan had the surreal sensation that he was being shuttled toward a premature and incomplete death.

"I've got car fare to carry us from here to downtown," Marty said as she dug in her purse when the two arrived at the railroad depot in Council Bluffs.

"Couldn't we walk instead of taking a streetcar, or is it too far?" Harlan asked with the dual purpose of saving Marty's coin and prolonging their time together.

"We could walk, but are you sure?"

"Yes. Please, let's spend these last few minutes pretending that we're just visiting the city to go Christmas shopping or something," he begged, reverting to his habit of fantasizing during his time with her when he knew it would be short.

Marty silently agreed to this proposal, and the two began to make their way toward Pearl Street. Enterprising merchants had already decorated their windows with shiny garlands and tissue paper ornaments which encouraged shoppers to part with their money in celebration of the upcoming holiday. They stopped to look in several windows, but as their feet took them closer and closer to their destination and the central spire of the Pottawattamie County Courthouse came into view, their mood turned somber and they lost interest in the bustle of commerce around them.

Nestled between the courthouse, the city's beautiful Carnegie library, and a row of stately funeral parlors stood a red brick building that had an almost medieval appearance about it. Except for the front, it was surrounded by a tall black iron fence topped with formidable spikes.

"There's the jail," Marty said quietly. "I suppose that's where we should go." She pointed to the thick wooden double doors at the front.

Harlan's stomach was doing somersaults. He wanted to turn back badly, but he knew that it was impossible for him.

The two paused and prayed one last time together.

"You don't have to go in with me if you don't want to. I understand," Harlan said a few feet from the doors.

"I'm going to stay with you as long as I can," Marty said. "If we get separated right away in there, you must promise me that you'll write us and keep us informed as to what is going on with you. We'll be sure to send you any reply we get from your mother or Ben.

"Keep your chin up and remember that you belong to Christ now. Nothing that they can do to you will take away the liberty you have in Him."

Marty reached a hand up and rested it on the side of his jaw. "Remember that 'even the very hairs of your head are all numbered. Fear not, therefore,'" she whispered; then she rose to her tiptoes and kissed him long and hard.

When she let go, they turned and rapped on the jailhouse door.

Chapter Thirty

December 2, 1935

Harlan and Marty were ushered into a hallway with a large grey-painted staircase in the center of it and a reinforced steel door at the back. Sounds of muffled shouting came through the door into the entry way, and the building felt cold and damp.

The jailer, a barrel-chested fellow with short hair and a somewhat unkempt appearance, ushered them into his office which was a relatively small room to the right of the front door. He indicated that they should sit in a couple of chairs that were across from his desk. "What can I do for you folks?" he asked with visible disinterest.

"My name is Harlan Jensen, and I came to confess to a murder."

Harlan and Marty had both figured that this statement would have earned the immediate attention of the jailer, but the man showed no obvious change in his demeanor.

"And who are you, miss?" the jailer addressed Marty.

"I'm Martha Meyer, his girlfriend."

"Oh." The jailer looked suspiciously at her. "I'm not usually the one to…"

The burden of Harlan's heart suddenly became too much to carry any longer, and, though he had not been invited to do so, Harlan began sharing the story that he had related to Marty and her mother the previous afternoon, this time revealing more details to the jailer, who listened but remained aloof.

When Harlan got to the end of his tale, the jailer leaned back in his chair and pressed his fingertips together. He leveled his gaze at Harlan and scrutinized him intently.

"What brings you in to tell me this now?" he asked.

The question took Harlan off guard, and he initially wanted to avoid answering it directly, but it seemed that honesty would obviously behoove him when talking to a lawman. "Well, two weeks ago I received Jesus as my savior, and since then I guess the Lord has been working on me."

"You got religion, eh?" the jailer said derisively.

"I guess that's one way to put it," Harlan responded, thinking that the jailer's words were utterly insufficient to describe what had happened to him.

"Now, what did you say the name of the dead fella was again?"

"Well, I don't know his first name. We all just called him Digger, but his last name was Conti."

"Where was he from?"

"I don't know for sure. I just always got the impression that he was from somewhere to the east."

"And whereabouts in Lewis and Clark State Park did you leave the body?"

"I'm not sure. It was dark, of course, so it was difficult to tell where I was. I do know that I ran along a lot of Blue Lake's shore before I got out of the park, so I was probably nearer the north side than the south."

"Now what day did you say you committed this murder?"

"Well, I'm not sure about that either, sir." Harlan was beginning to feel rather foolish. "See, when you're in the CCC, if you're just a plain worker like I was, you don't pay much attention to the calendar, just the days of the week. I imagine it might have been a Thursday," Harlan said, lamely.

"And no one else was around who could vouch for the truth of your story?"

"Like I said, Ben Jensen was in our tent, but that was a ways away by the time Digger and I started to fight for real."

Did I dream all of this up? Harlan began to wonder as the jailer's questions made his story sound more and more flimsy.

The jailer studied Harlan over the narrow rims of his glasses for a moment. Then he got up and retrieved a couple of binders from the top of his file cabinet. One binder was filled with wanted posters, and the other appeared to be a collection of official bulletins. The jailer studied the papers in both for a short time, but apparently didn't find anything that caught his interest.

"Tell me again what the relationship is between the two of yous," the jailer instructed, removing his glasses and using them to point at Harlan and Marty.

"Well see, after I ran away from the park, I rode the rails for awhile, just anywhere so I kept moving. I stayed a couple times in a hobo jungle here and there, but mostly I was on the trains when I could be, and I happened to ride on the tracks that cut through the north part of the Meyer farm. I was getting real hungry that afternoon, and I saw this farm that was well-kept, and I thought I might get a bite to eat in exchange for a little wood splitting or some other odd job, see. So I jumped off the train there."

"What day was that?" the jailer interrupted.

"Thursday, October 24th," Marty supplied.

"And you've been living there ever since? Today is December second. Just how much wood did they make you split for that one meal?" Marty and Harlan grinned nervously for a second, thinking that the jailer was making a joke, but a single glance at his humorless face assured them that it was a serious question.

"Well, sir, I came to find out that Marty's dad had had a stroke about a month before I happened onto their farm; then he died after I arrived, and they were in need of a hired man. One thing led to another, and, well, Marty and I fell in love. Fact is, we intended to get married, but then my conscience got to working on me about Digger, and I..."

"Young man," the jailer started with a distinct lack of patience in his voice, "you have come into my office this morning and confessed to murdering a scummy delinquent, but you can't tell me his name, you can't tell me where you disposed of the body, you have no witnesses, and you can't even tell me on what day this alleged murder happened. Your mug ain't on any wanted poster that's been sent here since the first of August, and your name and description ain't on any of the bulletins that the state has sent out during the same length of time.

"This jail ain't no hotel. You can't come in here and give me some song and dance just to make me lock you up so that you can get three squares a day and a place out of the wind to lay your head at night since it's gettin' on ta be winter."

Harlan looked at Marty out of the corner of his eye. He couldn't believe what was happening.

The jailer shifted his focus to Marty and said, "I don't know what you're mixed up with this bird for, missy, but I think it's about time you both got out of my office." With that, the jailer rose from his desk to show them out.

Confused notions were swimming about in Harlan's brain. The jailer had said that he wasn't a wanted man, so all of his fears about being found out were baseless. The jailer had also effectively poked holes in his entire confession, making the cloud of guilt that he had been living under so long seem as if it had been a figment of his imagination. Now, the jailer was basically throwing them out of his office. Didn't that mean that he and Marty could just go home and rest in the fact that without judge or jury he had been exonerated? Harlan shifted to rise out of his chair in obedience to the jailer's invitation to leave, but Marty stayed him with her hand on his forearm.

"Harlan," she whispered, "I want to be able to walk out of here just as badly as you do, but if we go now, you're always going to wonder and feel guilty even if you're truly not. I...I don't want half a man."

Harlan sat back in his chair again. "Sir, I've been sleeping in a warm bed with a full stomach for over a month now, and I'd be crazy to want to leave Marty and the life that we were planning together to spend even a single night here. I'm telling you the truth, and I'd appreciate it if you would take me seriously."

The jailer studied his face for a moment and then returned to his desk and picked up the phone. "Hello? Get me the Monona County sheriff's office, please."

It became rapidly apparent to Harlan and Marty that the chairs they occupied were among the most uncomfortable in the world. Hours passed while the jailer made several phone calls and waited for people to call him back. Deputies brought in a tough-looking fellow who had been caught shoplifting for the second time at Beno's, a popular department store in downtown Council Bluffs, and the jailer had to put his research aside to process the new detainee. Marty was escorted to the opposite side of the building to wait in the kitchen with the jailer's wife while the new arrival was searched and fingerprinted.

Both Marty and Harlan were wide-eyed when they were reunited in their adjoining chairs. The two were alone in the jailer's office because he had had to go deposit the new prisoner in his cell and they obviously did not present a flight risk.

"They don't give them silverware to eat with—just a spoon sometimes!" Marty gasped in a barely audible whisper.

"They also don't give them uniforms to wear," Harlan said. "You get to keep your own clothes, but you have to give up your belt and shoelaces."

"Why do you suppose they do that? You couldn't dig your way out of here with those things."

"They are afraid you'll hang yourself with them," he answered.

"Oh, Harlan, you wouldn't..." Marty's memory had flown back to Harlan's escapade in the barn loft two weeks earlier.

"No, not any more," he assured her, patting her wrist. "You don't have to worry about that."

The jailer returned presently, looked at Harlan and Marty with disdain, and generally gave the air of being disgusted that he had to waste his time with them.

At noon, neither Harlan nor Marty were offered anything to eat, the jailer citing the fact that he could not use county funds to feed just anyone who came along. They took turns making use of the restroom that was behind one of the two doors immediately to their left. Then, the afternoon dragged on miserably with the lawman's attitude growing more and more sour toward them.

"What time does the train leave to take you back?" Harlan asked in a low voice.

"Quarter after four," she answered. "I wish we'd driven ourselves, or better yet, we should have made arrangements for Charlie or Roy to come and help Mama with the chores, and then I could have stayed the night with Aunt Amanda and Uncle Otto."

"But who would have thought we'd have had to wait this long?" Harlan whispered.

The jailer's eyes met Harlan's with loathing; he had obviously heard Harlan's complaint, and he opened his mouth to address it. "If you really did kill someone, you'd better get used to waiting because that's all jail is, buddy. Waiting. You's either waitin' to get out, or you's waitin' to die. And when somebody is in jail for committing murder, it's usually the latter, so I'd hurry and get my..." His phone rang, interrupting his tirade.

"Pott. County Jail...Yessir...You don't say!" The jailer's eyes narrowed on Harlan. "Got it." The clipped phone conversation was over, and the man replaced the receiver on its base, rose from his desk, and crossed the room to lock the office door.

"I didn't believe you 'cause I had a fellow in here just last week who confessed to a crazier crime than yours just so he'd have a home for a while," the jailer spoke to Harlan with new respect in his voice, and Harlan felt odd about the change. "That was the sheriff on the phone. Harlan Jensen, you're under arrest for the murder of Diego 'Digger' Conti."

The next few seconds were a blur as Harlan was divested of his belt and bootlaces and they were given to Marty. She managed to squeeze his forearm affectionately before she was rudely shooed from the room so that Harlan could be searched. Tears ran down Harlan's cheeks at the realization that he would most likely never see her again, and her last memories of him would be watching him be manhandled by this strange jailer.

After his fingerprints were taken, the jailer opened the narrow steel door to his left, revealing a small cube of space with only a can in it, and beyond that a narrow passageway which was sort of a lop-sided "L" shape.

"You'll have to wait in here until I do some rearranging," the jailer said gruffly.

The door slammed shut, and Harlan was left in near darkness. The temporary blindness he experienced while his eyes adjusted served to heighten his other senses, and the first thing he became aware of was the sound of multiple masculine voices speaking at once, echoing against the stark jailhouse walls. In addition to regular conversation, he could hear occasional laughter alongside the repetitive utterances of someone who was obviously suffering from mental illness, and because it had been so long since he had heard any profanity, the swear words seemed to jump out at him more loudly than anything else.

As his eyes adjusted, he could see some grey light coming from the far end of his skinny dungeon, and he began to timidly walk toward it. The source of light was a barred gate which opened into a tall room with large barred windows up high on the walls. Harlan walked timidly toward the light, noting that if he'd had anything to eat at noon, he doubted that the odors that were greeting his nose would have allowed him to keep it down. The dank smell of unwashed men and stale bedding mixed with tobacco smoke and dampness couldn't quite mask the stench of human waste.

Upon reaching the gate, Harlan looked out—and up. He couldn't believe his eyes. To his left was a three-story cylinder made of steel bars, and inside of it were men in wedge shaped cells. At different spots in the exterior of the cylinder he could see a hand or arm protruding from the bars, and one disembodied arm at the very top was engaged in writing some sort of vandalism on the ceiling outside the cylinder. Everything was covered in a dismal gray enamel paint and was even more cheerless than he imagined jail could be.

Doors somewhere above and behind him creaked open and clanged closed, and then Harlan heard the jailer's voice bellow, "Gonna roll!" Immediately, all of the hands and arms were pulled into the cylinder as if by vacuum, and, much to Harlan's astonishment, the pie shaped cells began to rotate within the cylinder.

"Johnson, Traft! You two are gonna be roomies," the jailer shouted, "so, Traft, get your stuff packed double quick."

A barrage of foul language poured forth from a mouth that had clearly smoked a number of cigarettes over the years.

"Shut up, Johnson; you'll be on your way to Fort Madison in a couple o' days anyhow," barked the jailer.

The mention of Fort Madison brought Harlan's emotions to the surface. He wanted to cry but thought it best not to show weakness. He felt his nose leaking profusely, though, so he brought his handkerchief out of his pocket and blew it. Suddenly, a man came from his left and stood just on the other side of the barred door, his towering frame almost completely blocking the light. Before Harlan could take a step back, the man's hands shot between the bars and grabbed Harlan's shirt.

"Ya got any smokes?" he asked threateningly, his foul breath hot in Harlan's eyes.

"I...I don't smoke."

Not satisfied, the giant groped him through the bars, leaving no pocket unturned and never releasing his grip on Harlan's person enough that he could have escaped. Not finding the desired object, the man threw Harlan back and disappeared from the doorway once more. Suitably afraid of being too near the door, Harlan receded into the shadows of his small cell. He could hear more doors open and close above his head, and then the door from his cell to the office opened once more.

The jailer commanded Harlan to walk backward toward the door with his wrists crossed behind him. Through the bars, the jailer attached handcuffs to his wrists and then brought him back into the office so that he could herd him up the staircase at the front of the building.

"We're going ta the third floor, where the guys who've done the worst stuff go, so just keep climbing," the jailer instructed.

Harlan climbed past the doors to the women's quarters, the juvenile cell block, and the infirmary and finally reached the third of the steel reinforced doors which he had figured out were the access points to the cylinder of cells he had seen from below.

The jailer opened the series of doors to give Harlan access to his designated cell and removed his handcuffs. The single lightbulb in the vestibule did little to illuminate the interior of the small room, but Harlan could see that he was not going to be alone once the warden left.

"I'll bring you a tick and pillow for your bed later on," the jailer said. "If I make you move, your tick and pillow go with you so that you can keep your own bugs."

"Sir, what happens next?" Harlan asked naively.

The jailer's face curved into a strange grin. "I already tole you what happens next: you wait—until you die."

Chapter *Thirty-One*

December 2, 1935

Once the jailer left the cell and all of the doors between Harlan and freedom had been bolted and locked, Harlan tried to assess his surroundings. In addition to the incessant noise and the awful stench, the looks of the place were also dispiriting. The wedge-shaped cell was extremely small, and Harlan realized that he could spread his arms and touch both side walls in the majority of it. A recessed area in the point of the wedge served as the toilet, and in front of that were a pair of bunk beds attached to one wall with a utilitarian wooden bench standing against the opposite side. An incomplete deck of playing cards was spread on the bench—along with a partially smoked cigarette—while a pair of laceless, worn out boots stood beside each other underneath.

Harlan's cellmate was lying in the bottom bunk under a thin, ragged blanket. A single dark eye silently examined Harlan, but it did not seem that its owner was hostile. In the scant light, Harlan could see that he was a slight man with particularly spindly arms and legs.

"Gonna roll!" the jailer shouted from somewhere below, and suddenly Harlan felt himself moving as if he were on a slow Victrola. The cylinder stopped when his section of it was facing the north side of the building so that instead of there being a floor on the other side of the bars, he looked two stories straight down and saw the door of the chamber he had been held in before being brought upstairs.

There was very little light on that side of the building despite the large windows, so Harlan judged the time to be somewhere after five o'clock already. The gathering grayness caused everything inside the jail to appear even more grimy than it actually was. This intensified Harlan's depression acutely, bringing to his mind a verse of Emily Dickinson's that his teacher Miss Stanton had made him memorize:

> *There's a certain Slant of light,*
> *Winter Afternoons –*
> *That oppresses, like the Heft*
> *Of Cathedral Tunes –*

Harlan felt that heft in his shoulders and buckled under its weight so that he fell with his face against the bars. He did not cry, but he wanted to; in fact, he knew he would have felt better afterward, but it seemed unsafe to show any such vulnerability this early in his incarceration.

What Scripture would Marty read in a situation like this? he asked himself. Harlan mentally searched what few Bible verses he had memorized in the last two weeks, and only two passages came to mind: "My grace is sufficient for thee" and "All things work together for good to them that love God." Neither of those passages offered much comfort, but he whispered them quietly to himself anyway.

"Ya gonna be all right there, blondie?" rasped the man in the bunk behind him.

Harlan turned around. "Yeah," he replied in a barely audible voice.

"What're ya in for? Mus' be somp'n bad if they brung ya direkly up ta the third floor."

"Murder," answered Harlan.

"Yer too pretty ta be a normal murderer. We got some time b'fore supper. Why don' ya tell me yer story?"

For the second time that day, Harlan recounted the sequence of events which led to him killing Digger Conti. His listener remained horizontal on the bottom bunk throughout the telling, and Harlan didn't bother to get off the floor where he had fallen near the outer edge of the cell. The two men were so near to each other that Harlan could tell his story in a low enough voice that he was sure none of the other inmates heard him. There was a certain amount of comfort to be gained in sharing the story with his cellmate, as it removed a barrier between them. However, Harlan was interrupted by the call for supper just after he had told of his flight along the shores of Blue Lake.

"Gonna roll!" came the jailer's call once more.

"Git away from the bars!" the man said hoarsely.

Harlan did as he was instructed just before the cylinder began revolving.

"I's here only a couple o' days when some dummy kep' his hand in there when the call came. Tore his hand off at th' wrist. Story was he did it o' purpose to be took ta th' infirmry. Thought he c'd ecscape from there easy."

"Did he?"

"Nope." The man threw the blanket off his left arm and revealed a bandaged stump where a hand used to be.

Harlan gasped loudly.

The man was amused by Harlan's shock and began laughing in an unsettlingly phlegmy gurgle. "Skeered ya, didn' I!" The guffaws transformed into a rattling cough that the man had a hard time bringing under control.

Harlan wanted to put some distance between himself and whatever disease gripped the man, but there was no where to go. The man sensed Harlan's discomfort, though, and endeavored to allay Harlan's fears.

"Don't worry; it ain't catching. After he sewn up my arm, the Doc examined me an' told me I's full o' cancer."

"Shouldn't you be in the hospital then?"

"Nah. Too fer along when it'uz caught, and my sen'ence is too long. I's one o' the ones the tur'key is talkin' about when he sez people in jail're waitin' ta die."

"I'm sorry," Harlan said sympathetically.

"I ain't. Least I ain't gonna be in this squirrel cage firetrap long."

The cylinder was turning in a clockwise motion then, causing the cell that the two men were in to be steadily working its way back toward the door where Harlan had entered. This time, though, a door was opened onto a small landing, where plates of food were being passed through a narrow hole by someone on the other side. A single lightbulb dimly illuminated this landing, casting more shadows than light. The jailer was under the lightbulb, calling a head count as the prisoners from each cell came forth to get their supper plates.

"Johnson! Traft!" the jailor shouted as the cell before Harlan's was called out. "You got a new shiner there, Traft?" Harlan could see the jailor stop the prisoner and look at his eye.

"No sir. Ain't new; it's about an hour old," Traft replied sardonically.

"You all right?" the jailor asked.

"Better than Johnson," Traft chuckled.

At that moment, Johnson walked under the lightbulb, and the jailer whistled in disbelief. "Two new shiners, for you eh? You two roomies having a little spat, huh?"

"We just had to get a few things straightened out if I'm going to have to be his bunkie. We're good now," Traft smiled.

When Johnson turned around to head back into his cell with his supper plate, Harlan could see by the look on his swollen face that he was still angry. Harlan was glad he hadn't been put into Johnson's cell!

The cylinder turned again, and it was Harlan and his cell mate's turn to get their supper.

"Jensen! Darby!" called the jailer when the door was evenly situated between the bunks and bench in the cell.

"Can ya sen' mine in wi' Jensen?" called Darby.

"Yup. How are you getting along?" the jailer asked Darby gruffly, but Harlan detected the slightest note of sympathy in his tone.

"Can't complain."

Harlan disembarked from the merry-go-round, retrieving two metal plates holding sandwiches made of bakery bread and some kind of wurst, a few pieces of raw carrot, and a canned peach halve on each. Two metal cups of water were passed through as well. Since Harlan had had no noon dinner, the meal looked delicious to him.

When Harlan returned to the cell, Darby was struggling to raise himself to a sitting position. The man's thick salt and pepper hair and whiskers made it difficult to distinguish his features very well in the dim light, but Harlan sensed something familiar about him. The strain and the change in posture caused Darby to suffer another fit of coughing.

When he had mostly regained control of himself, he croaked, "Here. Shove these cards over." Darby motioned with his stump that Harlan should clear off the wooden bench so he could sit down. While Harlan was bent over completing the orders, the cylinder moved again, causing him to lose his balance and hit is head on the steel wall behind the bench.

"Gotta always brace yerself during mealtimes 'round here," the veteran prisoner advised.

When the rotation stopped for the next men to get out and retrieve their supper, their cell was illuminated by the lightbulb on the landing where the jailer's wife was passing the food through the slit. Harlan and Darby sat down across from each other, Harlan on the wooden bench and Darby on the edge of his bed. When Harlan bent his head to give thanks for the food, out of the corner of his eye he glimpsed the fingers of Darby's right hand. They were so black with filth that they looked like the fingers of a coalminer, and Harlan was never so glad to see anything in his life.

"I know you; you're Dirty Darby!" Harlan cried, almost lurching forward to hug the man in front of him.

"Shhh!" Darby quickly scolded.

Fortunately, Harlan's exclamation coincided with the jailer's shouting of another set of names so no one else heard it.

"You saved my..."

"Shut up, you idget!" grumbled Darby, kicking Harlan lightly.

"You okay in there, Darby?" the jailer called.

"Jus' fine, jus' fine!" Darby called back. "Jus' havin' ta learn the new buck a few table manners is all." Then to Harlan he hissed, "Keep it down, boy. If the tur'key thinks we's friends, he's boun' ta separate us!"

"But you saved my life. Don't you remember?" Harlan was speaking fast now but more quietly. "After I ran off from the park, I hoboed around for a while, but I didn't know much about surviving. You were at one of the jungles I stopped at early on, and you made a big pot of soup with a chicken that you had *borrowed*, and you gave me a bowl with a whole wing in it because you said it didn't look like I was going to live through the night without some food. Do you remember?"

"Boy, I fed so many youngins in jungles an' Hoovervilles o'er the last six years, no way I c'n 'member all."

"It was the worst soup I ever tasted, but it was what I needed that night," Harlan chuckled. He really didn't know Darby at all, but he was so glad to see a familiar face that he felt immediately bonded to the man.

"It 'uz only th' worst soup ya ever tasted 'cuz ya ain't been here long enough ta taste this woman's cookin'," Darby said, motioning with his stump toward where the jailer's wife was dishing up the food.

"What are you in here for?"

"I's in a jungle near n' Bluss here an' a cuppla guys got in a fight. One 'uz hurt bad, so I borrowed a gen'leman's car ta take 'im to the hospital."

"Just stealing a car got you to the third floor?"

"Well, it weren't so much stealin' it as it wuz wreckin' it. I don' know how ta drive, ya see."

"But still," Harlan shook his head.

"Wunst they had me, they had a rap sheet on me long as my arm." Darby held out his mangled left arm and looked at it. "Actully, it 'uz closer ta as long as yer arm," he laughed, once more ending with some deep coughs. "I borrowed a lotta stuff o'er the years."

Both Harlan and Darby chuckled.

"I's awright, though. I'm gittin' too ol' to be Robin Hoodin' aroun' anyways. I ain't got long lef' anymore, an' at least this way the couny will bury me rether than the buzzards eatin' my carcass."

"You look much rougher than you did just a couple months ago. Did something else happen to you?"

"This, that, and t'other. Life's hard on th' outside. There must be more ta *yer* story too. From the looks o' ya, ya ain't seen the inside uva hobo camp or a rairoad car fer some time. Ya e'en smell like ya had a bath recent."

Harlan told Dirty Darby about his stay with the Meyer family and how they had played a part in leading him to faith in Christ, but he left all of the details about his relationship with Marty out since they were too difficult to talk about.

"I's glad ta hear ya found some reeligion; makes me feel like it 'uz awright that I kinda prolonged yer life a leetle with that soup. 'At way, I kinda did ya a good turn if ya hafta go to th' gallows now. Now, as fer me, it's too late, but you's got some time ta kinda make up fer what ya done."

"That's not the way it works at all," Harlan said. He would have liked to explain further, but in the cell next door Johnson and

Traft engaged in a shouting match that was so loud that Harlan and Darby's conversation had to come to a halt.

After they had finished eating, Darby immediately crawled back under the covers of his lower bunk and fell asleep, apologizing to Harlan for not being better company, but saying that he tired out so easily these days and that sometimes it was very difficult for him to sleep at night.

Having Dirty Darby for his roommate completely changed Harlan's attitude about being in jail. He still wasn't happy about his incarceration, of course, but how else could he explain being made into the cellmate of a man who had helped him during his time as a hobo other than to say that it was a miracle from God? Harlan no longer felt abandoned, and this was definitely a cause for celebration, so he stretched his legs in front of him and entered into a time of prayer.

The evening wore on slowly, especially since Harlan expected the jailer to come at any moment with the tick and pillow for his bed. He also was hoping for a blanket since it seemed to be getting colder in the cell as the evening progressed. There was a lot of other activity in the jailhouse that Harlan could hear, and he assumed that the jailer was too busy or had otherwise forgotten to bring him any bedding, but he didn't know how to summon him to remind him, either.

Harlan lifted himself into the metal bunk and lay down, trying to get comfortable. The bed was exceptionally hard and cold, and the sounds and smells of the jail were certainly disconcerting, but Harlan eventually felt himself dropping into a light slumber. He didn't know how long he'd been asleep when a loud ruckus from the next cell erupted.

"Hey!" came Traft's voice, several decibels above what would allow others to sleep. His shout was accompanied by the sound of running water. "What the?"

"Serves you right for roughing me up earlier!" Johnson screamed back.

Traft roared, "You think two black eyes are bad? You'll be lucky if you can even *hear* tomorrow morning let alone see it when I get done with you!"

The whole cell block erupted in shouts, cheers, and summons to the jailer in response to the beginning of another fight between Johnson and Traft.

Dim electric lights were lit on the third level and the jailer's now familiar "Gonna roll!" echoed through the cavernous space just before the cylinder began to turn, this time much faster than what Harlan had experienced before.

"Break it up, you two!" the warden shouted. "Hold him, Traft!"

Harlan deduced from the noises that Traft had gotten the better of Johnson once more and was detaining him so that the jailer could handcuff him through the bars, thereby making it safe to unlock the cell.

"What happened here?" the warden shouted.

Using very colorful language, Traft related that he had been asleep when Johnson decided to exact his revenge by urinating on him as he lay in his bunk.

In response, the jailer announced, "Johnson, you're going to solitary."

All manner of clamor ensued while Johnson was removed from the cell and Traft was allowed to clean up as best he could. Amidst that, Harlan heard Darby rustling around in the bunk beneath him.

"Where's solitary?" Harlan whispered.

"He uses th' cell ya wuz in 'fore he brung ya up here," answered Darby.

"Why would Johnson have done something like that?"

"He's in fer killin' some people in col' blood an' is headed to Fort Madison purty soon where he'll hang fer sure. He's hopin' thet Traft'll kill 'im 'fore he hasta leave cuz he's got nothin' to live fer anymore. Them type o' guys er' the most dangerous cuz they got nothin' ta lose."

This statement scared Harlan because he guessed that he too was headed to Fort Madison to hang. What did he have to lose?

Chapter Thirty-Two

December 3, 1935

At breakfast roll call the next morning, the jailer noted Harlan's lack of bedding. "If I haven't delivered a tick and pillow to you before the noon meal, you be sure and remind me," the man commanded. Harlan noticed that there was some kind of compassion in the man's tone, and figured that the fact that he hadn't complained about the neglect he suffered might have gone a ways toward making the jailer respect him a little.

Again, Harlan retrieved the meal plates for both his cellmate and himself.

"How are you today, Darby?" the jailor asked the sick man.

"Not many days lef' now," Darby said simply, stifling a coughing spell. "I'm 'fraid I need some more rags ta use fer hankerchiffs."

"I'll see what I can do."

When their cell finally rotated around toward the large windows on the south side of the jail house, Harlan could see Darby more plainly than he had at any time the previous day, and he was shocked at how ill the man truly looked and wondered that he'd had the strength to sit up at all.

There was a great deal of noise in the jailhouse in the light of day. Some of the men in the lowest tier of the cylinder were permitted to walk about freely in the bull pen, a few of them taunting Johnson mercilessly. Harlan could hear card games being conducted in some cells, in another cell an inmate was reading a racy book aloud to whomever wanted to listen, and there was the repetitive droning of the mentally ill detainee.

Late in the morning, the now familiar call sounded from the jailor warning the men that he was going to turn the cylinder, and Harlan and Darby's cell was brought around to the east side where the access door was open on the other side of the bars. Much to Harlan's surprise, there stood Roy Schoening on the landing with the jailer.

Harlan's first thought was that something awful must have happened to Marty.

"No, she's as well as can be expected under the circumstances," Roy assured him. "It's her mother who's beside herself."

"Why?"

"I'm not sure exactly. She said something about being confused by what she felt God was telling her and what has happened to you. I don't understand all of the details, but I understand that she's very busy praying for you."

After hearing that the Meyers were all right, Harlan's next reaction was one of embarrassment at having Roy visit him in jail, but Roy quickly put Harlan at ease.

"I went to go visit you this morning at Meyers' and heard the news. Brother, I wish you had told me all about this earlier, but I understand why you didn't. I just wanted to let you know that if ever there was proof of the transformation Jesus made in someone's life, this sure looks like it to me. Praise God for the depth and sincerity of your repentance!"

"Thanks, I guess, but I didn't turn myself in to impress anyone," Harlan said with a nervous glance at the jailer. "I just couldn't live with my conscience anymore."

"I'm not surprised, given the way the Holy Spirit convicts you; I saw that in the barn loft first hand, remember?"

The jailer interrupted them curtly, "I hate to break you two lovers up, but I ain't got all day."

"Sorry," Roy apologized. "Here, Harlan," he said, pushing a paper sack through the bars. "This gentleman said you could have everything in that bag."

"Thank you," Harlan said.

The jailer cleared his throat.

"Gotta go. We're all praying and will do our best to keep track of what happens with you."

With that, Roy turned to leave and the large reinforced door clanked shut behind him.

Harlan sat down on the bench and opened the paper sack. He could see Dirty Darby's single eye focusing on him as he did so. The first things Harlan pulled out were a pencil, a pad of paper, and a few envelopes along with a matching number of postage stamps. Next, he removed a small piece of pink stationery that had obviously been folded neatly until the jailer had examined it. Harlan opened it and discovered that it was a note from Mrs. Meyer. Though Harlan's reading had improved quite a bit since he and Marty had been studying the Bible together in the evenings, he still had difficulty reading, especially if the text was handwritten. Thus, he absentmindedly read the note aloud as he slowly deciphered it.

Dear Harlan,

I am in near constant prayer for you as recent events don't seem to line up with what I think God is leading me to believe in regard to your future with us.

The Lord keeps directing me back to the following passage of Scripture, but I can not figure out why.

"God setteth the solitary in families: he bringeth out those which are bound in chains."
Psalm 68:6

*I wanted you to know in case it helps you understand
something I've misunderstood.*

Much love,
E. Meyer

Harlan did not understand how the verse could be significant and laid the paper aside because the bag still felt heavy. He put his hand down in the bottom of the the dark sack and pulled out a small rectangle.

"Roy's pocket New Testament!" Harlan whispered aloud in disbelief. "It's the one he had with him in the hayloft two weeks ago." Sure enough, when Harlan opened the tiny book, he could see Roy's careful underlining and circling. Harlan was excited to have this small copy of part of God's Word, and he couldn't wait until the cylinder of jail cells was rotated again so that he would have better light by which to read the tiny print.

"Them people ya run onto out'n the country're the real McCoy when it comes ta bein' Christians, huh?" Darby asked. From his place in the lower bunk, he had a clear vantage point to the expressions on Harlan's face, and he could tell how happy the visit and the small paper sack of gifts had made Harlan.

"You bet they are," Harlan agreed.

"Read us th' twenty-fifth chapter of the Gospel of Saint Matthew startin' at verse thirty-five, an' I bet we'll see 'em," said Darby in a gravelly voice.

Harlan did as he was told. "For I was an hungred, and ye gave me meat: I was thirsty, and ye gave me drink: I was a stranger, and ye took me in: Naked, and ye clothed me: I was sick, and ye visited me: I was in prison, and ye came unto me."

Harlan was flabbergasted, and a lump came to his throat. "You're right! They've done every one of those things for me," he observed. "How did you know about that passage? Are you a believer?"

"I wouldn' call me a Christian," he answered, "but I do know th' Bible purty well."

This didn't make any sense to Harlan.

"Whaddya make o' that note the missuz sent you?" Darby inquired.

"I don't know. I wish I had more than just a New Testament here so that I could look up the verses on either side of that Scripture to understand it better," lamented Harlan. "But let's get back to you: I don't understand how you can know the Bible so well and not believe it."

"I didn' say I didn' *believe* th' Bible. I do. I said I ain't a Christian."

"Why not?" asked Harlan quizzically.

"Well, in church I was always taught that ta be a Christian, ya gotta *be* good an' *do* good, and that ain't never been my style."

"Being good and doing good don't make you a Christian; they are just things you do *because* you're a Christian. You become a Christian when you place your faith in Jesus Christ. Remember Ephesians 2: 8 and 9? 'For by grace are ye saved through faith; and that not of yourselves: it is the gift of God: Not of works, lest any man should boast.'" Harlan had learned that much in the last two weeks.

"James 2:26: 'For as th' body without th' spirit is dead, so faith without works is dead also,'" quoted Darby. "It's too late fer me."

With that, Darby started on a severe coughing spell—the worst he'd had yet—and Harlan was alarmed to see blood mixed with the phlegm that Darby wiped on the rag he was using as his handkerchief.

"He'p me...sit...up," Darby requested.

Harlan put his hand on Darby's back and pulled him forward. As he did so, he felt the sharp angles of Darby's shoulder blade beneath his clothing. There was no muscle to speak of between the skin and bones.

Darby's rag was completely saturated by the time the coughing was under control, and Harlan was concerned about what they would do if another bout of coughing occurred before more rags arrived. Moments later, he was glad to hear the jailer's "Gonna roll!" signaling the beginning of the noon meal.

Even though they would be eating soon, the coughing spell had taken a lot out of Darby, and despite his sitting position, he fell asleep during the rotation of the cylinder and did not awaken when it was Harlan's turn to retrieve their plates.

"Here is your bedding," the jailer said as Harlan disembarked the rotating cell.

"Did you remember the rags for Darby?" Harlan asked, pointing to the dark red rag in the sleeping man's hand.

"These were all that my missus and I could find for now," the jailer answered, handing Harlan three cloths.

"Those aren't going to last very long."

The warden hushed his voice and spoke to Harlan as if the two were co-conspirators. "Neither is he. For the second time, you're watching a man die, Jensen, and it looks to me like it's happening fast."

Actually, it's the third time, Harlan thought silently.

The gravity in the jailer's voice made Harlan feel a sense of urgency. He was haunted by the fact that Dirty Darby could apparently know the Bible so well but not have trusted Jesus Christ as his savior. The verses that the two exchanged seemed to be at odds with each other, but Harlan knew that the Word did not contradict itself; it was he who was ill-prepared to explain it.

Harlan got back into the cell with the two plates of food, and as Darby appeared to be asleep, he whispered his prayer before eating. "Lord, I thank you for this food, and again I thank you for putting me in a cell with someone I know. But I most especially thank you for Roy Schoening, the Meyers, and all the wonderful Christians I've met over the last few weeks that You used to lead me to faith in Your Son. I thank You for Your faithfulness to me.

"Lord, I also pray for Darby. Give me the words that he needs to hear in order to change his mind about having faith in You. Please, Lord, before it's too late. I pray these things in Jesus name, Amen."

Darby began to stir a few minutes later when Harlan was almost finished eating the nondescript casserole that was the noon fare.

"I've got your dinner here," Harlan said, handing the elder man his plate.

"Thanks."

Darby managed to get a few bites into his mouth, but then paused.

"You all right?"

"My arm is jus' awful heavy," he mumbled.

Harlan finished the last of his own dinner and laid his plate aside. Then, he scooted the bench forward so that he was within reach of Darby. He took the man's plate of food from his lap, pulled the piece of casserole apart into bite-sized chunks and began feeding Darby. Without silverware, this was an awkward and intimate act which was humbling for both men. At intervals, Harlan even held Darby's cup to his mouth so that he could drink.

After about half of the casserole was gone, Darby waved his hand to signal that he was through eating. "Thank ya. Thet'uz real kind."

"Just think of it as returning the favor. You fed me when I needed it; I'm happy to do the same."

"Sorry I ain't better comp'ny, but I's awful tard." Darby lay down and tried to burrow under the covers of his bed, but it was obvious to Harlan that the declining man was struggling, so he bent and covered Darby up.

The cylinder was situated such that Harlan and Darby's cell was on the south side, so there was now plenty of light for Harlan to be able to read the fine print in Roy's pocket New Testament. He took it out and began thumbing pages. Harlan didn't know whether it was the knowledge that Christmas was coming soon or just what it was, but he felt drawn to Luke's gospel and began reading at the first chapter. The familiar story of the second chapter grabbed his attention so firmly that he just continued reading after that, feeling as if his eyes were being pulled continually toward the next words.

Harlan guessed it to be about two in the afternoon when he was summoned to the bars of his cell, put in handcuffs, and then taken down to the booking office where a man who identified himself as being somehow connected to Monona County waited to question him.

The first question he was asked was whether he could afford to hire his own attorney. Of course, Harland could not, but he also couldn't see why he needed one. He knew he had killed Conti, and he was prepared to suffer the consequences, no matter what they were. Harlan was told that an attorney would be assigned him eventually, but in the meantime, since he was willing to make a full confession, he re-told the same story regarding the particulars of Conti's demise.

The man in the office that morning listened much more attentively than the jailer had, quickly taking notes on a pad of paper.

"And when did you say all of this happened again?" the man quizzed.

"Late September, I think."

"What did you do after you ran off?"

"I hid for a while wherever I could, walking in the darkness until I got to a set of railroad tracks. I rode the rails for some weeks, staying in hobo camps every so often, but mostly keeping on the move in every direction."

The man narrowed his eyes as he listened to Harlan, seeming to gauge whether Harlan was believable. "How did you end up here?"

Harlan related an abbreviated account of his time on the Meyer farm and how he had felt convicted to turn himself in.

The man shifted uncomfortably in his chair, like he didn't trust everything he was hearing. Then he asked, "What were you doing on November seventh?"

Without pausing to think, Harlan answered, "Shoveling corn into the crib at Meyers'. That was the day that all the neighbors got together to pick Mr. Meyer's corn for him."

"How come you can't tell me the exact day that you murdered Diego Conti, but you can tell me what you were doing on November 7th?" the man asked suspiciously.

"Because Mr. Meyer died the next morning. I don't think I'll ever forget November 8, 1935."

"How did he die?"

"Massive stroke."

The man seemed to have trouble believing that Harlan was being truthful. "Can anyone corroborate your story?"

"What do you mean?" Harlan asked. He'd never heard the word "corroborate" before.

"I mean is there anyone who could vouch for the fact that you scooped corn all day on November 7th?"

"There were a good twenty-five men who would have seen me there, I suppose. I don't know if anyone ever got a full count. Roy Schoening scooped corn alongside of me all day. Of course, Mrs. Meyer and her daughter Martha saw me before and after the picking bee," Harlan said. "Why?"

"What about November eighth then? Where were you then?"

"I was at Meyers' all day. Mr. Meyer died about mid-morning, and then a bunch of the neighbors dropped in for the rest of the day."

"Anybody able to verify all of that?"

"Same ones as before."

The Monona County man seemed angry and gave Harlan a look that he did not know how to interpret.

"How'd it go?" Darby asked when Harlan returned to his cell.

"It was strange." Harlan shook his head. "After I told him all about killing Digger, he kept asking me a bunch of questions about where I was on certain days in November. I don't know what that had to do with anything."

"What'd yer 'ttorney say?"

"I didn't have one. I don't really need one when I know I'm guilty."

Darby shook his head and clicked his tongue. "Yeah, but soun's ta me like they's tryna pin another murder on ya. Iffn they kin git two on ya, yull hang fer sure."

Harlan had figured that the gallows would be his fate all along, but Darby's words made him uneasy just the same.

Harlan crawled up into his bunk and resumed reading the book of Luke in the remaining afternoon sunlight while Darby fell back to sleep below. Just before the light waned beyond the point where Harlan could see the fine print, he came to the middle of the twenty-third chapter.

That's it! That's Darby's answer!

In seconds, Harlan was kneeling on the floor, gently shaking Dirty Darby's shoulder to rouse him.

"Let me alone!" Darby snapped, trying to muster the energy to roll over.

"No. Don't go back to sleep. I know why it's not too late for you to be saved! Think about the thief on the cross. He had lived a bad life, but he came to faith while being executed next to Jesus. And Jesus said to him, 'Today shalt thou be with me in paradise.' The thief didn't have time to do good or be good in order to *earn* his way to Heaven, but Jesus himself told him he was going there. That's proof that it is by grace through faith. Darby, I think you're hanging on your cross. Invite Jesus into your heart before it's too late!"

Dirty Darby stared at Harlan but didn't say a word.

Chapter *Thirty-Three*

December 3 - 25, 1935

Darby's condition had visibly deteriorated when the jailer took supper roll call. His breathing was becoming shallow and staggered, and he no longer really had the energy to cough.

"You've got to be in pain, Darby. You want to go to the infirmary? We can have the ol' doc come and at least give you something to make you more comfortable. At least the bed in there might be a little softer," the jailer offered upon seeing him.

"Jus' be a waste," Darby responded without opening his eye. "Jensen'll take kyeer of me."

The jailer shot Harlan a question with his eyes.

"We'll be all right," Harlan responded with a nod.

The officer left them alone then, and Harlan endeavored to spoon some of the vegetable soup that constituted their supper into Darby's mouth, but after only a few sips Darby refused any more.

"You ought to try to eat," Harlan said kindly, his concern for Darby obvious.

"Don' think it'll make any differnce. I ain' gonna see tomorry, Jensen."

"You don't know that," Harlan argued.

Darby responded by merely shaking his head.

Harlan finished his own supper as deep darkness descended upon the jailhouse, and as he did so, he prayed fervently for the man who was slipping away in front of him. The darkness and the warm soup eventually got the better of Harlan, causing him to fall into a light slumber while still sitting on the wooden bench across from the lower bunk.

"So ya think that e'en the thief on th' cross gone to hea'en, huh?" Darby whispered, startling Harlan awake.

"I *know* it," Harlan whispered back groggily.

Darby didn't say anything more, but Harlan resumed praying for the man.

Lord, keep working on him. His heart is softening! Only You can draw him into Your love. Move me to action if there is something I need to do or say to urge him along.

"I think ya might be right 'bout ther bein' nothin' we ken do ta git to Hea'en," Darby whispered. "I's jus' goin' o'er some Scripture in my head, an' I 'membered Titus 3:5: 'Not by works o' righteousness which we ha' done, but according ta His mercy He saved us, by the washing of regeneration, and renewing of the Holy Ghost.'

"Jesus tole' Nicodemus thet ta git ta Hea'en ya hafta be born agin. How d'ya think thet happens?"

"I think the first thing you do is repent of your sins," Harlan answered. In that moment, he knew that he should feel nervous about saying the right things to Darby—answering his questions in a way that would convince the man to come to Jesus. Instead, Harlan felt as though he were not the only one in control of the words he said, and he actually felt relaxed. "I think that means that you turn away from your sins."

Darby was silent for a moment. "In my case," he reflected, "I think my worst sin 'uz rejectin' Jesus all these years. I think erpentance means thet I also hafta change my mind about my sin. Somewhere's it sez ta let everone know thet God has made Jesus both Lord and Christ. I b'lieved thet, but I didn' make Him *my* Lord and Christ."

Darby's voice began to waver a little, and Harlan detected that he was struggling to keep his emotions in check.

"'Cuz o' my own bullheadedness, I wasted my whole life," Darby croaked.

"Don't waste these last few hours, then," Harlan urged. "Receive Christ now. Repent and trust Him. Ask Him to be your master and savior," prodded Harlan.

Dirty Darby, there in the bottom bunk of a dingy, dark, steel jail cell prayed like he never had done before, and when the peace that comes only from the Holy Spirit entered him, he fell asleep— no longer dirty with sin. Once Harlan could tell by the man's rhythmic, shallow breathing that Darby was out, he prayed his own prayers of thanksgiving. Feelings similar to the relief, peace, and joy that he experienced on the day of his own conversion washed over him again, and he felt like he had a new understanding of the celebration in Heaven which occurs when someone comes to saving faith in Christ Jesus.

What had he read just a few hours ago when he was reading through Luke's gospel? The parable of the ninety-nine sheep with the hundredth one lost spoke of the shepherd's joy at bringing the lost lamb home. "Rejoice with me," the shepherd said to his friends and neighbors, "for I have found my sheep which was lost." And Jesus said, "I say unto you, that likewise joy shall be in heaven over one sinner that repenteth." Harlan smiled. There was celebration in Heaven as well as inside a tiny, pie-shaped jail cell in the middle of a small city in Iowa.

Harlan's own jubilance reminded him of the unbounded joy that Mrs. Meyer had exhibited on the morning of his own conversion just a couple of weeks earlier. Of course, he couldn't remember Mrs. Meyer without remembering her daughter. With a pang, Harlan thought of Marty. Not even two days had passed since he had last seen her, but it seemed like they were separated by a lifetime. With his life now completely wrapped up in the consequences of the sins he had committed before coming to the Meyer farm, it was as if those few turbulent but beautiful weeks spent with the Meyers were some kind of colorful dream. The only thing that made them real for him now was his faith in Jesus. That faith, even though still in its infancy, now defined everything about him: his actions, his outlook, and his future destiny.

Thank you, Lord, for your grace. It is sufficient for me.

Darby stirred again.

"Do you need something?" Harlan asked.

"Thet lady," Darby whispered, struggling to catch enough of a breath to form words, "who wro' thet...Psalm ta ya:...'He sets the sol'tary...in families.' He...did thet ta both of us. He put ya...in their family...an' then He...put us tagether...ta bring...both of us...home ta Him. She 'uz right...'bout thet...havin' meanin' fer ya. He...ain't done yet, though."

"What do you mean?" Harlan whispered.

Darby did not respond. Instead, Harlan could hear his shallow breathing resume the pattern that indicated he was asleep.

Harlan thought about what Darby had said. He was right. God had put him in the Meyer family when he was most alone in his life, and just when Harlan was being torn from them and put into what he thought was going to be a very lonely time in jail, here was Darby. Sure, he didn't know the man well, but he was a familiar face, and now they were brothers in Christ. But it did not make sense that he had been wrested from the Meyers and now Darby seemed to be ebbing away before him. Why give him two families, only to take both away?

Harlan crawled up into his top bunk and lay down. The thin tick and pillow had come with a scratchy wool blanket and were an improvement over the cold plate of steel that constituted the bunk, but they still were not so comfortable that they induced sleep right away.

God setteth the solitary in families, Harlan thought to himself.

What did the other half of the verse say? He would have to look at Mrs. Meyer's note again in the morning light.

Family. When he thought about that word, Harlan couldn't help but remember his mother, and he was sure that she would be in despair once she learned of his fate. When would the letter that had gone out in Monday's mail reach her?

"I'm sorry, Mom." Harlan spoke in a barely audible whisper. "Jesus has forgiven me for everything. I hope you can too."

Harlan figured that the night had become the very early hours of the morning since the jailhouse was remarkably quiet. Men snored loudly in some of the cells, and the bare gray walls and steel bars served only as surfaces from which the sounds could bounce and echo. Occasionally, he could hear an inmate talking in his sleep, but even that was muffled by the fellow's own arm or bedding. Harlan drifted into near unconsciousness. He did not know how long he had been in that state when he became aware of some kind of struggle going on beneath him.

In his drowsiness, Harlan first believed that the noise was coming from one of the two cells directly beneath the one he and Darby occupied, but then he understood that the noise was coming from Darby himself. Harlan scrambled down to the lower bunk, and could tell even in the pitch darkness that Darby was struggling to catch a breath.

Harlan felt about on the wooden bench until he located the one remaining clean rag. Then his hands sought and found Darby, pulling him up into a sitting position. With a thump on his back from Harlan and all of the strength that the dying man could muster, Darby coughed up the mass of phlegm and blood that had been stopping his airway.

"Thank ya," Darby whispered. "That's th' last un. Don' hev th' strenth ta do it agin."

Harlan prepared to lay Darby back down on the bunk.

Darby protested. "Nah, keep me upright. Hurts ta lay down."

Doing his best in the blackness, Harlan attempted to prop

Darby's back against the wall to which the bunk was fastened. His attempts were futile, however, because Darby no longer had control of what little muscle remained on his frame. Not knowing what else to do, Harlan crawled into the bunk with Darby, holding him in a sitting position.

"Bless...ya," Darby said between faint breaths before dropping to sleep again.

Though it didn't seem possible, the jail was even more quiet than it had been earlier, and each of Darby's breaths rang loudly in Harlan's ears—until there in Harlan's arms, with hours still to go before daylight, Darby exhaled one last time.

After a few minutes of silence which assured Harlan that Darby had indeed expired, Harlan wriggled out of the bed and lay the man's body gently on the bunk. Harlan reflected with irony that he should cry, but instead, he could feel himself smiling. Darby was with Jesus, whose biography he had known well for a long time, but with whose grace he had only recently become acquainted.

The jail seemed to come to life earlier than it had on the previous morning, with men shouting, laughing, and squabbling throughout the three-story cylinder. After Darby had passed, Harlan thought maybe he should alert the jailer right away, but he didn't know how to go about that without the whole cylinder of men being disturbed, so he resolved to wait until the breakfast roll call to let the jailer know that Darby was gone. Harlan figured that the jailer would not be surprised, and he could see no danger of being accused of foul play, so Harlan pulled the blanket over Darby's face and climbed up into the upper bunk where he didn't have to stare at Darby's corpse.

"Jensen! Darby!" the jailer called when their cell had been rotated into place.

"Just Jensen now, sir," Harlan said quietly.

The jailer's demeanor changed instantly. "What time did it happen?"

"I don't know, sir. My guess would be about three o'clock."

"You all right to stay there with the body until we get breakfast distributed?"

Harlan shrugged. "I guess it doesn't bother me any."

"I'll be back as soon as I can."

Harlan returned to his cell and crawled up into the top bunk to eat his breakfast.

"Jensen!" he heard someone say from behind him once his cell was rotated to the opposite side of the landing.

"Traft?" Harlan asked.

"Yeah. Did I hear you say Darby's gone?"

"Yes. In the night."

There was a long pause, and Harlan heard a sniffle from the other side of the wall.

"He was a good guy," said Traft finally.

Harlan thought about that statement for a second. Dirty Darby hadn't been any better than anyone else. By the world's standards, he was probably a lot worse than most people.

"No, he wasn't," Harlan finally answered, not whispering anymore. "But he died a forgiven man, and that is all that counts."

Harlan hoped that his statement would pique Traft's curiosity and open the door for him to share the Gospel with the giant in the next cell.

Breakfast had long been over and Harlan had begun to wonder if he were going to have to live indefinitely with a corpse in the lower bunk of his cell when the jailer's "Gonna roll!" sounded. His cell was rotated around to the access point on the east side again, and both the reinforced door and the barred door of the cell were opened. Two men in uniforms stood with the jailer on the landing.

"Sorry 'bout the delay, Jensen," the jailer said evenly. "Some important business came up. Gather up your stuff and come down to the office. These fellows are here to remove Darby's body. You can leave your bedding."

Harland thought it odd that he was told to leave his bedding and that he was not put in handcuffs when he was exiting his cell, but never having been in jail before, he realized that he was very naive regarding how one was operated. Gathering the contents of the paper sack that Roy Schoening had delivered the previous morning, Harlan followed the jailer to his office, where the door was shut behind him and he was face-to-face with the law man from Monona County again.

"Jensen, this man is the reason you had to sit so long with a corpse in your cell this morning," explained the jailer.

"Huh?"

"Jensen, we're letting you go."

"Diego Conti—or Digger, as you called him—didn't die the night you strangled him," said the man who had come from a couple counties to the north. "He regained consciousness sometime later, just as ornery as ever. We were able to find Ben Jensen still with the CCC, and he filled us in on the details that Conti had come back to camp sometime later looking for you. Ben, thinking as best he could on his feet, convinced Conti that *you* had been the one killed by Conti's hand during the fight and that Ben had hidden *your* body in the woods. Ben used this lie as leverage to keep Conti at bay, and the two agreed to just say that both you and Conti had deserted.

"Ben Jensen was relieved to find out that you are still alive, but he was even more glad to hear that Diego Conti is dead."

Harlan was having trouble following all of this. "So I didn't kill Digger Conti, but he's dead all the same?"

"Yup. Digger Conti died in a bar brawl up in Whiting on November 7th. He had found a job picking corn for a farmer up there, and once he got paid, he went into town to blow his stash on booze. Got rip-roaring drunk and started running his mouth like he was apparently known to do on occasion, and when another bar-patron had had enough and told him to shut up, Conti broke a beer bottle and came after the other fellow with a shard of it like he was going to cut his throat.

"Problem was, nobody in Whiting knew or recognized the other customer, and he hot-footed it out of there after leaving a bullet in Conti's gut. So when we heard that someone had confessed to murdering Conti, even though the dates weren't jiving, we had to hold you and investigate the lead. You're free to go."

Harlan stood there stunned.

"Do you want to call someone, son?" the jailor asked, pointing to the phone.

"No, I...I," Harlan's mind was working as quickly as it could. "I want to go back up to my cell and give a little book to Traft," he said finally. "And then I'll just go, if that's all right."

The jailer tossed the Monona County officer his keys. "You can take him up while I finish the paperwork for his release."

It was getting dark when Harlan brushed the snow from his clothes. Without laces in his boots, quite a bit of the white stuff had gotten down inside them when he had jumped off the train, but he didn't care. Below him stood the beautiful Meyer farm. Well-kept flowerbeds and a weedless garden were buried under a layer of snow, and smoke curled out of the kitchen chimney.

Harlan spanned the back pasture as fast as his legs could carry him. He climbed the fences of the assorted feedlots and barn pens agilely and arrived at the back door of the house panting hard; the dog, who was very glad to see him, stood beside him as he knocked firmly on the screen door. While he waited for an answer, Harlan took out his release papers and held them in front of his chest as proof that he was not an escapee.

The door opened, and there stood Mrs. Meyer.

"Hello, ma'am. I'm sorry to bother you, but my name is Harlan Jensen, and I just jumped off the train next to your back pasture, and..."

Expressions of both shock and joy crossed Mrs. Meyer's face.

She opened the screen door to him, and her eyes quickly scanned the paper that Harlan held out in front of her. With an ecstatic screech, her strong arms scooped him into the kitchen.

"Praise God!" she shouted, hugging him tightly, feeling his arms and cheeks to make sure he was real. "He bringeth out those which are bound in chains!"

"Where's Marty?" Harlan asked after she had calmed enough that he could make her understand him.

"She's over at Louise's helping her make some Christmas candy to try to get her mind off of all of this with you. She'll be home in time for milking. Go get yourself cleaned up and shaved so you don't look like this when she gets here!"

There was that certain something about Mrs. Meyer's voice that made it obvious that she was accustomed to being obeyed, and Harlan didn't know if he'd heard anything quite so nice in the last several hours.

"Would you please pass the potatoes, Mrs. Jensen?" Elsie Meyer asked three weeks later at Christmas dinner. She was seated at her own dining room table, a radiant smile crossing her lips even though this was the first Christmas without her husband at the head of the table.

Both Mrs. Viola Jensen—a tall, matronly lady—and Mrs. Martha Jensen—a petite, spritely newlywed—reached for the bowl of mashed potatoes between them. As their hands brushed momentarily, they dissolved into happy giggles. Seated between them at the head of the table, Harlan—both husband and son—beamed at the three women seated with him, secretly hoping that it wouldn't be too long before some boys were born to keep him from being so horribly outnumbered.

Notes from the Author

I hope you enjoyed reading *He That Covereth His Sins*. While Harlan Jensen, the Meyer family, and their neighbors were all completely fictional, the world they lived in was very real. Astute readers from West Pottawattamie County, Iowa, and specifically those from the town of Underwood, will recognize many familiar names and places. For example, my great-great aunt Ella Klopping was indeed substituting in the Underwood Post Office in the 1930s before becoming the full-time post mistress a few years later. She was also truly living beside the Milwaukee Railroad tracks and feeding as many as seven hobos per day.

The dance hall at Weston still stands, but no dances have been held there for many years. However, the Phoenix Theatre in Neola has undergone a recent renovation, and movies are once again shown there on weekends. Council Bluffs' unique Squirrel Cage Jail was in continuous use from its construction in 1885 until 1969. One of the eighteen rotary jails originally constructed in the United States—only three of which stand today—it is now a museum open to the public.

The Civilian Conservation Corps (CCC), one of the most popular programs in President Franklin D. Roosevelt's New Deal, did indeed build a lodge at Lewis and Clark State Park in 1936; however, I have no idea whether they would have actually sent a small group ahead in the previous year to scout the logistics of the endeavor.

The rest of the cultural and historic events mentioned alongside the story of Harlan Jensen were also based on real life during the Great Depression from the stories that I have listened to all my life. If you ever get the chance to ask me about them, I hope you have pre-planned a method to get me to stop talking!

Of course, the most important aspect of *He That Covereth His Sins* is the truth of the Gospel of Jesus Christ, and I hope all of my readers are blessed with its illustrations of the grace and peace available to us only through him.